CN01635780

DOGS AND WOMEN ALLOWED

DOGS AND WOMEN ALLOWED

Emma Briggs

First published in 2024

ISBN (paperback): 978-90-9038498-6
ISBN (e-book): 978-90-9038713-0

Book designed and typeset by InsideStudio26.com
Internal illustrations © Victoria Heath Silk
Pawprint illustrations © Chinch, Shutterstock.com

To Dad

For letting Hackkett, Love, Bashit, Rough and Bushrod come to life again.
Although they never really left us now did they?

Just like you, always there somewhere.

Of all the hazards, fear is the worst.
– Sam Snead

CHAPTER 1

'Righto. Ball washers sorted. Let me see what's next.' Peckers Wood's President Harry Bashit peered over his specs at the other men in the golf club's main study, taking in what he'd be faced with the coming year. Standing to his left: Ben Chipperfield, the soon to be appointed Golf Club Captain. A handsome, dark-skinned, twenty-something oozing confidence, Ben's hands hung loosely in his trouser pockets. His sharp-shaven dark skin was in stark contrast to the bright polo-necked shirt under the seemingly casually thrown-over jumper, emphasizing the broad square shoulders, pulled backwards. Trying hard to look casually indifferent, but today overdoing it, turning the usual compelling attraction into annoying cocksureness, causing a niggle of foreboding to creep up the President's spine.

Bashit turned his head slightly, focusing on his Secretary Reggie Rough. Colourless, is what came to mind when zooming in on the pasty blob in front of him. Blond hair, waxlike face with the beige sports jacket and slacks blended in. Huddled in one of the floral-patterned chintz chairs, Rough resembled a mound of pale-yellow mashed potato shoved to the far side of an abandoned plate, rejected, with no other destiny than to be scraped onto a heap of leftovers, ready for a passel of vicious, hungry pigs to feed on.

Poor chap. Bashit shook his head internally, wishfully thinking the surge of adrenaline caused by the exciting new responsibility might light some fire in his young Secretary's balls. Perhaps he should order his old crony Lieutenant Retired Bushrod to slap these boys into shape, push them around a bit before the season really started. Bashit quickly dismissed the idea, noticing Bushrod theatrically pulling a dog hair from his sleeve, the corners of his fleshy lips pulled down, a look of intense horror in his beady eyes.

Good grief. Bloody drama queen.

The President zeroed in on the task ahead of him, knowing he had built up the tension to an almost unbearable level. But he just couldn't resist prolonging the obvious agony a little longer by slowly feeding the last bit of the apple cake to his dog Percy, wickedly wallowing in the misery his extended intermezzo was causing the others.

But the fun had to end. Time to move on. 'Ben Chipperfield.' His clipped voice whipped through the heavy atmosphere. 'Congratulations. Club Captain it is.'

A collective sigh of relief rippled through the study. Bashit wiped his hand on his crisp linen napkin, and smiled – ever so slightly - before he reached towards his old fountain pen waiting for him on the desk's cracked green leather top. 'When I figure out where to sign this wretched thing, that is.'

The two younger men exchanged a quick look. 'It's right-hand side, bottom. Sir,' said Reggie Rough, pointing towards the piece of paper.

'Don't just sit there, Roughie!' Bashit thundered, using the nickname for his Secretary that had stuck with him since boarding school. 'I didn't appoint you to just dangle and hover.'

Roughie stumbled towards him. 'Please allow me to assist you,' he said, turning the page and pointing at the dotted line, the tremble in his voice synchronizing perfectly to his shaking index finger.

'Right,' President Bashit grumbled. 'Good show.'

The fountain pen flowed over the paper while the bold signature appeared, slowly but surely. 'Fetch my stick, Bushrod,' the President ordered, making the club's treasurer stand to attention, 'so I can stand up while I shake young Chipperfield's hand.'

Ben stood and grabbed the old palm that was stretched out to him. 'Thank you very much, President Bashit. I am so proud.'

'So you should be. Just make certain I won't regret signing that piece of paper. Make Peckers Wood Golf Club proud by getting that Best Regional Team's Medal back where it belongs. Here. In our prize cabinet.' Bashit pointed towards his own chest and stabbed it a couple of times before he continued. 'Charmers was useless during his year, and coming in second was bloody unworthy to our reputation.' Bashit warmed his hands by the blazing fire, feeling a shiver shoot through his body. 'Rather chilly today.' He looked towards his fellow board members and the newly appointed Club Captain, wiping sweat from their foreheads. 'Are you alright, boys? You seem flustered.'

'We're fine, sir. Just a tad warm in here, that's all.' Roughie felt the drops trickling down his tight collar, his neck so bloated from the heat that his tie felt like a noose, making it near impossible to swallow the rising bile, thinking it must be a hundred degrees in the President's study. 'Could we have a word about our next meeting now, sir? The one with Mrs Van Dycke and Miss Hackkett?,' he asked surreptitiously, now perspiring heavily. 'It seems a little complicated, the whole issue.'

'Complicated?,' Bushrod piped. 'Bloody nuisance you mean.'

The President ignored the Treasurer's comment, leaned on his walking stick and hobbled towards the window. This side of the room had the best view of the clubhouse, showing the golf club's first tee at its prime, surrounded by white and mauve hydrangeas, in full bloom, and the fairway, wide with oak trees all the way up to the elevation of the green. At the moment, this idyllic scene was obscured by that young Hackkett girl. As she bent down to tee up her ball, the back of her long slim legs beamed towards him. Her bottom stuck out while she was taking her stance, and under that tight top, her bosom showed itself in her back swing, disappearing in her follow-through. Bashit sighed and shook his head. How different from the picture his father would have seen before him.

A deep breath filled his lungs, and he exhaled, forcing himself to remain calm. Looking back at bygone times wasn't the answer, so he might as well be open to this whole palaver. 'What are your thoughts about these ladies playing the course so much lately?'

Roughie mopped his brow again, trying to buy time to find a right response that wouldn't ignite the President's firy temper. 'Well, can't say I'm overly thrilled by the whole idea.' He paused again slightly, thinking he actually hadn't given it much thought. 'But what choice do we have? It is what it is, nowadays.' As Roughie answered, he realized that he hadn't encountered enough women on the course to actually say anything plausible about it. 'We might as well try and make the best of it?'

The words came out cautiously while he slowly joined the President at the window, halting a good foot behind him. Together they watched Philly Hackkett walk towards the green, pick up her ball and set off towards the car park.

'At least we don't allow them in our quarters.' Bushrod snorted. 'Do you know there are clubs where they roam all over the entire clubhouse, by themselves?'

Good Lord. Perish the thought. President Bashit shook his head and turned his eyes to the first fairway again, following the young woman walking back towards the car park. 'How is our candidate Lady Captain, Miss Hackkett doing, Chipperfield? I gather you and her are getting on quite nicely?' President Bashit suddenly spun round and stared at Ben, who quickly averted his eyes. 'I heard some rumours about you two being more than friends. Whatever that means this day and age.'

'Yes, President. That is one item Roughie and I wanted to talk to you about.' Ben said, guardedly. 'Sorry you had to hear it on the grapevine.' The embarrassment briskly disappeared, and the familiar arrogance was back. 'But please let me point out that my relationship with Miss Hackkett will in no way cloud my judgment on the first Lady Captain's future accomplishments,' he assured the President, holding his head up high. 'So, I thought it might be wise to talk about strategy, about what we expect from such a position?'

'Expect? Strategy? From a woman?' Bushrod's voice came up again. 'Not being a pain in the backside. That's all as far as I'm concerned.' A deep grunt escaped his throat. 'Why should we care about what women are up to? Let them be, for goodness sake. As long as they keep to themselves and don't bother us with their nonsense.'

'I agree.' Bashit's head bent towards his Secretary, who was back in his usual seat, in his usual slumped position. 'Any input on that strategy, my dear fellow?'

Roughie felt his cheeks go bright red. Input? He never needed to give strategical input before? And now that the subject was on women, he suddenly was being pushed. The sweat started to gush from his pores again. His mouth opened and closed, not finding the words that should come out to add something constructive.

'Chipperfield? Any input?' The President's chin went up, as if he was trying to mimic Ben's posture.

Ben wiped the back of his hand over his face. 'Well, I was hoping to put some goals towards the proposed Lady Captain. To see how she goes?'

'Good lord.' Bushrod sat down on the Chesterfield reading chair next to the fire place, his movement causing the old leather to grunt, like a muffled objection to the heavy weight. 'You two don't have clue when it comes to handling women, now do you?' He shook his head in disbelief. 'Hoping women set and achieve goals is nothing more than delayed disappointment. They're not capable of forward thinking, you know.'

'They can't help it.' The President's walking stick pointed towards Ben and Roughie. 'Their heads and brains are smaller than ours,' Bashit proclaimed, while thumping the expensive silk carpet with his walking stick. 'But let me tell you, with females, there is one strategy that never fails. It's the pretend strategy.' President Bashit's voice lowered to a conspiratorial whisper. 'Just pretend to listen, pretend to involve, give them something trivial to occupy their minds, pretend it's something hugely important and then just ignore them.' A wagging finger came towards Ben. 'Trust me, it prevents a lot of headaches.'

Roughie parted his lips, longing for the courage to speak, but his voice again didn't want to come.

'Anything else, Roughie? I see you are, at least, tempted to utter some words?' President Bashit sat up and flicked through the notes in front of him, trying not to show his rising impatience and resume the business of continuing the meeting in a professional manner. 'We will deal with this women matter later this afternoon. As for now, Roughie, do you have something positive to share with us, to end this trivia?'

'No, sir,' Roughie whispered, trying to get up from his chair, but stumbling on account of his wobbling knees. 'I think we've cleared everything.' He steadied himself, holding on to the chair's back, letting the crisp, dry touch of the chintz cool down his burning hands.

'We have?' President Bashit turned his papers. 'I am quite sure incoming correspondence is on the agenda for today.' He tapped his index finger on the desk. 'Yes. Here it is.' He glanced at the trembling man in front of him, feeling the familiar sense of rising impatience. God, how he hated sloppiness. If only Roughie would sit down, stop hovering and get on with it.

'Yes. Of course it is. Very well.' Roughie swallowed, realizing postponing looming trouble would get him nowhere. 'I think, we have the thank you letter from the widow Spencer-Downe. She really was touched by the little wreath and kind letter we sent, and she would appreciate it if the credit note for the left-over six-month cost could be sent to her urgently. With the actual reimbursement, of course.'

'Credit note? Reimbursement?' Bashit inquired, exchanging a quick look with Bushrod.

'Yes, what's that supposed to mean?,' Bushrod asked, obviously flabbergasted. 'Are you saying we have to pay back his remaining fee? On what grounds?'

'On the grounds he's unable to play due to circumstances,' Roughie explained, feeling extremely uncomfortable. 'The circumstance being, he's…,' Roughie voice turned into an embarrassed whisper, '…well, you know, deceased.'

'Yes, I think we do realize the poor man is dead, Roughie.' President Bashit's face turned an angry shade of red. 'Bushrod, did you know about this? Is it in our rules?'

'I haven't the foggiest, Bashit. Sorry. Haven't seen or touched the financial rule book in a hundred years,' replied Bushrod, clearly mystified. 'But I will look into it.'

'Good,' Bashit said. 'And please, sometime this century, if it's not too much bother. If we have to reimburse every member that kicks the bucket before the 31st of December over the coming years we'll be bankrupt before we know it.' Bashit glanced at his watch and tapped it. 'Chop chop, there's more to cover, and I haven't all day.'

'Right.' Roughie slowly released his grip from the chair's comfortable steadiness and let himself slide back in his seat, trying to ignore the acid that seemed to be burning a hole in his chest. He pulled an envelope out of his inside pocket, and the piece of stationary inside appeared slowly, sticking to his trembling fingers as he tried to unfold it. He swallowed, cleared his throat and tried to speak. 'It's a letter,' he squeaked.

'Yes. I can see that,' Bashit sighed. 'I'm not visually challenged, Roughie. Who from?'

'Lavender Thorneybush.'

'God Almighty.' President Bashit slumped again and raised his eyes towards the ceiling. 'Don't tell me the damn woman is complaining again? What's she on about now?'

'She's so frightfully nouveau, that Thorneybush hag,' Bushrod sighed dramatically, 'always flaunting their so-called wealth. Absolutely ghastly. Driving that flashy electric car.' He shook his head and tutted. 'And let's face it, she's nothing more than a plumber's daughter, for heaven's sake.'

'Quite.' Ben agreed, as he stood up and walked towards the window facing the first tee.

'At least he pays her fees on time,' President Bashit added, 'which can't be said of all our dear members.' A hard stare went towards Bushrod, who quickly began inspecting his nails.

'Let's have it then. What's in the letter?' Bashit returned to his chair and watched the twitchy Secretary unfold the paper further, his damp fingers nearly dropping it in front of Percy who was snoozing gently and ignoring all the tension.

'It's a…,' Roughie muttered while wiping the unrelenting torrent from his forehead, '…sort of, well, resignation.' He shook his head, making drops fly of his forehead, narrowly missing Bushrod. 'Miss Thorneybush writes she is resigning from the club. Sir.' He passed the printed e-mail to Bashit, his right hand now shaking uncontrollably.

What in earth was Roughie on about? Bashit snatched the paper towards him and started reading. No-one had ever resigned from this golf club. It must be some kind of mistake, he thought, while his eyes moved from left to right, quickly scanning the document in front of him.

'Is she giving up the game?' Bushrod asked, sounding muddled.

'No.' Roughie slumped back down in his chair and rubbed his head. 'She's leaving Peckers Wood for Goodlie Golf. You know, that new club, up the road.'

The study went absolutely still, the only sound coming from Percy, letting out a hardly audible fart while moving his nose towards his backside and sighing contently. Bushrod started flapping his hands violently, shooting a dark look at President Bashit, who ignored him, looking completely lost. An old-fashioned checkered handkerchief appeared from Roughie's trouser pocket, and he started mopping his brow, moaning softly.

'Did you know about Goodlie, Bushrod? Isn't it more your neck of the woods, where they are?' Ben asked carefully.

'I heard rumours,' Bushrod said, nodding slowly. 'But I never thought they were serious about developing an actual championship course.'

A loud cackle escaped Bashit. Championship? Goodlie? His large, purple nose crumpled up in disgust while contemplating on the ridiculousness. 'Bloody nerve they have, calling themselves a golf club at all! I heard they greased the palm of some local politician and got their hands on a couple of acres of farmland. Chased a bulldozer over it, stuck 18 flags in the ground and now announce themselves the region's best golf experience!'

The President rolled his eyes thinking of the drawings one of his Rotary friends managed to show him of that monstrosity of a clubhouse they were planning to build. Modern architecture they called it. Absolutely abysmal. They must have bribed the whole council to get planning permission. He threw the letter on his desk in an annoyed flick of his wrist.

'Really? What a naughty thing to do,' Roughie said carefully, while he pulled a dog biscuit out of his trouser pocket and slowly coached Percy towards him, trying for some postponement so he could compose himself. He glanced back at the printed e-mail, carefully drew it towards him and read on carefully. 'It says here they will have 18 holes championship, 9 holes par 3, a driving range, pitch & putt course, a special section for lessons, tennis court, a swimming pool and a wellness area.' He put the letter in his lap and stared at Bashit. 'Quite impressive, if I may say so, President.' His last words came out in an embarrassed whisper.

Ben nodded, his dark face looking glum as he addressed the group of men. 'I think we need to take this seriously. What if more members decide Goodlie is the better option?' He turned towards Bushrod, who suddenly resembled a dying fish, his mouth opening and closing again, the colour of his face slowly changing from dark pink to a steely grey.

'I beg your pardon, Chipperfield,' the Treasurer hissed. 'What on earth makes you say that? How could anything be a better option to Peckers Wood?' Bushrod sat up straight, unfolded his knees and pulled his shoulders backwards. 'Complete and utter nonsense, President. There is nothing better than our fine institution. And I say that as a proud board member. We have nothing to worry about. So the Thorneybush woman is leaving? Well, good riddance I say.'

Roughie picked the letter up and squinted. 'Another thing worth mentioning, perhaps. Lav, Miss Thorneybush, will be Goodlie's Lady Captain. It says here she has quite a section already. And that it is a wonderful opportunity for her, one she would never have gotten here.'

'Quite right,' Bushrod exclaimed, his voice more authoritarian than ever. 'Over my dead body. Someone like her? Here? Lady Captain? Not a chance.' He stared at the President. 'Frankly, I'm having second thoughts about that whole, to be quite honest, rather silly Lady Captain initiative. Being a Peckers Wood representative is a humongous task that comes with huge responsibility. Saying I'm not quite certain ladies are up to that is an understatement, if I'm rather frank.'

Bushrod was about to set off in a torrent, but was cut off by a thundering 'Silence!' from Bashit who was now standing behind his desk, his hands firmly planted on the leather upholstery. 'We are running out of time, and I have had enough of this women subject. We will end this meeting now, and we are not reconsidering the position of Lady Captain.' He paused for a second before speaking again in a whisper. 'Females are moody creatures, and I do not wish to light a spark under them, thank you very much.' Another pause followed. 'Especially in this current brave new world we find ourselves in.' Bashit resumed in a grave voice. He sat down again, slowly, and inhaled deeply before eyeing the other two men. 'And I gave my word to Anthony Hackkett that I would initiate this and so we will. It's a minor thing, we won't be paying too much attention to this whole sheep-headed initiative anyway. It will probably have solved itself before the year is over.'

'Alright, Bashit,' Bushrod grumbled. 'But remember… we've been perfectly fine for more than two centuries. Our good members won't be amused if this lady nonsense turns into, heaven forbid, us being forced into…*changes*.' His voice quivered, whispering the last word.

The President stared at his Treasurer, sighed inwardly and waved towards the door. 'Let me handle this. Roughie, Chipperfield, the two ladies should be here in 10 minutes. Go and arrange some more refreshments, will you?'

The two older men waited for the heavy panelled door to close behind the two younger ones sent off to sort out the housekeeper Miss Snuggs for some more tea. The President limped to the far back end of the study, followed by the Treasurer and Percy, the lurcher still munching on the treat his master had tossed towards him.

Bushrod picked up a pair of binoculars from the President's desk. 'Your dog might think he has something tough to chew on,' Bushrod said slowly, while pushing away Percy's head with an irritated shove, pulling the heavy curtain aside and resting the President's antique binoculars on his nose. 'But what about us? I mean, look at them.'

The Treasurer squinted through the old glass and concentrated on the scene in the car park left of the first fairway. Two identical, slightly plump dark-haired young women in matching navy trousers and pink pullovers, took brown leather golf bags out of the boot of a battered Jaguar and threw them on two tired-looking trolleys. A small, tan and black scrawny terrier with one lopsided ear pulled towards two other women, walking in front of them. Both were thin, one with her black hair pulled backwards in a severe bun, wearing black slacks and a bright red top with matching shoes, their shine showing they were carefully polished; the other one, now bending down, kissing the dog while her bright orange curls cascaded over her face. Starting to stand up straight again, she tossed her pony tail back, facing him, revealing her body. His heart skipped a beat. Her eyes seemed to look right through him as the others also turned in his direction.

'Good Lord. Look.' President Bashit's face crumpled up in disgust. 'Now Wonder Woman shows up.' He snatched the binoculars from Bushrod who grabbed the heavy curtain for support and fell towards his old friend, only just regaining his posture.

Bashit sighed dramatically and aimed towards the car park. What in earth were they up to? Chatterboxing. Trust women to dillydally and waste precious playing time. He put the binoculars down and shook his head. At least young Miss Hackkett and her friends seemed to like dogs. He looked down at the large loving droopy eyes that were staring at him.

'No good will come of this, Bashit. They will want things. Have opinions. Things *we* do not want. Opinions *we* do not share. Believe me.' Bushrod released the curtain and staggered back to his chair, the defeated look on his face matching the slump of his usually straight back.

The President joined him, trying to ignore the ominous dread he felt rising in his gut while he thought of Anthony Hackkett's letter in his left top drawer.

CHAPTER 2

17th of May, 2022

Dear Harry,

How much I enjoyed our nine holes together. Wonderful to be out on the course again. *Extremely* impressed by your excellent handling of that nifty new fairway wood, must try one myself soon as my long iron shots are the saddest ones imaginable.

My sincere apologies that I again bothered you with my ramblings about Dorothy and the funny spells she has suffered ever since Philly left for university and threatened she might start her career up north. Quite the nightmare it's been, putting up with the wife's never-ending gloom and despair over the last year.

But times have changed for the better, now that my darling daughter decided to move back to the village as soon as she got her degree and started her new position. And, again, as I mentioned before, not only her career opportunities, but also Philly's warm feelings about being able to play a course like Peckers Wood with her dearest friends were of great service to her return. The young ladies seem to regard their time on our fairways and greens as an invaluable part of their happy young existence.

Dear Dorothy has since, thank God, made a remarkable recovery and is back to her chirpy old self. She picked her feather duster up the moment Philly moved into the High Street flat she shares with Prudence Love, and the wife instantly turned the dark hovel our crumbling old cottage was becoming into the lively shack it used to be before our bairn left.

So grateful you grasped I desperately want to hang on to this reappeared cheerfulness and need to cling to every opportunity to keep my daughter near to my other half.

So, my dearest and oldest friend, I am forever in your debt now that you finally agreed to formalize matters and now create this Lady Captain occasion I suggested to you. Knowing my offspring, she will grab this with both hands, get stuck in and will never want to leave Peckers Wood (and thus us) ever again.

Yours sincerely,
your faithful friend Anthony Hackkett

P.S. Philly and Dorothy have been yakking about PW needing a Lady Captain for as long as I can remember. Are like Cheshire Cats ever since I told them your plans. The wife's happy, our child is happy, so I'm happy. Thank you so much. You *are* a life saver.

CHAPTER 3

200 yards to the entrance. Please drive slowly.

Philly's hands felt clammy on her steering wheel. She tried to ignore the tingling feeling in her stomach and threw her hair backwards. Tilting her chin upwards somehow made her feel more confident. Her yellow sports car nearly seemed to drive itself, curling into the familiar turns towards her destination. She pushed the back of her head into the neck rest and looked up. The watery yellow blob above her was trying to get some warmth towards her, but was defeated by cumulus clouds blocking the light in the sky, looking like giant cotton balls rolling over a bright blue surface. Her car's engine rumbled, the low roar sounding like a long-troubled growl after being pushed to its limits, the ominous sound intensifying the apprehension flowing through her veins.

150 yards to the entrance. Please drive slowly.

Her foot hit the brake, making time for a quick pause at the familiar gap adjacent to the bushes running along the 15th where her father used to hide the car and sneak her in at dawn every Sunday. Philly stopped, closed her eyes for a couple of seconds, trying to ignore the frenzied butterflies that were now dancing up and down in her gut. She forced her mind back to her childhood, concentrating on just two sounds: the woodpeckers drumming their midday rattle and the 'swoosh' of her clubs. Her eyes opened and became fixed on the mirror, checking her face and reassuring herself she looked okay, before turning back towards the road. The final familiar bend came into view, towards the lane leading up to the gate. The thick may thorn hedge nearly hid the coloured signpost on the left.

100 yards to the entrance, please drive slowly.

The cast-iron gate appeared and opened, two ancient oak trees on each side towering over it, their dark branches touching each other in the middle but not obscuring the elegant building at the far end with its distinctive, paired chimneys and large wooden door. Philly shifted gears and maneuvered her car to the far end of the car park. She checked her mobile for time, deciding she could just squeeze in a couple of holes before her friends would arrive.

Her friends.

She stepped out of her car and pulled her gear out of the boot, suddenly feeling sick, as a wave of insecurity flashed through her, unwillingly forcing her to contemplate what could happen if this whole thing went pearshaped.

Her friends would be fucked. She would be fucked.

What if she didn't make it? What if Bashit just laughed and threw her out? What had they, she, been thinking? Her right hand held on to her golf bag for support, her left hand clutched her stomach, trying to calm it but failing, no matter how she pushed and stroked the strained area above her belly button. She inhaled deeply through her nose and exhaled, letting the air out through her mouth, slowly, suddenly noticing her mobile buzzing in her front trouser pocket. She pulled it out and concentrated on what popped up in front of her.

Mum, it said, revealing her mother's smiling face. She tapped, waiting for the message to pop up.

Hi darling.
Tiger Woods says your will can move mountains.
Good luck. X Mum.

Her thumb moved over the screen, absorbing the words in front of her. Tiger was right. She walked boldly towards the first tee, as her stomach calmed down, and her will fired up.

CHAPTER 4

Playing a couple of holes had done Philly good, relaxed her a little. Her bag was now safely strapped on her back, as she strolled the shortcut towards the ninth, following the path along the pine trees towards the far end of the car park leading towards the clubhouse. Her eyes followed the familiar roof lines and the mixture of stone, brick and wood in its Georgian symmetry. The roses in front of it were in full bloom, in all sorts of shapes and shades, seemingly smiling at her, reflecting the afternoon's sun like multi-coloured Christmas lights, illuminating the copper plate in front of the heavy door.

Peckers Wood Golf Club
since 1806
Members only
Trespassers will be prosecuted

Her gaze moved towards the reserved parking spaces on the right. Ben Chipperfield's car shone proudly in the middle with its nose nearly touching the gold and green sign saying 'Club Captain Only' in bold curving letters. She quivered slightly with a feeling of lust mixed with pride. The casual flirting and occasional sex between herself and the club's most eligible bachelor during the last year had turned into something more sustainable with them both agreeing on being exclusive, which suited her more than fine.

Philly pulled her eyes away and peered towards the clock standing alongside the first tee. If Pru and the Bangers arrived on schedule, there would just be enough time to go over the afternoon's big event. She couldn't believe it was actually happening. Her mother had rung her like what seemed a million times over the last week, wishing her luck and telling her over and over how proud she was of her.

Lady Captain. Being of service to the Lady Section. At the prestigious and so stunningly beautiful Peckers Wood Golf Club.

But it wasn't in the bag yet. A short gush of wind caught the flag on the 18th green at the other side of the car park, causing it to flap, its cloth making a ticking sound on the pole. One, two, three, four. Philly counted to the rhythm. One tick for each stroke on each hole. One beat for every pound in her chest.

She shivered for a moment, despite feeling the warmth radiating off the cobble stones beneath her, and turned towards the sound of a car heading her way. Philly had known the two Banger sisters for more than 20 years, since kindergarten. The inseparable pair sat behind the front window of their ancient green Jaguar, both with the usual large grins on their pretty tanned faces. As always, they were accompanied by Maggie, with her little paws resting on the dashboard, her body quivering as Birdie Banger snapped on the blue leash and carefully placed her beside the car.

Philly stepped towards them, bent down to stroke her little friend, her coat's soft touch under her fingertips calming her. Maggie stretched and licked her face, wagging her tail fiercely.

'Good grief, Freckles. That is so horrid.' Philly's best friend Prudence Love suddenly appeared from behind the bushes, calling her by the same nickname she had been using since they were six years old. 'Don't you dare kiss me now.' She carefully pulled white plugs out of her ears and a finger moved to Maggie. 'She just cleaned her lady parts with that tongue before she decided to smooch you.'

'Thanks for that thought, Pru.' Philly hugged herself, unconsciously, suddenly feeling uneasy, as if the car park's atmosphere wasn't quite right somehow. As if something, or someone, was watching her.

'What's the matter?,' Pru asked. 'Nervous?' She looked at her friend giving an encouraging nod. 'We do understand. Having you as a Lady Captain is a huge step forward for us. It's going to be so wonderful.'

'Nervous? No. I mean, yes, a bit, to be honest.' Philly shivered again and turned towards the clubhouse. 'But I just had the uncanny notion someone was looking me over. From up there.'

The four of them now stared towards the window Philly was pointing out, clearly noticing a curtain being pushed quickly towards the middle, trying but failing to block a figure behind it, holding binoculars. Maggie shook herself and started to yap, tugging her leash towards the direction the girls were staring at.

A quick glance was exchanged by the Banger sisters, eyebrows raised.

'Yuk. A peeping Tom.' Bogey Banger crumpled her nose. 'Some old dirty little man.'

'Oh, my God,' her sister Birdie guffawed. 'Getting off on Philly's backside. Our future Lady Captain, showing off her bottom French kissing Maggie.' She slapped her sister on her shoulder while they fell onto the bonnet of their car and slid off simultaneously, collapsing in heaps of wheezing giggles.

'Goodness gracious me. You two. Stop it,' Pru hissed, sounding embarrassed. 'Remember where you are.' She pulled the Banger sisters up and pushed them towards the side of their car, making certain they stayed upwards. 'Varilla the Gorilla at six o'clock. Pack it in.' Philly saw Pru indicate towards car park.

'O super. Is that bitch Thorneybush with her?,' Birdie asked, her giggle suddenly disappeared as she looked over her shoulder, trying not to stare at the stocky figure coming towards them.

'Nope,' replied Philly, shaking her head, feeling annoyance creeping up. 'All by herself now. And what the fuck is she wearing? There must be a million moths huddling in that outfit.'

Varilla Van Dycke's hand was up in a wave as she came towards them, her muscular calves straining under her tweed skirt as she picked up speed.

'Ah, Philomena, Prudence,' she said, dragging out Philly and Pru's full names, making them sound ridiculous. 'Here you are. Good. I wanted a word.' Varilla turned to the Bangers, who were trying desperately not to laugh but failing. 'What's so funny?,' she asked, her small pig -like eyes narrowing.

'Nothing,' they replied in unison. Pru shot the sisters a dark look, her brown eyes nearly black with warning. 'We were just changing our shoes and getting ready to play a few holes, Varilla, that's all. What is it you wanted to discuss?'

Varilla took a deep breath and pushed her chest out. 'I think we can safely assume that I will be appointed Lady Captain within a couple of hours, and I thought it a good idea to be bold and daring right from the start. Show Bashit what I am made of.' She stared at the Bangers who started to wheeze again.

'Did she say hairing, darling?' Birdie nudged Bogey, who fell forward laughing, clutching Maggie and trying to muffle her coughing sounds into the little dog's coat.

'Hahaha. Bold and hairing. That doesn't make sense,' Birdie squeaked, while dropping her face next to her sister's.

Varilla snorted and turned her attention back to Philly. 'But as I am all for democratic leadership, I thought I would just brush my idea past you.'

'Brush!,' the Bangers sisters squeaked together, now sliding off the car again in hopeless uncontrolled laughter.

'Varilla,' Philly said, trying to ignore the Bangers while looking down at the short, square figure in front of her, 'you're not there yet, now are you? Aren't you just a little presumptuous?' She stepped backwards sensing Pru behind her looking furious, her usually pale white face now flushed with red blotches. 'But, please, enlighten us, knock us for six with your brilliant plan.'

'Yes. I see.' Varilla's chest came forward again. 'But I want to hear your idea too. Assuming you have one, that is.' Her voice went up a notch, and she flicked her head back. 'President Bashit will expect you come up with cutting edge suggestions, during our meeting. If, in the very unlikely event, you will be appointed, he can get a feel for your leadership and creativity.' A short finger waved at the group. 'Much needed, for the future Lady Captain.'

Philly and Pru exchanged a nervous glance. 'Fuck,' Philly whispered towards Pru. 'I didn't prepare for that. Now what?'

'Be silent,' Pru whispered back through clenched teeth. 'Something will come to us.'

'God I hope so. I feel screwed already.' Philly suddenly wanted to slap Varilla in the face but composed herself, gesturing towards her friends, making them listen to her adversary, who was clearly enjoying the misery oozing out of Philly's pores.

Four pairs of eyes focused on Varilla, who took a massive breath. 'I will demand preferred times for the Ladies Section on Sundays.' She blurted out. 'Try and better that! Ha!' The small eyes were pitch black now, eyeing the other women, one by one, with deep contempt. 'Imagine us gals. Being able to tee off before lunch, just like the men.'

A long silence followed. Her friends were gawping at Varilla, their mouths wide open. Preferred times? Teeing off with the men? Philly couldn't believe what she just heard. She tried to catch her breath. 'You will never pull that off,' she piped.

'I will pull it off. I am sure of it. Positive. Deadly positive.' Varilla tried not to look smug but failed. 'And when I will,

I will not only step into history as the first Peckers Wood Lady Captain, but as the one that showed the rest how things are done around here.' She stepped back towards the Philly's car and crossed her arms in front of her. 'I am dying to hear your suggestion, Miss Hackkett. Assuming you have one, that is.'

Birdie shot a look at Philly, now looking despairing, and took a large stride forward, dramatically clearing her throat. 'Well, Varilla. To tell the truth, Philly was just asking us how we might feel about finally having a Ladies' room. So we don't need to change here in the car park, or in the kitchen's loo.'

'I was?,' Philly mouthed, exasperated.

'Yes. You were,' Birdie mouthed back.

Varilla grabbed her sides and pretended to double up in mock laughter. 'That is truly hilarious. Bashit, the club, spending money on us? Forget it. Lav and I have asked him a million times.' She stepped away from the car and pushed her face in front of Philly's. 'Can't wait for his reaction to this, what do you call it, joke? He'll be quite shocked, realizing that someone clearly as mad as a bag of ferrets is actually competing with me for the Captaincy.' Varilla pulled away and started walking towards the driving range, leaving a stunned group of women behind her. 'See you at five sharp, Philly.' Varilla's voice rang out over the car park. 'Can't wait to see the look on board member's faces when you share your brilliant plan.'

The gravel under Philly's feet crunched as she spun round to the Bangers. 'What the fuck? You bloody nitwits! Do have any idea in what position you have put me? Put us?' Her hands flew to her face and she groaned. 'Oh my God. Bashit will go ballistic.'

'Yes, he probably will,' Birdie replied with a grin. 'But when the stupid berk figures out he has no other option as to grant our wishes…' They balled their fists and started to move them up and down, again crying with laughter, and then moving their hands up to their eyes, pretending to gaze through a binocular.

Pru shook her head in wonder. 'Goodness gracious. You two are something else.'

Philly started to pace, feeling the nerves that were now seriously causing her stomach to turn. Her hand pressed hard on her abdomen, trying to calm it down. But fireballs were shooting holes in her stomach, as some kind of forewarning for the penetrating bullets from the firing squad she was obviously facing.

'Don't you dare get your knickers in a twist now,' Pru said, grabbing Philly's shoulders and shaking her friend carefully. 'You will make a professional appearance at the meeting.'

'Of course she will,' Birdie assured her.

The two sisters stepped forward, dragged Philly towards them and gave her a big wet kiss. 'Good luck, Captain. Knock 'm dead,' Bogey whispered. 'If anyone can pull this off, it's you.'

'Just be certain you ask for the Ladies Room, Philly,' Birdie Banger said, suddenly sounding serious.

CHAPTER 5

The walk from the car park to the clubhouse seemed much shorter than usual. Philly had tried to postpone the agony, but Varilla had leapt past her with an unusual spring in her step. She tried to swallow the bile in her throat, closing her eyes for a moment, getting her thoughts aligned. Why hadn't she seen this coming? Why didn't she think of a plan, a strategy to present during this meeting she had been wanting ever since she was a child? Why, for fuck's sake, had she allowed Varilla to get the better of her?

Because, Miss Hackkett, you assumed this opportunity would fly your way by itself with no effort from your part whatsoever. Not good enough, young lady. Not. Good. Enough.

A voice from the past rang through her head, causing her to relive that embarrassing moment in her secondary school's cold office after she came second in the annual debating contest. Being forced to listen to the obvious disappointment, feeling the shame hearing the head mistress tut about. How on earth was she going to tell her parents? Did she realize how disenchanted this would make them feel?

She had never come in second ever again.

And she certainly didn't intend to get beaten by that filthy cow today. Or tomorrow. Or any day. Philly squared her shoulders, shook her hair back and stepped forward to catch up with the short woman in front of her.

The main door was open, leaving no time to hover. The two women stepped into the great hall with the large white marble statue of a male golfer in the middle, his club in mid-follow through pointing towards Bashit's den - the clubhouse's beating heart. Varilla's sharp knock on the President's study entrance exuded confidence, making Philly stand up straight as she stepped over the threshold, after hearing Bashit's voice ordering them to enter.

She heard the dark oak door close behind her, sounding ominous, suddenly making her feel like an alien in this dark ancient man cave smelling of smoke, polish and Scotch. She shivered, despite the heat coming from the roaring fire, and tried to pull herself together by zooming in on the tiny holes woodworm had left in the dark panelling next to her.

One, two, three, four. Times two makes eight. Add four make twelve. She added the little dots up slowly, trying to synchronize her crazed heartbeat to her slow counting rhythm. The holes started to swim in front of her eyes, forcing her to focus on the row of black and white photographs showing a very young Bashit caddying for his father while playing with a famous St Andrew's board member.

I will not come second.

'Miss Hackkett, Mrs Van Dycke.'

The clear voice snapped Philly back to the present when she turned her attention to the President, his sharp blue eyes were staring right at her. She really just wanted to throw up, preferably over Varilla standing next to her looking annoyingly sure of herself. But it was time to face the music.

President Bashit pulled himself up on his stick and beamed towards the two women. 'Please do sit down,' he said, pointing towards the two dark green club chairs in front of the desk. 'I trust you found your way comfortably here to my quarters?'

Varilla Van Dycke sat down and nodded vigorously. 'Yes, sir.

Of course. I took the route you instructed.' She turned towards Philly. 'So I could be absolutely positive that I wouldn't be in anybody's way, risking members becoming uncomfortable. And I escorted Miss Hackkett, so she wouldn't get lost.'

The sharp upper-class voice cut through the study, accompanied by a condescending look towards Philly, making the room's awkward atmosphere even worse. Varilla rearranged herself in the chair, crossed her stocky legs and pulled the ancient tweed skirt over her knees, causing the others to stare at the long black hairs on her legs, stuck upwards under her brown stockings. Philly sneaked a look at Ben, who turned away, his expression giving away he was trying not to giggle.

'And President Bashit, thank you for this meeting. I am so looking forward to this new chapter,' Varilla said, while stroking the tweed pattern covering her upper legs. She swallowed, cleared her throat and stared at the baffled looking Bashit opposite her. 'I would like to take this opportunity to speak by quoting Dwight. D. Eisenhower.'

'You would, would you?' Bashit pulled up an eyebrow. 'Well, Mrs Van Dycke, don't let us stop you, off you go then.'

'Thank you, President.' Varilla smiled and rattled on. 'He once said, "*without integrity, no real success is possible, no matter whether it is on a section gang, a football field, in an army, or in an office.*"' She gulped for air and continued. '"*Honesty and integrity are two important ingredients which make a good leader. How can you expect your followers to be honest when you lack these qualities yourself?*"' She blurted out, paused and stared hard at Lieutenant Retired Bushrod. 'Especially on the golf course. Leadership. So important when being Captain. So important for Peckers Wood, the fine institution I love with all my heart.' The last word was emphasized by a dramatic flutter of Varilla's eyelids, her right hand clutched to her chest.

'Good lord.' Bashit quickly looked at Bushrod who suddenly dropped his face in a large blue handkerchief and started wheezing, loudly. Ben had turned away and was now busy inspecting the watercolours at the back of the study, clearly too embarrassed to face the group. Roughie had escaped, mumbling something about having to find Miss Snuggs for more tea and biscuits.

Philly started to feel better, sensing the effect Varilla's drama was causing. Her heartbeat slowed down a little and a flutter of careful excitement crept up her spine.

'Miss Hackkett? Any thoughts from your side?,' Bashit asked, clearly exasperated. 'Tell me, what's our club's appeal to you? Why are you here?'

Philly straightened herself, encouraged by her new found confidence. 'I adore the game, Mr President,' she said, concentrating hard to keep a normal pace to her words. 'And not only the game itself, but everything that comes with it, my friends, the fun we have, the competitiveness, how we learn, become better people by respecting rules and etiquette, and to be able to enjoy the beautiful surroundings. I just can't imagine my life without it, and I wish my good fortune on everyone. And I hope I can contribute in a meaningful way. To be of service to the club's future and its members.' A quick glance went towards Ben, who nodded to encourage her to speak further. 'It would be my wish that as many people as possible can enjoy the benefits of the game and of club life.'

'Well, well, Miss Hackkett. How noble of you. But you do realize most of us had to wait for ages to become members? We still have long waiting lists and harrowing selection procedures. Peckers Wood is a place for the happy few, and many members wish to keep it that way.' A long sigh escaped Bashit. 'Anything else?,' he asked, clearly indicating he had heard enough.

'Well, maybe it's a good idea if we listened to your thoughts first? Before getting ahead of ourselves? Maybe you would like to inform us on the votes?,' Philly suggested, turning her head sideways to Varilla, who tried to dismiss her with a mocking look.

'Yes.' President Bashit pushed his glasses further up his nose.

'Excellent suggestion.' He took a deep breath that seemed to stay in his chest forever before he began eyeing the notes in front of him and stared at the two women for a few seconds before he began. 'As you know, to become appointed Captain at this club, one needs at least 60% of the votes.' The papers ruffled in his hands. 'And, as far as I know, we've never had to check towards this rule during the Peckers Wood's long history because the vote for Captain has, as it should be, always been unanimous.'

'Hear, hear,' Varilla said, flashing her long teeth at everyone.

'That is...,' Bashit's words came out slowly with the emphasis on the last word, dragging it out, '...up till now. Alas your section, all the seven ladies we have on our membership list, didn't seem able to come together on the subject. The fact of the matter is, that you, Mrs Van Dycke, managed to get one vote in your favour.'

'What?,' Varilla gasped and jumped up, making Percy crawl under the desk and shiver. 'This can't be right.' Her face turned from bright pink to deep purple. 'I demand an explanation!'

Bashit ignored her outburst and addressed Philly, who was trying to remain calm and not leap up and cheer. 'And Miss Hackkett, you, got four.'

'What a bloody sham. You need to call for a recount!' Varilla was now sobbing, her head in her hands.

Bashit pressed on, unresponsive to Varilla's tantrum. 'Your one vote, apparently came from Miss Thorneybush, which I will now declare invalid,' the President said with his voice becoming louder with each word, 'because she felt the need to bugger off to ghastly Goodlie!' He shouted the last two words, causing the group to jump and cringe at the same time.

Bashit gave Varilla a hard stare during which she sat up carefully. 'Well, Ladies. The rules are explicit. Miss Hackkett. Congratulations on your new position. Lady Captain.'

Bashit stretched his right arm out, waited for Philly to stand up and reach towards him. He shook her hand while his bright blue eyes bore into hers. The silence that followed was overwhelming. No-one dared to speak, even Percy remained motionless. Breaking the tension, Bashit pulled back and waved a finger in the air. 'But, Mrs Van Dycke. Life isn't over. As your friend Eisenhower used to say, "for every obstacle there is a solution. Persistence is the key! The biggest mistake is giving up!"

His mischievous grin at the end of his speech made Philly smile, despite the flutters that were building up in her stomach again. 'Hear, hear,' she quietly concurred while sitting down.

'I do understand this isn't what you were hoping for, Mrs Van Dycke. But you have a second shot, you know. For next year.' Bashit pulled himself up, wobbled a little, found his balance and moved towards the other end of his desk, leaned on the side and bent over slightly. He crossed his arms over his chest, closed his eyes, as if deep in thought, opened them again and glared at Varilla, before deliberately turning to Philly. 'This is a major responsibility, for any representative of this wonderful institution. Empathy, sportsmanship, management skills, profound financial insight, excellent social skills. Being a true ambassador for Peckers Wood. With its future in mind. Club before self. Those sorts of things.' Bashit opened his eyes. 'Even for the women. Are you with me, Miss Hackkett?'

Philly nodded, attempting to look in charge, trying to take it all in. Was this really happening? Was she really on the verge of becoming Peckers Wood's first Lady Captain? 'Absolutely, President Bashit,' she said clearly. 'I am deeply honoured.' Hearing herself speaking here, in this room with its history, she nearly burst with pride.

'Good.' Bashit pointed towards Ben. 'Chipperfield. Please read the Club Captain's responsibilities out loud. So we all understand what we await concerning your position.'

Ben pulled his mobile from his pocket, tapped, scrolled, cleared his voice and eloquently stated the outlines about what was expected of him in terms of leading and organizing events, ensuring safe and enjoyable play, upholding rules, etiquette and traditions, being Peckers Wood's public face, chairing committee meetings, organizing prize givings, club occasions, providing the board with reports and be the playing Captain to the premier men's scratch league team.

'Well put. Thank you.' Bashit paused dramatically and addressed Philly. 'I have the fullest confidence that young Chipperfield will have everything under control. So you, Miss Hackkett, can concentrate on keeping your Lady section, containing all six lady members, on the straight and narrow.'

'Hear, hear,' Ben said, giving Philly a reassuring nod.

'But, before I end this meeting,' Bashit continued in a somewhat friendlier tone. 'I am sure you both had some kind of request or topic for coming year you wanted to share with us? Something special for the ladies? Like a new mat, for the driving range? A pink one, perhaps?' Bashit added a little wink to let Philly know he was quite aware of the female colour preferences.

Philly stared at him, not knowing how to react, other than nodding slowly. Had she understood correctly, had Bashit really said what he said? Her mouth started to fall open, ready for her to retort, but she controlled herself, seeing Ben shake his head ever so slightly.

'Good.' Bashit pointed at Varilla. 'As the result of this meeting might have come as a disappointment for Mrs Van Dycke, I will do my best to make the grapes a little less sour by making certain both your requests are met.' Bashit's smile nearly looked genuine. 'What can I do for you both, Mrs Van Dycke, Miss Hackkett?,' he asked in his sweetest voice.

CHAPTER 6

Her armpits were starting to get moist, and her mouth felt as if she was trying to suck water from a spoonful of dust. Witnessing Varilla making an utter fool of herself caused Philly to want to crawl under the President's desk and hide forever with vicarious shame. Why did the stupid woman go on about these damn starting times? Didn't she pick up on the throbbing veins in Bashit's neck and the froth that was starting to build up in the corners of his grey lips? Or the way the piercing eyes were narrowing with every argument Varilla added to make her case?

'Well?,' Varilla asked defiantly, 'when can we start Sunday mornings?'

Oh my God, Philly thought, watching Bashit inhale and stare at Ben, who intervened quickly, obviously sensing looming disaster.

'Varilla, we will have to discuss it with our starting times committee,' Ben said sternly. 'That's how it works.'

'Okay. Fine.' Varilla slumped back in her chair and sulked. 'But I won't be fobbed off, you know. I will be on your case right after the meeting. Don't you forget it.'

Bashit's eyes spread wide open revealing his emotion of utter contempt, and Bushrod looked as if he were about to combust.

'What about our Lady Captain. Any request?,' Ben asked carefully, turning to Philly, obviously wanting to quickly steer the attention away from Varilla.

Philly tried to collect herself while her thoughts raced to her friends, probably now waiting for her in the car park, eager to find out what triumph she had come up with. She just couldn't disappoint them. 'I would like a proper Ladies' room,' she blurted out, noticing her armpits getting sweatier by the second. 'So we don't need to change in the car park, can retreat after our game and not bother Miss Snuggs in the kitchen every time we need the loo.'

A death-like silence enveloped the room, followed by a thundering stumping noise.

'I beg your pardon?' Bushrod suddenly was on his feet, charging towards her. 'Kitchen not good enough for you? Retreat after a game?,' he thundered. 'Whatever next? Lounging on the men's bar's terrace, sipping a cognac? Smoking one of our cigars?' He shook his head in despair and sat down, shaking his head. 'Bloody nerve.'

Ben and Roughie exchanged a quick glance and looked away, obvious embarrassment oozing from their faces. Varilla's expression had turned from grumpy to horrified. Her hand was over her mouth, her body still, as if frozen in shock.

Purple blotches had raced up Philly's neck, now creeping up to her cheeks, making her face burn. She turned to Ben for support, but he was facing the floor, hands behind his back. Her eyes were drawn to President Bashit, noticing him grab his stick and slowly rise, looking demented, inhaling sharply through his blue veined nose before clearly stating the meeting was over and that he would come back with his reaction in his own time. That the ladies were dismissed, ordering Roughie to show them out with an annoyed flick of his wrist and at the same time shooting a warning look at his Treasurer.

—

The thick carpets in the hallways were like springs under Philly's feet, so eager she was to escape the clubhouse and its awkwardness. She jumped over the entrance's threshold and banged the door behind her, pausing for a second under the rose arch to breathe in some fresh air, noticing Varilla slipping out after her, not acknowledging her presence, evidently longing solitude and not wanting further embarrassment. Philly's hands covered her face. Ben hadn't even congratulated her. And she thought he would be so proud of her. Philly sighed, feeling a niggle of disappointment. But in all fairness, the study exploded before he had the chance. As expected.

God, she should have known better, she told herself, letting a low groan escape her. 'What on earth are we going to do?,' she whispered while shaking her head slowly. She hadn't even started and already made things worse.

A familiar sound of yakking came towards her. Maggie. Philly opened her eyes and watched her friends hopscotching down the path, following the little dog running in front of them. Pru reached her first and congratulated her with a peck on her head. Bogey stepped towards Philly and hugged her, her soft body and strong arms oozing comfort. 'Amazing job. Captain!'

Philly nodded carefully. 'Not quite certain how this meeting went though.' She stared at her feet. 'Not entirely sure I nailed the Ladies' room request. Bashit and Bushrod weren't overly enthusiastic about the idea.' She giggled, letting the nervous tension out. 'And Varilla's preferred times bummed as well.'

'Serves her right. Very silly idea from the start,' Bogey said.

'Never mind the Ladies' room. That will sort itself out,' Birdie added, putting her arms around the two of them and squeezing them tighter together. 'Philly? Go and see your Mum and Dad. Make them both prouder than proud, drive home, let beautiful Ben congratulate you with a good old bonk and all will be bright and beautiful tomorrow.'

Philly nodded slowly, taking her friend's advice in, trying to calm down. 'Where are you off to?,' she asked, watching the Bangers getting ready to leave.

'Nipping by our utterly yummy Caddy Master to pick up some new balls,' Birdie replied with a mischievous grin on her face.

'Ow. Splendid. Always worth the trouble,' Philly smiled. 'Lucky you. And then what?'

'Home,' Bogey said. 'We need to catch up on some emails, and Maggie has a backlog on her socials, her followers are so impatient.' She raised her eyes. 'And we're going to sell Granny's old coin collection online. Decided to swap them for cryptocurrency. Coins aren't any good to us. Can't buy anything with them.' She shook her head. 'And Granny loved doing cryptograms.'

'Yes,' Birdie nodded. 'Definitely.'

'My goodness. Poor Granny.' Pru shook her head in wonder and gave Philly a questioning look, who returned the same expression, fighting a giggle bubbling up from her stomach. As if Granny Banger didn't leave those two with enough dosh already.

'Right. I'm off to Mum and Dad,' Philly said, rummaging for her car keys. 'What about you, any plans? Want to join me?,' she asked Pru.

'No thanks, I need a run.' Pru looked away and twisted her earplugs in. 'To let some steam off. See you when I see you.' She glanced at the Bangers, turned on her heel and ran towards the car park.

The tight winding road from the club to her parents forced her to go slow, navigating the turns and making sure her brake was under her foot. Philly leaned into the neck rest, trying to relive the afternoon, the thought of the maniacal Bushrod and the probably consequential laughter in the men's bar made her heart race, pumping blood towards her head, building up hot flashes that flew to her cheeks.

Her hands gripped the wheel, and the car turned to the side of her parent's cottage. The sight of the medieval facade instantly relaxed her muscles and dropped her heart rate to a normal level. She stepped out of her car, walked to the iron fence with the tired piece of string that had been there forever, and followed the path towards the French doors at the back of the cottage facing the back of the garden, with the putting green in full view.

She held back for a moment, enjoying the fuzzy feeling the scenery gave her. That lovely patch of grass where she and her father had spent hours and hours, perfecting grips, distance and ball speed. Where she had invited her friends to come over and play. Where they had long conversations while her father had challenged them on so many levels.

That seemingly endless, carefree life. Without her self-inflicted heavy work schedule, eager to be the best business controller her boss could ever have.

Philly snapped back to the present, tripping over an uneven flagstone, making her pause just long enough to give her a few moments to take in the flower beds which oozed her mother's odd touch in gardening. The poppies and corn flowers in the unkempt border, kept smiling at her through the wafer-thin petals. Fat, hairy bumblebees were flying from one flower to the other, giving off their soothing buzzing sound. The smell of honey, nearly tangible, again took her back to the days when Mum let her pick the wild flowers and arrange them in one of the many vases that she kept in the pottery shed. Where she could watch her grandfather and Dad have a putting match on the green. Where she had tried Dad's new putter. Where she had felt the thrill of the best feeling in the whole wide world for the first time.

She smiled to herself despite the afternoon's shame rising again in her stomach and walked towards the kitchen window.

She stopped in front of it, seeing her parents together. Rays of early evening sun had re-appeared, filtering through the dense foliage and into the kitchen, seeming to illuminate the faded coppery grey on her father's head, nearly making it look like it did when she was a little girl. Bright fiery orange it once was, with specks of gold, like her own, but now it seemed faded, even in this light.

As her father bent his head towards his plate, Philly could clearly make out the last auburn-coloured strands between the grey, falling forward as his head moved along to the movement of his right fingertip, slowly sliding through the leftover gravy on his plate.

She turned her attention to her mother standing behind the kitchen sink and nodding towards her father. He was clearly concentrating on something in front of him, causing her mother to smile and toss the dishcloth she had been using towards the range. Her eyes went soft, as she cocked her head and stepped towards her husband. Carefully, she touched his left cheek and bent over his shoulder, her right cheek now very slowly moving towards her husband's left temple, her right hand cupping his right shoulder, squeezing it gently. The greying copper head moved under her mother's touch.

Philly watched, seeing the tip of her father's finger having now left the plate, covered with congealed, glistening gravy and sticky tomato ketchup. He pointed it towards Sniggles, their dog, who licked it gratefully.

That familiar fingertip. The one that used to push Philly's curls behind her ear when she snoozed against her father while watching telly, the one that waved at her when being told off for doing something stupid or pointed at her mother before tipping his lips with it, when the two of them, father and daughter, shared something private. Their special secrets about their clandestine outings, like squeezing through the rhododendron bushes at Peckers Wood and unseen by anyone play a few holes at the turn, just after dawn, before the members would arrive.

Her mother pulled her husband's plate towards her and held it up, high enough to be seen from the window.

I hart PPW, the gravy wipes read. Philly blinked, swallowed a lump away and stared at her parents. *I love Polly Pitching Wedge.*

A long kiss followed, making Philly back away in embarrassment. Time to make some noise to announce her arrival before things would get worse.

CHAPTER 7

'Who voted for Varilla?' The long silence in the Hackkett's warm country kitchen was broken by her mother's voice, while stroking Sniggles the old Rottweiler, his head resting on her lap.

Philly sighed and smiled ruefully. 'Lavatory Thorneybush.'

Mrs Hackkett smirked at the old joke and tickled the old dog's chin.

'A bit of a bummer though. I really thought you had the unanimous vote in the bag.' Mr Hackkett sighed and smiled ruefully. 'I bragged about you being Captain at the Turner's sweet shop, you know. And at the delicatessen. And the book shop.'

Mrs Hackkett smiled and winked at Philly. 'Lavender would never have voted for you now, would she?'

Philly shook her head while her mind raced back to her early childhood, picturing herself, sitting next to her mother, at this very kitchen table.

'Are you sorry for what you've done?,' her mother had asked, looking sternly down at her, the naughty little girl with the orange hair. Philly could still feel the red patches burning on her cheeks. *'No. Maybe.'* She swallowed, feeling the redness turn to deep purple. *'Should I be? It's just Lavender Thorneybush,'* she had said, leaning back in her chair, trying to calm down by staring at the potted geranium in front of her, eager to forget all about

what happened to her after her first day at primary school. To when she came home, being sent directly to her father in the drawing room, where a massive bollocking followed because Head Mistress Clapp had rung him about the frightful frog fiasco. When she had run to Mum in the kitchen who had listened calmly to her admitting what she shoved into Lavender Thorneybush's knickers. And then told her that this was unacceptable behaviour. That if she wanted to remain being Mum's best friend, she could not be cruel to animals. *'Imagine how Mr Frog must have felt, being stuck in Lavender's underpants?,'* Mum had said. *'Extremely uncomfortable, most likely. How would you feel if someone did that to you? Poor Mr Frog.'* And when she convinced her she should apologize to old Head Mistress Clapp for calling her a stupid cow. That it was very cruel to assume all cows were stupid. That neither head mistresses nor cows deserved being bullied. Nor did poor Lavender Thorneybush. Her mother had pointed her finger at her. *'Just promise me you'll be good. Look at me. No pissing about, Philomena Hackkett,'* she had said, very sternly.

No pissing about. Her mother had been right. She always was. But come on. Poor Lavender Thorneybush? Who had called her Silly Philly Fanta from the moment she stepped into the classroom? And kept hissing it at her every chance she got? Luckily nice little girl Prudence who had been appointed to sit next to her had helped holding Lav down so she could shove the frog down her pants without harming it too much.

'Well.' Her father's voice behind her brought Philly back to the present. 'A Peckers Wood Lady Captain in the house. How super exciting.'

The kitchen went silent again, Mr Hackkett holding Philly's hand, blinking away the happy tears, the only noise coming from Sniggles, snoring, now lying against Mrs Hackkett's legs.

'Right.' Philly pulled her hand away. 'And about time too.' She glanced at her mother who was starting to look dark like she always did when the subject of Peckers Wood and women came up. 'But enough of that. What is new with you two?,' she asked, trying to change the subject.

'Your mother beat me yesterday. Not that's something new,' Mr Hackkett said in an attempt to catch his wife's attention. 'We played nearest to pin, pitching at the back of the garden, and Dorothy Hackkett beat me. Again.' He shook his head. 'And still she won't come with me on a green fee.'

'I see,' Philly said carefully, aware of her failure of turning things around, and her mother looking annoyed again.

'Play with the wife? At Peckers Wood? Not a chance.' Her mother's voice sounded taut. 'And I myself really don't see the added value, spending my time and money being surrounded by a bunch of misogynist mastodons,' she said while glancing at Philly. 'Don't get me wrong. I'm proud of you becoming Lady Captain, but how you and your friends put up with those men at that obsolete golf club with its prehistoric traditions, I do not know.'

'I beg your pardon?,' Mr Hackkett said, mockingly. 'Are you suggesting I am some sort of dinosaur with a grudge against women?'

Mrs Hackkett picked up a clean cloth and threw it towards her husband. 'Whoops. Sorry. No, not you. Which is a miracle, knowing the board and its staunch followers. Come on, you know as well as I do they put up with the girls because they have to, not because they want to.' She turned to Philly. 'This isn't breaking news to you, is it?'

Philly shook her head, thinking about all the jokes and puns she had to put up with over the years, making her smirk. *Why shouldn't you let women play golf? Because they can't drive.* Ha bloody ha. So lame. But still causing hysterics in the pub.

'Tell me, why do you think the men act like they do?,' Mrs Hackkett asked.

Her mother's question snapped her back to the conversation. 'I don't know. They just think we are a bunch of silly creatures who don't understand what the game is all about, I suppose. That we don't grasp what sportsmanship is, competition spirit, or how important scores are. That kind of nonsense.' Philly shrugged. 'As if we just walk around the course talking about curtains and stuff. And then go home to paint our nails.'

'O come on you two!' Mr Hackkett raised his eyes towards the ceiling. 'Don't be so bloody sensitive.' He pointed a biscuit towards Sniggles who snatched it and swallowed it down in one go. 'But now that we are on the subject, and everything seems so god damn awful, why do you put up with us at the club?'

'Because just like you,' Philly replied, leaning towards him, 'we girls think the course is sensational, the surroundings take our breath away, and we get to play the game we love the most in the world, together, as best friends.'

'And don't forget there are some yummy young men skulking about.' Now Mrs Hackkett giggled and winked at Philly who turned red. 'Anyway. Miss Hackkett, Mr Hackkett, why don't you two sod off together so I can do a good clean up in here after your father's culinary adventure?'

Philly nodded, moved towards her father and put her arm around the tall figure. 'We have some time to ourselves. A putting match? Outside?'

'Nope. Too damn hot. Telly.'

'Right. Telly it is. Let's take the scenic route,' she said. 'At least you'll be out in the sunshine for a couple of minutes. That won't kill you.'

'No. But the nagging about the club will.' Mr Hackkett pushed Philly out of the kitchen door and out onto the small patio where small birds were splashing about in their baths next to the gold fish pond. He took her arm and pulled his daughter towards him, standing still for a while, enjoying the peace and quiet.

The squeeze of his fingers round her hand made Philly look up at him, seeing the familiar eyes turned towards her. She focused on the specks of brown in the green between the long lashes, just like her own, noticing a slight smile coming up.

'Listen, old girl,' her father said, brushing a curl from her face, 'I'm really proud of you.' He paused for a moment. 'You girls will be fine, just keep your heads down.'

'Our heads down? Why? So we won't be tempted and dare to look the men in the eyes?,' Philly smirked.

Her father wagged a finger at her. 'Please don't play the victim, Philly. It doesn't suit you.' His voice went grave. 'And make Varilla your priority. Your six ladies, your section, needs to align. Don't forget Mrs Pushet.'

Philly nodded and looked at his hand, simultaneously stroking the blue veins with her thumb. 'Sure. If you say so,' she said absentmindedly.

The old hand remained still, and her father's eyes turned towards hers again, this time looking serious. 'Listen, light of my life, why do you girls dislike Varilla? She seems harmless to me.'

Philly averted her look and tugged him gently, forcing her father to start walking again. They moved from the patio along the garden path at a slow pace before reaching the drawing room's back door.

'Must be difficult for her to connect with you lot, being, what is she, about 10 years your senior?'

'8 years. She's 33. And it's not about age,' Philly admitted after the moment of silence. 'She's pompous, self-centred and smug. Not nearly in Lav's league, but still.'

'No. Really?,' Mr Hackkett said, a familiar teasing twinkle popping up in his eyes. 'Bit like your best chums the Banger sisters then?'

'Ha, bloody ha.' Philly shot him a dark look, opened the door and pushed her father inside. 'Not funny, Dad.'

Mr Hackkett smiled and settled in his chair. He pulled a cushion behind his back and bent forward to pull out a box from the shelves next to him. A worn tape disappeared in the ancient VCR machine, and the telly above it flashed itself into action, just a split-second before Peter Allis's soothing voice filled the room, making her father's face light up. Philly pulled a chair up next to him and watched her dad become transfixed with the action on the screen, as if he was seeing it for the first time instead of the seemingly endless times they had enjoyed this together.

She glanced round the room, trying to suppress her emotion about the day's events by concentrating on the old pictures. All her academic achievements, carefully framed. A black and white snapshot of Pru, the Banger sisters and herself in their newest school uniform. And of course, her mother's most prized possession: a tattered copy of the letter she wrote to President Bashit when she was nine years old, challenging him to tear down the *'No dogs or women allowed'* sign which had hung at Peckers Wood Golf Club's gate for nearly two centuries. Bashit surprisingly honoured her request after she was invited for an interview at the club. Philly smiled, remembering how grown up she had felt, walking up to the clubhouse and announcing herself to the valet. And how President Bashit actually seemed interested in what she had to say. That he had even asked Mrs Snuggs, the silent disapproving housekeeper and grandmother to her current replacement, to bring them flapjacks to go with their tea because he knew that they were her favourites. How he had made his secretary take notes on her arguments on why girls were just as capable as boys, and how towards the end of the meeting, he told her all about the new puppy he and Mrs Bashit had recently acquired, showing her its adorable little face beaming from the framed picture on his large imposing desk.

She had felt so important, sitting there in the large flowery chair with President Bashit listening to her points about girls being good sports, future champions and how they could be of added value to the club. She didn't know at the time that her mother had threatened to involve Mrs Rough, married to Mr Rough, one of the most rich and influential men in the club. Through her husband, Mrs Rough had insisted that Philly and President Bashit should take down the sign together, make it a special moment, a statement that showed the club was ready for its next step. The fact that the much sought-after, brand-new driving range was constructed almost simultaneously with this memorable event was quickly dismissed as a coincidence.

The little ceremony had been her mother's proudest moment. She had even forked out for a new golf outfit for Philly: pink sweater, white polo shirt, checked trousers and new golf shoes thrown in. Philly had never felt so proud, standing there, feeling the spikes under her feet while she and President Bashit turned the screwdriver towards the sign together, the cameras clicking behind them.

And now, nearly twenty years later, Peckers Wood was ready for yet another step into the future. The appointment of the first Lady Captain. Philly smiled to herself. She would make it work. She would show her Lady Section was ready to grow. Together with her friends. The itchy feeling of unease that had bothered her all day suddenly disappeared from her stomach, making her feel happy and relaxed again.

She leaned towards her father and turned her attention to the telly, watching Seve Ballesteros win the 1987 Ryder Cup for Europe for the zillionth time, seeing her father's hand fly into the air like it did countless times before. 'I can never get enough of this, Philly, never.' His elation was so familiar, so comforting, just like the joy in his eyes.

She bent over and hugged the skinny shoulders. 'Yes. I know.' She squeezed a little tighter, not wanting to let go, savouring the moment of having her father all to herself, just like during the good old days. The old VCR clicked and spitted the tape out.

'Ah, there you are.'

Philly felt a tinge of disappointment, followed by guilt, when her mother came in carrying a tray, and settled herself on the arm of her father's chair. Her index finger with the ever-present coral pink nail varnish slid thin pieces of cake between her husband's lips. They seemed so absorbed in each other. So absolutely perfect together.

Mrs Hackkett turned to her own tea and took a few sips before she gave Philly a knowing stare. 'It's Saturday night, you need to be out, with your new boyfriend.'

'Absolutely. Bugger off,' her father uttered, fiddling with the VCR and not looking at either of them.

'Give my regards to Club Captain Chipperfield. Bring him over for supper sometime.' Mrs Hackkett stood up and walked her to the back entrance, clearly wanting her daughter to leave.

The door closed behind her, and she rested her head against it, hearing the lock turn, shutting her out of her childhood comfort and sending her out into the real world. Philly inhaled, trying to figure out what the best approach would be, making her think of the Bangers. She stretched and squared her shoulders. Yes. Bonk beautiful Ben. Best advice ever.

CHAPTER 8

Keys rattled, and Philly pushed open the squeaky kitchen door. She closed her eyes for a moment and breathed in deeply, letting the small flat's familiar smell of slightly burnt toast and Ben's scent drift up her nose, soothing and arousing her at the same, chasing the images of the afternoon's awkwardness from her brain. *Fuck Bashit*, she thought. *And Bushrod*. Or rather not. She was going to fuck her new boyfriend instead. Just like her friends had suggested.

She undressed, stepped into bed and pretended to sleep hearing Ben come in, but through her eyelashes watched him toss his shoes towards the corner and throw his blazer on top of it. The wooden floor boards creaked under his weight as he tiptoed to the chair opposite the bed and sat down, looking at her, on her back, naked, her long hair spread over the white cushion. One arm stretched towards his side, the other arm crossed over her belly button, just under the hollow in her stomach. Her legs slightly apart, one leg straight and the other slightly bent.

She opened her eyes a little and stared at him, sitting there. So absolutely beautiful, so stunningly handsome, gazing at her, now starting to undress slowly, showing his erection growing, his thumb tugging the elastic band of his briefs, and they went down over his legs quickly. She watched him lean backwards, his eyes still on her, his cock hard and upright.

'Hay, sailor.' Her fingers moved downwards, between her legs, feeling excited. 'Are you saving that for me?' She started stroking herself, slowly.

He was on her in a flash. His hands in her hair, moving her face towards his. His tongue in her mouth, finding hers. Her legs wrapped around him, and she tugged him close, gasping, feeling his cock sliding into her, pushing herself towards him, making him pull her on his lap. His mouth found a nipple, causing her to moan as he sucked it and pushed himself deeper. Her arms forced his head towards her, her long hair falling over him. She started to ride him, slowly at first but picking up speed with every thrust. Her back arched backwards, letting her nipples bounce in front of him.

She knew he couldn't hold it any longer. Philly let go of him as he fell backwards, his eyes never leaving hers. His arms stretched towards her, and he pulled her next to her, with his hands going through her hair, turning his face toward her.

'God, I love you.' He closed his eyes and wrapped his arms around her. His lower lip quivered. 'So much.' The embrace tightened. 'Whether you're Lady Captain or not.'

'Right.' She tried to loosen his arms and looked at the face next to her. His dark eyes had a troubled look, the long eyelashes fluttered suddenly.

'Ben? What's the matter?'

A silence followed, his eyes still on hers, making her feel awkward.

'Ben?'

'Please tell me you're not really asking for a Ladies' room.' She heard him whisper, desperation clearly sounding through his words. 'Bashit was beside himself with rage after your meeting. He kept yelling about traditions. Bushrod kept on ranting about women knowing their place.' Ben rolled on his back and covered his face. 'Oh my God, I've never seen them so upset.' A long sigh followed his desperate whisper. 'What a cock-up.' His fingers started rubbing his eyes. 'Jesus, Philly. Fucking hell. You should have let Varilla fall flat on her face with that preferred times nonsense and left it at that.' His head rolled towards her. 'What in the hell were you thinking?,' he asked.

'What do you think? Justice, of course. Not wanting to fall flat on my face. Showing no ambition at the beginning of my year. Not wanting to be upstaged by my rival,' Philly pouted. 'I just didn't want to look like a loser.'

'Right. I see,' Ben sighed. 'At least I think I do,' he said, confusion sounding through.

'Good. Thank you. And now we're on the subject, there's something else I want to talk to you about. Something that happened at the club. Something worrying.'

'Oh God,' Ben groaned. 'Really? Can this get any worse?'

Philly frowned. 'Besides being insulted and belittled by Varilla the Gorilla and being yelled at by a demonic Treasurer I had another traumatizing experience.' She pulled herself up and straddled him. 'We, Pru, the Bangers and I, were changing in the car park, and I felt watched somehow.' She shivered and continued. 'I looked towards the clubhouse and distinctly saw a man with binoculars, checking us out. A peeping Tom.'

'You're joking.' Ben sounded concerned but looked distracted. 'That's disgusting,' he said slowly, now stroking her upper legs and trying to focus on Philly's face instead of the pink nipples pointing towards him. 'Are you sure?'

'O, yes,' Philly nodded. 'No doubt in my mind. I bent down to tie my shoe laces and saw him with his binoculars pointed at my bum. There is a voyeur among the good members of Peckers Wood.'

'Good lord.' Ben managed to tear his eyes away from her breasts and stared at her face. 'That's serious. I will have to inform Bashit the minute I see him.' He shook his head and let out a long moan. 'That will set him off again. But don't worry, and tell your girls I will make sure the culprit is found and taken care of.'

Philly waved a finger at him. 'I trust you to see to it, Captain Ben. That this will never happen again. I sincerely hope that the Club Captain won't condone this kind of nonsense. Otherwise I, Lady Captain, will have to call for a meeting with the board.'

'God, no. Absolutely not,' Ben said while his head shook fiercely.

'Come here, you big lover.' Philly started to grin. 'Let's do seconds and talk about Bashit later.'

She felt Ben go hard again and whisper 'I want you so much, Philly.'

She moved down, sliding her hand over his cock and bending her head towards it. 'Good,' she whispered before going down on him.

CHAPTER 9

To: secretary@peckerswood.co.uk
From: banger@home.co.uk
Cc: President@peckerswood.co.uk
Subject: yucky creep

17th of June 2022

Dear Secretary, darling Roughie,

Just a little note from one of your favourite girlies to let you know we were REALLY, REALLY FRIGHTENED today. And still VERY, VERY UPSET. Just can't stop crying. Have faces like chewed up toffee, after today's billion tears.

All because we have a BEASTLY YUCKY CREEP at our golf club. Who stares at us. Whilst changing shoes in the car park. Through bins. From the clubhouse. At our bottoms. And our chests. It's ABSOLUTELY HORRID.

Do realize we are unbelievably drop dead gorgeous and is virtually impossible not to stare at us. So, I thought it might be a good idea if you made sure we are not always in clear sight, when changing. Otherwise it might get FRIGHTFULLY OUT OF HAND.

What if your fabulous mother is also stared at by this PERVERT when she comes to visit you, and she throws a wobbly in front of Bashit? Or, if this filthy person indeed has a BIZARRE fetish, and pounces on poor old Varilla? One CANNOT IMAGINE what might happen next.

What if it reaches the newspaper?

Thousand cuddles and kisses,

Bogey B.

PS My sister just mentioned we might need a little room, for us ladies to change and stuff. So we won't be seen. Or heard. That would be just perfect for me too.

CHAPTER 10

Roughie inhaled deeply, feeling nauseous after finishing the last email and closed his laptop with a slow push of his index finger. He leaned backwards, feeling the old leather chair creak. He slowly exhaled and closed his eyes, forcing himself towards some happy thoughts to chase the feel of unease away.

His mind drifted back almost 20 years to Dimple House's kitchen, the sisters' home, but then still Granny Banger's, instantly feeling its warmth and the smell of apple crumble. He could still see the two sisters sitting opposite of him, huddled together, giggling naughtily and looking so adorable in their school uniforms, with their angelic round faces shining above crisp white bows, tied around their little necks. Their broad smiles revealed the large gaps where their front teeth would soon appear, but now causing them to lisp in such a sweet way.

Granny Banger had ticked them off, warning them to be kind to that nice young man who came to visit and wanted to be their friend. So they had run towards him and crawled on his lap, kissing him, telling him he was their new buddy, while begging for a cuddle and a game of hide and seek. During this game, they always frightened him to death, popping out of dark hideaways with high-pitched screams when he least expected it. They would fall over with laughter as he turned grey with fright, which they saw as a new opportunity to smother him with kisses and tickle him until he couldn't do anything but wiggle and giggle underneath them until he had to surrender for yet another game. He never resisted. Because he just couldn't. Not then. Not now.

He slowly sat up, feeling a little better, reached for his top drawer and stroked the large yellow envelope inside. He flipped it open and turned it upside down, catching the pictures with one hand and spreading them out on his desk, revealing the sisters, from left to right, starting as little girls with chubby brown legs under pleated skirts and evolving to curvy young women in tight jeans tucked into green wellies, throwing sticks for a pack of dogs that were following them to catch.

Every once in a while, he would send a picture to Mr and Mrs Banger, working all over the globe, always on some documentary, ever since the girls were small. All those years ago Mr Banger had made him promise to keep an eye on, what he called, his two little mischiefs Burdine and Bogine, the names that were hard to make out correctly, especially with their front teeth missing. Mr Banger said that they were in fine hands with Granny, but could do with some masculine guidance, now and then. Although he was only three years older than the girls, Roughie had felt so grown up and important when Mr Banger kissed his daughters goodbye and vanished to Peru with Mrs Banger. After their departure, the sisters had sulked for a while, but Granny had managed to cheer them up with a plate of fish fingers and chips and had suggested Roughie should take them off to Peckers Wood's new driving range to hit some balls. Granny reassured him she had talked to Bashit, and that he was fine with the girls coming, as long as chaperoned by Roughie.

So they went out to the club as much as they could, during school holidays and weekends. When they were still in primary school, Roughie had squandered all his pocket money on buying the sisters ice creams and lemon squash. They nagged him all day long, wanting to use his clubs instead of their own, unrelenting in begging for longest drive competitions and, embarrassingly so, winning nearly all of them. When they were all at boarding school and came home for what now seemed endless long hot summers, the girls used to strip to their underwear and jump into the lake, fishing up balls, throwing them at him at blinding speed, and then climbing out of the water, hitting the balls back in again and repeating the whole exercise, all day long. His pocket money seemingly disappeared even faster, as the craving for ice cream and squash had now turned into demanding sparkling white wine and endless packets of salt and vinegar crisps, which they gobbled up, huddled against him, a sister on each side, trying to get dry after their swims, their underwear clinging to them, not leaving anything to his imagination. Roughie knew he should tell them to put their clothes back on, but he never did somehow.

His left hand moved to his favourite picture of the two girls - on the 18th green in tight tops and pleated golf skorts, high white knee socks with little bows just under tanned knees, their arms around each other and blowing kisses into the camera, bent over, just enough to reveal their tanned breasts, nearly falling out of their tops. He had made copies of that picture and several others, selling them at school and to the youth members at Peckers Wood, enabling him to buy the girls whatever they asked for when the three of them were together, which, if he didn't have to train for the youth competition, and they weren't hanging around Philly and Pru, was always.

Bobby Long and Henri Sweet never caught on that he watched them secretly, jerking off together behind the shack at the fifth, hanging over the pictures they had spent their summer job's wages on. Roughie smiled to himself. Those two were still smitten, after all those years. But the sisters kept fobbing them off, obviously not interested at all, despite all the tricks Long and Sweet were trying on them.

His index finger slid the pictures towards the left, all except for one. His very favourite. Roughie's right hand moved to his crotch, trying to push his slowly growing erection down, feeling embarrassed and excited at the same time. He stared at the image, feeling himself grow rock hard in his palm. He swallowed and blinked, focused on the pretty young woman, staring at him from his desk, making his hand go up and down slowly, picking up pace concentrating on the figure in the tight uniform, the sweet face with the kind violet eyes staring into his, the light brown freckles on the straight nose. Roughie pulled a tissue from his drawer, stuffed it into his underpants and cleaned himself up after coming with a short shudder. He stared at the pictures showing the sisters, shook his head and felt himself go limp.

A deep moan escaped him, feeling the dread rising. But he eventually rose and set off down the hall towards Bashit's study for the meeting called by Ben.

CHAPTER 11

Another log landed crookedly on the fire's core, causing the wood to smoke, making the President's study feel even more oppressive.

'A voyeur, you say.' President Bashit cleared his throat and fiddled with the poker. 'Are you two quite sure, Chipperfield, Roughie? I find that very hard to believe,' he said, turning away from the fireplace and staring over his glasses at the row of *Golf Illustrated* copies stacked next to the old hardcover encyclopaedia. 'I mean, honestly. Among our good members?' He paused for a second and looked away. *What lowlife would do such a thing, he thought. Behaving like some oversexed little monkey?*

Ben stood up and walked towards the little sassed window at the back of the study, pushed the thick curtains aside and sighed wearily. 'Are you calling Miss Hackkett and Miss Banger liars, Bashit?' he asked, turning round and sighing again. 'They were very clear about what they witnessed last Saturday you know. There, in that car park. Late afternoon.' He turned to Roughie who was fiddling about with a piece of printed paper.

Last Saturday? President Bashit suddenly felt nauseous. Late afternoon? He took his handkerchief from his pocket and wiped a couple of droplets from his forehead. 'What exactly did they see?,' he asked, his voice sounding a little less confident than usual.

Ben cleared his throat and glanced at Roughie, who was now slumped forward, inspecting the carpet's elaborate pattern, clearly very uncomfortable. 'Philly said she saw a man, maybe even two, with binoculars, looking her up,' he said slowly. 'And her friends confirm that. While they were bent over, greeting their dog, tying their shoe laces.'

'I see,' Bashit replied, still not sounding his usual assured self. 'But they didn't recognize these individuals?'

'No. But if they had, I would have had them by the balls.' Ben walked back to the desk and stared at President Bashit. 'And I would have moved heaven and earth to have the pieces of filth expelled. Publicly.'

Pieces of filth expelled? Publicly? 'That's a bit harsh, don't you think?,' President Bashit whispered. 'I mean, these men could have been, well, you know, just have been interested in the cars, or something.' The handkerchief moved over Bashit's forehead again. 'I am sure this is some kind of misunderstanding.' Sweat was now pouring from the older man's face that turned into a ghoulish pasty colour.

'I'm not convinced, President,' Ben said. 'And I am not amused. I want your word that you will do everything in your power to be certain that this won't happen again.' He sat down in the flowery antique chair opposite the large desk, while continuing his stare at the puffing man in front of him. 'So what do you suggest we do, to be certain that these voyeurs don't have the opportunity to take pleasure from staring at innocent women changing in our car park?'

'Good grief.' President Bashit fell backwards and put his hands over his face. Trust bloody women to make everything complicated. He groaned and watched Ben walk to the window sill at the back of the study. 'Any bright ideas, Roughie?'

A long silence followed.

'Well.' Ben sat down, looked over the car park and turned back to President Bashit. 'We could do a thorough investigation.

Grill all the members that were here last Saturday, check tee times, figure out who was where and when during the afternoon.' He stared towards the cars again. 'Shouldn't be too difficult. Then we find the bastards, squeeze a confession out of them and then, I suppose, ring the police.'

'The police?,' Roughie whispered, hardly audible.

'Yes.' Ben nodded. 'You know the Chief Constable, don't you, President? Isn't he in your Rotary Club? Good to have friends in high places to help us conduct a professional investigation.'

Ben stood up again and slowly walked over to the Victorian chest of drawers in the study's far corner. 'I mean, there's motive, we've already covered that. The perpetrators are clearly oversexed,' he said slowly, carefully touching the items on display: the silverware, the antique paper knife, the binoculars. 'And, then we need to cover means.' He picked the binoculars up for a second and put them down again, very slowly.

'I see,' President Bashit squeaked. 'And what else?'

'Well, let's have think.' Ben's voice sounded thoughtful. 'That leaves us with opportunity, President. And I think we can assume we have opportunity in spades.' Ben shrugged and continued. 'I mean, the women are here every weekend, bending over to tie their shoe laces, wriggling their bodies trying to get into their attire, all while in their cars. Reaching over into their car boots, tugging heavy golf bags out. Pushing their chests out, trying to pull their bags into position.'

The President suddenly sat up. 'Really, Chipperfield?' His voice had returned to normal again. 'How very perceptive of you. Good to know you are keeping such a close eye on the ladies. The Chief Constable will be very interested to hear your points of view.' He pointed his stick at the young man in front of him. 'With your particular interest in Miss Hackkett.' The President's chin came down, and he peered over his glasses, locking Ben's eyes. 'Does poor old Hackkett senior know? That you are drooling over his daughter? Like some overse…' The stick came down slowly, the soft thump emphasizing the last words.

A hot flash rushed up towards Ben's face, and he pulled at his jersey, trying to release the sudden tightening tension it was causing. He sat down carefully, trying to swallow the lumps away that were boiling up in his throat and to avoid the cold, cunning eyes boring right through him.

'But, Chipperfield. I get your point. Let's look at this situation objectively.' Bashit's right hand came up, and he pointed his finger at Ben. 'First, let's be frank about it, half of our members become oversexed little monkeys when confronted with good looking, wriggling women. I mean, who can blame them?' The hand moved upwards, now with two fingers sticking out in a V. 'Two, we have binoculars lying all over the place. Most of our members hugely enjoy the occasional bird watching.'

Ben swallowed again, trying to ignore the nervous giggle that was building in his stomach. He looked away and nodded silently.

A deep sigh escaped the President. 'In order to avoid jumping out of the frying pan and into the fire, we need to tackle opportunity. So the guarding foxes may be relieved from their duties, so to speak, Chipperfield.' The cold stare was still on Ben's face. 'Get a move on, then you two. Chop, chop.' The President looked up. 'Solve this cock-up for once and for all.'

'By doing what?' Ben asked, clearly mystified.

'By making sure they have a bloody hen-house, where they can wriggle among themselves privately, you birdbrains.'

CHAPTER 12

'Philly? Is that you?'

'Yes.' Philly held the phone against her ear and rolled back towards Ben. 'How can I help you?,' she asked, nestling herself against the warm, dark body next to her and glancing downwards, seeing their skins together, hers milk dotted with cinnamon sprinkles against Ben's creamy, chocolate glow.

'You haven't forgotten, have you?'

'Forgotten what?' Philly opened her eyes wider, taking in the scene of the flat's bedroom, strewn with clothes and tapas boxes, the sour smell of the leftover white wine in the two cut glasses on the nightstand making her stomach turn.

Birdie sighed. 'Finishing the Ladies' room transformation of the old tool stable? Making sure the plumbers have done their job properly? Please tell me you'll be there. After all the trouble Roughie went through to get it mucked out and painted?'

Philly shot up. 'Yes. Of course. Give us half an hour.'

'Good.' Birdie left a short pause before she continued. 'Why don't you ask Ben to make you a coffee? Might speed and sober you up.'

The call ended abruptly, the embarrassment of being caught rising up in Philly's body. How fucking uncanny that Birdie knew she was in bed with Ben. She shook her head, remembering last night's sweaty escapades.

'Freckles?'

The door opened slowly, showing Pru's face, peeking in and asking if she was ready, crumpling her nose in disgust. 'God. That's quite a pong you two have brewed up in here.' Pru pushed the door and stepped inside, looking ready for a hard day's work in a crisp T-shirt and pair of faded designer jeans. 'And cover him up, will you,' she whispered loudly, shielding her eyes and waving her hand towards Ben's naked body.

Philly grabbed a pillow and threw it at her friend. 'Greenkeeper's shack still standing, is it?'

'I don't have the foggiest what you're talking about.' Pru shrugged and looked away, trying to hide her burning cheeks from her friend and telling her to move her behind and get dressed so they could keep their promise to the Bangers to be outside in 20 minutes.

'You know I loathe to be late,' Pru said throwing a sweatshirt towards her friend.

Pru put the bucket down and knelt down next to Mrs Pushet who was on her knees vigorously moving a hard sweeper up and down the floor. She told the older lady to take a rest and let her finish the last bit of scrubbing. The Bangers moved towards them, a mop in each hand, ready to finish the floor and plug in the fridge and microwave. Philly was nearly done with the telly and said she would fix the light.

'My word, Maggie,' Mrs Pushet said, while looking round and holding the little dog to her chest. 'Here we are in your very own Ladies' room. And it looks super.' She smiled warmly. 'I'm so pleased you asked me to tag along. I'm having great fun with you girls.'

Philly looked down at them, feeling proud. It all looked exactly how she imagined it. A nice crisp and bright room, large enough for a party but not too big to feel uncomfortable with just the six of them. A spot in the middle to slump and relax, combined with a decent table and chairs to eat properly or conduct a meeting. On a tiny budget and with a lot of creativity, they managed to make this old stable into something rather decent in a couple of days.

Bashit had kept word, got a team of handymen in who worked quickly under strict supervision of Lash Johnsson, the Caddy Master. The forgotten damp toolshed had been cleared and stripped down to its bare wooden floor boards. The dirty walls had been painted white. Brand new electric sockets were now in place, and a dividing wall was put in hiding the new loo and shower room from sight. Roughie had also chipped in, by accompanying the Bangers to an IKEA shopping spree for mountains of cushions and rugs, where he reluctantly agreed to adding a small kitchen unit.

Mrs Pushet put Maggie down, walked over to the fridge and pulled a bottle of wine from the cardboard box. 'Bugger the tea,' she called out. 'Pru, why don't you fetch my bag. We need to celebrate.'

Wine glasses appeared from the large scruffy handbag, and Pru wiped them carefully before passing them to Bogey who promptly filled them up with sparkling wine and raised her glass to the women around her.

'To us,' she said. 'And to our darling President, protecting us from oversexed little monkeys.' She paused for a moment and smiled at the confused looking Philly and Pru before she continued. 'And of course to suddenly well willing Chairmen and Secretaries.'

Mrs Pushet started to giggle. 'You are wicked, young ladies,' she said, winking at the Bangers.

'Who? Me?,' Bogey Banger asked, innocently. 'I wouldn't call myself that. We just must make the most of opportunities that are presented to us.'

Their attention turned to the door, hearing a soft knock. 'Who's there?,' Birdie Banger asked.

'It's Secretary Rough. Roughie. Can I come in?'

'No,' Bogey Banger replied. 'This is the Ladies' room. You're not a lady.' She winked at her sister. 'We too can play that game,' she whispered.

'What do you want?,' Birdie Banger called out.

'President Bashit instructed me to do an inspection,' Roughie replied. 'To see if you're not wrecking the place and, if everything is in order, to hand the extra set of keys over.'

'Fair enough. Come in then.'

Roughie pushed the door open, choked as if his breath was cut off by the chlorine mixed with turpentine and took in the scene in front of him. Philly, up on a ladder fixing a light bulb. Pru Love, on all fours, folding an electric cable over a skirting. Next to a familiar-looking coffee table, he noticed the plastic chairs the Bangers found at a car boot sale on their way back from their trip to that ghastly furniture department store. Some rather decent framed photographs of women in old fashioned dresses swinging a hickory club, hanging above a sofa. A box with six bottles of white wine, perched on an old fridge. Maggie's basket sat next to it with a new blanket. Everything looked neat and tidy, rather homely somehow with the flowers and plumped-up cushions.

Seeing them in the room it suddenly all seemed to make perfect sense, this Ladies' room. It must have been so inconvenient for poor Miss Snuggs to have to put up with them bursting into the kitchen all the time, wanting to use the loo and boil the kettle. He had surreptitiously asked Ben why the Ladies didn't have their own quarters up till now, but Ben had just dismissed it, pointing out there hadn't been much point as there were only a small handful of women roaming around anyway. Setting up the red tee markers for them had been hassle enough, Ben had added, as if to illustrate his point.

‘Well,’ Roughie said while he covered his face with his handkerchief trying to block out the mix of intoxicating smells, ‘it seems to be in order.’ He passed the keys over to Birdie. ‘Good luck.’ He gave Bogey a quick wave, turned on his heel and left quickly.

CHAPTER 13

To: secretary@peckerswood.co.uk
From: btwo@home.co.uk
Cc: President@peckerswood.co.uk;
Bcc: vvdycke@home.co.uk
Subject: Ladies' room

17th of July, 2022

Hi Roughie,

It's us again. Just short note from your darlings. Dying to give you another gazillion kisses for solving the beastly creep booboo. YOU ARE SO SUPER GREAT.

New Ladies' room is FAB. Adore it. And so does Maggie. Even have telly. Had SUPER JOLLY time watching the Open this weekend. Maggie loves the Open. And WE love YOU.

Philly is over the moon with it. All the ladies are. Well, nearly. She is sooooo clever, getting this done. Anyways, Philly asked us to ask you, when you see our MAGNIFICENT President, to be a darling and pass a couple of our gazillion kisses to him? To say thank you?

Super lots of cuddles and kisses,
xxxxxxxxxxxxxxxxxxxxxxxxxxxxxxxxxxxxxxxxxxxxxx
Birdie & Bogey Banger

PS Do you know Varilla hasn't been in the Ladies' room yet? We thought that was QUITE BIZARRE. You haven't told her not to, have you? Because there really no reason why she wouldn't be welcome. Although she never helped us decorate.

PPS Maybe Varilla doesn't like decorating. And in her defence, it is quite difficult to decorate if one doesn't have ANY TASTE. If you do run into her, please tell her she is absolutely welcome to drop by.

PPPS Has Varilla talked to you about the preferred times yet? Because we haven't heard anything?????? If you do hear and want to pick our brain on the best approach, during a lovely sunny lunch, let's say next Saturday, absolutely totally fine. We will pick you up at noon.

Toodles!

CHAPTER 14

A soft tap sounded, followed by the familiar squeak of the President's study's heavy oak door opening slowly. 'Mr Rough? President Bashit?'

'Yes, Miss Snuggs, do enter.' Roughie caught the door and held it open.

'All right for me to come in and bring you the tea you requested?' The pretty young woman's voice lingered slightly. 'Or should I come back in half an hour? I realize I'm a little earlier than usual.'

'No, Miss Snuggs. Please continue. Perfectly fine.' President Bashit watched her quickly laying the cups out, pour the tea and arranging the chocolate tarts, letting an annoyed sigh escape him, making Miss Snuggs look up. 'I'll be out of your way in ten seconds, Mr Bashit.' She whispered. 'Sorry I was early.'

'No, no, Miss Snuggs. It's not you. Take your time.'

Miss Snuggs blushed. Deep crimson patches appeared on her cheeks while she sneaked a look at the man at the other side of the study, looking so handsome in his beige slacks and creme sweater. So in control. Deep in thought, gazing at her. She breathed in, sharply, through her nose, letting the room's scent tickle her throat.

Her eyes closed for a second, taking in the smell of polished mahogany combined with Secretary Rough's aftershave, making her knees go wobbly. Her eyes opened again, lingering on the image of Mr Rough wiping droplets of sweat from his forehead. They seemed like little diamonds to her, before realizing Mr Rough must be feeling hot, like herself. She was feeling very hot too.

'Are you alright, Mr Rough?' she asked carefully. 'Should I switch on the air-conditioning for you?'

'No thank you, Miss Snuggs.' Roughie paused for a second before turning towards the girl in front of him. 'Or do you need some fresh air? You do look quite flushed, are you alright?'

'Yes. No.' Miss Snuggs felt her back go damp. 'Yes. Sorry, Mr Rough. Maybe it's my tight uniform,' she said, tugging at her frilly apron. 'Sometimes I think it might be better if I wore something else, maybe like a top and neat trousers.'

'I see.' Roughie turned crimson and stared at Miss Snuggs's chest.

'Let's stick to the uniform for now, Miss Snuggs,' President Bashit said gravely. 'It suits you just fine.'

'Yes, Mr Bashit.' Miss Snuggs gathered her tray feeling giddy, sneaked another look at the man staring at her bosom, trying to catch his eye but failing. She composed herself and closed the door behind her softly.

Roughie stared towards it, deep in thought. Why couldn't all women just wear a uniform? Preferably the same one. That would solve a lot of issues. He rubbed his temples. Just like at school. Matron had always worn the same uniform. And she looked damn fine in it, too. Just like Miss Snuggs.

'Roughie?,' President Bashit called out. 'Snap out of wherever you are and pay attention. Show our guests in.'

'Yes Sir.' He stood up straight and opened the door, seeing the small man waiting for him just at the end of the corridor. He checked his watch. Yes, right on time, perfect. He had a feeling this new accountant he had selected was just the chap they needed. The soft carpet bounced under his feet as he approached the mahogany bench and bowed slightly.

'Mr Rough?' The accountant stood up and offered his hand. 'How do you do?'

The handshake was firm, and the small eyes were set on Roughie's, making him feel queasy somehow. 'I think I see Mr Bushrod approaching,' Roughie mumbled, feeling relief while waving at the large figure rushing towards them. 'Please follow me.'

Roughie tried to ignore the tingles that started in his intestines, concentrating on the surrounding pictures of all the important men that had contributed at making Peckers Wood what it was now. The dimmed light made the stern faces lining the panelled walls nearly look friendly, seeming to follow him with their eyes. They looked Roughie over with wonder in their faces, while the light crept in through the heavy curtains blended the pastel colours of the antique furniture and the heavy Persian carpets.

The President's study was open, and Roughie led the accountant in, guiding him towards the large desk. A beaming Bashit stood behind it, held out his hand and invited the accountant to start his presentation while Roughie dealt with the tea and the pastries.

'So you are telling me we are in dire straits?' President Bashit yanked his glasses off, tossed them on the large mahogany desk in front of him, leaned forward and squinted. 'And how, may I ask,' his voice turning into an angry hiss, 'did that happen?'

'Well,' the little bold man on the other side of the desk started tutting, 'more antique furniture for this study, refurbishing the men's lounge and bar, a steam room in the men's changing room. These things cost money, sir.' A short finger came up, wagging at Bashit. 'Money you don't have.' Rat-like eyes moved towards the others in the room. 'You,' he commanded, his finger moving from one person to the other, 'being the management, should work towards a more frugal approach.'

'More frugal?,' President Bashit whispered, raising his eyes upwards. Good Lord. He already said no to fixing that dodgy ninth green and to replacing the gravel towards the first's pathway. How frugal could one get?

The accountant's briefcase snapped shut with a sharp click, making Bushrod and Roughie flinch simultaneously. 'Let me be frank,' the bald man said clearly, turning towards Bashit, 'considerably less fee-paying members than last year, a major contributor pulling out and moving his business to a new competitor, more extravagances. If you don't get more money in, get the income flowing, you will go into history as the President that led Peckers Wood Golf into bankruptcy.'

Bashit felt the familiar angry fire rise from his intestines. What was this awful little man thinking? Standing there, insulting him. In his own study. In this club, his father, his grandfather and their forebears before him, built from scratch. The sound of crackling wood coming from the large open fire seemed to enhance the embarrassed silence in the study.

Bashit grabbed his walking stick and smashed it on the large desk. 'Money? How dare you take that word into your foul mouth!,' he yelled. 'Gentlemen don't discuss money. This is an institution where us gentlemen honour traditions, good manners.' A piece of froth flew from his lips towards the accountant, leaving a white speck on the small man's brown suit. 'Get out!,' he hissed, yanking the walking stick towards the door. 'Get out and never come back here, you tedious, useless little man!'

The study's heavy door closed with a bang, leaving Bashit sitting upright in his chair, staring at the perturbed-looking men in front of him. He started to speak, slowly. 'When we are finished, you,' he cocked his head towards Roughie, 'get to that computer of yours and draft a letter to that miserable little weasel's superior.' The words came out faster, accompanied by beats from the walking stick, being slapped on the desk, in rhythm to the movement of Bashit's grey lips. It suddenly flew from the desk and pointed towards Roughie. 'Tell him that if he ever lets that imbecile near me again, I will retain another office. And you,' Bashit bellowed, his stick flying towards Bushrod, 'as the bloody treasurer. What in hell's name is that bloody accountant on about?'

The old chair protested with a loud creak as Bushrod shifted his weight, looking extremely uncomfortable. 'Well, I say, yes, what can I say?,' he stammered, trying to avoid the cold stare from behind the large desk. 'You know, chip of the old block and all that. Just hanging on to tradition, you know.'

'What in earth do mean?,' Bashit asked, clearly becoming exasperated.

'I suppose, you know, when I took over from father, he just told me to keep signing the bills, like he always did, not to worry too much.' A deep sigh escaped Bushrod, and he gave Bashit a pleading look. 'You always knew we don't have a clue when it comes to finances. Mother takes care of all that. It's like you said, gentlemen don't discuss money. So I don't.'

A loud snort thundered through the study. 'Quite right, Bushrod, quite right. Indeed.' Roughie tried to sit up straight while he addressed the President. 'How dare he. That nasty accountant. Talk about money. Here, in your study, President. The core of our club values. In front of your father.'

Bashit turned round towards the painting above the fire place. The formidable-looking man in the picture stared back at him, his dark blue eyes cold, just like the woodpecker's, perched on his shoulder. 'God help me,' he whispered, more to himself but loud enough for the others to hear. He turned, seeing Roughie suddenly go light green, while looking at the notes in front of him and fingering his inside pocket. He might as well focus on important things. 'Roughie, please make sure the item is on the agenda for next meeting.'

‘What item, sir?’

‘The M-item, Rough.’ President Bashit waved towards the door. ‘The M-item. Now, for the relevant issues. The ones that actually matter.’

‘Yes, President?’ Roughie stood up and squared his shoulders, as if standing to attention.

‘Our committee meeting. The one we’re still preparing. What’s on the agenda?’

‘Ah, yes.’ Roughie unfolded the piece of paper from his pocket, eyeing the items. Evaluation of the new driving range balls, Sweet’s request on water bowls for the dogs, the new blazers for the Regional Competition team and Mrs Van Dycke’s request. Roughie swallowed, wiped his forehead and decided to start with the latter. ‘The women’s request for preferred times on Sundays,’ he squeaked.

Bashit shook his head in misery. Was this lad seriously wanting him to put that request to the committee and turn themselves into a bloody laughing stock? Bashit pulled himself up, ready to leave for the board room. ‘I suggest you and Chipperfield handle that too.’ The President hobbled towards the door. ‘And with that, Roughie, I mean, make the preferred times nonsense go away. Otherwise, I might have to make some board members go away.’ He turned and stared at his Club Secretary. ‘Do you get my drift?’

Roughie nodded, stealing a glance at Ben, who was looking miserable.

‘Good.’ Bashit grabbed the brass door handle and leaned on it for a second. ‘Because, gentlemen, if this doesn’t evaporate into thin air, I might be forced to dismiss that whole Lady Captain silliness.’ The old, blue veined hand turned, and the heavy oak door opened. ‘Imagine how Miss Hackkett would feel.’ Bashit tutted and the cunning eyes stared at Ben. ‘Or worse, your future father-in-law.’

CHAPTER 15

Philly's bag was leaning against the large oak tree at the ninth green, waiting for her to finish her put and move on towards the next hole. She picked it up, slid her arms through the loops and pushed it into position, letting the weight pull her shoulders back, relieving some of the tension she had been feeling caused by a long week at work. The clubs rhythmic ticking sound helped her mind relax with each step she took along the path leading to the 10th tee. The buzz of the first nine's score started to kick in, softening her muscles further.

She slowed down a little, looking up, taking in the variations of shades of green leaves, from bright and light to dark, nearly black. The rays of late summer sunshine illuminated parts of the fairways through the trees, lengthening the shadows behind the bumps and hollows and showing the greens with the flags flapping on their poles, inviting her to play them again.

She reached for her driver while making the sharp turn towards the tee box and started swinging it in front of her with her left hand. Right to left, right to left.

A familiar figure was already on the medal tee, also practicing a swing, slowly, meticulously moving her club upwards, checking the angle of the club face in its highest position.

Philly waved her driver as a greeting. 'Done working?,' she asked Pru, her attention drawn to something behind them.

'I thought the sisters were joining us?' Pru asked. 'Where the devil are they?'

'They cancelled. Something about a liquid lunch with Roughie.'

'Good Lord.' Pru smirked. 'Whatever for?'

'No idea. But by now they'll be passed out at the side of their pool so I don't think we'll see them anytime soon.'

A soft humming sound reached them, and Philly looked over her shoulder, seeing a buggy rolling slowly in their direction with two familiar figures in it, waving and pointing towards the seats behind them.

'Hi, you two. We saw you walk up,' Roughie said. 'It's getting dark. You'll never make it back in time. Join us on my inspection round?' He leaned towards them, looking conspiratorially. 'We need to talk to you about important club matters.'

Philly's eyebrows shot up while she stared at Past Club Captain Charles Charmers' serious-looking face and gave Pru a quick glance who was already tying their bags to the back of the buggy.

Roughie's foot came down, starting up again, rolling towards the next tee. 'I do this every day, you know,' he said, breathing a distinct waft of white wine towards them with each word. 'My favourite chore. Letting Peckers Wood's beauty inspire me.'

The wheels touched the soft fairway and rolled gently over the first hump, showing the diffused evening light filtering through the trees, illuminating the bunkers around the green, making them look like small golden ponds.

Roughie made a sharp right turn, steering around the ninth back tee and following the path alongside the eleventh fairway, pushing the buggy to its max, climbing up the hill towards the 18th back tee on the top. He turned its front towards the lake, now changing from copper to black, the soft white sheen coming from the moon clashing with the sun's last rays, just lighting the flag at the 18th green at the far end of the lake. The trees seemed to fold around the water's edge, as if trying to protect it, accompanied by a gentle woodpecker's drum. The heather behind the green was turning from mauve to dark purple.

'This never ceases to amaze me,' Charmers confessed, breaking the silence. 'Isn't it beautiful?'

Philly nodded. 'Yes. It is. Stunningly beautiful.'

They sat still for a while before the past Club Captain spoke again. 'We need to discuss something awkward.'

Philly shot a worried glance at Pru and swallowed, feeling uneasy.

Charmers turned and faced the two women behind him, telling them that they gathered there was no support among the Ladies Section for preferred times. Which they thought was frightfully uncomfortable, as they, with Ben, nearly went to the committee to put the request forward.

'Thank God we didn't. Especially for Ben's sake,' Charmers said, shaking his head. 'Quite frankly, we assumed, quite wrongly it seems, that Mrs Van Dycke's wish was supported.' He looked apologetic while turning to Philly. 'But it now turns out it wasn't? Imagine what Ben what have looked like in front of the starting times committee?'

'What do you mean?,' Pru asked.

'An unsupported request. Varilla was adamant about her point, and it is common policy to never address such important issues without the full support of your rank and file,' Charmers explained as Roughie released the break and let the buggy roll towards the 18th fairway. 'But today we learned there is no backing from the rest of the section.' He sighed and sternly told them never to let this happen again, leaving Philly and Pru silent, not knowing how to react.

Roughie's foot came up again, slowing the buggy down, carefully passing the practice green and jumping over the concrete ridge towards the path leading up to the car park. 'Make certain your Ladies understand how club matters are handled. You wouldn't want members start thinking you really don't grasp how things work around here, now do you?'

Roughie steered towards the Ladies' room and stopped. 'Well, this is you.'

Charmers stepped out and offered his hand to Pru, who looked baffled. 'Thanks for listening, ladies. All is well now we nipped your little starting time screw-up in the bud. You just needed a little coaching.' He squeezed Pru's hand and gave her an encouraging nod. 'But don't worry your pretty little heads. Roughie here will inform Ben and will let Bashit know that this preferred times request is dealt with.' He turned to Philly. 'You just need to tell your pal Varilla and find a way to align your section before any other bright ideas spring up without you knowing and the section consenting.'

Charmers helped Philly step out and stared at her chest for a second. 'Have a nice evening, you two.' He said with a grin, before getting in next to Roughie, and the two of them disappeared into the night.

Philly stared after the buggy, feeling bewildered, watching the hunched figures turn into a dark grey blob. What the fuck was this all about? 'Bloody hell. Needed some coaching,' she muttered, pushing the Ladies' room door open.

Pru shrugged. 'But how do they know there's no commitment for Gorilla's idea? No-one ever asked me.'

Philly shook her head and pulled her mobile from her pocket. 'Nor me.' She moved her thumb over the screen. 'But I'm starting to grasp what's going on,' she whispered while reading the message in front of her.

CHAPTER 16

To: secretary@peckerswood.co.uk
From: banger@home.co.uk
Cc: President@peckerswood.co.uk; phackkett@home.co.uk; vvdycke@home.co.uk
Subject: Preferred times

17th of August 2022

Dear Secretary, darling Roughie,

Just a short note from your Banger besties to thank you for the SUPER lunch the other day. So glad we forgot to stop at the Chasty Chicken and had to proceed to the Gourmet Garage instead.

Absolutely ADORED the 12 course amuse menu and all the drinkie poos that went with it. Simply DIVINE. And we are ABSOLUTELY CONVINCED that our darling President will sign the bill so it doesn't have to come out of your pocket money.

As discussed, we hereby confirm the results from the exploratory RESEARCH we talked to you about, in writing, about the assumed support for preferred times. Our dear Mrs Van Dycke is right, we also FIRMLY BELIEVE in democratic process, just like she does. So here the preliminary findings are:

Philly: Nay. Everybody knows she wants to sleep in on Sunday's because she is totally worn out after bonking Ben Chipperfield all Saturday night.

Pru: Nay. Everybody knows she wants to spend Sunday mornings in the caddy shack perfecting her weak grip on firm shafts.

Mrs Pushet: Nay. Doesn't care what time of day it is so tees off whenever she feels like it.

Us: Nay. Don't see the point. Course is PRACTICALLY EMPTY after one PM. Suits us fine. Back in time for loads of DRINKIE POO'S.

So, in short, the outcome of our thorough investigation is: Preferred times for us girls? NO THANK YOU. We leave it to you to break this news to our darling President Bashit and we will tell V the G.

God speed.
Yours FOREVER, BS (Banger Sisters)

PS. We are considering advising Mrs Van Dycke on USEFUL Sunday morning activities. Like taking a bath and shaving one's legs.

PPS. And arm pits.

PPPS. And (not that WE understand how) plucking one's long black hairs from one's chin.

CHAPTER 17

A fat drop of rain left a dark mark on the flagstone in front of her right foot. Mrs Pushet sighed and stuffed the little roll-up fag back in her trouser pocket. How she loathed smoking out in the rain, the thought of getting soaked took out the pleasure of feeling her muscles relax and letting her mind drift to happy thoughts.

Her back ached as she stood up from the hard wood garden furniture. The girls wouldn't allow her to have a puff in the new Ladies' room, finely pointed out by Pru. The girl was such a stickler. Mrs Pushet shook her head. Maybe Harry was up for some R & R. Would do him good. The poor man seemed so stressed lately.

She looked over her shoulder, checking if she was alone, so she could sneak through the back door and take the short cut through the back hallway towards the President's study. Everything seemed deserted. Mrs Pushet climbed over the low rhododendrons and bent down so she could crawl under the conference room's window sill unnoticed. The window was slightly open, and she heard a familiar voice shouting.

Bushrod.

Mrs Pushet crouched down and tried to follow what he was going on about.

That piece of shit. Apparently he found a totally berserk Varilla at his doorstep demanding the public execution of the Bangers sisters and everything that went with them. Mrs Pushet heard a soft voice in the distance, sounding strangely metallic, obviously coming from a speaker. '*Yes, I understand you think they are slippery as eels covered in Vaseline, and yes, I do understand you feel they always seem to get away with murder.*' Definitely young Philly Hackkett's voice, uncharacteristically demure.

Mrs Pushet giggled, despite Bushrod's earlier tone. She heard Philly again. '*Indeed, sir. The Bangers are my friends. And maybe not quite like eels, but….*' Bushrod had cut her short with the sharp interruption that he wanted to remind Philly that preferred times on Sunday were definitely off the table. 'Yes,' she said, sounding beaten. 'Understood. Definitely.'

'You keep an eye on your section and for God's, and all our sakes, keep those creatures out of our sight.' Bushrod's voice again, before ending the call abruptly.

Bloody condescending twat. How dare he lecture her lovely girls that way? Mrs Pushet's muscles tightened. She would make certain he got what was coming to him sometime soon.

Hands planted firmly in front of her, Mrs Pushet escaped on all fours and made it to the back door unscratched. Its door handle clicked under her hand, indicating it was unlocked, and the old lady slid through, quickly picking up pace, pushing herself stealthily against the hallway's wall as if trying to avoid sudden gunfire.

The study's door was closed, and she leaned towards it, wanting to pause for a few seconds to catch her breath. Yet her weight caused the door to open, and she flew forwards into the dark den, only just remaining upwards after catching her toe under the carpet's edge. She regained her posture and blinked a couple of times, trying to get adjusted to the darkness, making out the antique desk and the leather chair behind it. The fire was on its last kindle, letting off a little smoke.

Mrs Pushet smiled. Well, well. Dear Harry was obviously away on some important golf mission. A wee fag here wouldn't make any difference, now would it? Over the last centuries a million ciggies must have been puffed away here. She walked over to the President's chair, stroked it a couple of times and sat down, leaning backwards, putting her feet on the desk, feeling extremely naughty. An elegant cut-glass lighter stood next to her left foot. She moved her leg, trying to pull it towards her, dragging a plastic-bound document towards her in the same motion, making it topple from the desk onto the carpet beneath it. She ignored it and snatched the lighter, lit her fag, took a deep drag and contemplated the conversation she had witnessed outside. Poor things. And, coming to think of it, she actually began to feel sorry for poor old Varilla the Gorilla as well. First that bitch Lav fucked off and left her to die, then her proposal went down the drain while Philly's materialized. The last drag of smoke filled her lungs and she exhaled, slowly, enjoying the moment.

The leftover stub was tossed into the fire, and Mrs Pushet bent forward, picking up the document she dropped earlier. She held it between her thumb and index finger, looking down on the cover. Realizing what it was, she started to read through it, faster with each page.

Oh dear, she thought. *This was bad. Really bad.*

But so very excellent at the same time.

The document found its way firmly under Mrs Pushet's arm as she made her way out of the clubhouse towards the Ladies' room unnoticed.

Pru carefully wiped her clubs down, put them in the boot of her car and stared at Philly, who was holding her mobile and looking miserable after her uncomfortable conversation with the Treasurer. Philly handed Pru the phone, showing her email she had just read.

'Look what the cheeky buggers did now.'

Pru nodded slowly, while she took in what she read again. 'Now what? Are we going to kill or kiss those two?'

The smart little device went back to its owner, who shoved it in her pocket and started walking towards the Ladies' room, passing the clubhouse and sticking her tongue out. Philly really didn't have a clue at the moment. But what she did know is that she had enough of all those fucking wankers telling her what to do and how to act.

She turned towards Pru catching up with her. 'We pay full membership fees. We should bloody well be allowed to do and act as we please. It's not like we don't grasp what it is we're here for, do we?'

'I agree.' Pru nodded and wiped her feet on the little mat in front of the Ladies' room door. 'But somehow, however annoying it may be, do they have a point?'

Philly slumped next to her friend. 'Spare me. How about a glass of wine and a think about how to handle all this crap.' Philly pushed the door, switched the light on as she entered the dark space, noticing a small figure on the sofa, hunched over a book. 'It's old Mrs Pushet.' She whispered to Pru who nodded and followed her.

'Mrs Pushet? Are you alright?' Philly asked, gently touching the grey hair.

'Oh my God, Philly Hackkett and Pru Love. Good heavens, you startled me. Yes, I'm fine. Just reading something I found lying about.'

Thank God the old girl was okay. What was she doing here, so late, alone? Philly pecked the old lady on the cheek and sat down next to her.

The pretty wrinkled face crumpled up in a wide smile. 'So wonderful you pulled this Ladies' room off, Philly. I love it. Glad I voted for you, I'm so happy with how everything turned out.'

'What are you reading?' Philly leaned towards Mrs Pushet and glanced at the document in her lap.

‘Excellent stuff. Numbers.’

‘Really?,’ Philly asked innocently and sneaked a look at Pru. ‘That sounds interesting. What are they telling you?’

‘That the Club’s figures don’t add up.’ Mrs Pushet started to giggle. ‘But that’s nothing new, now is it? I mean, honestly. Most of the men I know here at the club aren’t even able to count to five, now are they?’ She shook her head in wonder. ‘Imagine one of them in charge of something important?’ Her face suddenly took on a frightened look. ‘That would be awful, no?’

Philly and Pru exchanged a bewildered look while Mrs Pushet looked down at her hands and examined her wedding ring, her face going soft and relaxed again, before standing up suddenly. ‘Listen, do you know most men shoot six when they yell four and write down five? Bloody hilarious if it weren’t so pathetic.’ She picked her handbag up, stuffed it under her arm and walked towards the door, a sudden angry look clouding her friendly face. ‘But it annoys me no end. I taught half of them math back in the day, when I was still in teaching.’ Her silver curls bobbed up and down as she shook her head and stood still for a moment, staring at Philly and Pru. ‘Give my love to the Banger sisters. I adore them. They are such good girls.’

Philly watched Mrs Pushet leave towards the door and turned her head sideways. The document the old lady had been reading was still on the sofa. ‘Mrs Pushet!,’ Philly called after the disappearing figure, ‘you forgot your book!’

Her small hand waved Philly off. ‘Never mind. I know it by heart. Do with it what you like, my darlings. And keep up the good work, you hear!’

Pru grabbed Philly’s glass and filled it up, while seeing Philly slump down, frown and open the pages. She put down the drinks and tried to look Philly in the eye, who avoided her look for a second before she spoke.

‘Pru?’

‘Yes.’

Philly looked at her dear friend who knew her inside out, could read her mind, feel her mood and had been at her side during the most daunting events in her life. 'It's the Club's financial results. And they aren't good.' She whispered while looking Pru over, her eyes dark and pleading. 'In fact, looking at this balance sheet, it really scares me.' Little buds of sweat that had suddenly appeared on her upper lip. Her fingertips felt numb as she started to rub her throbbing temples. 'Look at this. If this is the trend, and it continues, our beloved Peckers Wood could get into real trouble.' She pushed the papers towards her friend, who stared down and inhaled sharply.

'My goodness.' Pru's index finger moved from top to bottom, while she quickly scanned the pages. 'If this is true, the club won't survive, Freckles.' She flicked the pages and read on. 'These look abominable. What in devil's name is going on?'

'And I bet neither Bashit, Roughie or Bushrod have a clue.' Philly stood up and began pacing. 'Mrs Pushet is right. They can't count to five, let alone make out a balance sheet.'

'But surely Ben knows and can steer this in the right direction?' Pru asked, looking desperate.

'I'm not so sure, to be honest,' Philly answered. 'He's an outstanding dentist, but hasn't the foggiest when it comes to running a business. No sense of money, whatsoever. I'm always explaining financial things to him. He's clueless on the subject.'

'Oh dear. I see what you mean.' Pru jumped up and also started pacing. 'That is scary.' She paused and stared at the wall in front of her. 'We need to do something.'

'Yeah, right.' Philly shook her head and pointed towards the main clubhouse. 'With that lot down there? The supposed superior half of our civilization? The ones that think we need coaching? Remember?' Her knuckles turned white as she clasped her upper arms, staring at her friend. They sat down again, next to each other, gazing at the papers, letting the situation sink in.

‘Right. Let’s stay calm and not jump to conclusions right now.’ Pru broke the silence, paused and stared at her watch. ’Listen. Could you talk to Ben and find out tonight, what’s really going on?’

‘You bet.’ Philly nodded. ‘And will let you know first thing tomorrow if our beloved club is on its last legs.’ She threw her head back. ‘And if we need to go and beg horrid Lav Thorneybush to accept us at Goodlie.’

‘Over my dead body.’ Pru turned her head towards Philly and stared at her. ‘Let’s pray we are underestimating Ben and Roughie. I would rather die than suck up to Lav. Or being submitted to that dire Goodlie joke of a course.’ She stood up, grabbed her handbag and opened the door. ‘I need to be off.’

‘Okay. Bye darling. Speak soon.’ Philly took their glasses, rinsed them under the small tap’s cold water, grabbed her bag, turned the lock after herself and kissed Pru goodbye. She waited for a moment, watched her friend walk into the direction of the caddy shack and crossed the path towards the car park, lingered for a moment, checking her mobile for messages and her work schedule for tomorrow. *Great if we could chat 10 minutes before acquisition meeting.* The Whats App from her boss stared at her. *So you can get me up to speed on tactic. Thx.*

Her thumb moved quickly, replying. *Of course, see you at 745. We’ll make a killing.*

She dropped the mobile in her hand bag and got into her car, her fingers tightening round the steering wheel while she took a deep breath. This could not be happening. Not now. Not when she finally had what she wanted and was looking forward to many happy years at Peckers Wood with her friends. Their beloved course, down the drain?

No. No. No.

The mere thought was too awful to even consider. Find out what is going on, Pru had said. That was exactly what she was going to do.

CHAPTER 18

The knife's tip scraped the wooden surface under the red peppers. Philly pressed harder. The even parts moved to one side, and she started cutting. Chop, chop, chop, flipping the knife in her right hand and diving her left into a colourful earthenware pot, pulling out garlic and pushing them together on the work surface. Her fist came down on the knife's flattened blade, crushing the cloves. Thump, thump, thump, letting the sharp garlic scent hit her, causing her eyes to water.

A large glass of red wine appeared in front of her, making her head move sideways, looking into Ben's dark brown eyes, staring down at her. The corner of his mouth was turned upwards slightly and his scent followed the garlic up her nose, making her insides go funny.

'I hope I'm not next.' He nodded towards the knife. 'Can I trust you with that or should I take it away from you?' He gently pushed her aside and folded his hand over hers. 'Here, let me take care of that. Before you hurt yourself. Have a sip of that wine. Will do you good.'

He tried to catch her eyes again. 'Everything okay? You seem very quiet.' He started slicing the tomatoes in front of him. 'Sorry for being late. But I had to run tomorrow's meeting past Bashit.' Ben's hands pushed the tomatoes and the knife towards Philly and pulled her against him. 'Everything sorted with Varilla and the silly preferred time fiasco, I gather? At least Charmers told me it sort of solved itself? Did it?'

Philly nodded, trying not to think about Bushrod or the Bangers, feeling a gentle tug at the back of her head, making her face Ben, while he put his warm lips on hers.

'Good girl.' She heard him whisper. 'Love you.' His hands moved over her body, pulling her closer, finding her tongue for a long kiss.

She closed her eyes, trying to enjoy the moment, but instead thinking of what he would have to say about the P&L, still in her bag. 'Absolutely. Dealt with and buried.' Philly finally replied, pulling away. 'But you might need to concentrate on something else.'

'I'd rather concentrate on you.' Ben sighed, letting his arms fall beside him in mock defeat and moving towards his chair. 'What's so important it presides over you and me leaving dinner for later?'

Philly reached over the table and pulled her laptop from its sleeve. She handed it to Ben, telling him to open a file named PW finance. A few clicks later, he groaned loud enough for Philly to turn and stare at him.

'What's the matter?,' she asked, innocently.

A stressed grunt blurted through his lips. 'Oh my God, Philly!' Ben's fingers went over his head, like they always did when he was annoyed. 'How did you get these? This is confidential information, board only. Certainly not for you to see.' He stabbed at the screen. 'What the fuck's going on?' He leant backwards in his chair and pushed the computer towards Philly who closed it carefully.

'Do you realize how bad it can get if this isn't turned around?,' she asked, returning to the sink and starting to clear some left-over crumbs. A slight pause followed, before she turned towards Ben, who groaned again.

'Jesus H. Christ. Ben. Please. Listen to me. Our club will go down the drain.'

'How do you know? It can't be that bad. Aren't you exaggerating a bit?'

'I do have an MBA, Ben. I do understand how businesses work. And this one clearly isn't.' Philly folded her arms and stared at the irked-looking face in front of her, now turning and nodding towards the stove.

'Dinner ready yet?,' Ben asked, his tone indicating he wanted to close the subject.

Philly nodded, pulled the chicken out of the oven and ignored his unspoken annoyance. 'We need to address this, talk to Bashit asap before someone outside your precious board finds out. And before Charles Charmers has another go at us about fucking rank and file.' The knife sliced the chicken in a quick flip of her wrist. 'We need to come up with a plan.'

'What do you mean, we?' Ben now sounded seriously irritated. 'The club's finances are none of our business. Bushrod takes care of them.'

'Really? Does he now?' Philly asked, sarcastically. 'He must have some wild strategy I don't quite understand. The club is in real trouble, Ben.'

The salad was carefully arranged, next to the roast chicken. One slice of white meat for her, the rest for Ben. She knew he liked her thin, one time he even ticked her off when he caught her allowing herself a little sugary guilty pleasure. 'We, Pru and me, do understand what Peckers Wood is all about, and I know we can make a decent business proposition out of it.' She said firmly.

'Don't go there, Philly.' Ben's voice was dark.

She turned towards him, now feeling her own annoyance rising up. She opened her mouth to let it out, but closed it again, seeing the ominous look on his face.

'Let Bushrod and Bashit deal with it. Back off.' Ben unfolded his arms, and his eyes softened. 'It's not that I don't believe in you, beautiful. But sometimes it's just better to not interfere and let problems solve themselves.'

'Problems never solve themselves.' Philly put the plates on the table and sat down, looking determined. 'And I am not letting our precious Peckers Wood go under. Over my dead body.'

Ben nodded absentmindedly, clearly wanting to end the discussion. 'Sure. Whatever you say. But don't say I didn't warn you.'

CHAPTER 19

President Bashit looked around the large mahogany table that had been here in the conference room, right in this spot, for over two centuries. Where great men had sat, in these chairs, managing the club in the fashion they were accustomed to. The gentleman's way, honourably. And now this. The lump in his throat wouldn't budge, however hard he gulped his Scotch down.

But he had managed. Professionally. He had been short and firm about it, not wavering although the worried glances had worked their way along the table at blinding speed, followed by soft whispering and the shifting of sitting positions, making the atmosphere extremely uncomfortable.

Bashit swallowed hard, feeling the discomfort run through his spine again. But, thank God, it was out. He had done his fellow board members right and put the question to the committee. The deafening silence that had followed his final words had seemed endless, the only sound coming from Roughie's fountain pen making soft scratching sounds. He had looked each and every member in the eye, one by one, pausing, leaving the room silent for a couple of seconds before he had continued. 'So let's take a few minutes to compose ourselves, have a refreshment and then share our views.'

The committee members rose from the table, the clinking of porcelain cups and saucers being put together was the only sound in the room. They sat down again, quietly drinking their tea, staring at him.

'Now, Gentlemen. Your thoughts.'

The men around the table started talking, frenzied, their voices raising volume by the second.

'I see. Bloody Goodlie stealing our members.'

'Mmm. Not thrilled by this, President. You got your way last time, with the unanimous yea to allowing green fees and visitors, but this might be pushing me too far.'

'I do understand,' he replied with a slow, understanding nod. 'But, what do we think about the board's request? Some expert to advise us, under our own supervision?'

The discussion started up again, the men talking fast and loudly.

'I agree with him. This could go awfully wrong. What if more members start to get silly ideas and want to leave? We need remain in control, in charge.'

And then Ben Chipperfield cleared his throat dramatically before raising his voice. 'I think we all agree on that. We need to decide if this is the route towards avoiding more members being dragged off to godforsaken Goodlie.'

Nods of agreement followed.

'As long as we draw the line somewhere.' Charles Charmers wagged his finger at President Bashit. 'I don't want some ghastly consultant breathing down my neck here in the clubhouse.'

'Good grief, old man, no,' he replied, raising his eyes towards the ceiling. 'Of course not. Perish the thought. No. They can do their work remote, online.'

'And we will only pay them if we agree with their evaluation and recommendations, I trust?' Henri Sweet waved his finger at him.

'Yes, of course. Roughie, you will draw up the contract?'

'Absolutely, President. Consider it done.'

'Good. What a nuisance already. Anyway. Gentlemen, let's take the vote. Yea or nay on this consultancy firm to advise us on our way forward?

Now alone after the contentious meeting, Bashit rested the back of his head on the chair's cool chintz and stared at his father's portrait, hanging above the fire place. The familiar blue eyes bored into his own, making the grey hairs on his arms stand up straight. The woodpecker sitting on his father's shoulder peered at him suspiciously, its beady eyes mocking him.

'These are trying times, father,' he whispered. 'What could I do? At least you didn't have to deal with this democracy nonsense. Having to put requests forward, taking votes, pretending allowing some overpaid consultancy firm to tell us what to do.'

Bloody hell. Yea to outsiders. Whatever next? He pulled his walking stick towards his chest and hoisted himself up. But young Chipperfield had a point. Getting these consultants in would prove to the committee that his views on club membership was sound, and that Peckers Wood would thrive under his, their, leadership. The report would shut everyone up, and he could get on with important things. Time to stop feeling sorry for yourself, he thought while he looked at Henri Sweet's suggestions and quotes on those exclusive bespoke dog bowls. He needed to catch up with things that really mattered.

CHAPTER 20

The driver made a sharp swooshing sound as it turned around Pru. She pulled the club back again, now stopping in mid-air. 'A consultancy firm? That's the solution?' She stared at Philly, who was tucking a pitchfork in her back pocket and nodding, looking grumpy with the corners of her mouth pulled down.

'It seems so. You go.'

Pru stepped onto the first tee and pointed her driver towards her target, one of the ancient oak trees' overhanging branches about 200 yards on the left of the middle. She turned, planted her feet firmly square, her arms straight in a perfect V-shape. Her back swing was slow, coming down she pushed her hipbone down, the V went through the ball fast and upwards, causing it to shoot towards her target.

'Shot.' Philly said, climbing up the tee box herself, pinning her peg next to Pru's. Another great drive followed, just a bit more to the centre of the par five's immaculately cut fairway.

They pulled their bags over their shoulders and started to walk, both deep in thought. The unexpected autumn sun warmed their backs and gave the final bloom of the hydrangeas a soft glow. Somewhere in the distance they heard the high squeak of a buzzard, and they looked up, watching it circle slowly, its wings pointed upwards, the large bird making good use of the breeze to float gracefully without effort.

Philly's ball had a perfect lie, sitting firmly on the grass's short surface. A slow, sweeping three wood would take her to the last hollow in front of the green. If she nailed her chip, she could write down her first birdie of the day. The thought made her feel better, making her chagrin leave her system, evaporating from her pores.

The fairway shot landed where she intended it. Her trusted pitching wedge did its thing, and Philly's desired score was secured with a tap in on the green.

'Four for you then?,' Pru asked, scribbling on a scorecard. 'Well done.'

'Thanks. Your five wasn't too shabby.'

The bags were lifted again, and the friends turned right, crossed the little wooden bridge over the brook and followed the path to the second. They saw a couple of deer shooting into the safe and dark woods.

Pru stopped, shook her bag from her shoulders, took her ball from the bag and turned to her friend. 'They never considered asking us, did they? To see if we could come up with a solution?'

'No.' Philly said, sounding short. 'Never crossed their minds. And Ben doesn't want to talk about it anymore. The matter is being dealt with, and that's that.'

'So now what? This could go frightfully pearshaped,' Pru pleaded. 'We can't let Peckers Wood die on us.' She swept her arm from left to right. 'I mean, look at it.'

Philly swallowed, seeing the ducks bob in the calm water of the hazard on the right, the eight's green flag flapping, just visible through the shrubs. The multicoloured leaves on the trees dividing both holes were bristling lightly, giving off a calming buzz. Two rabbits were sitting on the fairway bunker's edge, as if waiting for them to pass, so the animals could get on with their tunnels, messing up the perfectly raked sand. She could just make out the second green, waiting for them, lit up by a ray of sunshine. A shiver of dread shot through her body, making her feel uneasy, realizing she needed to take action.

'Right.' Philly pushed her driver back in her bag and stepped off the tee, seeing the Bangers driving towards the car park behind them. 'We need to inform the section asap. They have a right to know what's going on, and I should be the one to tell them.' She picked her bag up. 'Let's pack this up before they hear it from someone else,' she said, leaving no room for debate. 'I'll get hold of the Bangers.' Philly picked up her pace, nearly running, indicating to Pru to follow her, taking the short cut over the eighth green towards the 10th fairway. 'You rustle up Mrs Pushet. She'll be able to trick Varilla into a meeting, I'm sure she's roaming around somewhere.'

'Righto.' Pru ran after her. 'Meet you in the Ladies' room in 15 minutes?'

'Yes. But try and get the others to join half an hour later. I have an idea I want to run past you first.'

The Ladies' room door opened, and an annoyed looking Varilla burst in, pushed over the threshold by Mrs Pushet with a determined grimace on the usually friendly face. Birdie Banger stuck her hand up in a wave, patting the sofa's seat between herself and her sister, signalling the old lady to sit with them, at the same time pulling a large brown paper bag from under her feet.

'Philly found us just after we nipped over to the supermarket to get all these yummy goodies.' The wrappers crackled being pulled open, and the smell of pork pies and sausages enticed Maggie to move over to Bogey who slipped her half a sausage before popping the other half in her own mouth.

Varilla let out an audible sigh and checked her watch dramatically, causing Pru to sit up and clear her throat. 'Well, Philly,' she said and fingered her strand of pearls for a second, moving the necklace up an inch, 'you needed to talk to us about something urgent?'.

'Right.' Philly pulled her laptop from her bag and looked round the expectant-looking women staring at her, except for Varilla, who was now slumped in one of the plastic folding chairs with a bored expression on her face, her tweed jacket crumpled under her arms.

Philly cleared her throat and got to it, explaining how Mrs Pushet managed to stumble upon some relevant information, what Pru and herself had found out, how worrying the situation was and how the club's committee had voted to get in a consultant.

She paused, taking a breath, feeling the awkward atmosphere build up by the stunned silence around her. She rested her eyes on the laptop again. 'Things aren't good,' she continued, explaining about the overspending and the member count going down steadily.

Pru was busy passing glasses of wine around the group. Varilla refused, waving the gesture away with an irritated sigh, causing the Bangers to raise their eyes upwards dramatically.

A glass went towards Philly, who gulped half of it down before elaborating further. 'Half of the members are so ancient they'll be falling off their perch in blinding speed within the next two or three years. Even now Bashit's social calendar is filled with funerals,' she said gravely. 'Soon there won't be anyone left for him, or for instance my dad, to have a game with.' Philly shook her head, looking out of the window into the sky, now dark blue with only a couple of golden whips of light showing the fading sun staring towards them. 'And,' she emphasized, 'what a lot of members don't seem to realize is that times are changing. Obviously dried-up waiting lists, rising competition.'

'What do you mean?,' Varilla asked. 'This is ridiculous!' She angrily pointed a finger at Philly. 'Bashit specifically said we have long waiting lists and harrowing selection procedures that go with them. So what's going on?'

'Nothing,' Philly said. 'And that seems to be the problem. We haven't had an application in ages.' She turned round and looked at Bogey. 'How many new members have you seen, say, during the last six months?

Another stunned silence filled the small room. Even Maggie remained motionless.

The sound of a plastic chair being folded aggressively made the group turn towards Varilla, who was up on her feet, wrestling with the unwilling object before chucking it in the nearest corner. One of her dark beige legs showed a ladder creeping up quickly, revealing the long dark hair on her shin. She grabbed her bag, a sombre look clouding her face, making the small dark eyes seem even more pig-like than usual.

'Losing members?,' she snorted. 'What utter bollocks. Do you know I had to wait on every single hole the other day?' She straightened her shoulders and looked at Philly defiantly. 'That's not because the course is deserted, now is it?' She rolled her head and stared at Pru. 'I'm leaving. I don't want any part of this nonsense.'

'Sit down, Varilla. We need you here.' A long pause followed, and Philly continued. 'I need you here,' she said softly, before regaining posture and carrying on. Varilla's face turned puce, clashing horribly with her purple jumper. Her bag flew over her shoulder, and she grabbed the chair, banging it towards the floor trying to unfold it again, leaving the other women looking at each other uncomfortably.

The laptop went back to Philly in silence. 'And let's not forget the effect Goodlie has,' she said gravely. 'I heard their member count is up to about 500. Some of which should have been ours.' Her finger tapped the laptop's cover. 'The way this is going, our beloved golf club will be six feet under faster than shit through a goose. Dead. Kaput.'

'Dead? I don't want to die.' Mrs Pushet's cry shot through the room. The old lady slumped forward, clutching a Dunlop golf ball in her little wrinkled hand and started to sob, softly. 'I can't live without you,' she bawled, her shoulders going up and down, the grey curls bobbing in the sob's rhythm. 'I love you so much.' The blobbing turned into wailing, making Maggie run towards her, trying to lick the old lady's wet face, pushing her up with her snout. Mrs Pushet fell backwards, tears now dripping from her little stub nose, caught by Maggie, trying her best to clear the drops away.

Birdie pulled Maggie away carefully and pulled the old lady towards her, rocked her gently, trying to get her to calm down. Bogey pulled a paper tissue from the paper bag and tried to clean the wet face as best as she could. But the old lady kept whimpering. 'Playing golf here has saved my life, you know.' A big tear welled up, and Mrs Pushet wiped it away carefully. 'When my darling Mr Pushet died, my heart broke. Literally. It nearly killed me. My GP said I should take up golf. Said it would be good for body and soul.' She pulled Maggie towards her again and kissed her snout before continuing. 'And boy, was he right. It's so lovely out here. I approached Bashit, and he was kind enough to introduce me the same week, and I started to play. After a month my blood pressure was like a young girl's, and my cholesterol level had dropped by half.'

'What?' A cry erupted from the corner, making everyone turn towards it. Varilla was on her feet again, her face now even darker puce than before. 'That fucking Bashit made you a member within a week?'

Mrs Pushet smiled. 'Yes,' she said. 'Bless him.'

Varilla shot up and pulled her jacket in place. 'I cannot believe it.' She screamed, making Maggie disappear behind Bogey. She clutched her bag to her chest and stumped towards the door, yanking it open. 'I've been on that bloody waiting list for five fucking years.'

The door slammed after her, making the teacups rattle in the kitchen sink and leaving an uncomfortable silence before Mrs Pushet spoke again, clearly not bothered at all by Varilla's outburst. 'And then you lot. My new friends.' The familiar warm smile appeared. 'Who play with me, have a chat and a drink with me. Making every day worth living.' The soft eyes turned dark, Maggie was pushed back to Philly, and Mrs Pushet stood up, suddenly. She turned towards to the small window next to the kitchen unit and pointed towards the clubhouse. 'And now these simpletons are ruining everything.'

Philly turned to Pru, who nodded slightly, urging her to share the plan they had come up with. It hadn't been rocket science, adding the numbers and doing the math. The problem was clearly caused by a slump in steady income. About 75 new members each year for the coming three years should cut it. That shouldn't be too challenging, what with a whole undiscovered target group at the club's feet like low-hanging fruit longing to be picked?

The whole idea sounded more perfect by the minute, Philly thought, while she lay out the calculations to her friends, all beaming with consent. Who needed a bloody overpaid consultancy firm while the obvious solution was staring them in the face?

CHAPTER 21

The silence was overwhelming, while the two clearly embarrassed young women stood up in front of him and left the conference room following his direction, obviously put out. The heavy door closed behind them with a hardly detectable sound, causing his fellow board members to address each other, clearly relieved by his stern approach.

'Unbelievable. How dare they.' Bushrod stood up to take the floor. 'Having the gall telling us how to run our club. Actively welcome female guests. Recruit more women members. Absolutely ridiculous,' he snorted and turned to Bashit. 'But you made our point perfectly clear, President. Well done.'

'Thank God for that,' Charles Charmers said. 'I've seen what they can cause when let loose when I played on the continent. Horrid. They just don't know how to behave. You know, speeding up play, no chattering on the green, that sort of thing.'

'Leaving the trolley on the wrong side. They do that all the time. Women have no sense of direction whatsoever,' Bobby Long added.

'God, yes.' Henri Sweet nodded his head. 'I've been there too. So annoying.'

'And teach them just to hit the damn ball instead of taking

ages with practice swings. That endless waggle, I watched them do.' Charmers threw his hands up in the air. 'Never understood the added value of that exercise.'

'And pretending they have to repair pitch marks. As if they can get a ball to stop on the green.'

'Yes. That is hilarious. If it wasn't so irritating.'

'And what about replacing divots? Pretending to. So silly. They wouldn't know how to cause a divot even if it hit them.' The men agreed and smirked.

President Bashit clasped his hammer and thumped it down, causing the noise to die down. 'Right, gentlemen.' He stared at the agenda in front of him. 'Next item.' The hammer pointed towards Henri Sweet. 'Let's have that presentation on the bespoke dog bowls now.'

The hallway's panelling felt cool under her burning cheeks. Philly turned her face towards Pru, who looked as if she'd just taken a punch in the face. They had felt so confident, standing there, in that grand conference room, sharing their PowerPoint and Excel with President Bashit and the board. With the calculations carefully put together on the spreadsheet. Showing the global trend on declining membership at private clubs, explaining the volume was mainly caused by male membership, it being so much greater in scale then female. That, with the increasing popularity of the sport among women, also globally, it made sense that this was a promising proposition. Clearly indicating how recruiting 75 women during the next three years would cause considerable financial spinoff and would balance the clearly worrisome books.

But they had been stopped before they could finish, feeling the harsh defeat when they looked round the group of silent and disapproving men after Bushrod had silenced them with a sharp dismissal, making Philly and Pru feel as if they were beaten on the 13th green during a match play game. They had been sent packing, the silly little girls not realizing what it takes to play with the big boys.

And although Bashit had addressed them in a polite manner, he hadn't wasted many words putting them into their place by stating very clearly that they should first concentrate on holding their new section together, before endeavouring on greater things.

Bushrod had stood up again, taking the floor, telling them, that before anything else, they needed to make certain that their section understood etiquette, which definitely did not mean stealing the club's books and throw rude assumptions at the board. How dare they presume the management hadn't everything under control?', the Treasurer had yelled before he practically threw them out by pointing out the direction of the door.

To say it hadn't gone well was an understatement. How on earth was she going to explain this fiasco to the others? Philly pushed herself from the wall and straightened her skirt and blouse, the outfit she chose so carefully, determined she had been to look professional.

Pru let out a long sigh. 'Jesus Christ, that was a nightmare.' Her hands moved over her head, pulling her already sleek hair tighter towards the carefully knotted bun in the nape of her neck.

'Yes. It was. I need some TLC,' Philly said. 'How about we change into something more comfortable and have a cup of tea with my Mum, try to get back to normal?'

'Great idea.' Pru nodded and closed her eyes for a moment. 'Exactly what I need right now.'

CHAPTER 22

'Well, you two. Tea it is. How lovely to see you here, so unexpected.' Mrs Hackkett wiped her hands on the towel hanging from the range and inspected the sullen faces in front of her, knowing instantly something was wrong. 'It's still sort of light. A game in the garden first? Like the good old days?' Her voice sounded kind while her eyes were staring into her daughter's, and she reached over, pulling Philly and Pru towards her carefully. A tight hug followed, squeezing the slim bodies against her own.

The comforting arms released them, and Mrs Hackkett gently pushed the two young women towards the kitchen door. 'Get yourself in position. We need to have some fun together before you leave me again for those exciting new boyfriends,' she said, while she grabbed a sweatshirt, wiggled herself in it and shot a glance at Pru, looking embarrassed.

They crossed the patio and started walking along the footpath towards the rusty iron gate, leading towards the pitch and putt tee. The clubs were already there, waiting for them.

'Right. Let's do the high ones.' Her mother said, passing pitching wedges to Philly and Pru. 'Show me what you've picked up from all dad's golf lessons. I want to see perfect short approaches.'

Philly concentrated on the ball, forgetting the miserable afternoon. Square stance, the grip of the club as it should be. Three quarter back swing and perfect impact. She noticed her mother smile, while in her follow-through. The ball stopped dead on the green, just behind the flag. Pru's ball followed, not far from hers.

'Wonderful shot, Pru, wonderful! Get your putter out, and sink the putt!' Her mother followed them to the green and watched them prepare. One potato, two potato, three potato. Eyes on the ball. And up they came. Two steps back, two steps forward, grip left, grip right.

Philly's hair fell forward as she bent her head. The takeaway was straight, the strike perfectly through the ball. The club went forward, followed by the quick stretch of her legs and the follow-through. Plop! The ball disappeared, straight in the middle of the cup.

'There is just no beating you two girls.' Her mother took her own putter and dropped a ball on the green. 'I will give it a try, but I don't even know why.' The ball arched away just in front of the hole. 'No. See. Missed.'

'One more time, Mum! Please, try one more.'

'Right, one more go. But that's it, you two.'

A perfect strike. A 10-yard putt this time. Curve to the left. Perfect rhythm. Plop.

'Great touch, Mrs H. You should really play more.' Pru said, crouching down on the green, examining her line while letting a long sigh escape her.

'What's troubling you two, Philly?' Her mother pushed down on her putter. 'You're not here just for the tea, now are you?'

Philly looked away from her mother and stared towards the pottering shed. Was it lame, scuttling off to her mother, as soon as things got a little complicated? Like two little girls, running away from the playground crying because the nasty boys wouldn't let them play with them? Wiping angry tears from their faces, feeling sorry for themselves?

'Are you listening?' Mrs Hackkett stared at her daughter and her friend, now both looking miserable. 'You two seem miles away. What in devil's name is wrong?'

'Sorry, Mum. It's Peckers Wood.'

'Alright,' Mrs Hackkett said slowly. 'Somehow this sounds serious. What's going on?'

'Yes. It is serious,' Philly answered. She grabbed her mother's hands and started telling her about the ride in the buggy with Charles Charmers and Roughie, how Mrs Pushet had somehow nicked the club's P&L, the stupid approach the committee had come up with, how the Ladies Section had agreed that recruiting more women was a brilliant idea and how Bashit and Bushrod had put them in their place, in front of the whole board.

'I see,' Mrs Hackkett said slowly. 'What did they say?'

'That we should start with getting our current section aligned before even thinking of interfering with the club's business,' Pru said. 'And that we should be grateful for having the opportunity at all to play a course like Peckers Wood.

Philly nodded. 'And come to think about it, the worst thing is, Bashit has a point. I mean, look at us. There aren't many courses like ours. Maybe we should indeed just be thankful, and pray this consultant figures something out to save the club.' Her knuckles turned white as she clasped her upper arms. She saw her mother's eyes go downwards towards her right hand, dangling her putter. Philly dropped her hands beside her body, stopped rubbing, and strained her arms in front of her, causing the muscles between her shoulders to scream out in pain. 'Mum, what were we thinking? The club is in trouble and us girls save the day? I can't even get our tiny section together for goodness sake.'

'My word.' Mrs Hackkett took her daughter's arm and guided her and Pru towards the wooden bench at the table. 'Sit down. Let's have a think. We have talked about great challenges before. This one is like all others.' She fell silent for a while, gazed at the putting green and continued. 'You need to figure out what you want, before you know what to do. Now. Tell me. What do you want for your club? What is your main goal?'

'We want to make sure our beloved Peckers Wood will still be safe and sound for future generations. By recruiting more women members. It makes perfect sense.'

'And, to be frank, as an added bonus, show the good gentlemen we are bright enough to have meaning towards our club's survival,' Pru added.

Mrs Hackkett nodded. 'That certainly is a goal, although I'm not quite sure it's realistic, my darlings.' Mrs Hackkett paused, stared at the wedding band on her left hand, stood up and started walking slowly, letting Philly and Pru catch up with her. 'It's all about showing you understand how the game is played, girls,' she said slowly, almost to herself.

Mrs Hackkett linked her arms around Philly's and Pru's and guided them away from the putting green and onto the garden's path. 'Before you go and leave me for the exciting times ahead of you, I have a little something,' she said softly. 'Follow me.'

They walked through the garden towards the pottery shed, where a large paper bag appeared from under the worn wooden table which Mrs Hackkett handed over with both hands. Philly felt the blood rush to her cheeks, while her right hand dived in and pulled the items out, one by one. A pair of golf shoes, worn but carefully polished. Pink checked trousers, two white polo-necked shirts and a soft pink V-necked sweater, all faded, frayed but clean. A glove, worn to the thread. Her mouth fell open. 'You kept all this?,' she asked, her voice barely a whisper.

'Yes, Philly, for you.' Her mother nodded. 'Listen to me,' her voice sounded conspiring, 'let these remind you of the boundaries you can break. You wore these, tearing the "No dogs or women allowed" sign from Peckers Woods gate. Let them inspire you. Look at them, feel them, whenever you need inspiration.'

Her mother's kind face suddenly became serious. 'And girls? Remember what Dad told you. If you want respect, show you can play the game of respect. And sportsmanship. Or in this case, *sportswomanship.* I really think that's all you need to inspire your girls to do.'

Philly nodded fiercely. 'Yes, Mum. Yes. I do understand. We do.' Her eyes went towards her mother's. 'And thank you.'

'Good'. Her mother gave a little smile and pinched Philly's cheek. 'Not quite sure about Varilla though. But maybe that will solve itself. Some things just do.'

'Yeah right.' Philly's eyebrows went up. 'We wish.'

'How are the Banger sisters, by the way?,' Mrs Hackkett asked. 'I haven't seen them in a couple of weeks.'

'Fine. Still weirdly enigmatic, oblivious of what is going on around them and impossible not to love.'

'Being themselves then,' Mrs Hackkett chuckled. 'I hope Varilla appreciates their character traits.'

'Not quite sure about that,' Philly laughed. 'It's miracle she hasn't killed them yet.'

'Come here and give this old woman a cuddle.' Mrs Hackkett wrapped her arms around Philly and Pru. 'Fail to plan is plan to fail. Remember?'

'I do.' Philly hugged her mother and breathed in the sweet smell that surrounded her, feeling one hand stroking her hair.

'Just focus, my lovely ones. On a way towards showing what you are really made of,' her mother whispered in her ear. 'And have lots of fun. Something tells me you girls will work it out.' She slowly released and pushed them towards the cottage. 'Off you go, make your poor old mother a cup of tea.'

CHAPTER 23

To: secretary@peckerswood.co.uk
From: bangers@home.co.uk
Cc: President@peckerswood.co.uk;
Bcc: vvdycke@home.co.uk
Subject: fact checking selection procedures female members

17th of September 2022

Dear Roughie,

It's US again, your 4ever besties. Just to say thank you for SUPER SUPS we had last evening and JOLLY GOOD of you to remember how all the girls became members at PW. Your memory is just AMAZING. So frightfully useful to have now we might want to expand further. But when the taxi driver dropped us off, we had a LITTLE TIFF about how it all exactly went, so could you be an ABSOLUTE DARLING and check if we aren't talking absolute poppycock? Because POOR OLD Varilla seemed quite UPSET after our last meeting during which we discussed SELECTION PROCEDURES. And you know we ABSOLUTELY ADORE Varilla and don't want her to feel unsettled, so we thought it might be a good idea we could put her mind at rest. Be a darling and check the following:

1. Philly

Exactly the same time the works for the new driving range started, right? Wasn't she technically the first woman? As soon as the club allowed them? She NEVER was on any waiting list, right?

2. Pru

Philly asked Bashit if she could bring a friend and he agreed. SO NOT ON ANY LIST.

3. Mrs Pushet

Had a chat with Bashit at Mr Pushet's funeral and THAT WAS THAT.

4. Us

Nobody has any clue on how we became members but we have been @ PW 4EVER. Might have something to do with you.

5. Lav Th.

Not quite sure. But there she was suddenly. Just before the dodgy watering system was fixed, remember?

6. Mrs Van Dycke (aka VtheG)

Wrote 5 letters, was REJECTED 5 times, threatened Bashit with equal rights committee inspection, was put on waiting list after harrowing interview with Lt. Ret. Bushrod, had to WAIT 5 YEARS and was fobbed off again and again, pestered husband into forking out for renovating chipping areas and new ball washers, was finally excepted because, quite understandably, poor President Bashit had FINALLY run out of excuses.

Loads of cuddles and kisses,
B&B B.

PS We do realize how insanely CLEVER President Bashit is. Imagine how creative one must be to think of 5 reasons for rejection. Quite amazing, wouldn't you agree?

PPS And, thinking about it, how INSANELY persistent Mrs VD is. We would have given up after one rejection. But that is because we are such softies. Unlike Mrs VD. She is never soft. Not even in HAIRY situations, like when getting one's fifth rejection letter.

CHAPTER 24

Philly stared past the figure in front of her, trying instead to focus on the multi-coloured oak leaves dangling in the slight breeze. Last night's alcohol and the lack of decent food and sleep was playing havoc with her stomach and her head, both telling her to keep still. After leaving her parents and dropping off Pru, Philly joined Ben, Henri Sweet, Bobby Long, Roughie and the Bangers at the pub, who for some reason were already in quite a jolly state when she showed up. Her forehead crumpled, half recollecting coming home to an empty flat and Ben taking her to bed, later to wake up to the noise of Pru stumbling up the stairs at four A.M.

The next thing she remembered was opening her eyes to the sound of her phone, and her voice groggily responding to the question her mother posed at the other end before stumbling to the bathroom for a hot shower, forcing two aspirins down her throat and managing to get herself to Peckers Wood and talk to her dad, now sitting next to her on the wooden bench behind the kitchen.

'You do realize this means Peckers Wood has again lost two members to Goodlie?'

Philly nodded, slowly, feeling the nausea getting worse.

'I sincerely hope you do.' Mr Hackkett's voice sounded

grave while he passed a steaming cup of coffee towards Philly who accepted it gratefully. 'I cannot imagine what Bashit will say when he finds out. Varilla and her husband are running towards Goodlie as we speak.' A short pause followed. 'She is really pissed off, Philly. Imagine assuming you are one of the chosen blue-eyed children for all those years and now finding out it's all a farce?' He shook his head and took a sip from his cup. 'I don't know how she grasped what's been going on, but somehow she figured it out.'

'O God, now what do I do?,' Philly groaned. 'I am so fucked.' She put the coffee mug down and stood up. 'I've been Lady Captain for a couple of weeks, and the only thing I have to show for it is losing a member from our already miniature section. Bashit will be beside himself with laughter, thinking of our recruitment proposal.'

'All the more reason you might want to show you're pro-active and give him warning.' Her father peered out of the window. 'Before Roughie prints out a resignation e-mail for him.' He narrowed his eyes and nodded towards the path leading up to the car park. 'If my eyes aren't deceiving me, he has just come in from his rounds, driving the buggy towards the clubhouse now.'

She dragged herself up the path and turned right, stopping for a second to breathe deeply, staring at the clubhouse. The bold-coloured roses in front of it had faded, their heads hanging, their petals starting to crumple, the leaves dotted with tiny specks of brown. The '*members only*' sign eye-balded her.

Trespassers will be prosecuted. Philly's shoulders drooped. *No shit.*

She managed to put one foot in front of the other and went inside. She gazed at the marble statue for a while and the impressive prize cabinet behind it with its carefully polished silver glaring at her. 'Follow the hallway, don't be a pussy, pull yourself together.' The voice in her head became louder, and she walked towards Bashit's door, distracted by some noise coming from behind the opposite men's bar and restaurant. She peeked in, noticing all the Windsor chairs had been pulled back from their tables. Miss Snuggs was hoovering under one of them, bending over to pick something up from the thick burgundy carpet. Roughie was behind the large brown bar with its shiny brass skirting staring at Miss Snuggs's bottom while absentmindedly buffing a pint glass. Philly pulled back, somehow feeling she was disturbing something private, and she turned round, feeling her feet slide over the parquet towards the thick carpet in front of Bashit's door. She knocked twice, the sharp tap sounding more confident than she felt.

'Enter.' Bashit's voice, not entirely unfriendly.

She pushed the door and stepped in, blinking a couple of times to get accustomed to the dark study, hardly making out the President standing behind his desk, leaning on his old wooden walking stick, Percy at his feet.

'Do sit down, Miss Hackkett.' A slight smile quivered round the grey lips. 'How can I help you?'

Philly swallowed audibly and cleared her throat. 'I wanted to inform you about the…' Philly stumbled for a moment but managed to pull her chin up and continue, '…the departure of Mrs Van Dycke. Sir.'

'Ah. Yes. I heard about that.' A long silence followed. The cunning blue eyes left hers for a fraction of a second. 'Well, Miss Hackkett,' Bashit finally said, 'I must say, I'm impressed. You certainly are steering your section in the right direction. Although I didn't expect you to be this ruthless in your tactic.'

'Excuse me?,' Philly asked, while narrowing her eyes, feeling confused.

'When I asked you to be true to our values and align your section, I didn't mean kick the poor Van Dycke woman out and bang the door behind her.' President Bashit's hand reached into his pocket and pulled out a white handkerchief which he moved over his lips, as if trying to wipe something away. A strange noise escaped him, and he coughed, using the handkerchief to shield his face, followed by a long hiccupping wheeze, causing the white cotton to bellow.

'President Bashit?,' Philly whispered. 'Are you okay? Should I call for someone?'

'No. No, I'm quite alright.' Bashit put the handkerchief back in his pocket and squared his shoulders. 'But let me read a passage from a letter to you,' he said quietly while unfolding a piece of paper and pushing his glasses up his nose.

'Quote.' He started reading the letter out loud, "'*...and that inadequate, spoiled girl you call Lady Captain, I mean, really. What a joke. Everyone knows she has absolutely no clue on how to run a disciplined section, show leadership or strive for any sort of athletic achievement at all....*" Unquote.' Bashit stared at Philly for a second before continuing. 'Quote. "*...even worse, as it seems to be Peckers Wood's way to create and wallow in an environment that thrives on sloth, I have come to the conclusion that the well-oiled machine of Goodlie far more fitting for someone as talented as Mrs Van Dycke who is not willing to associate herself with the amateurish ways of so-called golf club Peckers Wood anymore.....*" Unquote.'

'That fucking bitch Thorneybush wrote that, didn't she?,' Philly spat out, instantly regretting her words. 'Sorry, Mr President. I shouldn't have said that.' She wiped her sweaty palms on her trousers. 'But what she's claiming now, it's uncalled for, and I feel personally offended by her lies about our club. I hope you excuse me, but it makes me glad she has sodded off to ghastly Goodlie.'

'Simmer down, Miss Hackkett,' Bashit said, waiting for Philly to regain her composure before continuing. 'But I see your point. And actually share it, I might add.' He leaned backwards in his chair, as in deep thought. 'Some nagging beast inside of me is eager for some justice. I mean, no-one should get away with insulting Peckers Wood and its good members. Certainly not Miss Thorneybush.'

'I should hope not,' Philly said, her voice higher than usual. Her face grew red with blotches creeping up from her polo-necked shirt. 'Accusing me of inadequacy, how dare she.'

Bushrod turned towards her, not quite able to hide his amusement. 'And what about athletic achievement? How does that make you feel?'

'Bloody angry, sir.' Philly jumped up and walked towards the desk, with her finger pointed at the President, making him move back. 'I have played her more than a dozen times, and she never came near me. Nor to Pru. And the Banger sisters would butcher her given the chance.'

'Don't point your finger at me, Miss Hackkett,' Bashit countered, waving at her finger with an annoyed flick.

'I'm sorry, sir.' Philly replied, as her cheeks flushed.

'Very well.' Bashit hoisted himself up. 'Make sure you keep steering your section by keeping it together from now on. If you lose more, you won't have anything left. You wouldn't want that, now would you?'

'No, sir.'

'Maybe you should seek atonement for your sins.' Bashit limped towards the door and held it open. 'By banging Miss Thorneybush, Mrs Van Dycke and their cronies off a golf course before reaching the 18th, for instance,' he said while manoeuvring his guest out and closing the door with a soft click.

Philly crept sideways, letting the back of her head rest against the wall, closing her eyes and trying to ignore the annoying thumping sensation in her brain. She pulled her mobile out. 09:30. Ben would be on his way to the club, wanting to tee off at 10. Pru had probably made him a coffee before pushing him out of the flat, thankful for having it to herself. Knowing Pru, she would have a long soak in a hot bath before their tee time at one.

Her thumb moved over the screen, finding her friend's number, and she waited for the familiar voice to appear.

'Freckles,' followed by humming, after listening to what she had to say. Then a firm 'Absolutely,' before ending the conversation with a 'Give me half an hour.' Philly felt herself relax slightly, closed her eyes again and took a deep breath, letting it escape her lungs with a long exhale.

'Philly?' The sudden sound of a male voice made her jump, instantly making her adrenaline pump, knowing she was somewhere she shouldn't be. 'What are you doing here?' Her eyes opened, and she tried to focus on the blob in front of her, shaping into a round human form, wearing a beige pair of golfing slacks and a pale pink jumper, amazingly matching its owner's skin colour. 'I'm on my way to Bashit,' the pink lump said, making her stand at attention and ignore her throbbing temples. 'You might want to make yourself scarce. If he sees you here, there will be hell to pay.' She slowly recognized Roughie, who leaned towards her and pulled her from the wall, with a simultaneous nudge towards the emergency exit.

'He knows I'm here,' Philly said, shrugging Roughie's hand off. 'We just had a meeting. About the Van Dycke's sudden departure.' She looked up, distracted by the sound of hoovering coming their way. 'And, I might add, Bashit wasn't un-pleased.' She said, waiting for a reaction that didn't come. Roughie's gaze was transfixed by the monotonous sound moving towards them, accompanied by Miss Snuggs, now bent over, her backside towards them, dragging a heavy chest of drawers towards her, making sure she could clean behind it.

'Roughie?' Philly snapped her fingers, trying to catch his attention. 'Bashit wasn't un-pleased.'

'I see.' Roughie's moist face moved towards her, obviously trying hard to concentrate. 'About what?'

'The Van Dycke's. Sodding off to ghastly Goodlie.'

'Oh, that.' Roughie shrugged. 'Nor am I. I mentioned it to him over the phone, and he said he had more important things for us to discuss.' The back of Roughie's hand moved over his forehead. 'Like Ben's strategy on winning the Regional Competition. And in doing that bringing the medal back where it belongs. In the cabinet of the region's best golf club. Peckers Wood. The place to be.' He put his arms around Philly and guided her towards the exit. 'Now, off you go. Chop, chop.'

CHAPTER 25

Pru had kept her word, like always, sorting out the meeting Philly asked for and making certain everything was prepared. After a quick WhatsApp chat, she knew that her friend meant business, wanting inform the section about Varilla's sudden resignation but also needing a breather after the encounter with Bashit. The short walk from the clubhouse to the 18th green had calmed Philly down, enjoying the beautiful views over the lake towards the 17th and the hill flowing between the 11th green and the 18th tee boxes. The autumn's sun put a hazy shine over the copper glazed lake, its water rippling slightly as the ducks bobbed around each other. The leaves were changing into warmer colours, announcing the start of another season; swallows were circling low, ready to leave for somewhere more exotic.

Philly looked towards the car park from her secluded spot, just making out Maggie jumping out of the old Jaguar, followed by the Bangers, carefully guiding Mrs Pushet's petite figure alongside them. She caught up with them, letting Maggie run past her, the little dog eager to find out what goodies the Ladies' room had in store for her.

The smell of fresh coffee and sweets welcomed them as they stepped in, and Pru was still busy laying everything out neatly, including a large piece of paper spread over the coffee table.

'Thanks, Pru.' Philly hugged her friend. 'How did you manage all this so quickly?'

'I just nipped past the sweetshop in the village. They're open Sunday mornings, and that pleasant young girl they have gave me the royal treatment.' Her head turned sideways, towards the Bangers, sharing the croissant Pru had just refused. 'I mentioned those two. Apparently, they are VIP customers.'

Philly let go of her friend and cleared her throat. 'Fore, everyone.' She pointed towards the plastic chairs and the sofa. 'Please sit down, we need to discuss something important.'

The Banger sisters huddled together, blending into each other, wearing matching outfits as usual, pulled Maggie on their lap and stared at Philly. 'You sound serious,' Bogey said. 'What's this all about?'

'Varilla,' Philly replied in her gravest voice, 'has left us, for Goodlie.' The last word came out in a gasp. 'I thought it might be good to break that news to you personally and discuss the consequences.'

'Nooooo.' Birdie dragged out the word, while raising her eyebrows dramatically at her sister who returned her look with the same gesture. 'Why on earth would she want to do that?'

Pru shot them a dark look before turning to Philly. 'How did Bashit react?,' she asked.

'Well.' Philly paused for a second, trying to piece things together before she continued, pointing out the President was just as upset as she was by Gorilla's offensive tone of voice. He also ticked her off for losing a section member and then, quite surprisingly, seemed to imply that some sort of revenge would be appropriate.

'I see.' Pru cut in. 'Did he in any way discuss how this adds to the decline of members? To the already dire financial outlook?'

Philly shook her head. 'No. Nothing. Not a word. Our meeting was,' she contemplated for a moment, 'quite constructive to be honest.' She looked at her hands, as if buying some time for her next remark. 'And after the meeting I bumped into Roughie. Same there. All he cares about is bringing the Regional Competition Medal back to Peckers Wood. And so do Ben and Bashit, I gathered.'

A collective sigh blew through the room. 'Men. Bloody typical. Can only concentrate on one thing at a time,' Birdie said.

'Stop!' The word rang sharply around the room, making the women turn towards the tiny figure huddled in a deck chair with her hands in her grey curls. 'Too much information!,' Mrs Pushet shouted out, clearly overwhelmed. 'One thing at a time!' She jumped up, surprisingly agile. 'Money. Members. Revenge. So much to do and so little time.' Her last words were accompanied by a long look towards the Bangers before she sat down with a thoughtful look on her face. 'Sorry for the outburst, girls. But I just need a recap to sort out what's going on.'

Pru exchanged a quick look with Philly who grabbed the felt pen and moved towards the large sheet of paper in front of them. 'I think what Mrs Pushet is telling us is: we need a plan. We need to figure out what we can do to turn things around.' Her face turned bright pink, remembering the board meeting. 'Without it being anything large or compelling. I don't think we will get away with that again.' She gestured towards the other women who got up and crouched around the paper. 'So let's go for something relatively small but with impact.'

'Right.' Mrs Pushet nodded. 'I get it. Let's start by answering some obvious questions. What is more attractive than anything?' She looked at Pru. 'Let's have it, you divine marketing wizard.'

'Success. Everyone wants to be around a winner,' Pru said.

'Exactly!,' Mrs Pushet exclaimed.

The group nodded, followed with hums of agreement. 'Yes,' Birdie said. 'Nothing more attractive than someone oozing the winner's attitude.'

Bogey nodded. 'Absolutely. Winners draw others towards them. I know.'

'Damn right,' Mrs Pushet said, drawing arrows from one topic to the other. 'And if my long-term memory isn't deceiving me, I can clearly remember when the club's member count increased quite dramatically.' She put the top back on the felt pen and sat down. 'It was Mr Pushet's finest moment, winning the Regional Competition in 1982.' A long sigh escaped the tiny figure and the pretty old face crumpled up in a bright smile. 'He was in the local newspaper with a picture of him looking as proud as a rooster, holding the medal. And after that, the applications flooded in. Every male golfer in the county wanted to become a member at Peckers Wood.' The smile turned into a naughty giggle. 'And I never got so much action in my life. He just couldn't stop humping me for weeks, he was so over-excited. Horny bugger.'

Four pairs of large eyes stared at the little lady in stunned silence, who was now pulling a roll-up fag from her purse and lighting it up with a Zippo. Mrs Pushet inhaled deeply, closed her eyes and let the smoke escape through her half-open lips. 'We need to gather that low hanging fruit that is dangling right in front of us,' she said slowly. 'Any suggestions on how, girls?'

The four of them gathered themselves and concentrated again.

'By creating a proud chicken,' Birdie said thoughtfully, pointing at the graphic outlines.

'Chicken I am not,' Mrs Pushet replied, laughing. 'And nor are you, right?' Her face went serious. 'My dear girls. We can pull this off.' She addressed Philly. 'I think we need to consider President Bashit's suggestion, my dear. Let's find out if our dear friend Lav is up for a challenge.'

CHAPTER 26

'Are you sure Maggie will be alright?' Birdie looked over her shoulder and backed the old Jaguar into the only open parking space in Goodlie's car park, narrowly missing the shiny new Mercedes on her left side.

'Yes,' Bogey insisted, crumpling up a crisp packet into a ball before stuffing it into her trouser pocket. 'Philly promised me she would take her on her round with Pru.'

'Who's feeding her?'

'Miss Snuggs.'

'Okay.' Birdie let out a sigh. 'That's a relief.'

'You weren't assuming I would leave her with the Anorexia Anonymous Twosome to beg for her din-dins?' Bogey raised her eyebrows at her sister. 'I'm not into animal cruelty, darling.'

'No. I know. Sorry.' Birdie grabbed her bag, pushed the car door open and got out of the car. 'Good lord, sis. Look at this. Ghastliness galore.' She stuck her tongue out. 'Remind me why we are here and not Philly and Pru?'

'You know Lavender loathes Philly and Pru and vice versa. Ever since primary school.'

They leaned against the back of their car, taking in the scenery. Five limited edition white Range Rovers, two Porsches, in front of a long line of mostly German cars. Lavender's sleek mauve BMW in the first row, nearest to the path towards the sign pointing towards the clubhouse, in front of a sign saying *'Lady Captain Only.'* An impressive row of large flagpoles with Goodlie logos flapping proudly in the breeze in front of the clubhouse. A large sign in front of it, also white, with flowing green letters. *'Enjoy Goodlie. Visitors Welcome.'*

'Bloody busy.' Bogey pointed towards a large group of people, surrounded by seemingly brand-new trolleys, carrying bulky, shiny golf bags with their brand names shouting at them in bold colours. Two carefully groomed young men in matching golf attire were giving directions while handing out green fee cards at the same time. One of them looked towards them and stuck his hand up before he sauntered up holding a clip board. 'Welcome to Goodlie. Wonderful to have you. What can I do you for?'

'We might learn to like it here,' Bogey whispered to Birdie before she flashed her broadest smile to the handsome boy in front of her. 'We have an appointment. Miss Thorneybush is expecting us.'

'Ah.' The young man smiled broadly while unashamedly checking out Bogey's chest and revealing a row of perfectly even white teeth. 'Lavender. Let me check.' A pencil appeared from behind his ear, and a white left hand flipped papers over the clip board. 'Yes. Here we are. Miss Banger one and Miss Banger two. That must be you.' He pointed towards a large 4-seater buggy. 'I will drive you to the clubhouse. Please.' The tanned right hand reached out to guide the sisters forward. 'Allow me.'

A waft of tangy aftershave drifted towards them as they sat down, and the buggy started to roll along the tarred paths between meticulously cut hedges, showing bold advertisement plaques at every curving corner, carefully placed in clear sight. The buggy started talking suddenly, making the sisters jump. *'You have reached your destination. Your destination is on your right-hand side.'*

The handsome boy laughed, watching the surprised faces behind him. 'Don't worry, it's just the iPad telling us we have arrived. Please, let me help you.'

The path forked into two, and the Bangers stepped towards large glass sliding doors, behind which was a huge white shiny reception desk. A group of people stood in front of it, including a pretty girl handing out pieces of paper. A large screen next to the reception flashed into action, making the sisters concentrate on its messages.

"Welcome to Goodlie, the region's first and best inland links."

"Four balls only. Repair pitch marks and rake bunkers."

"Rakes sponsored by Timeless Tiles, www.timelesstiles.com."

Bogey stared at Birdie. 'What the fuck is an inland links?' she asked. 'The nearest sea is a hundred miles away.'

The screen flashed again, moving towards the next image.

"Order your beverages and bar food online at www.goodliegolfsnack.com when you reach the 7th or the 16th."

"Enjoy our plate of the day, vegan burger with ginger sauce, now only 19.99."

'That sounds a bit of a nuisance,' Birdie said. 'Henri told me Miss Snuggs has their drinks and snacks ready when the men finish their round. Which isn't too difficult as they always have beer and scotch eggs.'

The sound of a buzzer made them look up towards the pretty girl who was smiling and waving, inviting the Banger sisters to move forward and approach her. 'You're here for Lav, right?,' she asked, before asking them to follow her past a glass facade with a large bar and restaurant behind it. The sisters moved through the area which was full with people talking loudly and watching large screens showing a football match, to a corridor with a row of doors.

'Looks like one of those ghastly lobbies one sees in business hotels,' Birdie whispered.

Bogey nodded. 'Absolutely dreadful,' she said while she crumpled her nose up.

The pretty girl knocked the white door, just under the sign saying 'Lady Captain Office' in green flowing letters and pushed it open, not waiting for a reply.

Birdie and Bogey stepped forward, cautious, holding on to each other, as if expecting something creepy to pounce on them. Soft pearly light filled the space stretching out in front of them, accompanied by the smell of patchouli, becoming stronger as the door closed, and the pretty girl's departure was audible by the sound of her quick steps on the stone floor moving away from them.

'Ah, there you two are!,' Lavender cried out. Her carefully streaked bob looked immaculate, emphasizing the roundness of her face. She wore green golf slacks and a white jersey, the gold embroidered Goodlie logo sticking out on her left breast. The patchouli became overwhelming, nearly suffocating them, just like the embrace that followed.

Birdie slowly let go of her sister and turned her body to Lavender, returning the welcome with a peck on the cheek before stepping backwards. 'Hi, Lav,' she said, while pushing a reluctant Bogey forward. 'So good of you to invite us.'

'Of course!' Lav smiled and turned, walking towards an enormous plexiglass desk with a sleek tablet perched in the middle, a white leather and chrome office chair behind it and two stylish bright green clubs in front, which were clearly meant for the sisters to sit down. She took her own seat, wallowing in the obvious awe of the two sisters, taking their time to gaze at the modern furniture, the light carpeting and the copies of well-known contemporary art hanging on the light pearl-coloured walls. 'Our dressing room and showers are just behind me, filled with lovely fluffy towels, shampoos, body lotions and state of the art blow dryers.' Lav's smile became larger, with a hint of evilness shining through. 'Far cry from Peckers Wood's car park and kitchen, wouldn't you say?'

The sister exchanged a look, no longer than a split second, before Bogey replied. 'We do have a Ladies' room now, Lav. With loos. And showers. Philly had that sorted the moment she became Lady Captain.'

'Ah, of course,' Lav sniggered. 'The abandoned tool shed you cleaned up yourself.' The snicker turned into a cackle. 'Varilla told me about that indeed. What a joke.'

'How is Go…I mean, Varilla, by the way? Settled in?' Birdie flashed her broadest smile. 'She left us in quite a hurry. We never even had the time to say our farewells.'

'Yah.' Bogey leaned forward, her head cocked sideways. 'Why did she leave, anyway?' she asked, slowly moving her head to the other side. 'And what about you, why leave so suddenly?'

An annoyed tut escaped Lav's carefully lipsticked mouth. 'Fucking hell,' she said, eyes narrowed. 'Isn't it obvious? Peckers Wood is nothing more than an archaic bunch of fossilized men who refuse to grasp that their so-called traditions and values are totally *passé*.' She paused for a moment, staring from Birdie to Bogey before she continued. 'It won't last, you know. Exclusive golf clubs. So last century. And on top of that, half of the members will be dead in ten years, and good old Peckers Wood with it. Why would anyone in their right mind join?' Lav shook her head and sighed. 'No, I, and Varilla in my wake, have made the right decision. We chose what we so rightfully deserve. Winners. Future proof winners.'

'Well, good for you.' Birdie's voice was as sharp as a knife, slitting through the darkened atmosphere, making Bogey sit up. 'Let's explore that a little further. We have an idea that might interest you.'

Lav listened carefully to what the sisters were telling her. A ladies competition. Interesting indeed, she thought, while contemplating on the opportunities spreading out in front of her. Might be practice for joining that county league she had been considering. But, more importantly, finally, the chance of putting that haughty self-assured Philomena Hackkett in her place. Along with that cold bitch Prudence Love who had never given her the time of day. Just like those moronic sisters, now sitting in front of her, looking at her expectantly with their pathetic drooping eyes. The four of them, always clinging together, so tightly knit in their own sad little protected outdated Peckers Wood world. Never missing an opportunity to shut her out.

The mere concept of showing them who was boss, here, on her own turf, under her terms, was too good to refuse.

CHAPTER 27

To: secretary@peckerswood.co.uk
From: banger@home.co.uk
Bcc: President@peckerswood.co.uk
Subject: Regional competition

17th of October 2022

Dear Secretary, darling Roughie,

Please don't be SUPER cross, just couldn't RESIST to sneak off to Ghastly Goodlie. Wanted to check for ourselves if it is indeed HORRID. Don't fret, were at our BEST behaviour, even though we were APPALLED by size of crisp bowls at the Ladies' room. The ones your FAB mum bought for us are SOOOO MUCH larger. (THUS BETTER.)

Wouldn't for the world trade Miss Snuggs's DIVINE cottage pie for the REVOLTING Goodlie vegan burger with ginger sauce that was the special of the day. Moth balls soaked in cat pee, more likely. VIOLENTLY SICK, after an hour, Roughie. Two bottles of QUITE ADEQUATE Chardonnay wasted. But we think the Ladies loo set us off, too. Frightfully hot in there. UNBEARABLE.

Even no relief from loo seats. Seem to be heated. Now have BLISTERS on cheeks. And, not a decent bar of soap in sight. Managed to scrub with that fairy liquid that comes out of those useless little taps. God knows why they want to do the washing up in the bath room.

But ANNYHOO. Bumped into good old Lav Thorneybush. She is head of Ladies Competition COMMITTEE. Had interesting CHINWAG about ladies regional competition OPPORTUNITY. And medal. And how VITAL it is. Discussed with Philly and Pru. They will consult you on this EXCELLENT IDEA. Sure you agree. Even ~~GO~~VARILLA loves it, it seems. (Quelle surprise, now she is batting for the other side.)

Love you.
B&B Banger

PS. Played 9 holes. Couldn't BEAR more. Course is DREADFUL. Asked for stimp. NO-ONE knew. Greens so slow it felt like hitting a vegan moth ball through stale cat pee.

PPS. Had pudding at Goodlie as well. Tasted like something the cat spat out after eating vegan ginger moth balls. Rushed to Miss Snuggs before going home. Her spotted dick with custard calmed our poor tummies down. Now QUITE CHIRPY again.

PPPS. Mentioned you to Miss Snuggs. Seemed to make her unsettled. Maybe you should try making her eat spotted dick. Convinced it will make her QUITE CHIRPY too.

PPPPS. Do hope you ADORE competition idea. Will take all our girl's time. Otherwise, we might all be MASSIVELY BORED and feel inclined to ask for MORE TO DO AT CLUB. Like becoming COMMITTEE MEMBERS.

CHAPTER 28

The Chinese take-away was carefully divided between the two plates. Philly put them on her small kitchen table and pulled Ben towards her. 'Your dinner, sir,' she whispered in his ear. 'Carefully prepared by…,' a drum roll on his back, followed a short silence, 'the Peckers Wood Lady Captain who will win the Ladies Regional Competition Medal.'

'What?' Ben's hand moved to his fork. 'Glad I picked up this food. Absolutely delicious.'

'Ben?' Philly sighed. 'Are you listening? Competition?'

His brown eyes stared at her, confused. 'Pass me the red sauce, will you?,' he asked, scooping up a heap of rice with his spoon and inspecting it quickly. 'What's this green stuff mixed in the rice?,' he mumbled, before sniffing it and stuffing the spoon in his mouth.

Philly stared at him, his obvious disinterest rapidly evaporating the elation she had experienced since this afternoon when she told her friends waiting for her in the Ladies' room they were good to go. They had been so excited.

She swallowed and forced herself back to that moment. When the Bangers rushed off back to their house and returned in their old Jag 10 minutes later, dragging a small desk from its rear seats, through the narrow door. And then pushing the white plastic chair behind it and announcing it the Lady Captains desk.

Her desk.

When Pru went outside, shoved the garbage bins towards the kitchen door and drove her car in front of the Ladies' room. 'A Lady Captain competing for a medal deserves her own parking space,' she said.

Her own parking space.

She breathed in deeply and stared back at Ben who was still fully engrossed in his supper. Close your eyes, she told herself. Feel the high, the adrenalin. It was pretty amazing, after all. Peckers Wood Golf Club Lady Captain Philly Hackkett competing for the Regional Medal. The Bangers had mentioned the possible next step, them joining the county league. That would be something.

'Ben.' She raised her head, defiantly. 'Mister Club Captain. We have a Lady Section now, so we need a competition. And the whole Lady Section agreed.'

'O, sorry.' Ben tore his eyes away from the food and pulled a can of beer from the fridge behind him. 'You are organizing a competition. That's nice, gorgeous.' He took a couple of gulps from the can and crumpled it in his fist. 'Does Bashit know?'

'No.' Philly felt her fighting spirit coming back to her. 'But I am sure I'll get his full support. And I would appreciate your support too.'

'Sure. No problem.' Ben attacked the omelette with his spoon. 'I think it's great you girls are trying to have a go at competitive golf.'

'Excuse me?' Philly felt a wave of annoyance bubble up. 'What do you mean?'

'Well. Not just trying to hit a ball in a straight line and see what happens.' Ben lowered his voice and waved a finger at Philly. 'This is different. This involves skill, strategy, course management. You will find it interesting once you start to get the hang of it.'

Fucking hell. Philly watched him stuff a heaped-up spoon in his mouth, leaving two rice grains stuck to his upper lip, making her feel disgusted suddenly. She reached over for a paper napkin and handed it to him. 'Any other advice, dear Captain? For us poor challenged girls?,' she asked, not bothering to hide the sarcasm in her voice.

'Did anyone mention you need at least six players?' Ben reached backwards for the fridge, pushed it open and pulled out another beer, not bothered by her sudden frostiness. 'That's one of the conditions to enter it as a registered match, the real deal. Among others. I assume you are organizing and playing under the Regional's rules, that is?'

CHAPTER 29

'Miss Snuggs! Where are you?' Bogey's voice rang out through the warm kitchen, her voice an octave higher than usual, as if talking to a little child. 'Where are our delicious muffins?' She whispered, taking her Monty coat off and throwing it on the nearest chair, followed by Birdie piling her identical one on top of it.

Miss Snuggs winced, hearing the high voice and seeing the Banger sisters move towards her. The freshly baked muffins dropped from her fingers and made a soft clicking sound, bouncing on the warm plate. A deep sigh left her through her nose as she stuck her red fingertips in her mouth. 'Stay calm Snuggsy,' she told herself. 'They don't bite. You have talked to them a million times, and they just want tea and a chat.'

'Miss Snuggs? Marvelous muffin person?' The last three words came out like a line in a song.

'Yes, Ladies?' Miss Snuggs pulled her shoulders backwards and started to pile the muffins in a paper bag. 'Your delivery?,' she asked, folding her hands around the warm bag and handing it to the two hovering women in front of her.

'Thanks. You're the best.' Birdie pouted her lips, blew a kiss and pulled the bag towards her. 'They smell heavenly.'

Birdie looked round and pulled herself up on the kitchen top, while Bogey grabbed a packet of crisps from a cabinet and started eating, slowly letting the sound of crunching flakes flow from her mouth. 'So, Snuggsy, what are you up to today? Anything interesting?'

Miss Snuggs couldn't stop the smile appearing on her face, thinking of what the day had in store for her. 'Well,' she said shyly, looking down at the floor, 'as soon as I'm finished with Mr Rough's lunch, I start mopping the floor in the men's lounge, do the toilets and clean the windows. Then I'm wanted at the Caddy Master, to help the caddies clear the driving range.'

'Right. Sounds like a full schedule,' Bogey said. 'We shouldn't keep you then.' Her face dropped. 'And bloody Philly is out pestering us, demanding to talk about training for the competition.' The sisters moved towards the back door, grabbing their coats, ready to leave. 'So we need to get a move on.'

Miss Snuggs nodded and waved, relieved they didn't want to stay, feeling her stomach tingle a little, thinking of Mr Rough's lunch. The best part of the day: walking towards Mr Rough's study with the tray. Knocking on his door and hearing his soft voice. Moving towards the desk and breathing the room's familiar smell in. Watching Mr Rough smile as he would pinch a sausage from the tray before she could put it in front of him.

She checked the carefully arranged items in front of her. A large glass of chilled white wine, two toasties with a slab of salted butter on top, homemade tomato ketchup, a pork pie, sausages and piccalilli she made herself. A little too bland, just like Mr Rough wanted it.

The linen napkin felt crisp under her palm before she carefully folded it into a perfect roll. The silver ring with PW looked just grand on it. Two more minutes, and she would walk up the stairs. Noon on the dot, like Mr Rough had instructed her. A shiver moved from between her legs to her tummy. She liked Mr Rough instructing her.

Her gaze left the floor, her burning fingers rested on the Formica workspace in front of the back window while she looked out over the fields. The meadow behind the clubhouse had turned a golden yellow after the warm summer, nearly hiding some left-over marigolds in their very last bloom. What if she dared to be a bit dangerous and pick some of them? They would look ever so pretty in a little white vase on Mr Rough's lunch tray? But no. It wasn't her place to go out in the field. The field was for the members.

Her mind drifted to last night when she watched Mr Rough drinking red vinos with Mr Sweet, looking ever so handsome sitting at the bar, pouring from the bottle she had fetched for him. He had left a little wine in his last glass. She could still taste it on her tongue. Her cheeks flushed remembering putting his glass to her lips and licking it. Her fingers moved to her lips for a moment. She closed her eyes and steadied herself. One and a half minute to noon. Time to go.

'Miss Snuggs?' The shrill sound of two identical voices startled her. 'We'll be off now and leave you to your loos and windows. If you bump into Philly, let her know we are on the course.'

She blinked, feeling herself being squashed into a tight hug. 'And thanks so super much for the muffins,' one of the sisters said. 'Maybe we will need some more.'

The other one looked into the bag, grabbed a muffin out and took a large bite. 'Yes. Definitely. More. Can we come over for a lemonade later?'

Miss Snuggs tried to compose herself, watching the sisters leave, still feeling the tightness of the four strong arms that had grabbed her, the sight of the clock spurting her into action, she sped into the hall and up to the familiar door.

'Mr Rough?' He hadn't responded to her knock, but he was in there. She saw him going in this morning. She knocked again. Nothing. 'Mr Rough? May I come in?' Miss Snuggs pushed the door with her elbow, slowly walked in and peeked towards the large mahogany desk.

There he was, behind it, staring at the computer screen with his head in both hands. He never noticed her putting the tray in front of him. She tiptoed out, carefully, not wanting do disturb him. Because Mr Rough was ever so important. And ever so handsome.

Noticing the tray on the desk, Roughie quickly closed his laptop and looked round his study, blissfully warm with the central heating on full blast. The soft leather sofa on the far end of the large, airy room looked inviting. He took his tray, stretched down on the sofa and stared through the French windows in front of him, where he could just make out the driving range and the practice green. Busy with gentlemen trying new routines, as always. He sighed. What he should be doing. Instead of all this annoying admin, like the competition committee, pushing him into retaining a new head pro.

And worst of all, he of all people had to make time for interviewing that new chap. Who did the committee think he was? Some kind of recruitment agency? Roughie snorted. Staff issues, what a bloody bore. He was far too busy and important to waste his time on something so, what was the right term, so, trivial? And that nonsense about that Lady Competition Bashit had been harassing him about. Whatever could Philly Hackkett do that would have any added value to the club? Bashit had dismissed his questions on the topic with a curt wave and a short "it's something trivial, Roughie. Lady stuff. Just deal with it quickly, will you?"

He swallowed. His heart beat went up a notch. The sofa creaked under his upright sudden movement, and he smiled to himself. Trivial. Lady stuff. He yanked his phone towards him and found Philly's number. She picked up after the second tone.

'Roughie.' The familiar voice sounded short but friendly.

'Dear Philly, it's Roughie.' He cleared his throat before continuing. 'As you gathered.'

'Yes. How can I help you?'

'As you might have heard, old Freddy Windim is taking early retirement from Peckers Wood. Can't say he will be missed enormously, but his departure, however, leaves us with something of a sticky wicket.'

'I see. Go on.'

'Yes. Well. Although our more senior members were not known to book more than one lesson a year on average with Windim, the men's competition team insists on a new head pro. Fortunately I received a tip from my dear old friend Banger Tosser, secretary at The Anglaise. Ted recommends a chap called Simon Hot who's been head pro there for four years but is looking to further his career elsewhere. Ted is willing to let Hot go immediately.

'Well. That sounds like a wonderful opportunity.' Philly's voice sounded pleased somehow. 'And I also need to talk to you and maybe Bashit about the ladies competition.'

'Yes.' Roughie swallowed and tried to build up some tension by pausing. 'The final decision on whether or not we retain Mr Hot of course lies with the board. But we are reluctant to move on without consulting you. As you know we value your opinion enormously.' He swallowed, hoping Philly couldn't hear the uneasiness in his voice, giving his obvious lie away.

'You do?' Philly's surprise sounded genuine.

'Absolutely.' He cleared his throat, relieved and convinced he had gotten away with misleading her. 'So, it would be greatly appreciated if you could spare an hour of your time in order to conduct an interview with Mr Hot and afterwards share your thoughts with me.'

'Great. Yes. Absolutely.'

'Perhaps you could take him for a spot of lunch?,' Roughie said, feeling confident. 'You can of course charge your expenses to the committee. You might want to consider The Chasty Chicken down the road. They do a perfectly good turkey sandwich.

'All right. No problem. Happy to do so. Just text me his details.' Philly's voice sounded shorter now, as if being distracted. 'Listen, I'm at work and need to go. I'll get back to you personally later, okay? I have the other thing I need to run by you. You know, competition?'

'If you must.' Roughie tried not to sigh but failed.

'Yes. I must. Will see you in your study. Bye, Roughie.'

The phone call ended with a short click. Roughie put the phone down, stretched his arms in front of him and checked his tray. Perfect. As always. That would keep him going until supper with his mother.

CHAPTER 30

Philly stopped just in front of Roughie's study, letting the heady odour of Black Opium drift up her nose, after managing to slip into the clubhouse unnoticed. She peeked through the opened door. There they were, sitting opposite each other. Mrs Rough, dressed like a mannequin ready to step on the catwalk, with that all too familiar determined look on her carefully made-up face. Roughie, slumped in his chair, a defeated look in his eyes.

Philly paused and took in the scene, concentrating on what was going on between mother and son.

'What do you think? Reginald? Are you listening to your mother?' Mrs Rough's voice carried through the study. 'Roughie! For goodness' sake! Pay attention!'

Philly grinned. Poor Roughie. Time for some lifesaving. She walked through the half open door and patted Mrs Rough on the back softly. 'Mrs Rough! You're back! How were the Bahamas?'

'Philly!,' Mrs Rough exclaimed. 'How did you sneak in here? Sit down girl, sit down. Before anyone sees you here.' She pulled a chair towards her and faced Philly. 'Bahamas were divine, as usual,' she said with a fat wink. 'But Philly, I cannot begin to tell you how much I enjoyed the delightful supper today, such a surprise. The food and wine were superb.'

Mrs Rough leaned towards her. 'I must admit I was a bit hesitant to meet Reginald here,' she said in a low voice. 'The last time I had lunch in Reginald's study, that vile Mrs Snuggs was still running the kitchen and bar. I distinctly remember she poured the wine like it was stale glue, and the shepherd's pie looked like something Percy had left behind the rhododendrons.'

Mrs Rough's beautiful face crumpled up in disgust, pausing and looking over her shoulder, towards the kitchen. 'But what a breath of fresh air her granddaughter is.' She whispered at Philly, while giving Roughie a knowing look. 'I took to the girl instantly,' Mrs Rough continued. 'How a place like Peckers Wood can hold on to her is a mystery to me. One might assume that such a well-mannered and beautiful girl could find employment anywhere.'

Mrs Rough clicked her tongue and turned her head towards Roughie. 'And I am sure she will make someone a good wife sometime soon. Beautiful and a good cook, what more could anyone want?' Her voice became more insistent with each word. 'And the honey-coloured hair with those amazing blue eyes? It baffles me that she hasn't been snapped up by some handsome fellow already.' She dropped back in her chair and let her hands fall in her lap, while raising her eyes to the ceiling, dramatically.

Roughie stood up. 'I need to go, mummy. Duty beckons, I'm afraid.' He bent over and kissed his mother on the cheek. 'I am sure you and Philly have lots to catch up on.'

'Roughie?' Philly gave him a knowing stare. 'Competition? I came especially?'

But the door closed behind Roughie, without a response.

Mrs Rough pulled a face. 'Duty beckons. What utter nonsense. He's avoiding us, Philly.' She poured the last of the wine into her glass. 'Let's ask that divine Miss Snuggs for another bottle.'

'What do you think, isn't she a wonder?' Mrs Rough rambled on. 'You know, if Reginald would present her as his fiancée, I would be thrilled to bits. But Reginald, alas, is such a snob. He finds people that work for a living quite beneath him. How I loathe that attitude. It's not as if he's from royalty, now is he?'

Philly raised an eyebrow. 'What do you mean, Mrs Rough? You could have fooled me, listening to you both, speaking the Queen's English.' She paused and cleared her throat. 'And you both having such beautiful manners, of course.'

'Oh, get off it, Philly. Everybody here knows about Mr Rough and myself. Sixteen I was, when I met him. Sneaked off, climbed out of my dorm room window to go disco dancing in the village.' The older woman's face moved close to Philly's. 'And there he was. Tall, butch, cocky and irresistible. Smelling of fresh sweat after a hard day's work,' Mrs Rough whispered. 'I opened my legs for him in a jiffy, and he got me pregnant right there and then.'

Philly choked and tried to swallow.

'But Mr Rough did the right thing. God rest his soul. Married me, put me in charge of the admin side of his little business and off we went, making pots of money, right from the start. And we worked our backsides off. Found a damn fine Nanny for Reginald and got on with it. We made our first million at 25. I will never forget the proud look on Mr Rough's face, the day he dropped Reginald off at that expensive public school he's always on about.'

'Right.' Philly swallowed another cough, trying to speak normally.

'You know, Philly,' Mrs Rough said, 'sometimes I wonder if it was indeed such a blessing that we could afford to send him to that place; although he did seem to adore his time there. Those boys seem to turn out as softies so often, don't you agree?'

Philly couldn't help herself nodding and giggled.

Mrs Rough sighed. 'I miss Mr Rough, you know. Such a shame, him toppling over just after the Chinese bought our potpourri business. Now I am left all alone, no one to spend all that delicious money with.'

'Mrs Rough?' Philly looked at the sad face in front of her. 'So, it is true, that you are filthy rich?'

'Oh, yes.' Mrs Rough nodded profusely. 'Absolutely swimming in cash.'

'Mrs Rough?' Now Philly looked down, feeling a bit embarrassed by what she wanted to ask.

'Yes, dear?'

'Does that mean Roughie is filthy rich too?,' Philly asked, carefully.

'God yes. He's got so much money his great-grandchildren won't even be able to spend it all. If he can bring himself to reproduce, that is.'

Mrs Rough stood up and took Philly's face in her hands. 'We both now he is not exactly James Bond, but he does deserve a loving wife.' She pinched Philly's cheek. 'My dear girl, if only we could find someone that understands and suits him. And would entice him to produce my grandchildren. What bliss that would be.'

She let go of Philly's face and set off towards the door leading to the hall. 'Let me find that lovely creature. For that bottle of wine I promised you. So we can really catch up.'

Philly turned her head, seeing Mrs Pushet waving at her. She stood up to beckon the old lady.

'Philly. Wonderful.' Mrs Pushet opened her arms. 'Give us a kiss, darling. How are you doing? And Prudence? And how are those adorable Banger sisters? I think I just saw them tiptoeing by?'

Philly smiled, imagining the two sisters. 'Hope not, Mrs Pushet. They shouldn't be skulking out here without permission. Bashit might see them and throw them out.'

'Pushy!,' Mrs Rough exclaimed. 'Also off the straight and narrow.' Mrs Rough bent down and clasped the little old lady in a tight embrace. 'You will join us and chat, will you?'

'So good to see you again, my darling.' Mrs Pushet beamed. 'Where were you off to now, Benidorm?'

'Bahamas.' Mrs Rough winked at Philly. 'Stayed with one of my delightful young gentleman friends.'

'Oh, goodie. Shagging something delicious in the sunshine.' Mrs Pushet nodded. 'Sounds just the thing to get one's mind off losing one's husband.'

Philly coughed again and her eyes watered, concentrating on Miss Snuggs running back to the bar while carrying two large wooden cases stocked with wine bottles. 'Indeed lovely girl, that Miss Snuggs,' she said, trying to change the subject.

'Yes. Divine,' Mrs Rough agreed while turning her attention to Mrs Pushet. 'Pushy, you always seem to know everything about everyone. What do you know about this girl's history?'

'Well. History.' Mrs Pushet let out a deep sigh. 'Yes. I'm up to par on that. Where to begin?' She looked at Philly for a moment before turning to Mrs Rough. 'I will tell you what I know. But I don't feel there is any added value in spreading the tale any further. If you understand what I mean.'

Mrs Rough and Philly exchanged a quick look and nodded towards the older woman in front of them. 'Understood,' Mrs Rough said.

'Let me say this young woman's life could have been very different if her mother hadn't died so early in life. I think little Miss Snuggs was three or four when she lost her Mummy to some dreadful disease and was forced to spend her childhood with that bat of a grandmother who did nothing to ensure the girl had a proper education, the opportunity to make some friends an enjoy her teens.' She shook her head, slowly. 'No, she was packed up to Peckers Wood as soon as it was legal for her to work full time.'

'That doesn't sound good. What about her father?' Philly asked. 'Where does he fit in?'

'The official version?,' Mrs Pushet snorted. 'The mother was caught fooling around with a young caddy on the driving range. When he found out she was pregnant he made himself scarce. Never to be seen or heard of again.'

Mrs Rough and Philly glanced at each other. 'Tell us more,' Mrs Rough said. 'Unofficially?'

'The President's son took her out on the driving range. At night, when no one was there. So he could get in her knickers again. They were hitting some balls when her father appeared. Ready to pull her home, by her hair. He startled the President's son so much the boy shanked his ball. Killed the father instantly. Hit him right on the left temple.'

'Good heavens. How absolutely dreadful,' Mrs Rough exclaimed. 'What happened next?'

'It was hushed up, of course. Word was the dad had a massive stroke and dropped dead.' Mrs Pushet said. 'The son got sent away to run one of the family's farms in Scotland, Mrs Snuggs was paid off so she would keep silent, and the caddy story was invented.' A slight pause followed, both Philly and Mrs Rough leaned forward, eager to hear more.

'And then the poor girl died a couple of years later. The whole thing was a nightmare. The club's darkest hour.' Mrs Pushet nodded her head, slowly. 'Yes. Died. Leaving dear little Miss Snuggs all by herself. Who, miraculously, turned out lovely. Despite being raised by that awful bat of a grandmother of hers. Who never wanted her. And still doesn't.'

Mrs Rough and Philly both stared at Mrs Pushet open mouthed, not knowing what to say.

The old lady continued. 'You know, I ran into that cow just last week. She had the gall to tell me she was fed up with her granddaughter still being single. Needs her married off. But what is the poor girl to do? In this village?' Mrs Pushet raised her eyebrows and glanced towards Mrs Rough. 'She will never be able to find something she can afford, poor thing. But what can one do?' She stopped talking with a shrug and a dismissive wave, clearly indicating the story was over.

Philly took her glass, gulped the wine back in one go and checked her watch, feeling the urge to end the tête-à-tête despite really wanting to sit and gossip some more. She needed to find Roughie and get the competition sorted. She turned and beckoned the two other women. 'Maybe you should continue in the Ladies' room before we get into trouble.'

The back entrance to the corridor opened with a squeak. The women slid past it and quickened, passing the marble statue, feeling the soft carpets slide over the parquet floor under the pressure of their feet. The space behind the large French clock offered an escape for a few seconds, just long enough to hear President Bashit's voice thunder through the passage.

'Miss Hackkett. Please. Do come in.'

Philly nervously managed a wave at the other women, urging them to go on. 'Go. I will see you later.' She stepped in front of the heavy panelled door, giving it a firm knock, touching the wood just under the copper sign stating this was the President's study.

'Enter.' The familiar voice reached her.

Philly pushed the handle, straightened her shoulders and stepped into the stodgy room. 'Sir, what can I do for you?'

The liver-spotted, bald head nodded slowly, and a blue-veined hand moved towards the leather club chairs in front of the desk. 'Yes, Miss Hackkett. Here you find yourself again.' The President's right hand went towards the walking stick's brass head, starting to rub it gently. His other hand moved to his purple nose, sliding the reading glasses down half an inch. His head went down a little, and the President's sharp eyes glared at Philly, unblinking, not leaving her face for a few seconds.

'So. Miss Hackkett, I thought we might have another chat. See how you are faring.' Something that resembled a smile appeared on the President's grey lips. 'I heard some rumours about a competition. Sounded rather unusual.'

Philly opened her mouth, but Bashit cut her short.

'Roughie dropped by.' The President's voice was neutral, as was the look in his eyes.

'I see.' The tingle in Philly's gut was starting to feel like a sour burn.

'Yes. He told me you were assisting him with the new pro selection. Jolly good.' The President's eyes left Philly and turned towards the window. 'We need someone that feels at home here, Miss Hackkett. Fits in.' A tense pause followed before Bashit continued. 'Before Windim, we had to let go of a pro. He didn't feel at home here at all and felt it necessary to voice his feelings to our members. His dismissal wasn't pleasant. At all. Unfortunate, as I greatly dislike unpleasantness.' Bashit was quiet again for a second before he carried on. 'So Miss Hackkett, you have your work cut out for you.' The cunning eyes came back to Philly. 'Make sure this Simon Hot understands what is expected from him. Be firm. But pleasant. About how we do things around here.' A long stare followed. 'We live and let live. Miss Hackkett.'

'Yes. Understood. Live and let live.' Philly nodded. 'I will. Certainly.'

'Yes. Well. I also gathered you were having a little chinwag with Mrs Rough.' The glasses returned again. 'Something to do with our dear Miss Snuggs, a little birdie told me.'

'Yes. Indeed.' Philly stared at the President. How was it even possible this man knew what had happened only 10 minutes ago? The blank look on his face revealed nothing, but it was clear he wanted Philly to elaborate. 'But nothing important,' she said, shaking her head. 'I can't even remember what we were discussing to be honest.' Philly shifted position. 'Just girl talk. We were discussing how lovely she is and deserves a little happiness, that's all.'

'Quite.' The President nodded. 'I agree. She is lovely, but still a bit, how shall I put it, innocent? Unacquainted, perhaps?' His head dropped to his chest, and he left a silence before he addressed Philly again. 'Miss Hackkett?' A pause followed before the President spoke again. 'Let's keep it that way,' he said kindly, but with a resolute undertone.

Philly nodded, realizing all too well what was expected of her.

'Good.' The President got up and hobbled back to his desk. His stick came up, pointing at the painting behind his desk, towards the grand looking man with the beady eyed wood pecker on his shoulder.

'My father.' President Bashit said. 'A great man. Insightful. Always showed great empathy. And discretion. Important ingredients for great leadership.' The stick came down again and the President continued. 'He taught me many important things. And I made him proud.' His hand went towards Philly, showing a signet ring, with the letters PW engraved in curving script. 'He gave me this just before he passed away and announced me President.'

'I see.' Philly inspected the ring. 'It's very beautiful.'

'Yes. It is. And it will shine on someone else's finger before too long. As soon as I have made up my mind on which member has shown the kind of leadership that will guide this club safely into the future.' The President pulled his hand back and turned towards Philly.

'Well, Miss Hackkett. What's all this about your rogue idea, this Ladies Competition a little birdie told me about?' A mischievous grin split President Bashit's face.

'Yah.' A wave of confidence suddenly came over Philly, like stepping on a tee holding a driver and knowing the shot would turn out great. She stared right into the President's blue eyes, detecting an amused glint, which made her even more eager to prove her point. 'We were thinking it would be nice to start a regional competition for Ladies. You know, start small, just Goodlie and us for now, see how we go.' She paused for a second and swallowed. 'It might be a first step towards entering county league, perhaps'.

Bashit's eyebrows shot up, and his eyes opened wide. His chin dropped to his chest, his eyes still firmly on Philly's. 'I suppose you think you have a chance of actually winning?' He chuckled and dropped his voice to an embarrassed whisper. 'Imagine how awful it would be if you needed to tell me, I mean the committee, that you lost. To ghastly Goodlie.' He was quiet for a moment before he continued. 'After your last encounter with us.'

'What do you think? Winning is exactly what I am going to do,' she said confidently. 'And I will present that medal to the committee personally.'

President Bashit returned her stare. 'I see. And what do you want from me?'

'Support.' Philly held his gaze, trying to win this obvious staring match.

'Well, Miss Hackkett,' President Bashit said thoughtfully, his eyes moving upwards towards the large painting of his father above the fireplace. 'Are you quite sure about this endeavour? It's not only about winning a couple of matches, you know. It's also about representing our club, and what it stands for.'

'I will bring that medal home, sir. And it will shine brightly in Peckers Wood's prize cabinet, proud to belong there, like we are, shining with delight because we are part of this club.' Philly bit her lip, seeing the President frown, hoping she wasn't overplaying her hand.

Bashit stood up and walked towards a low chest of drawers, reaching for one of the silver-framed pictures showing Severiano Ballesteros holding up a silver cup. 'Do you know what our dear friend Seve said? *To give yourself the best possible chance of playing to your potential, you must prepare for every eventuality.'* He gave the picture to Philly, who stared at it, feeling emotional suddenly. 'Keep that for a while, Miss Hackkett. Put it in your Ladies' room. Let it inspire you.' The President sat down again, leaving the room silent.

Philly stared at him and back at the picture, not believing what she just heard. Bashit, giving her something he coveted, from this study? Her mouth went dry, she knew she had to say something intelligent, but a soft '*Thank you, you're the best*' was all she could manage.

'Don't thank me, thank Severiano. He really was the best.' President Bashit looked at Philly. 'Well. Make sure you prepare yourself and your team, Miss Hackkett. One step at a time. Put the ghastly Goodlie women in their place. Before you contemplate on anything grander.'

'Thank you, sir,' Philly said while she stood up, feeling her knees wobble. 'I'll scuttle back to the ladies then.' She bowed her head slightly and fled towards the exit, clutching the photograph under her arm tightly.

CHAPTER 31

Pru turned left at the large oak tree, leaving the car park behind her. She pulled her jacket's collar up, feeling the evening's late autumn wind getting colder and making her shiver, a strange sensation when combined with the excitement that was rising up in her body. The path forked into three. She took the right, not concerned by the fading light, knowing her way towards the little stone cottage with the two chimneys on the roof, a miniature copy of its larger brother the clubhouse. The front door was open, revealing who she was longing for. He was waiting for her with a long, thin twig in his hand, his belt buckle already open, like the top button of his golf slacks, showing a dark line of hair rising towards his belly button, the sight making her knees turn to jelly.

She swallowed, picked up her pace and walked up towards him, stopping an inch in front of his body, not daring to look in his eyes, but inhaling his earthy smell deeply, knowing what was to come, the thought shooting raw excitement to her groin. Her head jerked back as his right hand quickly grabbed her pony tail, and his left hand arched her against him, her crotch against his, feeling him go hard.

'Kit off and on the bed,' he whispered, sliding the twig along her bum and slapping her with it, causing her breath to quicken. 'Now!'

She ran to the tiny bedroom, its bed stripped to the sheet, undressed and lay down on her back, legs slightly open, watching him come in, slowly, and looking her over from head to toe. The twig moved to her face, its tip resting on her forehead before sliding down slowly, first to her left nipple, whipping it in slow movements until it was nearly sore and moving down between her legs, stroking gently, making her twitch and moan.

'Your stance is too narrow,' he said, kneeling in front of her, still stroking between her legs and pushing her knees further apart with a quick, sharp tug. 'Open it.' The command was short, and she pushed her legs apart as far as she had ever done. 'You need to work on your rhythm.' His voice was low and slow as two of his fingers slid into her. 'Move your hips. Like I taught you.' He shoved deeper, and she started to jerk up and down. 'Faster,' he demanded, before bending down and licking her for a few seconds.

'I want to come,' she moaned, moving her head from right to left. 'Please.'

'No.' His head came back and his fingers slid out of her. 'Keep your head still. This lesson isn't over yet.' He stood up and undressed, not moving his eyes away from her, seeing the hunger in her. 'I want to feel your grip. It was too weak the last time.' His cock moved towards her mouth, and she opened wide, feeling it slide in and out a couple of times before he grabbed her hand and folded her fingers around it. 'Follow my lead,' he whispered, moving his own hand between her legs and started to rub her slowly. 'Not too fast.'

She couldn't hold it any longer. Her back arched, and she came, violently, screaming out while he turned her over, pulled her against him and thrust hard a couple of times, pushing her body close as they fell sideways together, holding each other still for a couple of moments. He reached under the bed with one hand, pulled a duvet over them, turned her around and kissed her gently, first on her lips, then moving to the tip of her nose and her forehead, while untying her hair and stroking it with slow movements.

'Marry me,' Pru said, her voice muffled against his chest. 'Please.'

'I can't afford you, Love.' Lash Johnsson pulled back a little and smiled at her. 'We've been over this.' He kissed her again.

'You don't have to. I can afford myself,' she whispered. 'And be the mother of your children.'

He chuckled, pushed her on her back and bent over her. 'You would be bored to death, sick of me before you know it. And then you'll be snatched from me by some handsome doctor with brilliant prospects.' His unusual light grey eyes stared at her, and he whispered, 'I'm just a humble servant to Peckers Wood and its members. Far beneath you.'

'I'm not a snob,' Pru pouted and snuggled against his warm body. 'And you have so much talent for the game. No need for you to be stuck here being Caddy Master for the rest of your life.'

'I don't feel stuck. And I owe it to Bashit. He saved my life, and as long as he is here, I am here for him. The place would be a shambles without me, and he would suffer from it. Specially now Windim is gone, and we have to find a new pro.' Lash pulled away and lay on his back for a while. 'I would be in and out of prison if he hadn't taken me under his wing.'

'I know.' Pru said softly.

'I mean, the man caught me in the act. Pushing his silver letter opener down my pants not realizing he was there in his study. And what did he do? Call the coppers? No. He gave me a job, taught me to play golf and some bloody decency. Personally. So again, I owe him, the man saved my fucking, sorry life.'

'I know. You told me. And I do understand,' Pru said again, moving towards him and wrapping herself around his warm body. 'But that doesn't mean you can't move on. Maybe Bashit would be proud of you.'

'Shut it, Love.' He pulled a string of her hair around his finger and tugged it. 'Or do I need to teach you a lesson again?'

'Yes, please.'

'Yes, please what?'

'Yes, please Master.'

Her mobile flashed, telling her it was past two a.m. She looked sideways, her eyes resting on the long dark lashes that quivered with each breath Johnsson took, longing to touch them but forcing herself out of the bed. She bent over, kissed his head and carefully ran her fingers over the thick black hair, making him grunt and turn over, unaware of her presence. She groaned and backed away from him, while her whole body was begging her to return, making her feel nauseous.

She reached out to the neat stack on the small wooden chair and pulled her clothes on, the fabric closing off the bodily warmth that had enveloped her like a large halo all through the last hours. Being near this man turned her brain to mush and her body into a ball of fire ever since that very first day she had crashed into him during one of her runs through the woods surrounding the course. She shivered, reliving the look in his extraordinary eyes, his smell reminding her of freshly dug up soil and the electric shock his strong hands gave her guiding her towards the caddy shack, wanting to be certain she was alright. The frantic love making that followed half an hour later, and again, and again, until they were both sore, inside and out, was something she had never experienced before. Never, ever, had she opened her legs so quickly, so wide, so eagerly, wanting to glue herself to him so he would never let go. Feeling, for the first time, the slumbering heat that she never acknowledged was there, somewhere deep down in her body, now wanting to erupt and spit out all the inhibitions that had been keeping her frigid and cold.

One time a colleague tried to set her up, and the feedback Pru received was not kind. *"Fucking Love was like sticking your dick into a freezer and humping dry ice."* Pru didn't hear this first hand, but nevertheless, it added to that feeling of humongous failure, so tired of waiting for a taxi after yet another one-night stand with some condescending twat going pearshaped, not knowing what in earth was so massively wrong with her? Going home, alone, wanting to cry desperately, but not being able to.

But now, suddenly, nothing was wrong. Everything was right. She would never be cold again. Ever.

The door closed behind her, and she started walking, the light of the moon just enough for her to find her way to the car park with only two cars next to hers, waiting to take her home. Home. Where Philly was. As always, since they had been together. At school and during all their holidays when her friend had taken her to her warm and predictable house, giving Pru a chance to escape her weird hippie parents in the forever icy and filthy country house, her mother and father, who were either too high or, as they called it, enlightened to care about mundane things like homeliness, structure and warmth, which she craved so much and got through Philly and her parents, who had saved her from freezing to death, physically and emotionally. But now, with Ben being in her friend's life and in their flat more often than not, Pru had feared the return of the dark loneliness she had felt whenever she couldn't be with Philly and her parents. When she was stuck at the large icebox house everyone assumed was home to her, she tried to fend for herself, feeling empty and afraid.

But not anymore. The gaping, painful, bitter void was finally filled.

Her car started with a low rumble, and she accelerated towards the gate, watching it slide open and inviting her to drive through it into the real world. Where her job, her responsibilities were waiting for her, bright and early. Her eyes moved towards her rear-view mirror and lingered on the image of Peckers Woods clubhouse for a moment. She blew a kiss towards it. See you soon, my love, she whispered before she turned left on the road leading towards the village.

The flat was dark and the wooden floor felt cold under her feet as she tiptoed to the kitchen, suddenly feeling hungry and wanting a snack before trying to get some sleep.

'Hey.' Philly's voice, loud and clear. 'Everything alright? I was starting to get worried.'

Pru jumped, feeling an adrenaline rush race through her body, realizing she had been caught.

'Jesus, Freckles. Why are you up?,' Pru gasped, trying to calm herself down and be unresponsive to Philly's question. 'I thought lover boy was staying.'

'He is.' Philly rolled her eyes. 'Snoring so loud the tiles are coming off the bathroom walls.' The mug of tea moved to her lips. 'How is yours, by the way?' The green eyes now rested on Pru, who averted hers. 'Come on, Pru. You're going to have to admit to it sooner or later. Might as well do it now.' She pulled a chair from the table and patted it, making it impossible for her friend to escape.

Pru sighed and sat down, looking at Philly in agony.

'Come on. Let's have it,' Philly said, her voice indicating she wasn't letting the subject go. 'I have a right to know why my dear "*eight hours a night*" friend has turned into a night owl, breaking all her rules and structures.' She started to smile. 'Although I have a feeling why.' The smile broadened. 'Jesus, Pru. I really don't know what the avoiding fuss is all about. I would fuck him if I could. He's drop dead gorgeous.'

Pru groaned, trying to chase the image of Philly having sex with Lash out of her mind and hugged herself. 'It's not just fucking,' she whispered. 'I love him. So much.'

'Excuse me?' Philly choked in her tea. 'Come again?'

'I do, Philly.' Pru swallowed, looked at her friend and began talking, like she had never done before, words flowing from her, not wanting to stop. About how relaxed she had felt with Lash, uninhibited, warm, not needing to rack her brain on what to do or say next all the time, but just being, thinking about him constantly when they were apart, how everything in her body just clicked into just the right place whenever he touched her. How protected she felt when he held her. How the thought of losing him made her want to die, right here, on the spot. On how she had imagined what their babies would look like.

'O, Pru.' Philly stood up and put her arms around her trembling friend. 'You, finally having a serious case of the hots and heavies.' Her head rested on her friend's. 'Good for you, girl.' She hugged tight and let go, sitting down slowly. 'How long has this been going on?,' she asked.

'A couple of weeks. Months.'

'Why didn't you tell me? We always tell each other everything.'

Pru shrugged, looking rueful. 'Maybe,' she paused, clearly struggling to find the right words, 'because we've been so busy, work, the ladies' section. Ben. We've haven't been able to chat, somehow.'

'Try again, girlfriend,' Philly replied. 'You're dodging. What's the hot water?'

Pru sighed and put her hands on her face. 'I thought you and your parents might think he's, I don't know, beneath me. And try to talk him out of me,' she moaned.

'Seriously?,' Philly said with a smile. 'And why would I want to do that? I'm not bloody high and mighty, you know that. And my parents certainly are not. Come on, Pru.'

'What will the jolly twosome have to say?,' Pru whispered. 'Me, having a liaison with a member of staff?'

'What? The Bangers? Does it matter?' Philly reached out and grabbed Pru's hand. 'This is about your happiness, not theirs.' She gave a squeeze, trying to get her friend to look at her. 'And come on, look who they're shagging? Bobby Long and Henri Sweet? Not exactly the Windsors, now are they?'

Pru shook her head and managed a smile. 'No. I suppose you're right. It's just,' she hesitated, 'Lash thinks he's beneath me. And that I'll leave him, get bored of him.'

'Bollocks,' Philly said firmly. 'Snap him out of that. It's not the nineteen hundreds, for crying out loud. And if you don't get it out of his pretty head, I will.'

Now it was Pru's turn to stand up and hug her friend. 'Thanks. You're the best.'

'Yah. And fuck the rest.' Philly rubbed Pru's arms for a few seconds. 'I'm happy for you. Enjoy yourself for a change. It will sort itself out.'

'Suppose you're right.' Pru let go and sat back at the table. 'How about you? Everything okay with Ben?'

Philly faltered for a second, thinking of her relationship with her boyfriend. Did she think about him all the time? Wanted to perish if he left her? Like Pru was obviously feeling about Lash? She thought she had wanted to die of boredom this evening, trying to concentrate on his, what he called instructions, showing her the perfect grip and swing holding the old hickory putter she kept in her bedroom. His never-ending blathering on his round today had nearly wanted her to smack him in the face. But, in his defence, the sex afterwards had been great.

'Absolutely.' Philly nodded. 'We're doing fine. But something he said to me is keeping me awake.'

'Okay.' Pru narrowed her eyes, noticing Philly's face dropping. 'You sound serious.'

Philly stuck her hand in her dressing gown's pocket and a piece of paper moved over the table, showing a brief list.

At least six team members.
No handicaps over 18.
Enough funds to cover lessons, lunches, suppers, drinks, transport.
Funds for acquiring a medal.
Commitment to play 36 holes in one day,

3 flights 18 holes foursome, 6 flights 18 holes single a day.
2 points for a win, one point for all square.

'Good grief,' Pru said, taking it in. 'I thought the Bangers had this covered.'

'Yah.' Philly nodded. 'So did they. I spoke to them this evening. The funds aren't the issue. If we put some money together ourselves, that is.'

'That should work.'

'But we all thought four team members and a spare would cut it,' Philly said, while she stared at Pru. 'How in earth are going to get an extra player, under 18 in time? We can hardly go out and recruit after the committee's ruling, now can we?'

'You counted Mrs Pushet in?,' Pru asked, almost rhetorically.

'God, yes,' Philly shrugged. 'Her playing handicap is 16 at the moment. And we know the poor old bird can play 36 holes, she's bloody tough.'

'What about Polly Pitching Wedge? I'm sure we could pull that off, if we line up your dad.'

'My mum?,' Philly gazed at Pru for a moment. 'I could run it by her when I see her, I suppose.'

Pru nodded and yawned. 'Listen, I'm exhausted and have a long day tomorrow. Let's chat about it later, okay?' She stood up and bent over to kiss her friend. 'Thank you. For being my friend,' she whispered in Philly's hair before stretching herself upwards. 'And we still have oodles of time before the competition starts in March.'

CHAPTER 32

The clubhouse's kitchen door was open, inviting them to peek in. 'Snuggsy?' The loud whisper carried into the warm space.

'Get out. No dogs or women allowed.' An amused sounding male voice came towards them.

'Fuck off.' Birdie put Maggie down who rushed forwards, trying to locate her friend.

'She's out on the driving range.'

Birdie pushed the door open and stepped in, seeing Henri Sweet, bent forward into the fridge. 'What do you mean?,' she asked, pushing him aside and peering into the fridge herself. 'She promised us we could fetch some more brownies to take with us to the Ladies' room.'

'Did she now?' Henri's hand moved over her backside, and he pinched it, nearly making her topple forward into the lasagna in front of her. 'God you look sexy. Give me a snog, and I will fetch the brownies from the men's bar.'

A long kiss followed, making Bogey cringe. 'O, gross. Either cut it out, or go and find a room. Disgusting, the pair of you.' She pulled the larder door open and grabbed a packet of salt and vinegar crisps. 'What's she doing out on the driving range anyway?,' she asked, attacking the bag.

'Assisting Johnsson. Apparently she helps out clearing up the practice balls, which is a nuisance. She's due for bar service at five and supper service at seven.' His face drooped for a second and lit up again while he pinched Birdie. 'I'll find those brownies for you and leave them at the Ladies' room door.'

Birdie pushed his hand away. 'Good boy. Chop chop, then. Off you go.' She shoved him through the door and closed it behind him.

'Well, well.' Bogey giggled. 'The pretty Miss Snuggs helping out Lash Johnsson.'

'Well, indeed.' Birdie winked at her. 'I wonder if Pru knows about that.'

'Maybe a little birdie ought to tell her.'

Bogey tossed the empty crisp packet into the bin. 'Let's go and check for ourselves first. Who knows what we will find out.'

They left the kitchen through the back and followed Maggie, taking the narrow path through the ancient beech trees towards the back of the driving range where they could hide behind the old caddy shack to have a good view towards what was going on.

Birdie whistled softly, making Maggie turn towards her, waiting to be snapped on her leash. The three of them scuttled towards the shack and crouched behind it, close together to keep warm, peering through the openings in the old wood, clearly making out Miss Snuggs next to Lash Johnsson, both holding an iron and hitting balls towards a row of buckets, in the middle of the driving range, that was scattered with hundreds of yellow balls.

'Bugger.' They heard Miss Snuggs say, after she hit a ball a yard left of the buckets. 'I missed.'

'A bit too fast.' That was Lash Johnsson's voice. 'Turn a fraction of a second later. Like I showed you yesterday.'

Clang. The distinct sound of a golf ball hitting an iron bucket followed. 'Yes. Much better.'

Clang. Clang. Clang. The Bangers flinched at every ball

hitting the buckets, while concentrating on Miss Snuggs who was clearing the balls at tremendous speed.

'Bloody hell.' Birdie turned to Bogey, who was staring towards the range open mouthed. 'How far is it, from her to the buckets?'

'150.' Bogey stood up and stretched. 'Let's go and have a chat with her.'

CHAPTER 33

To: secretary@peckerswood.co.uk
From: banger@home.co.uk
Bcc: President@peckerswood.co.uk; cherie@rough.co.uk; plove@home.co.uk
Subject: Complaint and observation on employee efficiency

17th of November 2022

Dear Secretary, darling Roughie,

Let's not chitchat and dive right in.

In all our years here, we have never been SO DISAPPOINTED as we are now. It pains us to tell you, but it concerns MISS SNUGGS in particular.

The other day, she promised us we could come to the kitchen to collect some snacks for us to consume in our BELOVED Ladies' room, and we found to our HORROR Miss Snuggs wasn't there, despite our clear instructions.

As it turns out, she was summoned to the driving range to clear up the MASSIVE AMOUNT of balls our dear members leave there every day, which we checked for ourselves and found was indeed true.

Once at the range, we tried to confront Miss Snuggs on her absence and the lack of snacks, but were fobbed off by that rather dishy LASH

JOHNSSON, who seemed TO USE HER FOR HIMSELF before she was due for bar service, loo cleaning, men's room and the steam room cleaning, supper service, washing up, kitchen cleaning and egg boiling for your breakfast tray for today.

Which she is now, as you are reading this email, probably putting in front of you, after which she will start to cook lunch, clean the loos again, vacuum the great hall, wash the caddy's overalls, prepare the bar for midday service, iron the caddies overalls, prepare for tea, polish the mahogany furniture in our magnificent President's study, poke his fire up, poke your fire up, do bar and supper service, after she has whacked a good part of 500 BALLS into a line of buckets with a BORROWED SEVEN IRON.

Roughie, this WILL NOT DO. We are shocked. How can you possibly expect this from poor Miss Snuggs? You know as well as we do it takes yonks to clear 500 scattered balls WITH ONLY A SEVEN IRON. To do the job faster in order to have time for all her chores, she needs at least a nine, seven, and five iron and a little wood.

We must INSIST you provide staff with the tools they need to do their job properly.

WHAT WILL HAPPEN IF MISS SNUGGS TOPPLES OVER, absolutely knackered after another seven-iron ordeal before bar service? We can't help out and do it, now can we? WE AREN'T ALLOWED IN THE MEN'S BAR. OR LOUNGE. OR ANY OF THE BOARD ROOMS. So, we fear that if Miss Snuggs has no other choice than to waste precious time having only a seven iron, you and our divine President Bashit might be left to poke your own fire and boil your own eggs.

Love you. Bir&Bog

PS. We thought it might be good if we took Miss Snuggs out on the course, so she can learn how to hit balls even further and straighter. Will save masses of time on driving range in future.

PPS. Another thing, we would like to invite a dear old friend from school. She is dying to play PW to have a break from her busy job, being the

CHIEF OF THE LABOUR INSPECTORATE. Will make certain we introduce you to her and President Bashit.

And Miss Snuggs. So she will remember your hospitality 4EVER. You will love her. I'm sure she will love you too.

And Miss Snuggs.

PPPS. When we take Miss Snuggs out on the course, you need to find volunteer to do bar service, ironing and loo cleaning. OR DO IT YOURSELF. Which sounds perfectly acceptable to us. Or, if you are really far too busy doing important PW stuff, it might be convenient to find some YOUNG SWEET GIRL from the village to help out for a couple of hours during the weekends.

CHAPTER 34

Damn Miss Snuggs. Pru turned and shoved her mobile under the pillow, trying to find the perfect position against the warm body next to her and shift the troubling image of the pretty blonde doing what she had just been doing to the man next to her.

'What's up, Love.' Lash Johnsson's hand moved from her breast and pinched the nipple. 'You're twitching.' He pulled her on her back and hoisted himself up so he could see her eyes, hastily avoiding his. 'Spit it out.'

Pru swallowed, trying to keep her voice calm. 'You never told me about Miss Snuggs,' she said slowly. 'That she works for you. With you.'

'So what?' Lash shrugged and kept his eyes on Pru's face. 'She helps me out now and then. Has done for years.'

'Are you shagging her?' Pru's voice turned into a whisper.

'Hell no.' Lash shook his head. 'Jesus, Love.'

'Do you want to shag her?' The whisper was hardly audible.

'Of course I do.' Lash started laughing as he felt Pru cringe underneath him. 'She's drop dead gorgeous, and I am a healthy bloke.' He reached out to her chin and pulled her face towards his. 'Listen, Love. I want to fuck the whole Lady section. And so does every Peckers Wood member of staff. It doesn't mean anything,' he admitted before kissing her.

'Poor Mrs Pushet.' Pru managed a giggle, despite the sourness in her stomach. 'You might need a gentler approach with her.'

'Hey, Love.' His voice was soft and he kissed her again. 'You're the only one I'm really fucking. And I love doing it.' He pulled her closer. 'And besides, the only bloke on the planet who has any chance with our dear Snuggsy is our dear Club Secretary.'

'I beg your pardon?'

'O come on,' Lash said. 'Haven't you noticed? She's been sweet on him forever.'

'You're joking.' Pru stared into his eyes and started to shake her head, slowly. 'Roughie? I never knew that? Does he know?'

Lash Johnsson shrugged. 'No idea. But he's so incredibly wet that he probably doesn't have a clue on how to get her into the sack.' He rolled on his back and pulled Pru on top of him, one hand on her left breast and one hand between her legs, starting to move up and down. 'Talking about wet,' he whispered. 'Is thinking about Miss Snuggs being fucked turning you on?'

Pru moaned as she felt him sliding in, closed her eyes and started to ride him.

'Or is it Rough?' His hand left her breast and slapped her bum. 'I might need to punish you, Love. For getting horny thinking of other blokes.' His hand moved upwards, and he pulled her hair, jerking her head backwards, making her breasts stick out. He pulled himself towards her, bit a nipple and pushed her on her back, spreading her legs open wide and wrapping them around his back, thrusting a couple of times before he pulled out, moved down on her, made her come before he slid back in and came himself, leaving her shivering underneath him.

'God, I love you,' Pru whispered. 'Please never leave me.'

Lash pulled her against him and started to rock her, gently. He remained silent for a while before he spoke. 'Snuggsy's a good girl, Love. She deserves something decent in her life.' His hand stroked her long hair. 'Maybe she needs a little help from more of her friends. Besides the Bangers.'

CHAPTER 35

Her mobile told her she was early for her appointment with Simon Hot so Philly decided to walk from her parents' house to the Chasty Chicken up the road. The exercise would do her good after the disappointing cup of tea with her mother who had refused her flat out, firmly telling her she had no desire to be treated as the easy way out.

The conversation had even gotten uncomfortable when her mother kept banging on about consequences on following the path of least resistance. That if their strategy on turning things around was to come crying to your poor old Mum, she had little faith in the outcome. Surely her clever daughter had a bigger and better plan thought out? Imagine what Bashit, Ben, and the whole male section would say when they heard that tired old Dorothy Hackkett was the only rabbit Philly could pull out of her hat? Talk about a major backfire, her mother had said.

But of course Philly realized to her own annoyance that her mother was right. Again. The solution should be something unexpected, something new. Although she couldn't, for the world, think of what that could be.

She took a sharp left, taking the shortcut through the village and stopping at the sweetshop, deciding to buy a large bag of toffee to stuff herself with later. The door was open letting the scent of sweets and biscuits drift out, making her feel excited, like a child.

'If it isn't young Philly Hackkett.' The familiar woman behind the counter smiled, took a brown paper bag from the counter and handed it over to a sullen looking teenage girl next to her. 'The usual, darling?'

'Yes, please, Mrs Turner.' Philly reached for some coins in her purse. 'The shop looks lovely, as always.'

'Thank you, darling. We just had your lovely friends in here, the Banger sisters. They always like to chat with my Lizzie.' The bag balanced on the young girls' hand, slowly being filled with the toffee by the older woman. 'And I have more time for decorating, now that my daughter is helping me during the weekends.' Mrs Turner stared at the girl next to her. 'Although she doesn't seem to enjoy it very much.'

'It's not fair, mum.' The teenage girl shrugged and shot Philly a desperate look. 'I was the best and now they kick me out just because I'm a girl.'

Mrs Turner looked at her. 'We've been over this, Lizzie. The boys feel uncomfortable having to push and shove you. It's different now you're so grown up.' The kind eyes went from the young girl to Philly. 'She played rugger since she was little, which was fine. But now, being the only girl in the village that plays, and...you know...her being fully developed...'

'Mum!' The word came out in desperation. 'Please don't!'

'Ah, I see.' Philly took the bag and nodded. 'Yes. That indeed might make the boys feel uncomfortable. And we don't want that,' she said, while giving Mrs Turner a wink. 'But I'm sure you'll grow to like working with your mother.'

The girl shrugged and pulled the corners of her mouth down, reached over to a big container and started tossing sweets into a shiny glass pot. 'If you say so,' she said, sounding condescending.

'Lizzie.' Mrs Turner gave her daughter a dark look. 'Behave.'

She moved towards Philly and sighed. 'She used to be such a sweet girl. But now? Quite a big mouth on her.'

'I'm sure she'll grow over it.' The brown bag was tucked under Philly's arm, and she waved to the two women. 'See you next week, Mrs Turner. Lizzie. Thank you and have a lovely day.'

She walked out, crossed the village green and turned towards the Chasty Chicken, already filling up for lunch, groups of people finding tables and grabbing menus. Philly quickly crossed to a small table at the far side of the bar, seeing a neat-looking man she recognized from his profile picture.

'Miss Hackkett,' the neat looking man said while he stood up and bowed slightly. 'Simon Hot. How do you do?' He reached over and pulled Philly's chair out, a carefully manicured hand gestured towards her seat.

Philly looked at the elegant figure in front of her. Ash-blond hair, carefully combed backwards. Small blue eyes, close together, set in a tanned, clean-shaven face, above a dark blue polo-necked jersey, buttoned up and tucked into chalk-coloured slacks with a smart leather belt. 'Please. Call me Philly.' She smiled, and Simon Hot returned it, revealing a row of perfect teeth.

'I will.' The smile got broader. 'And Simon. Please.'

Philly swallowed, trying not to stare at the bulky biceps that kept rolling under the polo shirt's tight sleeves with every movement Simon Hot made. Sneaking a look at his long fingers, she noticed they were bare of jewellery of any kind. She started talking, asking questions about his professional back ground, his motivation, his teaching approach, which he elaborated on calmly and professionally, only pausing for the waitress passing out their food.

'So. You've had a good run as a teaching pro. Quite impressive, the clubs you've served,' Philly said, trying to summarize while pushing the last of her salad towards the side of her plate. 'But tell me. Why Peckers Wood?'

Simon sat back and stared at Philly for a moment. 'Very good question,' he said while pausing for a sip of his mineral water. 'Before I spoke to Ben Chipperfield, I was under the impression that Peckers Wood was a club for over privileged traditionals hitting the little white pills over manicured fairways before retiring to the clubhouse for cigars and cognac.' He set his glass down and continued. 'Silly me, as it turned out. The Club Captain invited me to the club for a game and introduced me to his team. Very impressive, if I may say so.'

'Really?,' Philly asked. 'Why?'

'Extremely motivated. Excellent pairing. All under 5 handicap and willing to work hard to be an all under scratch team. Which I am now helping them with. And looking forward to the challenge immensely. And the course? One of the best I've ever seen.'

'Yah. I agree.' Philly nodded while concentrating on Hot. There was something about him that made her feel cautious, but she couldn't put her finger on it.

'It will take all my time, but it will be worth it,' Simon said confidently. 'If they manage to bring the Regional Medal home, we can start on bigger things. Like the national amateur competition. Where all the top teaching pros are at. Which means more money.'

'I see,' Philly replied, feeling her discomfort rise.

'Increasing income is my main objective, Philly,' Simon admitted. 'This is my job, my livelihood. I work for a living.'

'I understand. So do I.' Philly nodded, dismissing her earlier unease. At least the man was honest about his intentions. 'And what about our team?'

'What team?'

'Our Ladies team.'

'No-one mentioned a Ladies team to me,' Simon said, sounding genuinely surprised. 'Does Peckers Wood have one?'

'Absolutely.' Philly paused for a second. 'Well. Sort of. Nearly.

But we are competing against Goodlie for the Ladies Regional Medal next spring.'

'I see. A ladies team. Interesting.' Simon Hot frowned. 'But what do you mean with nearly?'

Philly sighed and looked at Simon, wearily. 'We need one more on our team. We thought four and a spare would be enough, but now it turns out we need six, which we don't have at the moment.

'And why are you competing for a medal?'

'Because,' Philly replied, sitting back and looking at the handsome figure opposite her, 'we feel we need to prove that we are worthy members, not just silly creatures frolicking around the odd green now and then.' Her facial expression became taut. 'And, more importantly, we think it might motivate other women to come and play, become members, enjoy the game, experience club life, its benefits.' She took her wine glass and emptied it. 'We love it. And we wish it on everyone.'

'Good for you,' Simon said.

'We want the Lady Section to grow, and with it, the member count.' Philly paused for a moment. 'You know, doing our bit towards the future, a bit of forward thinking from our side. Maybe even enter the county league.'

'I see your points. All of them. Would be good if someone could help you along.'

'But you could.' Philly leaned towards him. 'Surely you could coach us too?'

Simon shook his head. 'No, sorry. I'm afraid that's not part of the deal I made today with Ben Chipperfield. The contract I signed says 70-30. Seventy percent of my agreed time goes to the men's team, 30% to teaching individual members.'

'You already signed a contract?,' Philly asked, clearly mystified. 'Then why are we having this conversation?'

'Well.' Simon shifted in his seat and looked down, obviously feeling uneasy. 'That's a good question. I don't really know. He paid my agreed retainer upfront as well. So, I must admit, I was a little surprised Rough asked me to meet you for an interview anyway.'

Philly fell backwards and ran her fingers through her hair. Here she was, assuming the club actually valued her input. Nothing more than window dressing, as it turned out. 'Bloody men,' she hissed just loud enough for Hot to hear who fell backwards and held his hands up as if wanting to shield himself.

'Maybe there's a solution somewhere. What's your goal?'

Philly shrugged and managed a weak smile. 'All my current players under 10 and at least a new one, ready to go before the spring.'

'It isn't impossible. Nothing ever is.' Simon Hot got up, hurriedly, as if he wanted to disappear quickly. 'Thank you for the pleasant lunch, Philly.'

'Right. It isn't as good as Miss Snuggs's cooking. Make sure you make friends with her.'

Simon bowed slightly. 'I will. And sometimes the way forward is as obvious as a selecting a seven iron for a 130-yard shot into a wide open green. You just need to visualize it.'

Philly shook herself, paid the bill and took off, nearly running back to the sweetshop while she managed to get hold of Bogey on her mobile, who confirmed what she wanted to hear. If she pulled this off, her team would be sorted. She forcefully pushed the shop's door, almost sending the little bell through the store, relieved to find it empty, except for its owner. She walked up to her and began talking, explaining what she had in mind.

Mrs Turner stared at Philly and stopped scooping the toffee into the brown paper bag, looking totally bewildered. 'My Lizzie? Helping out at Peckers Wood?' She asked, nearly rhetorically. 'Tell me why again?'

Philly smiled and explained once more, how the Bangers sisters had been chatting to Lizzie a couple of times about golf, and that Lizzie had seemed so interested in why the sisters loved playing it so much.

'Well, well. It certainly doesn't sound like my Lizzie?' Mrs Turner shook her head in disbelief. 'She doesn't seem interested in anything at all, especially since the rugger disaster. I can hardly get her out of bed and into the shop, not that she's really of any help. And her school results are down the drain even though they always were so excellent.'

'Could it be she's just a bit disappointed by the whole rugger thing, Mrs Turner? She's only 16 years old. Life can be jolly tough at that age.' Philly broadened her smile further, trying to be understanding. 'It might do her good to work somewhere else, you know, a fresh pair of eyes, putting things into the right perspective,' she said, while she bent forward towards the counter. 'And she will get the opportunity to play a little, chances are she might even enjoy it. Take her mind of the rugger boys.'

Mrs Turner looked thoughtful. 'So you are actually telling me the Banger sisters recommended Lizzie to you and to Mr Bashit?'

Philly nodded. 'Yes. And President Bashit likes the idea of a local girl, someone trustworthy, to help Miss Snuggs.' She reached out towards Mrs Turner and touched her hand. 'It's only for a couple of hours, Saturdays and Sundays. A regular weekend job in a safe environment.'

'You don't have to convince me, Philly Hackkett.' Mrs Turner gestured to the door behind her. 'If you can manage to get that pain of a daughter of mine motivated, she's all yours.' She shook her head slightly. 'I have enough to deal with without some annoying adolescent bugging me.' The door opened slightly, and Mrs Turner stuck her head through. 'Lizzie? Please be kind enough to move your backside in here.'

The door opened wide, and Lizzie appeared, pulling her rubber gloves off with a surprised look on her face. 'Dishes are done, Mum.'

'About time, Mrs Turner snorted. 'Philly Hackkett here has something to ask you.'

Lizzie glanced at her mother before her dark grey eyes turned to Philly. 'Me?' She asked, clearly apprehensive. 'What about?'

'About an opportunity.' Philly shoved her handbag under her arm. 'But I was thinking, could I take Lizzie for a cup of tea, Mrs Turner, across the road? So we can have a chat?'

'Take her where ever you need to. As long as she is back by six.' Mrs Turner nodded towards her daughter. 'Understood?'

Lizzie stared from her mother to Philly, clearly asking herself what was going on. 'Yes. I guess,' she said slowly. 'Understood.'

'Excellent.' Philly took the young girl by the arm and guided her out of the shop. 'Thank you, Mrs Turner. See you later.'

A paper tissue appeared from Philly's handbag for the embarrassed-looking young girl at the other side of the small table. She took it with a trembling hand and wiped away an angry tear as she told Philly about rugby, why the boys didn't want to play with her anymore and how terribly lonely she had been since.

'I'm so sorry, Lizzie.' Philly took her hand and squeezed it for a second before Lizzie pulled it away. 'But you can hardly blame the boys. I do get why they started to feel uncomfortable.'

'I'm sure it's just because I was better than any of them.' Lizzie's tears stopped, and her voice became defiant. 'And they couldn't cope with that. So they blamed it on my boobs,' she whispered angrily. 'Said they distracted them.'

'Get used to it, my darling.' Philly started to giggle. 'And by the way, boobs are excellent for distracting when you need them to.'

Lizzie joined in the giggle, despite herself. 'That's what the Banger sisters said.'

'I bet.' Philly gave Lizzie a fat wink. 'They have the best pair of distracters in the world,' she said while she looked at her hands. 'But tell me, why do you feel lonely? Don't you have friends at school?'

Lizzie shrugged. 'Not really. The boys are idiots. The girls are kind enough, but we don't have much in common. I really like sports, and they really like to talk about boys, check their socials and put make up on. I don't know what to talk about with them.'

'Right.' Philly smiled. 'And what about your parents? You help your Mum in the shop. That must be nice, doing that together?'

'Not really. It sucks, actually.' Now it was Lizzie's time to avoid Philly's look and stare at her hands. 'Sorry. All she does is nag. I can't do anything right.' Another tear appeared, rolling over her nose into the tea mug. 'And I really am trying. But we just seem to piss each other off all the time.' The paper tissue folded over her nose, and Lizzie blew it loudly.

'I see.' Philly tried to catch Lizzie's eyes but failed as the girl stared down at the table, clearly feeling extremely embarrassed.

'And what about your dad?'

'Buggered off to fuck the dark witch.'

'I beg your pardon?'

Lizzie sighed, rolled up the tissue and stuffed it in her trouser pocket. 'His girlfriend. My so-called step mother. I hate her, and she hates me.'

'I see.'

'No, you don't.' Lizzie suddenly sat up straight. 'Your parents are super nice.' Her index finger shot towards Philly, in an accusing way. 'Mine suck.'

'Yah. Well.' Philly started to feel uncomfortable, eager to change to subject. 'But let's get back to this job I was telling you about earlier, at the golf club? How do you feel about that?,' she asked, while shifting in her seat. 'Pay isn't great, but lessons are included. Might be fun.'

'Fun?,' Lizzie said, leaning forward and raising her eyebrows. 'Wait on all those old people playing that stupid game? How is that fun?' Lizzie raised her eyes upwards dramatically, but suddenly a small smile appeared. 'Although I like Mrs Pushet. She tells me rude jokes when she's in the shop and thinks my Mum can't hear her.'

Now Philly raised an eyebrow. 'Does she now?,' she said. 'She must like you too then.'

Lizzie chuckled. 'What's the biggest thing a man has in his trousers a woman doesn't want on her face?'

'No idea. Tell me.'

'Wrinkles.'

'Very funny. Cheeky Mrs Pushet.' Philly put her hand up and gestured the waiter towards them. 'Righto. Let's get out of here,' she said while she pulled her credit card out. 'I need to check in on my parents. You can come with me, and afterwards I will show you around that silly golf club with all the geriatrics. So you can make up your mind about this new job.'

'Will Mrs Pushet be there?'

'Without a doubt.'

The heat from the Hackketts' kitchen hit them as Philly pushed the door open, sudden but also comforting, like being hugged by a warm, soft body after a chilly, wet walk. Sniggles was lying against the range on his back, his lips hanging from his jaws revealing his pink gums and his paws into the air, so relaxed he wasn't even bothered to wag his tail hearing them come in. Mrs Hackkett stood behind the large table, her hair in a messy bun, her flour-covered hands counting mince pies and putting them into plastic containers.

Lizzie breathed in deeply, taking the kitchen in, suddenly feeling ravenous, realizing she hadn't eaten anything since breakfast and noticing a large apple pie, smiling at her from behind Mrs Hackkett.

'Hi Mum.' Philly bent over and kissed her mother. 'What

did you think this morning? Another four weeks before X-mas, let's get cracking or we might not make it?'

'Absolutely.' Mrs Hackkett looked at Lizzie and gave her a quick wink. 'Hello dear,' she said and turned to her daughter. 'Winter is at our doorstep, and your father was good enough to get the oven going so there was no stopping me.' She reached over to the pie and cut a big chunk. 'Would you like to try, Philly?'

'No thanks.' Philly shook her head. 'But my new friend here might like some?'

'Of course she would.' Mrs Hackkett tapped the chair next to her. 'How wonderful to see you, Lizzie.' A plate appeared with a spoon and fork and a large pitcher with cream. 'And you look like you need it, my dear. So skinny. You're even thinner than my dear daughter.' She pulled a chair out and guided Lizzie towards it. 'Please tuck in, and tell me if you like it.'

The warm dough melted with the warm apple as it hit her tongue, and Lizzie started chewing, slowly and carefully. 'It's delicious,' she said quietly as she scooped the second helping on her spoon.

'Good. There's plenty more where that came from.' Mrs Hackkett sat down and took the mug Philly passed her. 'So, Lady Captain, what's up? Any luck on the competition team?'

'Well.' Philly nodded towards Lizzie who was totally absorbed by the pie in front of her. 'That depends. If young Lizzie here is up for a new challenge.'

'What new challenge?' The kitchen door opened, revealing Mr Hackkett coming towards them and bending down to kiss his wife and daughter. He stared at Lizzie, munching on the pie, her eyes half closed, nearly in trance. 'Aren't you the rugger girl?,' he asked, narrowing his eyes as he pointed towards her. 'I'm sure I've seen you play a couple of times.' He turned to his wife. 'And pretty damn good she is, too. Throws the ball a hell of a long way.' His eyes returned to Lizzie. 'But I haven't seen you lately. You haven't chucked it in, I hope?'

Lizzie shrugged and blinked, her eyes searching for Philly, clearly not knowing how to react and waiting for the other women to comment to save her from having to explain.

'Let's just say there weren't any other girls for Lizzie to play with. And the boys felt she was getting too, you know, old, for them,' Philly explained. 'And rugger's a bugger by yourself, isn't it?'

Mr Hackkett smirked and rolled his eyes at Lizzie, who couldn't help smiling despite feeling like crying. 'Bugger indeed,' Philly's father said, slicing a generous piece of pie for himself and sitting down next to Lizzie. 'I was really down in the dumps when I had to stop playing. My knees, you know. My doctor told me to concentrate on golf. Better for the knees and a very similar sport, he told me.' A piece of pie disappeared in his mouth, and he chewed for a while before he continued. 'Which I thought was a joke. Golf. A sport? Compared to rugby? Nothing more than a bunch of ugly old men in ridiculous clothes walking round a field at the pace of retired snails.'

Lizzie coughed, nearly choking, and tried to compose herself, not daring to look at Mr Hackkett, who was now waving his fork at her, clearly in deep thought.

'But it turned out the good doctor was right. It is similar. How you swing at a golf ball is very much like a good throw. It's all about body separation and getting back towards the ball early enough.' He returned the fork to his plate and cocked his head towards his wife and daughter. 'Not that they understand,' he said conspiratorially. 'But I'm sure I can prove my and the doctor's point to you. You'll get what we mean.' Mr Hackkett stood up and gestured at Lizzie. 'Eat up. And follow me. I will show you.'

Lizzie stared at Philly, who was smiling and shaking her head. 'You go with him Lizzie and make his day. I will come to rescue you in half an hour.'

Lizzie looked down at her hands, wrapped around the club, feeling awkward. Her knees were slightly bent, and she pushed her left knee forward taking the club into the air, just like Mr Hackkett had told her.

'Keep your arms straight, and now go down, and let your hips do the work for ball speed, just like on the rugby field.'

The ball jumped from her club, taking a slight left turn and ending up in the long withered grass behind the green. 'Sorry, Mr Hackkett.' Lizzie looked at the man in front of her, apologetic and noticed him staring at her, open-mouthed. 'That didn't go very well,' she said quietly, feeling the waves of embarrassment rise up in her stomach.

'Lizzie!' Mr Hackkett reached out towards her and took the club away from her. 'That was truly amazing,' he said and passed her another club. 'I've never met someone that actually managed to hit the ball the first time they took a swing at it.' He stepped back and explained the change to a shorter club and what that meant. 'Now, do exactly as you did just now, but try to end as if you want your right hip bone to point at twelve o'clock, and make your arms as long as you possibly can.'

The ball flew up in the air and landed behind the flag, about a hundred yards from where they were standing.

'Wow,' Mr Hackkett exclaimed. 'What a super shot. Well done.'

'Thank you,' Lizzie replied, feeling the elation she knew from the rugby field.

'How did the impact on the ball feel, Lizzie? Like hitting a rock or more like sweeping through a spring?'

'Like a spring.' Lizzie nodded. 'Yes. Definitely.' She looked at Mr Hackkett. 'Is that good or bad?'

'How did it make you feel?,' Mr Hackkett asked. 'Good or bad?'

Lizzie pulled herself up straight and gave the man in front of her a long stare. 'Good,' she said. 'Really good.'

'Right.' Mr Hackkett passed her another club. 'Let's take this further.'

CHAPTER 36

A meeting request. Complete with an agenda. From the Lady Captain. Which he could hardly refuse. With Miss Snuggs being one of the subjects. President Bashit swivelled his reading chair away from his guest Hot towards the study's fire and licked the last of the chocolate cake from the corner of his mouth. He stared at the orange and black tongues flaring towards him, suddenly thinking of his late missus, the memory of her revived by the request on the printed email in front of him.

It was Mrs Bashit, who begged him before she died to take the girl in and offer her a job so she would be safe, under his supervision. In the comforting surroundings inside Peckers Wood's gates, far from the evils of the real world outside ready and waiting to gobble the gullible girl up, eat her alive. He remembered his initial protest, knowing well he would lose the struggle in the end.

She'd been a tough old bat, his late wife. She had played along with that whole caddy charade, protecting the family, their good name, knowing she would have to abide to the dismissal of their son to Bonnie Scotland. He was still there, supposedly managing the farm, but in reality leaving the real work to his surprisingly able wife while he was idling his days away on some or other links.

Bashit closed his eyes for a moment, reliving the moment he had decided to push his son out of their everyday lives and not feeling sorry for it. The late Mrs hadn't resisted him, though it was as agonizing as putting her little boy on the train to boarding school, feeling her heart being ripped out. She would grin and bear it. Again. Because she knew she had no choice. Because she knew it was for the best. Making him feel guilty, knowing it would come back at him some day. She used it in the end, to push him into showing his compassionate side, which she knew he had. Somewhere.

Pure blackmail, he had said. To which she only laughed mockingly, knowing she clearly had him by the balls. Like the young Lady Captain had now, he certainly realized after his morning tea with Roughie.

He turned, coming back to the present by the determined knock on his door and stared at the slick-looking man in front of him, who was typing on something that looked like a device from outer space.

'Hot, dear fellow. Why don't you open the door for our Lady Captain?,' Bashit asked. 'And please stay. This won't take long. We can resume our meeting after Miss Hackkett has left us.'

He rested on his stick and hoisted himself up, greeting the Lady Captain and inviting her to sit down in one of the leather clubs. The longtime President watched her zip open some kind of folder and produce the same kind of outer space something or other Hot was using.

'Yes.' He heard himself saying, while he sat down. 'Indeed. I agree. Miss Snuggs could do with some R&R.' He forced himself to nod and smile. 'Yes. Indeed. I do remember our little chat the other day. There is nothing better than playing golf with friends. The Banger sisters were more than welcome to take her with them once in a while,' he said, assuming this would be all.

Wrongly, as it turned out. He should have known better.

Because yes, now the Hackkett girl was banging on about lessons. For that regional Ladies competition they seemed to have entered. And why the ladies weren't included in Mr Hot's retainer and that he should repair that major mistake.

'I beg your pardon?,' he asked, genuinely taken aback. But she kept rattling on, not noticing his interruption, about how convenient it would be if Miss Snuggs would join in, talking about killing two birds for a couple of hours during the weekends. And how it could all be solved by employing a young girl from the village to take over some tasks while Miss Snuggs was out playing. With her new friends. Getting energized, fully prepared for her work.

Good lord. He felt his hand go up, and it seemed to work, stopping Hackkett in mid-sentence. 'Hang on. Just a minute. We can't afford more domestic staff,' he argued, using his most autocratic voice. 'The committee agreed on stretching the budget for improving our chances on winning the Regional and with that we have reached our max.' His hand made a dismissive gesture, as if he were waving the annoying questions away. 'And Bushrod will never agree.'

But the Hackkett girl just wouldn't stop, claiming it would only take a couple of pounds each weekend next to stretching Hot's retainer and that she wouldn't accept this couldn't be arranged, the sound of her voice making his blood pressure rise as fast as his annoyance level.

He turned to Hot, asking him rhetorically what he should do now, tear Hot's retainer apart and dismiss the whole winning the Regional and its potential for the National?

Hot had abandoned the outer space typing thing and suggested, after clearing his throat and swallowing, that it might be an idea to take a moment and think about some possible solutions. What if he would ask Lash Johnsson to coach the Ladies team, which Miss Snuggs could join in on? He heard that Lash Johnsson was thinking about taking his teaching further and seemed to understand what ladies needed. Would that be an idea?

Bashit carefully looked at the Hackkett girl who actually seemed interested. He persuaded Hot to go on, to bide some time for himself to regain control of his temper, sarcastically asking if Hot might have some more interesting suggestions.

Hot managed a smile, glanced at Bashit and carefully mentioned there perhaps, yes, there might be some youngster in the village who would willing to do some work in exchange for some free lessons and a couple of green fees? Surely Miss Hackkett could mull the Lash Johnsson idea over with the ladies, and might they already have someone in mind who could help out?

Bashit closed his eyes for a moment, trying to banish the image of his late wife that kept popping up, now standing in front of him, bending over, her right hand between his legs, increasing pressure and breathing fire onto his face. He nodded and opened his eyes again. 'Yes. As a matter of fact, I think that sounds quite reasonable.' The grip on his balls released slightly, the image of Mrs Bashit faded, slowly. 'A perfectly acceptable solution,' he said as he watched his late wife disappear into thin air.

CHAPTER 37

Birdie shivered and pulled the electric heater's cord, its glow turning the Ladies' room slightly orange. 'It's getting cold,' she said, while sitting down on the sofa next to her sister.

Mrs Pushet nodded, pulling her cardigan closer. 'Can't say I'm enjoying winter. Today the wind was so lazy it went right through me.' A giggle escaped her. 'But!,' she exclaimed, lifting the white tip of her finger which looked dead with cold, 'we have something, someone, to warm us up during the coming months, haven't we Pru?'

'Yah, Pru. Your lover boy is our new teaching pro?' Bogey grinned. 'What a great idea. I can't wait for him to perfect my grip.' The last three words came out in a shriek.

'On his firm shaft.' Birdie giggled and started to wheeze. 'I hope he will help me turn my hips faster.'

'Towards his pole.' Bogey was now bent forward, nearly choking with laughter. 'Maybe he will let me try his wood.'

Philly grabbed a pillow and chucked it towards the two sisters. 'Shut it, you two. You're so bloody witless.' She stood up, put the electric fire up a notch and passed cups of tea round the small group. 'Now. We need to discuss a couple of things. Our team, Miss Snuggs and her replacement.' She looked at Pru who was examining her lips in a small mirror, pretending not to notice the sisters. 'And we have some gossip that might interest you.'

'Oh, goodie,' Mrs Pushet piped. 'I love gossip.' She turned to Pru and whispered. 'Is it about you and that dashing Lash Johnsson?' The old lady started to giggle. 'You should draw the curtains in that caddy shack, darling. More people might see and find out about you two,' she said while nodding towards the others. 'Do they know you are bonking him?'

'We do now. I know I would bonk him given the chance,' Bogey answered, not fazed by the dark look Pru shot at her.

Mrs Pushet giggled. 'Gosh, yes. So would I.' She leaned over towards the Bangers. 'I saw his wood, you know. Very nice it is, too,' she said, trying to continue but being stopped by Birdie putting her finger over the older lady's lips, seeing Pru's face turn from furious to frantic.

'I think we need to change the subject of gossip to Miss Snuggs,' Philly said, looking at Pru. 'And what her feelings about a certain Club Secretary are.'

The group turned towards her in silence, trying to take in what she was implying.

'Excuse me?' Mrs Pushet sat up and carefully put her tea mug in front of her. 'Feelings? Miss Snuggs? For the Club Secretary?' She started coughing. 'Our Club Secretary? When did that happen?'

'It's true,' Pru said, her cheeks turning dark red again. 'Lash told me. She fell in love with him the moment she laid eyes on him.'

'But that's years ago,' Mrs Pushet added, starting to sound desperate.

'I know.' Pru shook her head. 'Sad, isn't it?'

'Sad?' Mrs Pushet threw her head back and covered her eyes. 'It's a bloody disaster! Mrs Rough could have been a grandmother to a whole shit-load of children by now!' Her hands pressed against her forehead. 'Why is that boy so slow?

The only thing that gets him excited is a golf ball hitting the back of the cup before plunging into the hole. Bloody hell.'

The Bangers exchanged a quick look.

'That poor Miss Snuggs,' Mrs Pushet said. 'Yearning for someone, working her backside of for him and getting nothing for it.'

'Quite.' Pru refused the biscuit Birdie passed towards her and stood up. 'Coming to think of it, she would be absolutely perfect for Roughie.' She moved over to Mrs Pushet and sat down next to her. 'I mean, she can cook, clean, mixes one hell of a Martini and looks utterly adorable.'

'I too think she is perfect,' Mrs Pushet said. 'And Roughie needs to get excited by the thought of plunging into her…'

'Thank you, Mrs Pushet.' Pru held up her hand. 'I think we get the drift.'

Philly stood up again and faced the group. 'And look at us. Always taking her for granted, finding it perfectly normal she's always at our beck and call. She deserves some happiness. And we should help her. And Roughie. And our dear Mrs Rough.'

Mrs Pushet nodded. 'I agree. Any bright ideas, anyone?'

The Bangers and Pru looked at each other in embarrassed silence before getting up from the sofa.

'We need to think,' Pru said, opening the fridge and pulling two bottles of wine out. 'But first, a drink. White, everyone?'

'Sure.' Birdie pulled a plastic bag from under her seat and started to unwrap miniature sausages and pork pies. 'Roughie and Miss Snuggs? How on earth can we get them together?'

'God only knows.' Bogey nodded and popped a sausage between her lips. 'But we might dig up some rough ideas,' she said with a wink at her sister with a wide smile on her face.

CHAPTER 38

To: secretary@peckerswood.co.uk
From: banger@home.co.uk
Bcc: President@peckerswood.co.uk; p.hackkett@home.co.uk; cherie@rough.co.uk
Subject: procedure

3rd of December 2022

Dear Secretary, darling Roughie,

Just a little note from your darlings to let you know we again are MASSIVELY overwhelmed by your creatively, wonderful idea of inviting that lovely girl Lizzie Turner to help Miss Snuggs out. Everyone is completely over the moon having her here, especially Miss Snuggs who can now FINALLY have some R&R on the course. And dear Lizzie seems so motivated, how INSANELY CLEVER of you and fab President Bashit to throw in lessons and green fees as secondary conditions.

We do feel, however, we need to approach this endeavour as correctly as possible. All new members have to play a round with you before course permission is granted, and we DO INSIST that this rule also applies to staff. As much as we ABSOLUTELY ADORE Miss Snuggs and young Lizzie, we cannot condone outrageous staff privileges such as being able to play the course without following PROPER PROCEDURE.

In order not to let poor Miss Snuggs wait too long, we took the liberty of wangling a starting time Sunday afternoon, between lunch and tea. Lizzie will take over at the bar, and we will join you on the course, remembering how much you used to adore playing with us gals. We will have sooooo much fun!

Love you. Bir&Bog

PS. Talking of procedure, you might want to check our rules on proper attire. Your darling mother noticed SOMEONE on the course clad in an old cricket sweater from school. She wasn't amused. Said the sweater seemed to have been attacked by an OUTRAGED GANG OF MOTHS.

PPS. You might want to hide your school cricket sweater from your mother before the sight of it turns her into an UNAMUSED OUTRAGED MOTH.

PPPS. We stumbled upon a lovely blue V-necked wind-proof jersey. Are under impression the DIVINE colour matches the beige slacks you wear all the time. Left it on your desk. Love to see you wear it to see if it indeed matches slacks. And that nice white polo neck your mother bought you for your birthday.

PPPS. Supermarket in town sells perfectly good moth balls. You might want to ask your mother to get you some. Will UNAMUSE THE OUTRAGED MOTHS trying to attack fab new blue V-necked jersey.

CHAPTER 39

'Golf lessons?,' Miss Snuggs asked, barely audible.

Philly examined her fingernails, tried not to get distracted by Mrs Rough, who was beaming at the astonished-looking young woman in the deck chair at the other side of the desk, and started to talk. 'Yes Miss Snuggs. We would like you to take golf lessons so you understand more of what we are up to here, and maybe join us from time to time.'

'But how would I be able to afford such a thing? And when should I take lessons?' Miss Snuggs' violet eyes seemed twice as large as normal. 'Are you sure this is for the likes of me?'

'Oh, yes, Miss Snuggs. This is absolutely for the likes of you,' Mrs Rough said, nodding profusely. 'And don't worry about the cost, it's all taken care of. Philly here arranged everything with President Bashit.' Her hand reached over to the young girl in front of her, and she gave her arm a little encouraging stroke. 'It's all part of the job now.'

Miss Snuggs swallowed hard and started to ramble. 'That is mighty kind of President Bashit, and you, Mrs Rough. And thank you so much Miss Hackkett. But I don't think it's possible, you see there's the cooking, breakfast, elevenses, lunch, tea, snacks, supper. And the cleaning, and I always see to Mr Rough, and...'

She was stopped by Philly, who raised her hand. 'We know how incredibly busy you are. And we all agreed you need to have some fun once in a while.'

'We found a really sweet young girl who can't wait to help you during the weekends,' Miss Rough added. 'When she is here, you can play golf with us.'

Miss Snuggs stared at the two serious-looking women in front of her, not quite knowing how to react to all the information that was being poured over her.

'Miss Hackkett.' Miss Snuggs swallowed nervously. 'Does Mr Rough know? That I won't be there to serve him?'

Mrs Rough stood up, walked towards the hunched figure, put her arms around her, crushing her face on the large diamond necklace. 'Yes, my dear. He knows. And is thrilled for you,' she said while pulling Miss Snuggs up on her feet. 'Listen, I had a rummage through my attic and found some old gear you can use.'

Miss Snuggs was spun round and pushed towards the corner, where a spotless bag holding shiny new clubs was standing. 'And I asked the girls if they could spare you some shirts and stuff.' Mrs Rough stared at Philly, who was trying to rip price tags from a bundle of clothes under her desk unnoticed. 'And shoes, of course.' A box appeared, revealing a pair of black and white golf shoes in mint condition.

'Another thing, Miss Snuggs.' Philly pushed the clothes back in the paper bag and handed it to their new protege. 'We are in training for the coming Regional Competition and thought it might be effective for all concerned that you join in.' Miss Snuggs's face that had turned from frosty pink to ash grey. 'But Mr Rough requested that you play with him first. Like he does with all the new members.'

Miss Snuggs nodded. Her face and neck were now turning to a shade of pale blue. 'I will be on the golf course with Mr Rough?,' she whispered.

'Yes. Coming Saturday. You will be stuck together for two hours at least. And the Bangers will join you.'

The floor creaked. Miss Snuggs's eyes rolled towards the ceiling before she slumped and fell.

'Fuck,' Philly cried. 'Mrs Rough, I think she just fainted!'

Philly jumped up and bent over the girl sprawled on the floor. 'There's a bottle of Scotch in the top draw of the desk, hold it under her nose and sprinkle some drops on her lips.'

She rolled the limp girl on her back, lifted her head up a little and watched her open her eyes again.

'Miss Snuggs, my love. Wake up.' Mrs Rough pushed Philly away, pulled the floppy body towards her and rocked it until Miss Snuggs was back again. 'Don't you worry about a thing, my darling,' she whispered in her ear. 'Mummy will take care of everything.'

CHAPTER 40

The maythorn bushes leading up to the tenth were shredding the last of their foliage, making them look like giant rolling boot scrubbers. The Bangers followed their curve up to the tee box, stopping at the wooden bench to hide from the wind that was causing the large fern trees to sway in elegant rhythm. Miss Snuggs was already there, practicing her swing just behind the water dispenser with Roughie watching her, leaning against a birch tree, lost in thought.

'Good afternoon, here we are,' Bogey bellowed over them as she walked up to Miss Snuggs. Her dark eyes went over Roughie's figure, clearly appreciating what she saw. 'You look yummy, darling. Excellent jumper.' She shivered for a second. 'Good to have, weather's turning really chilly.'

Miss Snuggs blushed and gazed at Roughie as Bogey put her arm around her and squeezed her a little. 'How are you feeling, this lovely brisk winter's afternoon?,' Bogey asked. 'Looking forward to your first nine-hole match? I must say I am looking forward to it immensely.'

Birdie flashed her even white teeth at her sister and mouthed: 'don't overdo it.'

'I must admit I'm a little nervous, Mr Rough.' Miss Snuggs' eyes darted from Bogey towards the first tee, feeling her heart pounding in her chest. 'Miss Banger, I assume you take the first shot?

'No, my darling, I will not.' Bogey shook her head and handed the four iron to her. 'You and Roughie are up first. He will go from the medal tee, and then he will escort us girls to our little patch over there.' She pointed towards the red markers in front of them.

'Really?' Miss Snuggs started to giggle, nervously. 'Oh dear. I hope I won't let you down.'

'You won't let me down, ever. Just remember what Mr Johnsson taught us. Keep your eyes on the grass in front of the ball, and let your hips do the work. Turn the shoulders, and make those beautiful little hands of yours go down and then fly towards the flag.'

Miss Snuggs blinked and stared at the tee box, noticing Roughie wanting to start. He hit his tee shot, stepped backwards and joined the Bangers towards the red markers, guiding Miss Snuggs between them.

The three of them watched the young girl on the tee closely, seeing her arms go back and firing her hips just before the club impacted the ball, letting her head follow the release of her hands.

'Wonderful shot, Miss Snuggs, wonderful!' Bogey clapped. 'Look, the ball is still rolling, can you see it? It just passed Roughie's ball, left of the flag.' She started walking. 'Now, sis, let's see if we can pop those in.' She waved at Roughie. ' You two wait for us at the next tee.'

Both balls hit the back of the cup before sinking down the hole. Birdie took them out and lobbed one towards her sister who caught it in mid-flight. The two of them collected their trolleys and set off on the short walk towards the red tee, where Roughie was busy wiping his putter with an open-mouthed Miss Snuggs gazing at him. Birdie clambered on the tee box, took a practice swing and addressed the ball, leaving her stance wide open. The impact that followed was massive, sending the ball from left to right, ending up just in front of the foliage at the back end of the driving range.

'Good Lord. How awful.' Bogey called out. 'You seem to have sliced that ball straight into the woods. Let's see if I can do better.' The ball took exactly the same flight.

Birdie shook her head. 'Sliced it into the woods as well, I'm afraid. Just about the identical spot. We both seem to have botched it up now, don't we?'

'Yes, totally useless we are. I think we will leave it to Roughie and Miss Snuggs to go and find those balls. Ball finding in the woods is far too strenuous for us, don't you agree?' Bogey stopped her trolley in the middle of the fairway and leaned on it.

'Absolutely. Far, far too strenuous.' Birdie nodded. 'I feel exhausted just thinking about it.'

Roughie followed Miss Snuggs into the shrubs and spotted his ball right in front of her, just under a leaf. He crouched to look at it, trying not to gaze at the freckles above the long slim ankles in front of him. Golden freckles. On pearly white legs. He glanced upwards and his mouth went dry, his eyes moving over the golf slacks, from ankles to the back of Miss Snuggs's knees, unable to stop his urge to peek at the slight curve of her thighs, wanting to reach out to and feel inside. To touch. To stroke them. With his fingertips. And then lick them. With his whole tongue. He felt his hand go forward, nearly touching Miss Snuggs. He made it stop, just in time, and forced himself to keep his head down and inspect the lie of the ball, noticing the other lying just a yard further.

He pulled himself together, tried to ignore his throbbing groin and selected his seven iron, tapped it neatly so it bounced back on the fairway. He turned towards Miss Snuggs whose cheeks were flushed like a pink rose in full bloom. He concentrated on her crotch, seeing it whip towards the left, forcing the ball out of the thick bushes and land next to his. Good God. He just wanted to lay her down, pull those slacks down and screw her senseless.

What an utterly disgusting thought.

His mouth grew acid, loathing himself thinking of dear Miss Snuggs that way.

'Oh, Miss Snuggs, be a darling and get those balls out of the hole, will you?' Bogey called out. 'Roughie will hold the flag for you. My sister and I will walk to the 18th tee.'

Roughie watched the small gloved hand reaching into the cup. His gaze went up and rested on the area where he imagined her breasts to be. His insides stirred while he envisioned the golden dots between Miss Snuggs breasts.

Breasts. He liked breasts. Thought about them every day. Sometimes twice a day. Ever since he saw Matron's when she had washed him during that time he had the measles. How he had wanted to touch Matron's forbidden breasts since then. Every day. Sometimes twice a day. Now he felt himself wanting to touch Miss Snuggs breasts. Again. Feeling his erection press against his trouser buttons. Again. He eyed them on the last holes, when she bent down to tee up for her drive. When wisps of her long golden hair had escaped her cap. When she pushed them out of her lovely eyes and strapped them behind her small ears. Just before she out-drove him again.

A sharp voice brought him back. He tried to focus on the Bangers, already driving off from the next tee, sending their balls over the lake towards the curve of the fairway leading to the elevated green. Both balls bounced to the left, sending them directly into the bunker adjacent to the reed.

Bogey shook her head. 'Now what have we done? Put both our balls in that impossible bunker. Sis, what must Miss Snuggs and Roughie think of us? We are not making things easy on them, now are we?' She flashed a smile at Roughie and winked at him. 'Chop, chop, darling. Mustn't be slow.'

They marched towards the fairway, Miss Snuggs in their wake. He ran after them and tried to catch the attention of Miss Snuggs who was walking towards the hollow right of the lake where the bunkers were nestled.

'Do you mind hitting out of the sand, Mr Rough?'

'Well. Let me see. Do I mind bunkers?' Roughie tried to concentrate but struggled at the sight of Miss Snuggs' adorably pink lips. 'I certainly prefer the fairway or the green, but I seem to manage in them. How do you feel about bunkers, Miss Snuggs?'

'I don't mind them at all.' Miss Snuggs shook her head firmly. 'We've been practicing with Mr Johnsson a lot, and he said I was doing great, getting out of the bunker. Last week I made a sandy.'

She slowly stepped into the sand and took her stance. 'If I remember to keep the ball on the inside of my left foot, open the club face and strike the sand about three inches behind the ball I am absolutely fine, Mr Johnsson said.'

Miss Snuggs took the shot, making the sand spray backwards towards him. Her face crumpled up in delight. 'See!,' she cried out. 'I love it when the ball flies over the flag and rolls back towards the hole.

'I do see.' Roughie tried to swallow but couldn't. 'Very good, Miss Snuggs,' he said coarsely, feeling his cheeks go crimson and suddenly started sweating. 'You sound as if you are enjoying the game.' His voice was barely more than a wheeze. 'Am I right?'

'Oh yes. And Miss Hackkett told me I should also try to watch it as much as I can on the TV. So yesterday, when I was preparing the lasagna for lunch, I watched a re-run of the Open on the little set we have in the kitchen.' She let out a contented sigh. 'Sometimes I wish I could be on the golf course for ever and ever,' she whispered. 'Do you feel that way sometimes, Mr Rough?'

His groin ached as his erection was pulsating, his balls now hot stones ready to explode. He made his biceps bulge and sucked in his stomach. 'Miss Snuggs,' he heard himself say in his lowest voice, 'please let me help you out of the sand and onto the green.' Her slim hand disappeared into his, giving off a comforting tingle. His other arm wrapped around her waist, as if it had a life of its own, not responding to its owner's usual awkwardness, but somehow, by miracle, carefully guiding her towards the side of the green.

Miss Snuggs bent over her bag and pushed a plastic container towards him. 'Would you like a taste of my cinnamon buns while we walk to the clubhouse? I made them myself.'

'Miss Snuggs, I would love to taste your cinnamon buns.' The words came out in a hush.

'They are quite sugary. Do you think they are too sweet?' Miss Snuggs cocked her head a little and asked, 'shouldn't they have a little more bite?'

'No, Miss Snuggs.' Roughie licked the excess sugar of the pastries before he took a big chunk in his mouth. 'They are perfect. Lovely and sweet. Just like you, with the perfect bite.' He stared at her, waiting for the usual wave of embarrassment to arrive or the inadvertently offensive statement to escape his lips like it always did when he tried to talk to women. But neither came. Nor did the usual dismissive dark look or the turn and walk away forever action. His lips moved again, letting more words flow out easily, like a ball flies after it has been catapulted forward by the club's sweet spot.

'There is some sugar on your lips. Let me help you get that off.' He heard himself say, feeling confident, strangely in control. His lips did exactly what he had always dreamed of, finding hers and opening them carefully, tasting the pink tongue he had seen so often, watching her concentrating on a task with the tip of it sticking between her teeth. His finger touched her cheek, burning under him. His head spun as he pulled her slim soft body closer, not thinking about it, just doing it, without any inhibition.

Heaven. Yes, definitely heaven. He felt her small hands cupping his bulging biceps. He pulled back and inch, slowly releasing her lips and took in the beautiful face in front of him. 'Thank you, Miss Snuggs,' he whispered. 'Thank you for a lovely game. I really enjoyed myself. We must do this again sometime soon.' Roughie heard himself say. He turned to see where the Bangers were. They seemed to have disappeared. He bent over and kissed Miss Snuggs again.

His mobile buzzed, indicating a Whats App.

No need for Miss Snuggs to come in till 5. We've got this.
X B&B.

He pushed it towards the young woman sitting opposite him, wearing his old cricket sweater and the long johns he wore at school, tucked into a pair of his grey woollen socks.

He took her straight home after their game, leaving their clubs in the locker room and tearing across the country lanes to the grand old house his father bought for him but hardly ever used, feeling more at home in the familiar comfort of Peckers Wood. But now he felt proud, calm and in control, opening the imposing front door, holding her hand as they walked up the main stairs to his bedroom, where they undressed in front of each other. His love for her grew with every piece of her body she revealed, wanting to kiss every patch of pale skin, every goose bump, every hollow. Their lovemaking felt so comfortable, so easy. It made him feel serene even, just following his instinct, feeling utterly relaxed and divinely elated at the same time, like striking the final put for the Championship and knowing it would fall, feeling the ball move along that perfectly read line, with no fear or doubt that it would do what it was supposed to do. It resembled the peaceful state of mind and body he experienced on the course, but never felt being with a woman.

Another galaxy from the guilt and embarrassment he usually felt after sex. The unsatisfying, technical fornication with distant-looking women who took his money after agreeing on what had to be done, what he could and couldn't do, on how to make him come. Sometimes it was fast, and sometimes didn't happen at all. Both situations left him limp and depressed afterwards, gushing apologies that were always met with cold indifference.

But not now. Now he understood what all those romantic fusses were about. What love-making meant. Why his life was worth living. When she had lain underneath him last night, blended into his body, so soft and warm, feeling a love he had never felt before as he came, holding her, like she was part of his own being.

And now, the morning after, after they both had slept like babies and made love again, it was like she had been there forever. His large kitchen that always felt so empty and cold now had a homely glow about it, caused by the angel at the old wooden table, who was eating the bacon and eggs she had made them expertly navigating on the brand-new Aga his mother had insisted upon. He reached out, wrapped his fingers around her hand and stroked the inside of her palm with his thumb. 'I love you,' he said out loud, realizing he never had done that before in front of a human being. Not to his mother, his best friend at school or even Matron. The only creature that had ever heard him utter these three words out loud was Imogen, the fluffy rabbit President Bashit had let him keep in the sheep pen at the back of the fifteenth just before he was sent off to boarding school. Imogen was always there, ready to listen while silently nibbling at a lettuce he stole from the vegetable patch Mrs Snuggs kept. Imogen was also pearly white, soft, beautiful and loving, like the girl sitting opposite him, now smiling shyly, the corners of the lavender coloured eyes turned up.

'I love you too,' she whispered, hardly audible, moving

her hand to her stomach while she swallowed. 'But I could do with another cup of tea.' The shy smile disappeared while she stood up.

He walked over to her, gently pushed her back in her chair and kissed the top of her head, letting her smell drift up his nose for a couple of seconds. 'I'll take care of that,' he said and put the kettle on the stove. 'What would you like to do today?,' he asked, grabbing her mug and kissing her quickly. 'You don't have to start until five. We can do anything you like.'

'Could we go and play 18 holes together?'

Roughie turned to the maid's clock hanging above the old range, telling him it was just after nine o'clock. 'Definitely. Excellent idea,' he said. 'We'll take a bath and be on the tee by half past ten.'

CHAPTER 41

The driving range was empty. Winter had really set in. Members were on the course, but it wasn't nearly as lively as it had been during the last months. The more serious ones were deep into their practicing routines on the pitching green, getting ready for the next season. The men's team had an intense schedule, and Philly and Lash had established their own, working around the men's set times on the practice greens. It was actually turning out great, even the Bangers were taking his direction seriously and even took to practicing independently.

The first half of her Captaincy year was nearly over, and it was finally going her way. Philly looked round, enjoying the Sunday's peace and quiet, contemplating Lav Thorneybush's email before her team would arrive. A practice match at Goodlie as a warming up before the real deal in March. It actually sounded like quite a good idea. Ben also agreed when she showed him the email this morning at breakfast. 'Good for morale,' he said. 'An opportunity to try out pairings and strategy. See it as a day out well spent.'

The long field, with its scattered patches of brown and yellow yardage markers, looked inviting. The team had been ready for weeks, expertly coached by Lash Johnsson who was no doubt banging Pru in the caddy shack right now as a perfect way to spend his lunch break.

Philly breathed in deeply, letting the winter's cold air rush to her lungs. Pru. Her best friend since forever. She felt happy for her, seeing her mellowing a little. Pru was clearly head over heels and spending more and more of her time in the tiny cottage, presumably dividing her precious free hours between sex and making sure the caddy shack was spotlessly clean and organized. It reminded Philly of how their flat used to be before Ben showed up every weekend, leaving a trail of mess everywhere he went.

Ben. Philly tried to analyse what she felt about him. Love? Fondness? Her mind drifted to his beautiful body and his suave posture, making her physically want him. The intoxicating charm he turned on when they were with others, like with her parents who seemed to adore him.

A soft ticking sound made her return her attention to the practice ground. *One, two, three, four, five, six, seven, eight, nine.* Philly counted to the rhythm, not sure about its source. She looked over her shoulder, noticing the familiar bent figure of President Bashit coming up the path, slowly but surely, huddled deep into a tired looking loden jacket, followed by the ever-present Percy.

'Miss Hackkett. I was hoping I would find you here.' President Bashit lifted his walking stick. 'And might I ask you to sit with me for a moment? I want to consult you on something.'

'You do?' Philly's eyebrows shot up in amazement while she stared at the unusually friendly looking face. 'I mean, yes, of course,' she replied while moving to the bench the President had sat down on.

'How are you, sir?,' Philly asked politely.

'Been better, Miss Hackkett. Spot of the old gout bothering me again.' The President's face was pulled into a grimace, indicating the discomfort he was feeling.

'Ah.' Philly swallowed a witty reply, knowing better than to spoil the obvious special moment between them.

'I do this every day, you know. No matter what the weather is like. Or however agonizingly painful my foot is,' President Bashit said. 'My little stroll. Letting Peckers Wood's beauty inspire me and sort out my inner demons.' The sharp blue eyes pierced Philly's while the President paused for a while.

Philly nodded, not quite knowing what to say but also not daring to look away.

'It always dazzles me,' the President said, breaking the silence. 'The sheer beauty. Even now, with winter at our doorstep.'

They sat for quite a while longer before President Bashit spoke again. 'You might have heard, Miss Hackkett, that my Club Secretary has suddenly taken to playing with a female?' He shook his head in mock surprise. 'Teeing off together Sunday mornings, no less?'

Philly froze for a second but managed not to show it. 'Ah. Yes. I am so sorry. I will talk to Miss Snuggs about that. Make her aware of the rules.'

'No, Miss Hackkett.' President Bashit shook his head again, now looking serious. 'I'd rather you left it.'

'Why?,' Philly asked, feeling confused. 'We fully understand we're not allowed before lunch.'

'Well,' the President shrugged, 'let me see. My dear Club Secretary. Chronically glum, chronically nervous, and, to be quite honest, chronically wet. On the whole, not very appealing, somehow.'

'Oh, President Bashit, I'm not sure that's quite true. I know a pretty girl that would certainly disagree. She finds Roughie's appeal irresistible. And the feeling is mutual, you know.'

'I do know.' President Bashit nodded and shot a wicked grin at Philly, lightening the atmosphere. 'Because somehow, suddenly, our glum, nervous and wet Rough has undergone a magic transformation and is coming up with all sorts of bright ideas. Absolutely amazing.' President Bashit whispered the last words, while bent over towards Philly. 'Getting her to play golf was very clever of you, my dear. The only thing that annoys me about the whole thing that I didn't come up with it myself.'

Philly started to giggle, feeling relieved. 'Maybe that's because the concept of a woman on the golf course doesn't come natural to you, sir,' she added.

The old man joined Philly in the giggle for a second. 'Don't push it Miss Hackkett,' he replied in a friendly tone. 'But well done. Three birds caught with one stone. Happy Secretary, happy Miss Snuggs and your team sorted out.'

'Ah, yes.' Philly managed to keep her voice even. 'I was planning to discuss the team's formation with you, but you concluded this already.'

'Of course I did. I have my sources. And I hear she's doing really well, despite a bit of nervousness in the beginning.' The President stared over the range, focused on two figures with a small dog walking towards them. 'Ready to start the team lesson, I see. How are you doing? Master Johnsson doing his best for all of you?' The amused glint in the old man's eye was undeniable.

'Yes,' Philly said firmly, not wanting to fall into the trap the President was clearly setting up for her. 'He's dedicated, loves the club, adores the game, has Simon Hot on his side and fully understands the importance of us becoming the best we can be. And the time and dedication it deserves.'

'I see. Talking about Hot, where does he come in?'

'In what?'

'In you becoming the best you can.' Bashit turned towards Philly. 'Any contributions from his side?'

'He said I can ring him whenever I want to. For advice on strategy.'

'Good show. Always have your strategy ready.' President Bashit shifted in his seat. 'Righto, Miss Hackkett, talking about time and dedication, would your section be interested in,' a dramatic pause followed, 'doing some committee work?'

Philly spun towards him, eyebrows raised, making certain she hadn't misunderstood. 'Right,' she answered slowly, trying to ignore the feeling she was being made fun of and starting to nod profusely. 'Yes. Definitely. I think we can be of tremendous value. We would love to.'

'Excellent. Come and see me in my study after your lesson,' President Bashit said. 'I would like to use your female attributes effectively in the club's best interest.' He paused and stared at Philly intently. 'We need something positive, something that will unite the members, off the course. And something tells me you girls are just the thing.'

The lesson had been great. Philly stacked the last basket under the ball dispenser and stretched her back.

The others were on the course with Johnsson, wanting to try out foursomes, with him standing in for her, playing with Pru, while she was due for her important meeting. The girls gawped at her when she told them all the good news. Lav's invitation and the President's staggering request rushed the positive energy running through them even faster.

The spring in her step took her to the clubhouse quickly, Philly gained more time taking the short cut through the kitchen's back door towards the great hall, and past the statue. She waited for the response to her knock on the door, pushed it open and greeted the men, who stood up for her. Bashit gestured her to take a seat in front of the large desk in which she sat down quickly, eager to hear what was in store.

The President turned towards her and smiled briefly, before returning to his notes. 'And now for the final item on our agenda: the Annual Christmas Dinner and Dance.' Bashit ruffled the pile of papers in front of him. 'As discussed after last year's party we held a feedback survey. Mr Rough, would you be so kind as to read some of the comments our dear members left for us to consider?'

Roughie looked round and put on his reading glasses. 'Well, let me see….Mr Herzog here says he will file a formal complaint at the Royal & Ancient if Charmers ever touches his wife again. Mr Rajput points out that the glasses of wine were, and I quote, "quite definitely even smaller than the miserable measure with which this club thinks fit to provide its members. No doubt things are getting from bad to worse," unquote. Mr McFarnac was upset because Percy ate his wife's Christmas cracker present. Quite a few members voice their disappointment over the fact that the mince pies were gone before they had any. And Mr Bottum had to buy new shoes because Percy was sick all over them. Apparently, he had scoffed all the mince pies. Percy, that is.'

'I see,' Bashit said, frowning slightly. 'Anything else? Maybe something more constructive?'

'There does seem to be some common ground. A significant number of remarks on the carol singing. Most members find the traditional songs tedious, it seems. Offensive even, not considering all feelings concerned. But Danny's Disco for the dance went down very well. Thumbs up from everyone.'

'Right.' Bashit nodded and scribbled a note on the pile of paper. 'Danny's Disco it is. Now about this party.' The President looked at Roughie and Bushrod and slowly turned towards Philly. 'Mr Rough and I had a word and I must admit he managed to convince me that, taking this particular situation in consideration, there could be added value to a modern approach, meaning…' Bashit paused for a second, 'involvement of the lady section.'

A tense silence followed the President's unusual hint of vulnerability, Philly glanced at Roughie who nodded at her, smiling encouragingly.

'The Annual Christmas Dinner and Dance is vitally important for the good spirit in our beloved club.' The President was silent for a few seconds before he spoke again. 'Do you get what I am on about, Miss Hackkett?'

Philly nodded quickly, feeling excited. 'Absolutely.'

'Good. Because it would be very insensitive of me to force this question I am about to ask you on any of the male members. Tree decorations, crackers, wrapping up gifts, dinner, dancing. Christmas is more a womanly thing, isn't it?' He paused slightly before continuing and turned to his treasurer.

'How about you, Bushrod? Any thoughts on the matter?'

The tall man jumped to attention. 'Agreed, agreed,' he muttered. 'Mrs Bushrod once left me to fend for myself during a Christmas when she had a bout of the shingles, and I must confess I found the whole affair extremely nerve-racking. Thinking about it now, I distinctly remember stuffing the turkey with the Christmas lights, shoving the infant Jesus doll in the oven and setting the tree on fire with the Christmas crackers.'

'O my God,' Philly whispered, trying to avoid Roughie's astonished look. 'Poor you.'

'Indeed.' Bashit pulled himself up and walked towards the window, overlooking the car park in the distance. 'Righto, Miss Hackkett. The Peckers Wood Annual Christmas Dinner and Dance. Are you game? Organizing the whole thing?'

'Yes. Definitely.' Philly nearly shouted out loud but controlled herself, swallowed and tried to ignore her burning cheeks. 'Leave it to us, sir. We will throw a super party.'

'Wonderful. I'm looking forward to hearing your suggestions and budget, which is not substantial, but I think you understand why.' A long stare followed, first at Bushrod and then towards Philly. 'And another thing, Miss Hackkett. I would like you to take this opportunity to…,' the President paused and gazed out of the window. '…without sounding outrageously rash, but to conceptualize things a little. Christmas traditions are frightfully important, but we are a golf club, after all.' His head turned, and he eyed the portrait of his father. 'Maybe the theme should be more, well, us. So to speak. More aligned with our sporting manner.' His face went serious. 'And, please listen carefully, I will only say this once. I'm a great John Lennon fan. A wise man, our John.' The President's eyelids briefly fluttered. 'Here at Peckers Wood, we choose to follow his kind advice. Have done for years, with success.' His attention returned to the small group in front of him. 'So. Imagine there's no heaven and no religion too. To keep things simple and friendly. You get the gist, Miss Hackkett. Don't you?'

CHAPTER 42

'Last Christmas, I gave you my fart.' The loud singing was followed by giggles. Pru and Philly exchanged a surprised look before they pushed the door to the Ladies' room open to find Mrs Pushet and Lizzie doing the washing up together.

'It's heart, Mrs Pushet. Last Christmas, I gave you my heart,' Pru said, while raising one eyebrow at Lizzie who avoided her dark look.

'I know! Don't be such a boring fart, young Prudence!' Mrs Pushet winked at the young girl standing next to her and started singing in a high voice, *'Frosty the Pervert, in a trench coat he did go.'*

'Thank you, Mrs Pushet.' Pru pulled the fridge open and pulled a bottle of wine out. 'I think we've had enough of the Christmas songs for now.'

'Leave some cookies out, I'm going to eat them all,' Mrs Pushet sang, nudging Lizzie who turned red.

'Please, Mrs Pushet, we've really had enough now.'

'No, we haven't.' The door opened again, letting in a gush of cold air, followed by Maggie and the Bangers, looking smug, clutching an iPad and an old-fashioned looking recorder. 'We've been so busy writing and practicing, but we think we now have the perfect Christmas carol for the party.'

'O my God.' Pru shook her head in misery. 'Whatever next.

But let's have it. What's your encore to flatulence and deviant snowmen?'

The iPad slid out of its cover into Birdie's lap, and Bogey wiggled her fingers over the recorder's little holes before gesturing the others to take a seat. Philly pulled Lizzie by the arm, inviting her to sit down next to her. The first notes to All Ye Faithful sounded, the Bangers stood up next to each other and Birdie started to sing, surprisingly clear and on key.

O Come All Ye Golfers
Joyful and triumphant,
O come ye, O come ye to Peh- heckers Wood.
Come and tee off lots,
approach the greens thereafter;
O come, we all adore golf,
O come, we all adore golf,
O come, we all adore golf,
At Peh-heckers Wood.
O play, team of golfers,
Play in exultation,
Play as much you can on Peckers Wood's lovely course.
Give to our club glory in the highest;
O come, we all adore golf,
O come, we all adore golf,
O come, we all adore golf,
At Peh-heckers Wood.
All silent! Ball, we strike thee,
new this happy morning,
O Golf! for evermore we all wish to play.
On the fairest way, with the flag appearing;
O come, we all adore golf,
O come, we all adore golf,
O come, we all adore golf,
At Peh-heckers Wood.

Lizzie glanced sideways at Mrs Pushet, waiting for some kind of dirty joke to appear from the old lady's mouth. But her old eyes were brimming with tears, singing the last words in a soft voice. 'Mrs Pushet?,' she whispered softly. 'Are you alright? Would you like a handkerchief?'

A folded tissue appeared from Philly's purse, and Mrs Pushet blew her nose loudly. 'Thank you, my darling. I just got a bit overwhelmed.' She wiped under her nose before returning the wet piece of paper to an uncomfortable looking Pru. 'That was truly beautiful, girls. Bravo.'

'Thanks, Mrs Pushet.' The Bangers huddled together, their eyes shining brightly above red cheeks. 'Philly? What do you think? Will President Bashit like it?'

Philly stared at them, trying the find the right words. 'I think...,' she said while slowly shaking her head, 'he will absolutely love it.' She glanced at Pru who looked stunned and turned back to the Bangers who were now in each other's arms, squeezing each other tightly. 'Not so sure about the recorder though,' she added carefully.

'No,' Pru said slowly. 'But honestly, the lyrics are super. I can accompany you on my German flute if you like.' A large smile appeared. 'I'm a bit rusty, but we can practice, right?'

'Yes!,' the Bangers cried out together. 'It will be perfect!' They shared a quick look and scuttled towards Philly, kneeling down in front of her with a pout on their shining faces.

'And Captain,' Birdie said while she pulled at her lower lip, 'we have some thoughts on fun things to do during drinks and dinner. So our dear members won't get bored.'

Bogey leaned forward and looked at Philly, her brown eyes begging like a little puppy waiting for a treat. 'Can we please show you?'

'I don't see why not.' Philly moved towards them and hugged her friends, peeked at Pru who nodded and pulled back. 'Go on.'

The iPad was pulled towards them again and a file called PWXmas appeared. Bogey tapped it, and up came a sketch showing Father Christmas bent over a putter with a sign on his back saying Beat Santa. 'It's like Beat the Pro,' Birdie said. 'You turn up, try to better the pro and you win. We just need some artificial grass and a hole thingy to put the flag in and off we go.'

'I like it,' Mrs Pushet said.

'Wait till you see the next one,' Bogey replied. The next sketch emerged, now with a scarcely dressed young woman resembling Miss Snuggs holding a bag of potatoes and a driver. 'Pelt the Potato.' Bogey pointed towards the woman in the picture. 'We ask Miss Snuggs to bake the potatoes so they feel like, you know, sort of mushy marshmallows, and ta-ta, here is our indoor longest drive competition. All we further need is a tee, a driver and some paper to protect the rugs in the main hall.'

'Great stuff.' Mrs Pushet nudged Lizzie. 'I bet you're good at that. You might win a prize.'

'You might too, Mrs Pushet. With your magnificent short game. This one's for you.' Bogey's index finger tapped again. 'The final one: Carry the Reindeer.' A large dog showed up, a quasi-Percy, wearing fake antlers and a red plastic nose. 'We need a green round piece of paper, a flag, some more artificial grass and a sand wedge. And ready we are to try and lob a ball over the deer.' She closed the image and looked round expectantly.

'Love it.' Mrs Pushet started to applaud, slowly followed by the others.

'We do need to think about manning and holding score and that kind of stuff.' Birdie turned to her sister who took over. 'Yes. And prizes of course. And who does the prize giving. There is still so much to do and so little time.' Bogey shook her head and sighed dramatically.

Philly sat up, excitedly. 'I agree! And honestly, well done, you two. But you might want to take poor Percy into consideration. Half the members here can't hit a decent chip, the poor old boy will be battered to death by topped Titleists shooting at him.'

'You're right. We need to sit down and perfect the sketches, but we'll be ready by next weekend.' Birdie jumped back on her feet and clapped her hands. 'Snacks everyone?'

'No thanks,' Pru and Philly said simultaneously.

Lizzie got up. 'Miss Snuggs just texted me. I need to take over so she can discuss the menu with you, Miss Hackkett.'

'Yes.' Philly nodded. 'And Lizzie? Please call me Philly. I'm your friend, remember?'

The girl blushed and left hurriedly, leaving the other women to their wine.

'Philly? Pru?,' Birdie asked, her head slightly cocked. 'Would you consider Miss Snuggs a friend too? We certainly do.'

'Absolutely. She's such a lovely person. One cannot help liking her,' Pru said.

'Then why do we keep addressing her as Miss Snuggs? Because she's staff? Lizzie's staff.'

Philly and Pru exchanged a quick look. 'You're right,' Pru said. 'But her Christian name, does anyone know?'

'Berny.' Mrs Pushet's voice popped up. 'Short for Bernice.'

'Ah.' Birdie touched her sister and nodded. 'It's Berny. Not Bunny.' She started to giggle. 'We had cocktails with Roughie the other day, and he was yakking on about her, calling her Bunny. At least that's what we thought.'

Mrs Pushet laughed and threw her hands up into the air. 'And I bet you kept having these images of her in a Playboy suit hopping around the kitchen table wanting to nibble at Roughie's carrot, and…'

'Thank you. We get it.' Pru's hand came up, and she shook her head, as if trying to force Mrs Pushet's thought out. 'And talk of the devil, here she comes now.'

The door opened, and Miss Snuggs came in quickly, shutting the door behind her, keeping out the cold. Strands of hair had escaped her usual tight bun, and her cheeks seemed rosier than usual, making the colour of her eyes stand out even more. Her uniform, hugging her body and showing off her curves, was covered with droplets of rain, now giving of sparkles under the artificial lights.

'Miss Hackkett,' Miss Snuggs said softly, while trying to wipe the droplets from her chest, 'I've started on the Christmas menu and the snacks. Shall we discuss it now? Is that convenient for you?'

'Yah. Absolutely.' Philly moved over and made a space. 'Please, let me see.'

Miss Snuggs swallowed hard. 'Well, we talked about the five course Christmas walking dinner so everyone can join in with the games Miss Banger already discussed with me. But if I set a couple of tables for the older members so they can sit down, would that be an idea? And you specifically asked for my homemade Christmas pudding and mince pies, I will see to those, and I just need to stuff 20 big turkeys and peel 500 potatoes for the mash, and I'm nearly finished with making the Christmas crackers, but there is still a lot to do. The fish pies, the water cress soup. The croutons, the Scotch eggs, the bonbons.' She turned her head towards Philly. 'I am so grateful Lizzie is there to help me once she breaks up for her holiday, Miss Hackkett, I really am.'

'Sounds wonderful,' Philly replied. 'But are you sure you will have enough time? It seems like a lot to do.'

Miss Snuggs shrugged. 'Well, it's not like Lizzie and I have other Christmas things to bother about, like shopping for party clothes and stuff. We have it easy. We just wear our uniforms.'

'Ah, I see. Of course,' Philly said. 'But what about shopping for presents? You'll need time for that, won't you?'

Miss Snuggs shrugged bashfully. 'Not really, Miss Hackkett. My grandmother doesn't bother with Christmas, and Lizzie's mum said she didn't want Lizzie to spend her money on silly gifts.' A shy smile appeared. 'And Mr Rough says I am the best present he ever had and forbade me to get him anything.'

'Right. Good for him.' Philly smiled and pulled Miss Snuggs towards her. 'I am really pleased with this. It will be great. And delicious.'

'Absolutely,' the Bangers said in unison. 'Super delicious. But also a hell of a lot to do.'

'Yes.' Miss Snuggs sighed. 'So I think I need to get going now, okay?'

Philly nodded. 'Yah. On one condition. Only if, from now on, you call me Philly, Berny. And call Miss Love Pru. And the Bangers, well, the Bangers I suppose.'

Miss Snuggs smiled politely. 'Okay. I'll try.'

Mrs Pushet poured her a glass of lemonade. 'Here you go, Bunny darling, get this down you. Let's chuck the Miss and the Snuggs, Bunny it is. It suits you. Soft, cuddly and adorable. And something tells me it will be Mrs Rough soon anyway.

CHAPTER 43

To: secretary@peckerswood.co.uk
From: banger@home.co.uk
Bcc: President@peckerswood.co.uk; cherie@rough.co.uk
Subject: Xmas party

17th of December, 2022

Dear Secretary, darling Roughie,

Isn't our delicious President Bashit utterly BRILLIANT, putting Philly in charge of the always SPLENDID Xmas Dinner and Dance? She's doing a spiffing job, involving all us girls, we are absolutely convinced you will be QUITE THRILLED with our contributions.

And, of course, with what your darling Bunny is planning for us, that five course dinner sweet Lizzie and herself will work on day and night! We were quite tingled hearing all the extraordinary goodies they are preparing. And Bravo to you, for being so awfully good about BUNNY NOT BEING ABLE TO GIVE YOU ANY ATTENTION AT ALL THE COMING FORTNIGHT. And imagine how utterly knackered she'll be after the party, poor thing. We jolly well hope she will take some time off so you two can have glorious fun together after New Year's Eve.

So, thank you, and our President, for everything. We are convinced this will be the most brill party ever.

Cheerio. BB

PS. Been yonks since we've hoisted ourselves in a decent party frock. Tried on the ones we used to wear in school, but they turned out a bit too snug. Will have to go on shopping spree and buy new ones that are less snug. Because extremely frightened snugness might evoke beastly C. Charmers, who tends to grope anything remotely snug.

PPS. Talking of Charmers, we heard some delicious gossip about him having a uniform fetish. You might want to warn Lt. Rt. Bushrod to forgo his uniform for once and wear a decent dinner jacket. God forbid Charmers gets a bit tight and gropes him. Imagine those filthy little hands on our darling treasurer. It makes us quite seedy just thinking about it.

PPPS. Are you wearing that dashing velvet dinner jacket you used to wear in school? Might be a bit snug too.

PPPPs. Just realize BUNNY CAN'T TAKE TIME OFF. Lizzie must be back at school just after the New Year, of course. Silly us.

CHAPTER 44

The lunchtime walk around the course with Maggie had done its magic, settling down the flutters in her head and stomach. Philly stepped over towards Ben, seeing him gaze over the lake alongside the 18th and shiver in his coat. 'I need to go.' Ben squeezed her against him, holding her tight for a couple of seconds before releasing her. 'Team meeting. Only two more months until the practice rounds.'

'Everything on track?' Philly pushed her hood back and wiped her hair from her face.

'Absolutely. I just need to be certain that our pairing strategy is the best way to go. But we might need to hustle things around.' He pulled her hood back over her head. 'Well. I am sure it will work it out, somehow,' he said. 'You try and keep warm out here with that wind whipping around the shack without me to hold and protect you.'

Philly smirked. 'I'll manage, thank you very much.'

She watched Ben set off towards the clubhouse, his feet carefully treading the frozen fairway path. Her hands were deep in her pockets, now comfortably warm and tingling. She pulled her head back, closed her eyes for a second and breathed the freezing air in, filling her lungs with the tangy freshness and pushed her shoulders downwards while her she slowly opened her eyes again, focusing towards the back of the 17th, taking in the breathtakingly beautiful scene. The light greyish tone of the frozen green was surrounded by trees covered with thin layers of white powder, like sparkling icing setting off a glittering spectacle in the afternoon's soft winter's sun.

It would be dark soon with the moon taking over, accompanied by the million Christmas lights twinkling, acting as silver dust sprinkled over them for good luck. Philly took another deep breath, now suddenly feeling jittery again thinking about tonight. Everything was planned and prepared to the last detail. This Christmas party was a breeze compared to anything she had ever organized at work.

Bashit had been over the moon hearing the whole road map and had, totally unembarrassed, wiped a tear away while listening to the Bangers and Pru rehearsing the Christmas carol. Even Bushrod the Bigot admitted that he and Mrs Bushrod were looking forward to the party and had increased the budget for the prizes to be won during the Christmas games.

Her mobile buzzed under her hand, telling her it was time for her last check and final meeting. She whistled for Maggie, waiting for the little dog to return from the lake chasing the unfortunate ducks around the ice now covering the whole surface. Maggie ran towards her, waiting to be picked up to be carried inside Philly's down jacket, knowing she would be safe and warm. Her small pointed snout sticking out above the half open zipper bobbed up and down to the rhythm of Philly's determined step towards the clubhouse where the two large pine trees adjoining the entrance were now giant galaxies brought to life by the thousands of little lights Roughie and Lash Johnsson had put in together perfectly without a single gap showing. Mrs Pushet had made the Christmas wreath hanging in the middle of the door looking nearly professionally done with real holly and large pine apples they picked along the fifth during their last round of team practice.

The heavy door opened, and Philly gazed in, momentarily taken aback by the scene in front of her. The great hall, now shining with greens, golds and reds, was more impressive than ever. The paintings, antique furniture and the marble statue looked perfectly at ease in the scene, as if they had been covered with the decorations forever. Everything was set up for the games, and the main bar was transformed into a shiny, glittering seventies discotheque. She waved at Danny the D.J., who gave her a wink and the thumbs up.

She moved towards the lounge and stood still for a moment, remembering the only slight hiccup in the process while watching Bunny giving directions to the caterer Mrs Rough had somehow, like a miracle, come up with at the last moment. “No daughter in law of mine is peeling 500 potatoes and stuffing 20 turkeys” was the indisputable comment when she inspected the menu and asked Philly why Bunny and Lizzie hadn’t any help. Bunny had protested and said it was no trouble at all. She was used to it, and Lizzie was a great assistant, and what about the vegan alternatives Philly had insisted upon, but to no avail. Mrs Rough had marched into Roughie’s study, dragged him from his desk and put him in charge of the bar, telling him in no uncertain terms that she had been looking forward taking Bunny and Lizzie shopping since the party was announced and did not wish this outing to be compromised in any way. Getting Bunny’s blessing for the caterer was part of the outing, which happened very quickly once Bunny saw the spotlessly clean kitchen. The caterer went over the menu with her, gently but surely, asking for her opinion and suggestions for every course.

And it had worked out, like magic. Philly smiled as she walked up to the two young women. ‘Everything under control?,’ she asked, lightly touching Lizzie’s arm, who instantly blushed and looked down at her feet. ‘It looks, and already smells, heavenly.’ Her eyes went towards Bunny, still scribbling on her clip board, looking serious. ‘I think it’s time for us to go to the Ladies’ room for the final meeting, and of course, to get dressed,' she said while turning to Lizzie. 'I've seen your frock. It's super. You'll look smashing, make sure you stay away from that groping Charles Charmers. If he puts his disgusting hands on you, I'll ask Ben to punch him on the nose.'

Lizzie giggled, feeling warm patches burn in her neck, still not daring to look at Philly. 'I have Bunny and Mrs Pushet with me, they'll keep me safe,' she said softly.

The women gathered at the main entrance and walked up to the Ladies' room in a comfortable silence. They had all done a super job. Everything was ready for the guests to arrive. All that was left to do now was to change into their party dresses.

Simon Hot and Lash Johnsson had left the Ladies' room and taken the greenkeepers and the caddies to the shack for a quick clean up and change into their costumes to make sure they were ready and in place. Bunny was assigned as supervisor for the food, Pru and Lash were in charge of the bar, Mrs Pushet and Lizzie would sort out the prizes, and the Bangers would supervise the greenskeepers and the caddies with the games. Philly had the job of all-round manager, making sure Bashit was kept in the loop if anything would deviate from the road map he so merrily agreed upon.

The Ladies' room was already warmed up, the dresses and accessories were neatly laid out, ready for them to pick up and change.

Lizzie was the quickest, hiding behind the loo's wall, embarrassed, not wanting the others to see her. She stared at her reflection in the shower room's small mirror, and to her own surprise, she was not disgusted by what she saw. A tall, attractive teenager with short black hair slicked backwards stared back at her, wearing a mid-calf, clingy black dress, with thin straps over her shoulders, emphasizing her collarbone. Her new white sneakers looked really cool, especially with the silver ankle bracelet Mrs Rough had thrown in. She peaked around the wall, watching the others getting ready. Bunny looked adorable in her ice blue flowing gown, resembling Elsa from Frozen, a stark contrast to Pru in an ankle length, high-necked sleeveless black dress, her black hair tied back in a severe-looking roll. The only jewellery she wore were a pair of small diamond stud earrings.

Mrs Pushet suddenly popped up next to her and pointed at Lizzie's feet. 'Gosh. I wish I had some of those. Jolly, snazzy, and comfy.' She pulled a face as she stepped into her black spiky pumps. 'These numbers are killing me already,' she said, looking Lizzie over who was staring at Philly, her lips slightly parted, the dreamy look in her eyes suggesting she was in another star system.

'Ravishing, isn't she.' Mrs Pushet put an arm around Lizzie's waist, causing the young girl to jump. 'Amazing how anybody with carrot-coloured hair and a whole body covered in a zillion little orange dots can be so deadly attractive.'

Lizzie swallowed, wanting to look in the other direction but just couldn't tear her eyes away. The centre of her new universe was now bending towards the little mirror on the kitchen worktop, fiddling with jade dangling earrings, visible now the long orange hair was piled up onto Philly's head.

'Bewitched, bothered and bewildered, are you?,' Mrs Pushet whispered.

Lizzie nodded quickly, embarrassed, not knowing how to reply to her old friend and suddenly feeling emotional. 'She's so perfect,' she whispered. 'I wish I was like her.'

'She's not perfect, just extremely lucky, being born where she was.' Mrs Pushet gestured for Lizzie to sit down and whispered conspiratorially. "Let me tell you a little story. After years of trying and being miserable, the Hackketts had given up on a baby. But then what do you know? Mrs Hackkett suddenly found herself pregnant. They were over a hundred moons, Lizzie.

And they gave this love child all they got. The warmest home, the best schools, golf, university. Not easy on a school head's wages.' The old lady looked at her young friend and cocked her head. 'Come on, my darling. Growing up like she could? Makes everyone turn out near perfect.' Mrs Pushet reached out and pinched Lizzie's nose. 'Don't berate yourself, my dear. Nothing is more boring than perfection.'

'Wow. That's deep, Mrs Pushet.' Lizzie sighed. 'But I wish I could play golf with her.' She went red. 'I mean, like her.'

'Right.' Mrs Pushet leaned forward. 'Well, Sporty Dyke, does your mother know?,' she breathed.

'Mrs Pushet!,' Lizzie hissed, turning from red to puce. 'You can't say dyke. It's offensive.'

'O fuck me.' Mrs Pushet shook her head and waved both her hands in the air, her face crumpled up in desperation. 'Everybody's so bloody twee lately. Give me a break.' She pulled Lizzie closer towards her and put her lips towards the young girl's ear. 'Listen, my budding gay companion. In my day, we just got on with it. Everything was fine. Everyone was fine. No matter what you turned you on. Or off.' The old wrinkled hand came up and touched Lizzie's hair. 'Mr Pushet and I had loads of delightful acquaintances back in our day. We've had such jolly times together, experimenting with all kinds of exciting stuff. Try Sexual, I think the term is now.' Mrs Pushet nodded. 'You know, Mr Pushet looked divine in my dresses. But he also couldn't bear the high-heeled shoes.'

The blood in Lizzie's face had now plummeted to her stomach, causing her face turn to white, and her mouth fell open despite her tongue somehow sticking to her palate.

'Don't be embarrassed, dear,' Mrs Pushet sighed. 'We were just, you know, more open minded than you lot are now. These days everyone has to have a label. I find that so dictatorial. What in earth does it matter what you are?' Mrs Pushet took her bag and rummaged around for a while. 'Just as long as you keep away from children and animals, are kind and respectful to others, you're a chum of mine.' She checked Lizzie's face who was still looking abashed. 'You haven't answered my question. Does your mother know?'

Lizzie nodded. 'Yes,' she whispered, trying to swallow, but her mouth was still too dry. 'And she's fine with it. But…' Lizzie stopped talking, staring towards the floor.

'But what?'

'My father and the dark witch call me Lizzie the Lezzie.'

'Jesus Christ,' Mrs Pushet muttered while she rolled her eyes. 'How droll. Listen, I've found my lighter so I'm stepping out for a quick smoke. Come and get me before I freeze to death.' A crumpled-up fag appeared. 'Everything will work out fine, okay?'

Lizzie nodded. 'If you say so.'

'I say so.' Mrs Pushet smiled and stepped outside.

CHAPTER 45

Philly slipped back into the bar through the French window, looking over her shoulder to make sure she was unnoticed. Ben had gone berserk when he saw her in her new dress. She thought she would never get it on straight again, after he nearly tore it off her body in the men's dressing room.

She put her hands towards her burning cheeks, trying to cool them down. The sex had been raw, primal even. Seeing him in his dinner jacket, handsomer and sexier than ever, the look of hunger for her had excited her wildly. She hadn't protested when he pushed her through the door, savagely tugging at her dress and getting annoyed by his failure to get it off. He had yanked it upwards, pushed her knickers aside and stroked her until she wriggled and moaned. He then spun her round, bent her over the washing basin before he grabbed her hips and pushed himself inside her, fucking her hard.

It turned out to be painfully awkward. Philly suddenly stiffened, feeling uptight, worrying about her dress, the party, all the people waiting for them. Ben came quickly with a forceful last thrust, causing her to bang her head on the cold tap.

'Oh God.' He sighed, slumped over her for a second, then pulling her to her feet. 'Sorry beautiful. I didn't mean to hurt you,' he said looking bashful. He tucked his shirt back in his trousers and straightened his bow tie.

'Did you come?' he asked.

She shook her head and turned to the mirror, not wanting to face him, fiddled with her dress, put it back where it belonged and checked her forehead, relieved to see she didn't have a lump on it.

'Sorry,' he said again, the bashful look disappearing fast. 'I will make it up to you next time.' The familiar gesture of his hand over his head, and he turned away from her, leaving her to find her own way back.

He was casually flirting with a group of middle-aged wives when Philly made it to the bar, his suave posture completely stripped from the excited rawness she experienced a few minutes ago. She stepped back, avoiding a couple of people closing in. Ten paces to escape the crowd, she thought, and onto the patio, for five minutes by herself, get a grip, go over all the witty vocab she would hurtle towards all the members and their wives wanting to talk to her. But familiar voices came towards her, stopping her in her tracks.

'Captain! Here you are! We couldn't find you. Isn't this Christmas dinner smashing? Even the vegan stuff is excellent.' Four large brown eyes shot upwards; two tongues clicked in perfect unison. 'It all is a super success. We've had so much fab feedback on the carol. It was a hit.'

'And have you seen the queues at the games? Everyone wants to take a shot.' Birdie giggled and whispered.

'And look at you, you look divine, old girl.' Bogey leaned towards Philly. 'Everybody says so. And poor Ben, drooling all over you, lost for words, what's that all about? You're not withholding sex, now are you?'

The Bangers screamed with laughter, exchanging a fat wink. 'We wouldn't withhold Ben sex, now would we, sis? No way. Yummy, hot brownie Ben.'

Bogey nodded. 'I'll say. Poor chap. Be good, Philly. Be good.'

The two sisters huddled against each other and looked at Philly expectantly. 'Tell us, Captain, how do we look? Aren't we adorable?' Their arms linked together, lips pouted. 'Bobby and Henri are droolie too. Can't wait for their rumpy-pumpy.'

'Yes, you are. Utterly adorable.' Philly smiled in spite of herself as she examined what was in front of her, automatically drawn to the glittering spectacle on top of each sister's head. Sparkling tiaras with little stones cut as golf balls, carefully woven into their thick long brown hair, streaked by an obviously, insanely expensive hair dresser, the long strands curling inwards where the outrageous shocking pink dresses were just a little bit too tight. 'And you've, we've, all done an amazing job. Everyone's so pleased. We've sure as hell shown all those members what we are made of.'

The Bangers nodded, their eyes welling up with tears. 'We have. There's no doubting our true value now.'

The sound of the people hushing each other and moving towards their tables reached them. She looked round and caught President Bashit's eye, telling her he needed her attention.

'Ladies and Gentlemen, dear staff,' the President paused and waited for Philly to reach over and hand the carefully wrapped up presents and the piece of paper holding the scores to him.

'First things first. A big round of applause for our dear staff and, of course, the Lady section.' The President beamed towards the crowd who started clapping enthusiastically.' I think we all agree this is the best Peckers Wood Dinner and Dance we've had in years. Well done, staff and ladies!' Another round of applause and a few cheers followed.

The President unfolded the piece of paper. 'And now, the prizes for the fun and games we enjoyed so much. Excellent stuff.' Bashit nodded, looked surprised for a second and continued. 'First prize, Beating Santa. It's Mrs Hackkett.'

Philly watched her mother stand up, wearing the dress she had worn to black tie parties as long as she could remember and still fitting into it. Mrs Hackkett gave a little bow, accepted the prize gracefully and gave Philly a wink.

'And now, Pelting the Potato. It seems young Lizzie has beaten us all.'

Bashit turned round and handed a present to the embarrassed figure behind him, while a loud cheer from Mr and Mrs Hackkett followed. 'Well done, Lizzie!,' they shouted towards her.

'Which leaves us with the final prize: Who Carried the Reindeer the Best?'

President Bashit paused dramatically before he continued. 'Mrs Bushrod!'

Clapping followed, a little more subdued this time. The large woman in a dreary light beige outfit sitting next to Lieutenant Rt. Bushrod stood up and marched towards Bashit, nearly saluting him after grabbing the present from his hands and tearing the wrapping paper off, revealing the box of expensive golf balls.

'Righto everyone,' The President beamed. 'I think we can safely assume the Ladies have shown us our place. Beating us here inside, during these fun little contests.' Bashit chuckled and gave Philly an amused look. 'Which proves more than ever that us men are utterly useless inside and belong outside, where the real game is played.'

'Hear, hear.' Charles Charmers nodded, his chant followed enthusiastically by other men around him.

'Yes. Brilliant. Wonderful. A last round of applause and off to the dance floor, everyone!'

The crowd broke up and started to move towards the discotheque area. Philly waited, letting everyone pass, leaving the Bushrods to lead the way, now both seriously cross-eyed, well into their third bottle of Chardonnay and trying to catch Danny's attention who was starting up his music.

Her eyes moved towards Pru who had a dark look on her face, just like Mrs Pushet, Lizzie and the Bangers standing next to her. Philly cocked her head towards them, catching Pru's eye and walked towards her group of friends.

'Everything okay? You look as if you have swallowed a giant lemon.'

Pru whispered, 'what the hell happened just now? I sincerely think Bashit doesn't realize how condescending that speech sounded.'

'Bloody hell,' Philly mouthed back, ruefully smiling at the same time and whispering 'neither do I.' She turned her gaze to the group gathering round the dance floor and noticed the President coming towards her. She set off towards him, not wanting him to reach the others, still fuming.

'Are you up for a dance, Miss Hackkett?,' he asked kindly, the familiar amused wicked look in his eyes as he spoke again. 'I'm no Fred Astaire, but I'm sure I can hop along to the beat.' The walking stick was carefully put aside and Bashit guided Philly to the middle of the dance floor, holding on to her for support. 'Steady on, Hackkett. I realize I am ancient, but not quite old enough to allow you to lead.'

Philly nodded and started to move slowly, feeling awkward, not knowing what to say.

'Well, Miss Hackkett,' Bashit shouted over the loud music. 'Congratulations. Excellent job done. I knew I made the right decision, asking you ladies to do your thing.'

'Yes. Indeed,' Philly shouted back. 'Thank you. For letting us do what we are born to do.'

The sarcasm in her voice seemed to go unnoticed by Bashit who kept his smile on his face. 'Wonderful dinner, fun with the games and now this dance. I, we, the board, are very pleased.'

'Good show. I will pass it on to the team,' Philly said and glanced over her shoulder, sensing her mother, coming towards her, followed by Bunny.

'Ah, Philly, I think Bunny deserves a dance with the President, and your father is showing off his newly acquired skills with Lizzie. Join me outside for a breather?'

Thank God, yes, Philly thought. 'Mum. Yes. Let's do that.' She let go of the President and gently pushed him in Bunny's arms.

'Alright then. I snatched a bottle and two glasses.' Mrs Hackkett turned towards the French doors, and they stepped onto the terrace, catching their breaths feeling the night's frost hitting them.

'The first days of winter.' Mrs Hackkett wrapped her arms around her body and shivered. 'Cold, dark miserable nothingness,' she whispered to herself, gazing out over the course, taking in the view, now like an impressionist painting composed with only shades of blacks and greys. She turned around slowly, her eyes moving to her daughter and taking in the image of her. 'Philly. You do look lovely. This dress really suits you. Wear it more often.' The flimsy fabric rolled between her mother's thumb en index finger.

'Thanks.' Philly smirked. 'I had to survive on two green apples a day, for two months, to fit into it.'

'I sincerely hope that's a lie.' Mrs Hackkett frowned for a second. 'Don't overdo it. A few pounds on you wouldn't hurt. As I keep telling you.

'So you do.' The tone of Philly's voice clearly indicated she didn't want to continue on the matter.

'Fantastic party,' Mrs Hackkett changed the subject while handing a glass of wine to her daughter. 'You girls nailed it.'

'We absolutely did.' Philly finally smiled and took a sip. 'But I somehow find it difficult to enjoy the moment and relax. After Bashit's speech.' She rolled her eyes. 'Bloody hell. And bloody ignorant me, thinking we actually stood a chance, and the board would notice we might be of real added value.'

Mrs Hackkett twirled her glass in her hand, seemingly pondering on her daughter's remark. 'Indeed. And Bashit probably thinks he's done the right thing and can tick off the "involvement" box,' she replied slowly. 'But, President and his board aside, the party, excellent management, involving the staff, insights on everyone's talent, making certain to get the most out of the input, well played dear.' A knowing look went towards Philly. 'It must have inspired you girls to take this strategy further.' Mrs Hackkett sat down on the window sill and looked Philly in the eye. 'Are you ready?,' she asked carefully.

'For what?'

'To prove Bashit and his compadres wrong? That you might be able to accomplish something major, something outside, in the real world? By beating Lavender Thorneybush and her cronies? It's only two more months until the practice match, which is a test in itself. To put her in her place, break her confidence, before the real thing. And give this club something to think about.'

'I know,' Philly replied, trying to feel assured but failing, instead sitting down next to her mother and gliding towards her for support. 'Lash is now training us twice a week. If we can get off work early we sneak in another half hour.'

'Right. You might need to step up.' Mrs Hackkett nodded and pulled her daughter towards her. 'You need this win, my dear. To wake Bashit and all those men up from their winter sleep. To get some kind of support, before the real season starts.'

Philly chuckled. 'Support. Yes, that would be nice.'

'Indeed. Because, if you botch this up, you and your girls will be confined to arranging parties for the rest of your Peckers Wood life,' Mrs Hackkett said.

Philly turned away, feeling somewhat anxious, realizing her mother was right.

'And, my dear, from what I hear, you'll need all the help you can get.' She looked over her shoulder, noticing the Bangers standing behind the window and gave them a wave. 'Mrs Turner came by to pick up Lizzie the other day, and she heard that Lav's handicap has dropped dramatically since a couple of weeks. Rumour has it she hits the ball hard, and every shot is as straight as an arrow.'

Philly shivered, suddenly feeling the cold penetrate her bones. 'Good for her then,' she said sarcastically. 'Makes a change from her usual preference for hooks and draws. Must have taken some effort to get that out of her system.'

'Right. Make sure you make the most of time you have the coming weeks.' Mrs Hackkett let go and stood up. 'I'm going to have a chat with Pru, the poor thing looked as if she had drunk a bottle of poison after Bashit's speech. And I haven't seen her for ages.' She winked at Philly. 'Must be all the practicing with the young master,' she said while she saw her daughter's face cloud over.

'Didn't see you and Ben with each other much, this evening. Everything alright? You two still on the straight and narrow?'

The frostiness of the open terrace suddenly seemed to increase. Philly stared at her mother, remembering all the instances she had told her how much her father and her liked Ben and were so looking forward to their next step. A step that now bothered Philly, like an annoying ache in her groin, not only caused by the rough sex earlier in the evening. She swallowed some bile away, making her mother frown.

'I don't know, Mum. We'll see how it goes.'

'I see.' Mrs Hackkett took a closer look, making Philly turn away. 'Want to talk about it?'

'Not really.'

'Righto,' Mrs Hackkett said cautiously. 'But if you do, you know where to find me.'

'Merry Christmas, mum.'

'Merry Christmas to you too, my darling. Take your iron every day and live on greens.' Mrs Hackkett moved forward and kissed her daughter. 'And for the coming two months, remember, keep your head down.'

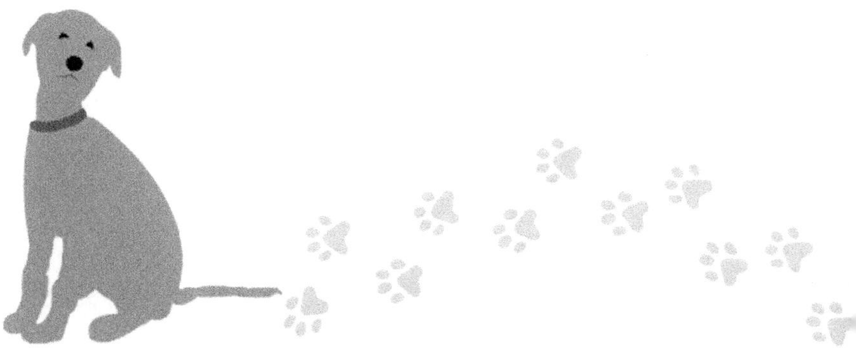

CHAPTER 46

Her mobile said February 19, ten past five. The sun would set soon, leaving the driving range too dark to properly see the yardage signs. Philly stretched, easing her aching muscles. 'God I am glad spring will start soon.' She turned to the nodding man next to her. 'These dark wet months since Christmas have just been so boring.'

'I agree.' Simon Hot stood up from the range's bench. 'But we've all used the time to our advantage.' He collected his bag and said his goodbyes, leaving her, feeling confident about the pairing strategy they discussed for the coming practice match at Goodlie. Pru and herself of course, Birdie and Bunny, Bogey and Mrs Pushet. Simon thought the physical and mental strength of the Bangers would help the more inexperienced players.

His advice had been helpful, although she hadn't seen much of him during the last six weeks. Time had raced by ever since the Christmas holiday, the last period off Philly had up till now. Christmas day was nice and quiet with her Mum and Dad, after Ben left to be with his relatives for a couple of days.

Her parents had been kind enough to include Lash in their usual Christmas Day invite for Pru. Philly smiled, thinking of the terrified look on the handsome face, finding them at the front door, a carefully wrapped box of chocolates clutched in

Lash's large hands. He had been very quiet during dinner, but had cheered up considerably after the long walk with Sniggles and her father, leaving the women to themselves. Pru was similarly silent, but she nearly cried after Mrs Hackkett assured her they really liked her new beau and that he seemed to be a lovely kind-hearted man.

The New Year started in a haze. She couldn't remember much of the party they all went to at the local pub. Ben was so drunk, he passed out in the kitchen, but Philly managed to drag herself to her bed. After their hangovers cleared the next day, they had left each other to it, Philly wanting to prepare for work and Ben needing to get a head start readying his dental practice. They hadn't seen each other much since then, with Philly working flat out and spending her precious spare time practicing all the new things Lash had been teaching them. Ben was taking on more and more patients and also wanted to be out on the course as much as he could. She had been so busy she realized suddenly she hadn't thought about him much.

She felt guilty she hadn't seen much of Pru either, but her friend was also swamped by her rising career and spending her free time with Lash. Even the Bangers seemed busier than usual, apparently gathering followers on Maggie's socials at blinding speed, growing the fortune their Granny had left them. They seemed to have an uncanny knack to feel what was about to be on people's minds. Philly shook her head. They never seized to amaze her.

She pulled her driver from her bag and grabbed the last ball in her driving range basket. Weight on the right foot, broad stance, head behind the ball, take away long, high, hips in and…'Whack!' The ball jumped and flew towards the 200-yard marker. They had practiced this shot over and over, turning it into driving competitions, trying to beat Bogey who was still by far the longest of them all.

The driver went back, and Philly pulled the cover her mother knitted over its head, making the pompom stand up. Her short irons looked dirty, worn out from the thousands of approaches they had shot under the expert eye of Lash, pushing them to do better, challenging them to try and hit the flag, teaching them how to spin the ball. Even the toughest bunker shots seemed a breeze now they all understood the drill of opening the club face and combining force with hand action.

Her mind drifted to Mrs Pushet, how the old lady had thrived during the lessons, not wanting to be outdone by her young friends, giving it everything she had in her. She had even taken to long walks, working on her stamina, taking Lizzie or the Bangers to encourage her.

And Bunny. Philly smiled to herself. She had turned out to become an amazing golfer. She even outdid the Bangers when it came to number rounds played. It was as if she spent every waking hour she could spare on the course, mostly with a besotted Roughie lagging behind her whenever Lizzie had the time to stand in at the clubhouse. Not even the fiercest gale would stop those two going out for a game.

They were ready to chop that fucking Lavatory Thorneybush into bits. All they needed to do was to get their admin on track.

Her attention was drawn to the path, hearing the sound of little feet coming towards her, followed by familiar voices. She turned round and clapped her hands, waiting for Maggie to run towards her. The little dog was followed by two identical figures, huddled deep into pink padded jackets, their long brown hair tied in flowing pony tails, jumping up and down with each synchronized step made by their pink golf shoes, causing the grey ending to the winter's day light up somehow.

'Hi, you two.' She greeted her friends and gave Maggie a cuddle. 'Glad we bumped into each other. I was wondering if you could do me a favour?'

'Absolutely,' Birdie replied. 'Just say the word.'

'The word is Lav. She asked me to get back to her on the arrangement for the match next weekend.' Philly sighed. 'But I am super busy coming week. Could you give her a ring?'

'No problem. I assure you she wants to gloat about the Saturday inspection round she arranged for us, and what we would like to have for dinner Sunday at their sublime restaurant?' Bogey winked at her sister. 'Jolly decent of her though, to let us get used to the course on Saturday before the real practice match on Sunday.'

'Definitely.' Philly nodded, glancing away from her friends. 'And she needs to know our pairing, something to do with registration in their system.'

'Right. Consider it done.' Birdie turned to her sister. 'We might go and see her and discuss this personally, what do you think, sis?'

'Excellent idea.' Bogey nodded. 'Can't wait to see the old hag again.'

The XJ Jaguar's engine rumbled as Bogey expertly navigated her through the mist of drizzle around the sharp bends leading to the motorway towards Goodlie. The white flags, now hanging limp at their poles, were hardly visible in the distance when they took the first exit. Goodlie's car park was nearly empty, and Birdie steered into the spot next to Lavender's BMW.

There wasn't any sight of the young men that had greeted them before so they locked their car and started to walk, huddled together under a large umbrella, following the path towards the large square building in front of them and turning right towards the entrance. The glass sliding doors opened, their sound breaking the silence in the reception area. The large flat screen TV showed a static image of the Goodlie logo, and the desk was empty with a notice stating the receptionist would be back soon.

'Now what do we do?' Birdie asked.

'No idea.' Bogey stepped towards the next door and peeked in. 'I think I see Lav sitting at the bar,' she whispered. 'Shall we go in?'

Birdie nodded. 'Might as well.'

The door closed behind them with a hardly audible click, and they tiptoed towards the large shiny bar, conscious of some men staring at them, as if they were a welcome distraction from the football match that was playing on another huge screen above the mock fireplace. The large space offered a view over the terrace and some of the course behind it, completely bare of trees, just a few shrubs and heather, an undulated fairway and lots of water hazards surrounding the large 18th green.

'Links my ass,' Bogey whispered to Birdie. 'As if the sea ever gets up to the greens. What a farce.'

Birdie tutted. 'And it goes round, not out and in. Farce indeed.'

They moved towards Lavender, who was sitting alone, bent forward, staring into a large glass with something orange in it, her bum sticking out the through gap in the back of the mauve velvet bar stool.

'Hi,' the Bangers said simultaneously, startling Lav who jumped and nearly knocked her drink over.

'Jesus.' Lav said, trying to compose herself, smoothing a loose strand of hair behind her right ear. 'You're early.'

Birdie frowned and checked her wrist watch. 'No. We're right on the dot.'

'Just being punctual, dear,' Bogey added. 'You said five, so five it is.'

Lav's eyebrows went up for a millisecond. 'Right. You found the bar, which here, you are actually allowed to enter. Must make you feel unsettled.' She waited for a reply, which didn't come. The two sisters just stared at her, expressionless.

Lav swallowed and continued. 'Before we get started, would you like a drink? I've ordered some sandwiches as a working supper during our meeting. Is that okay?,' she asked, nearly rhetorically.

The sisters looked at each other for a couple of moments, as if they were contemplating on what Lav was offering. 'Drink's a bit early for us, but why not?,' Bogey said. 'What are you having?'

'Campari Spritz,' Lavender replied, while she beckoned the spotty looking youth hanging at the end of the bar checking his mobile. 'We all drink it here, very much the rage.' She looked the sisters up and continued. 'I don't suppose Miss Snuggs knows how to mix a decent one? Probably never heard of it, the poor girl. You might want to enlighten her. It's Campari, prosecco and some sparkling water. Bottled, of course.'

'Gosh. Sounds rather ghastly.' Birdie crumpled her nose up. 'I can't stand prosecco. Or bottled water. Gives me heartburn.' She leaned towards the bar and checked out the offering at the back. 'I'll have a Gin & French. No ice.' She turned round at Bogey. 'What about you?'

'Same,' Bogey mumbled, looking at the menu on the bar. 'These sandwiches we're having,' she said while tapping the plasticized paper and looking at the boy mixing their drinks, 'could you cut the crusts off ours?'

'Oh, yes please.' Birdie nodded and stared at Lavender, who was gaping at them, nearly open mouthed. 'Bunny always cuts our crusts off.'

'Bunny?' Lav frowned. 'Who's Bunny?'

'Miss Snuggs of course,' Bogey said. 'Our friend. Plays in our team. Roughie's girlfriend. You know who Bunny is.'

'The bar girl?' Lav stared at the two sisters. 'You must be joking.' She was quiet for a moment, clearly needing time to take this new information in. 'She's shagging Roughie? Jesus.' Lav took a large gulp from her drink. 'He might not be God's gift to women, but that bar girl? Surely, he could do better than her?'

The sisters exchanged a dark look. 'He's God's gift to her, and she to him,' Birdie said pointedly, the sharp edge to her voice now sounding like a newly cut razor. 'We are all quite thrilled for both of them.'

'And she plays on your team?,' Lav rambled on, not taking any notice of what Birdie was saying, as if she was talking to herself. 'You must be fucking desperate.' She returned her attention to Birdie and Bogey, both with a dark look in their large brown eyes. 'So what are you bringing here next week?' Lav bent over towards the two women next to her. 'Skinny bitch Princess Spoilt, Morticia Adams, a demented old bag and Bunny the bar girl. Christ Almighty.' A pointed index finger with a dark purple gel covered nail pointed at them. 'And remember, no dogs allowed. So that nasty piece of scruff stays at home.'

'Right.' Bogey stood up from her stool and checked her watch. 'Let's get this show on the road.' She stared at Birdie who was nodding profusely. 'We need to make a dinner reservation at eight, can't keep the boys waiting.' She beamed at Lav. 'Just tell us the rest of the drill, and we will make certain we will be here next week with all the details, right on time, like lean, mean golfing machines.'

CHAPTER 47

Philly had already collected their gear from the locker room the evening before and was eagerly waiting in front of the flat, waiting for her partner. She leaned on her bag and glanced up the High Street, its shops' usually bright facades shrouded in semi darkness. Clouds were rolling high up in the sky, leaving gaps for the last stars and the first light of day. The weather forecast was promising, a mild and dry weekend was at their doorstep. A little red robin was perched on a bench, popping its chest out and singing its sweet and mellow song, making Philly feel calm and relaxed.

The Volvo rolled towards her and stopped. The car door was pushed open, revealing Pru smiling at her, waiting for her to hop in. 'Birdie just texted me,' she said, turning the car and navigating through the narrow street. 'Apparently Mrs Pushet was nowhere to be found at home, bit of a panic, but Lizzie found her at the club scoffing left-over shepherd's pie in the larder when she came in for work this morning.'

'Oh my God. Is she alright?' Philly gasped, feeling her heart skip a beat.

Pru nodded. 'Yes. Totally fine. Had her clubs ready, bag packed, standing in the car park, waiting for the Bangers to collect her. Who are now on a mercy dash from Mrs Pushet's house to Peckers Wood.' She signalled and turned into the narrow road leading up to the long lane to Roughie's Victorian country house. 'Some kind of miscommunication, apparently.'

They turned right through the iron gates, rattled over a sheep grid, along a sweeping lane dividing the lawns leading up to the ochre-coloured building covered in ivy. Bunny was waiting there, the grand entrance with its stairs leading up to a plateau making her look tiny while she stared at her mobile and talked, a large icebox hanging from her arm.

'Is that her snack? She needs to cut down on those.' Pru giggled. 'I thought she was getting a little matronly when I watched her play just a while ago.'

'Must turn Roughie on though. He's into Matrons, remember?' Philly pulled a face.

'That's great, Lizzie. So you're alright? Yes, wish you were here too.' Bunny started loading her gear into Pru's car. 'Mrs Pushet safe and sound, on her way? Good. Bye now. Yes. Thank you. Just let me know if you need anything.'

'Everything okay?,' Philly asked, noticing the worried expression on Bunny's face. 'What's in the ice box?'

'I packed us tea,' Bunny said. 'Bogey asked me, and I thought, you know, just in case the food is really as awful as they say it is.' She climbed into the back seat and nestled herself next to the stack of golf bags, neatly arranged on top of each other. 'And just checked if Lizzie is okay. She wishes us good luck, and your father sends his regards.'

'My father?,' Philly asked, looking over her shoulder.

Bunny nodded. 'Yes. He's helping out today until Mrs Rough takes over the evening shift. So Lizzie and your dad can practice a little on the driving range.'

Pru looked sideways and caught Philly's surprised expression. 'Lizzie must be doing really well,' she said. 'Your Mum mentioned the other day that she comes over quite a lot.' She circled round the mirror pond and picked up speed.

Philly nodded. 'That's right. And they enjoy having her. Said it's like having a granddaughter. And it gets me off the hook now and then.'

'Lucky Lizzie, spending time at your house,' Pru said, while turning the wheel towards the junction leading up towards Goodlie, noticing an old Jaguar coming up behind her. 'The Bangers are on our tail. With Mrs Pushet in the back.'

'Excellent.' Philly crossed her arms over her chest. 'All aboard and ready to check out this course. So we can smash those Goodlie bitches tomorrow.'

Philly looked over the 18th. In all honesty, the course wasn't as bad as the Bangers had led them to believe. A friendly lad had assisted them, showing them where to leave their bags in the locker room and explaining how to get to the first. The first hole had been easy, just a straight drive and a seven iron to the far end of the undulated green. The rest of the course was slightly more challenging, with lots of steep bunkers and slow hard greens that were slightly bulgy instead of hollow, making it hard to stop the ball. The fairway grass was higher than they were used to, but nothing they couldn't manage. And the wind, not hindered by trees and mature shrubs, caused a challenge from time to time.

But she had managed to get to the 18th in 73. She eyed the last hole's curve around a large water hazard, bending from left to right. From the tee the par 5 looked intimidating, trailing along the dark lake, with six bunkers in play for the first and second shot, leading towards a slightly elevated green in front of the clubhouse's terrace. A drive, slightly faded, would cut it. Then a five wood to carry the bunkers, leaving a ¾ pitching wedge to the green. Her eyes moved to the card she was holding. All the distances were pencilled in, with the little numbers for the clubs she used and how many putts she had needed. If she could pull this one off, she would come in at 78.

'You're up.' Birdie signalled at Bunny to take the tee. 'After that fantastic two you just made.'

Bunny nodded and pulled her driver out, briefly concentrated on her line and took her stance, eyes firmly locked on her ball all through her short back swing and impact, followed by a long release. The ball rocketed forward, carried the first bunker and landed in perfect position for the next shot.

'Great swing, Bunns,' Birdie said while she turned to Philly. 'You or me?,' she asked.

'You go,' Philly answered. 'Try and better that. I dare you.'

Birdie's ball landed next to Bunny's, rolling just a bit further. Philly smiled and pushed her tee into the hard soil. Her driver felt better than ever, lying loose in her palm, ready to smash the dimples. She hardly felt the impact as she went through the ball, her tee peg flying behind her feet. It felt so good, watching the little dot fly in the sky and landing on the spot she had envisioned.

'Four more to go,' she said as she picked up her bag and slid her arms through the loops. 'And well played, both of you.'

Birdie glanced at her. 'We're not there yet, Captain. It ain't over till it's over.'

The five wood that followed was as good as ever, leaving the final short shot she had in her mind. She waited for Bunny and Birdie to approach, both leaving a 10-foot distance to the pin. Her eyes narrowed and she concentrated, keeping her eyes on the grass behind the ball during her practice swing. 100 yards to go. Easy.

She pushed her feet down and clenched her core, short swing, arms straight, and *'Hi! Philly!'* rang over the course towards her.

Lav's cry pierced her brain just as her hips wanted to move forward. Her hands should have gone down reaching the ball, and her eyes were supposed to have seen a divot fly into the air. But instead she felt the hardness of the ball shoot into her fingers, making them numb instantly. Birdie shouted *'Fore!'* at the top of her voice, as Philly's ball flew towards the terrace, not even touching the green, narrowly missing the two ducked women standing at the edge, and disappearing in the dense foliage against the wall leading up to the stairs.

'Holy cow.' Philly heard Birdie gasp and giggle at the same time. 'You nearly assassinated Varilla.'

'O dear.' Bunny let go of her club and started running towards the two women, still crouched down. 'Mrs Van Dycke! Are you all right?,' she yelled.

'O my God,' Philly groaned. 'And my ball is probably unplayable.' She glanced at Birdie who was trying to compose herself. 'We'd better go and see how they are.' She shook her head and started walking. 'Fucking bitch. Yelling in my back swing.'

Bunny had hoisted Varilla back on her feet, now helping her to brush grass from her jacket and was apologizing profusely. Philly reached them and held her hand out to Lav, waiting for her to reach out but refusing it flat out, shooting a dark look at Birdie, who was walking towards the green to pick the other balls up.

'I sincerely hope this was the only flier you hurtled towards any of our members,' Lav said, clearly not intending to sound funny or ironic. 'I invited you here to play this round, in my name. So your bad shot will be on me. You do grasp that concept, do you?'

'Yes. Of course.' Philly nodded, feeling a distinct urge to attack Lav, claw her eyes out and feed them to the crows that were gathering on the fairway behind them. 'I am so sorry. Please accept my apologies.' Her attention was drawn to the stairs, seeing Bogey, Mrs Pushet and Pru running off them, looking worried.

Lav spun round to Bunny and Varilla, snatching Bunny's hand and tearing it off Varilla's back side. 'Stop that, you idiot, you're making things worse.'

'No, Lav, really, she's not. She's only trying to…,' Varilla protested, but was cut off by Lav's curt 'Shut up!'

Birdie stepped forward, put her arm around Bunny and thrust her other hand towards the shell-shocked looking woman in front of her. 'Hi, Varilla,' she said warmly while she nodded towards the others to follow her lead. 'It's really nice to see you again. Thank God our Lady Captain can't aim. She might have finished off Lav forever. Hope you're alright.'

Varilla nodded, clearly lost for words. 'Yes. Thank you. I'm fine,' she whispered.

'Good.' Bogey came towards her, put her arm around her and lead her up the stairs. 'Let's finish that drink we were having before Lav so rudely dragged you away. I was really enjoying our chat about the ways of Goodlie and its members.' Her smile flashed at the others. 'Fascinating stuff.'

CHAPTER 48

The Goodlie restaurant was empty except for their party. The last remaining member of staff was stacking glasses behind the bar, looking fed up. The mock fire had been shut off, and the screen above it was dark.

"Well, ladies, we need to be off." Bogey nodded to Varilla next to her and stood up from the dining table. 'Mrs Pushet is dead tired, and we have a long day ahead of us tomorrow.'

Bogey pushed the chair back and walked up to Lav, sitting next to Mrs Pushet, who had her head bent forward, snoring softly, obviously fast asleep. 'Thank you for a lovely supper, Lav. The lentil pie was truly something else,' she said while she tugged at Mrs Pushet, who woke up and looked round, obviously not having a clue on where she was.

'Yes. Divine.' Birdie quickly put her mobile away, joined her sister and flashed Lav a smile. 'And I'm looking forward to tomorrow so much, can't wait to play this splendid course again.' She reached over and pecked Lav on the cheek. 'You and Varilla are playing Philly and Pru, right?'

'Yes,' Lav said haughtily. 'Captains play captains.' She looked at Varilla before addressing Philly, who was talking to one of the other Goodlie ladies, not taking notice of Lav's nasal voice. 'And if my sidekick holds it together for once, it should be a walk-over.' A distinct waft of Limoncello drifted from Lav's mouth, making Birdie turn away quickly.

'Right. I'm sure she will,' Birdie replied with a sweet smile on her face. 'But you never know with this game, now do you?' She turned to Varilla, who looked miserable. 'Could you help us with Mrs Pushet and lead us to the Ladies' room so we can get our stuff?'

'Sure.' Varilla sighed and stood up, her short stocky body bent forward, showing the creases where her tweed skirt had crumpled under her bum. She took the back stairs towards the basement, followed by the three women she used to know so well. She was strangely relieved by their unexpected friendliness towards her during drinks and dinner, being really interested in how she was getting on at Goodlie and what her new teammates were like. She had actually felt safe being with them, their bubbly presence made her feel relaxed instead of being on guard all the time.

They passed the reception area, now dark and abandoned, towards the Ladies' room. She reached for the door, pushed it, waiting for the lights to switch on automatically to illuminate the bold colours of the spotless area.

'I'm starving.' The silence was broken by Mrs Pushet, who flew towards the ice box Bunny had left and opened it with a quick tug. 'That lentil pie was utterly inedible. I wouldn't even feed it to the pigs.' Her hand dived in and pulled out stacks of sandwiches, thick with layers of cuts of cheese and a box filled with home-made raspberry tart. 'And that tired tinned fruit for pudding, goodness gracious me.' Mrs Pushet held out a sandwich towards Varilla. 'Here, old girl. You look as if you could do with some comfort. There's enough for everyone.'

Varilla couldn't help herself. She snatched the food, and her long teeth sunk into the bread, the cheese's rich taste combined with the slightly salty taste of the home-made dough making her mouth water. The smell and the texture immediately brought her back to the fifth tee at Peckers Wood, the spot where she consistently used to open the package Miss Snuggs always made for her as a snack during her rounds. She sighed deeply, not aware of the Bangers staring at her intently and started to chew slowly, savouring the moment. Absolute heaven.

Birdie suddenly touched her, making her flinch.

'Varilla,' Birdie said kindly. 'It was really nice seeing you again.' She squeezed Varilla's arm, an apologetic look on her face. 'Listen. I know we've had our differences, but we think it's rather a shame you left us.'

Varilla's mouth fell open, revealing the last of the sandwich stuck on her tongue.

'And don't let Lav get to you too much. You are so much the better player.'

'And person,' Bogey added, nodding towards her. 'Lav's a bitch, and she doesn't deserve you.'

Varilla's jaw dropped further, not believing what she had just heard, but instantly feeling the pain Lav's constant flak had caused her.

'We're off now.' Bogey's voice snapped her back to the present. The Banger sisters suddenly looked as if they were eager to go with Birdie guiding Mrs Pushet towards the door, and Bogey handing her a raspberry tart.

'See you tomorrow, and good luck keeping Lav on the straight and narrow.' The Bangers gave a quick wave, stepped out and closed the door behind them.

The emptiness of the room caused Varilla to suddenly feel abandoned. She looked round, bit into a chunk of tart, swallowed hard and sighed. *What a nightmare this had turned out to be*, she thought to herself, feeling a sudden tear well up. She wiped it away and got up, exiting the stuffy room and walking along the bleak basement corridor up to the back entrance. She longed for the fresh air, following the footpath towards the locker room where she could sit down outside and take some time to pull herself together.

Her limbs tensed while she went over the events of the awkward evening. Lav with that fucking smug look on her face, bragging about all the wonderful things she had accomplished being the Lady Captain. Banging on, at the top of her annoying voice, how the whole committee at Goodlie was super thrilled with all her improvements. How she had transformed the Ladies Team, despite the fact that poor Varilla had obviously found it so challenging to fit in and show some added value, but was now working so dapper towards at least some progress. And slyly implying that it was all due to her, as if the rest of team didn't exist. Or matter.

Her face went from cold to burning hot. Varilla felt vicarious shame, thinking of Philly and Pru exchanging knowing looks, with every sentence Lav uttered while she looked round, making sure her faithful team members were staring at her in awe, obviously oblivious to the hidden insults in Lav's comments. Varilla shook her head. Stupid girls. With their identical streaked bobs, Botox foreheads and pearly white capped teeth. The things they do for money, she whispered to herself.

Her recollection was interrupted by a strange noise coming from the tack room. She crept towards it, slowly, making sure her steps went unnoticed. The four voices she made out, two male and two female, sounded familiar somehow. Varilla inhaled and pricked up her ears.

'*Don't stick that bloody big torch in my face,*' one female voice hissed.

A darker sound, obviously a man. '*Bend over some more. I can't find it.*'

'*Yes, I can feel it now.*' The other female hiss became more insistent. '*Push it towards me. More, more!*'

The other male's sound, soft, but clearly tense. '*Grab it, put it in, drill it deep. Deeper. If you don't drill deeper, we will never get it off.*'

Varilla exhaled, feeling her heart race in her throat. What in heaven's name was going on? She concentrated again, now hearing one woman whisper.

'Now it's too tight. That won't do the trick. Add some more lube. Yes, that's much better. Now rub it, slowly, not too fast.'

'Put the rubbers on, we need to be careful!' A short silence, before the first voice sounded again. *'Now twist, turn and yank. Harder!'*

'I can feel it sliding in now, yes, that feels absolutely perfect.' The second woman whispering again, but now obviously more satisfied.

'Are you sure you want to go all the way?' The sound of the male voices was getting more familiar.

'Yes. I am bloody sure.' The woman again, but now in a louder whisper. *'We can easily do it another eight times before my legs go numb.'*

'Show me your torch again. I need to see the shaft's tip before I can start blowing.'

'I don't want to overdo it. Grip more to the right, this is too much.'

'Right, be careful. Nice and slow.'

'God, my knees are giving up on me. I need to stop. Bobby, can you take over?'

'No prob old boy. Come on, darling, four more to go. Just grab the shaft and start easing it in.'

'Bobby? Bloody hell.' Varilla slid forward carefully, hid behind the trash can in front of the tack room and peeked in. Yes, it was quite clear. Birdie Banger, her sister, Bobby Long and Henry Sweet. All over each other, at it in the bloody tack room. She shook her head, clearly confused. Why here? Why not go home and shag those men in a comfortable bed? Was this some kinky new fetish she hadn't heard about yet?

Varilla crept back carefully, feeling excited and dirty at the same time, making certain she wasn't seen or heard, leaving them to finish whatever they started. She wondered if Philly knew about this particular foursome. She could go back to the Ladies' room and enlighten her since they were probably just on their way there. She contemplated for a second on how this piece of information would set off Philly and Pru. *No, Varilla, go home.* She told herself. Let it go. None of your business, really. The last thing you want to do is confront them, fucking up their budding sympathy towards you. She pulled herself away and tiptoed back to the car park, noticing Mrs Pushet waiting in the Banger's Jag giving her a friendly wave, looking surprisingly chipper.

CHAPTER 49

The mobile's blue light shone at her. 5th of March, 8:30. What a damn horror, oversleeping on the most important day of her life. Lav picked up speed, now nearly running towards the locker room, a panic rising in her stomach. She had slept right through the alarm, waking up feeling dizzy, not knowing what day it was before realizing she was due on the first tee in half an hour. Her whole schedule fucked up by a useless alarm clock, her having to leave Varilla to welcome the others, hand out the scoring cards and tee times and make sure everyone could hit a few shots at the driving range before the match. That was her job. She was the Lady Captain, not that hopeless Van Dycke.

She stopped, feeling something odd and noticing her locker wasn't closed properly. Damn that good-for-nothing Varilla for not paying attention yesterday, she said to herself while she yanked her bag out and started checking for balls and tees. At least those were in order.

'Pull yourself together, Lav!,' she said out loud. 'I'm the Captain! I have the lowest handicap and will bloody well show those miserable Peckers Wood misfits how this game is played!'

She straightened her back and pulled her chin up, settling down the nervous flutter she was feeling. This was going to be the match of her life; she could feel it in every fibre of her being. She was going to chomp those two incompetent women into bits, inhaling their shameful sweaty smell when they would have to concede at the 15th knowing they hadn't a chance in hell against her. Not now and certainly not during the real match.

She could nearly feel that medal in her palm. Those emaciated idiots Philly and Pru wouldn't be able to ignore her supremacy any longer. Lav bent down to zip up her bag, clenched her teeth and marched through the locker room door towards the first tee where they all were, the Peckers Wood team and her own girls, huddled together waiting for her. She walked past them, greeting them curtly with her eyes firmly fixed on the first fairway, her head held high, pushing her card in her back pocket and looking over her shoulder. The team had followed her, and she heard some hushed whispers. Those moronic Banger sisters were lagging behind as usual, for some reason in fits of giggles.

'Hey, Lav. You made it.' She turned round towards the soft kind voice. Philly had suddenly appeared behind her with a smile on her face, putting her arm over her shoulder, the touch making her flinch.

'We need to be off. What shall we do? Toss a coin or throw a tee?,' Philly asked.

'Throw a tee. And Varilla drives the uneven holes,' Lav answered, nodding towards Varilla who hurriedly brought a tee over. The peg went up in the air and landed at Lav's feet, indicating Goodlie had the honour of choosing who was driving first.

'Have a good one,' Philly and Pru said simultaneously.

She indicated to Varilla to take the tee with a flick of her right hand, noticing her teammate's hands shaking a little gripping her driver while checking the point she was going aim at. The ball flew from her club in a perfect flight.

'Great drive, Varilla.' Pru nodded towards her.

She noticed Varilla turning round and looking at her, obviously waiting for some kind of compliment, needy as the silly woman was. Lav snorted and made way for Philly, who took her stance and hit an equally perfect shot.

Lav pushed her trolley and trotted towards their ball in the middle of the fairway. 150 yards straight to the pin, she made out on her distance watch. A breeze. A slow 5 iron would do the trick. Her favourite approach.

She pulled the club from her bag with a confident tug, somehow noticing it didn't feel as it always did. A bit heavier than usual somehow. Lav shrugged and wiggled the club in her hands. Must be her imagination, the new set still took some getting used to, she thought, while peering towards the flag. She stepped behind the ball, pushed her heels downwards, concentrated on the ball and took her club away. Her back swing felt perfect, downward rhythm just as it should be, her head still, eyes on the divot, before following the ball's flight towards the pin.

'I think you hooked it out of bounds,' Pru shouted toward her. 'You might want to ask Varilla to hit a provisional just to be on the safe side.' Lav looked towards the left of the course in amazement. *What the fuck had happened? Had she fired her hips too late? Had she been leaning towards the right?* She turned towards Varilla who was standing behind her with a petrified look on her face. 'What in hell's name are you doing, standing there, you twat?,' Lav yelled. 'You know I can't stand people in line with my back swing. Get the fuck away!'

The provisional dropped at her feet, and she felt eyes pricking in her back while she stepped aside for Varilla, who hit a wonderful shot, leaving the ball five yards from the pin. She glanced towards the first tee, seeing the others watching her, except for the Banger sisters who were facing the car park.

Philly raised her eyebrows at Pru, not daring to speak, witnessing Lav's drive shoot left, straight into the damp grass of the 4th, just in front of the massive bunker blocking out the view towards the green, some 250 yards further. Another drive massively hooked, just like the one on the second, where the ball hit a post and shot to the right, ending up in the middle of the artificial lake. And the little approach Varilla had left Lav on the third wasn't much better, Philly thought, recollecting how it had bounced to the left, violently hitting the hump leading to the green. What in hell's name was wrong with her?

Pru's drive had again been fine, lying safely left of the brook with just 130 yards left for Philly to carry to the green. Lav threw her driver in her bag and stomped off, followed by Philly, an embarrassed-looking Varilla running after them, nearly in tears.

'That lie's awful,' Philly whispered to Pru, catching up with them, staring at the minuscule patch of white staring at them through the dense grass.

'We might want to deem it unplayable,' Varilla suggested, sounding meek.

Lav sighed dramatically, put her hands on her hips and stamped her left foot. 'No, of course not, you moron.' The last two words were uttered in a low whisper, but loud enough for Philly and Pru to hear before turning away, horrified. 'Just play the damn shot.'

A pitching wedge was yanked from Varilla's bag and thrown towards her. She caught it just in time and bent forward to inspect the ball again. Her feet came down behind the ball carefully, and the club came up, face open, the inside of Varilla's right wrist bent towards the target. The club face shot at the ball with huge force, making it nestle itself even more firmly in its tight hollow. Varilla stared at it and turned to Lav, looking devastated. 'Sorry.'

'Jesus.' Lav pulled her club and shoved Varilla away. 'You killed it. You need to hit through it, not at it.' Her feet trampled the grass, she addressed and wiggled a couple of times before swinging back. The club came down in perfect rhythm to her hips and swooshed through the grass. The ball never moved.

Lav's face remained expressionless, repeating her set-up.

Pru gasped. 'That wasn't a practice swing,' she said, staring at Philly who was shaking her head.

'Never mind.' Philly shrugged. 'She'll never get it out. We'll be 4 up in a jiffy.'

The second swoosh followed, again leaving the ball motionless. Lav straightened herself, checking if Philly was watching her and turned puce. The club came up again, now in front of her face, clutched tightly, and it came down with a thump, causing the ball to disappear fully into the ground, while Lav was whimpering '*miserable shit fucking ball*' while she fell on her knees to claw the abused Titleist out of the trampled grass with her carefully manicured hands.

Philly walked back from the car park towards the eighteenth green, Pru's car keys rattling in her trouser pocket. Lav had run off home, hardly taking time to shake Philly's hand on the tenth. The round had been awkward, to say the least. Lav got more aggressive with every shot she made, making the hooks get worse and worse, hurtling verbal abuse after every miss hit.

She stared over the water hazards overseeing the course, the fading light casting shadows over the humps and hollows. Pru was walking from the 18th and taking the short cut towards the green, Varilla at her side. At the far end of the course she made out Mrs Pushet's tiny figure, pushing her trolley, followed by one of the sleek-haired bobs. Her mobile buzzed, telling her Pru had won, and that the Bangers were one up, that they were safe to assume the practice match was in the bag, and it might be nice if they bought the Goodlie team a drink and some snack before they went home to Peckers Wood.

Why not, Philly thought. Now that Lavatory had fucked off home, they might even have a good time.

CHAPTER 50

'They did *what?*' President Bashit's draw dropped.

'Took Mrs Thornbush's clubs apart and adjusted the heads. Or fiddled at something that buggered them.' Roughie blushed and stared at the ink pot on the President's desk. 'Apparently she hooked every shot she made.' He cleared his throat. 'Sir.'

'And she never caught on? How she suddenly became a hooker overnight?' The President's voice was no more than a wheeze.

'No,' Roughie said. 'Not as far as we know.'

Bashit fell back in his chair. 'Who saw her play?'

'Well. Let me see. Mrs Pushet, Prudence Love, Philly Hackkett, the Banger sisters, Bunny, the Goodlie Ladies team and the six flights at the adjoining holes of course.' Roughie swallowed. 'Sir.'

'Good Lord.'

'Indeed. So, we can safely assume all golfers in the northern hemisphere are in the loop by now. That Miss Thorneybush is indeed a hooker, that is. Not on what caused it.'

'I see.' Bashit grinned slyly. 'My word, Roughie, I would have given my right arm to see Lav Thorneybush leave the course with that colossal loss under her belt. But I must admit I do feel sorry for poor old Varilla Van Dycke.' He coughed, trying and failing to suppress the laughter that was now bellowing out of him. 'Miserable Thorneybush having to come in losing 10&8. Twice. Oh my God. This will have me tickled for weeks.' Bashit sat up, trying to regain control of himself again. 'I would like to speak to Miss Hackkett personally and alone, Roughie. Please set it up for tomorrow.'

'Yes Sir.'

Philly felt sick. No matter how much she swallowed, the big lump in her throat wouldn't budge. Her pounding heart got louder with each beat as Ben's sharp words chased round in her brain.

He had burst into the flat after his practice match, finding her alone after saying goodbye to the team. She was still wallowing in the joy the victory at Goodlie had given her and the compliment from President Bashit that had followed and excitedly had told him all about how she and Pru had won 10&8, how Bunny and Birdie had managed to scrape a win with one up and Bogey and Mrs Pushet had given it their best squaring their game.

The singles were equally worth mentioning. Her win was the largest, beating Lav 10&8 again and all the others winning by a small margin, except for Mrs Pushet, who only lost with one down. Bashit had actually said they had made him and Peckers Wood proud. And hearing him say that, had made her, and the whole team feel so good, all of them literary glowing.

But Ben had managed to kill her elation very quickly, leaving her feeling icy cold, having exclaimed loud and clear how she had made his position extremely difficult when he found out what the Bangers had done after hearing Bobby and Henri boasting about their prank to Roughie at the club. They managed to shut the two up, but it was virtually impossible for him and Roughie to keep it from Bashit. He thought her section's behaviour towards Lav was hugely unbecoming any Peckers Wood member and was disappointed in her and hoped she understood that he, as the Club Captain could be held responsible for this fuckup. Did she realize that this was cheating?

Cheating. The word rushed through her brain again, making her cringe with shame.

Ben hadn't stopped at that. He had droned on, how she should not assume that he would go and speak to Bashit on how to handle this debacle. That he left it up to her to sort things out. That she should, for once, put her ego aside and try to act according to the club's gentleman's culture. If she knew what that meant. And that he was off for nine holes with her father tomorrow morning and would not mention the whole shambles to him. To protect her. But that he expected her to come up with a solution and was going to bed. Alone. The last sound she heard was the door slamming behind him.

Her mobile buzzed. Philly groaned, reading the text message.

Bashit wants to see you, 7 pm tomorrow. RR.

Bloody hell, she said out loud. What a fucking disaster. Ben absolutely livid, and Bashit will expel us all. No boyfriend, no team, no medal. Silly Philly Fanta and her team can only win by cheating. And that would of course mean no Peckers Wood anymore. Ever again. The last thought made her gasp and want to vomit. She pulled herself up, tried to breathe normally and calm down. Just go to bed, she said to herself. There's nothing to be salvaged now.

The bedroom was dark, and she didn't bother to turn the light on. Her right hand followed the contour of the bed, and she fell down on it, pulling the cold, crumpled duvet over her head and her knees towards her chest, clutching them with both arms. The distant church bell that she heard every hour during the long night sounded omnious.

CHAPTER 51

The wheels of her car skidded as she sped towards the entrance of the club, the shrill sound of her surround system popping up, suddenly making her headache worse and sending an icy shiver from her toes to her hair seeing the familiar name.

Ben.

Shit.

Time to face the music. Philly pushed the button on her steering wheel, picking up the dark sound of Ben's voice, flying around her car. She listened in silence, not daring to interrupt, feeling tears well up.

'I know, I feel terrible as well. We shouldn't fight.' She yanked the mobile out of its cradle as she turned her car into her parking space. 'I will. Of course, I will. I totally understand and consider it done. See you later.'

She turned off the engine and sat back, going over the Ben's request and feeling confused. That was a weird change of tune. He hadn't sounded angry at all anymore. Not even remotely. Just said she would have to be a good sport and make sure Lav would be cured from her annoying hook as soon as possible. And that he wished her good luck for the meeting with Bashit, that she shouldn't be stressed out about it too much.

She stepped out of her car, noticing a beige lump emerge from the behind the old oak tree at the far end of the garbage bins. 'Philly!' It called out. She froze, seeing it coming towards her. 'It's me!' Roughie's face appeared in the faded light of the early evening. 'I need to talk to you about the Lav fitting fiasco.'

'Oh Lord.' Philly groaned and put her hands over her face. 'What a fuckup. I am so sorry.' Her hands came down and she looked at Roughie with a pleading look in her eyes. 'And now Bashit will cut me to pieces, and throw us all out for cheating.'

'Well.' Roughie whispered. 'I don't know. He just told me he wanted to talk to you in private.' He moved towards to her. 'Off the record, Philly, Bashit had hysterics when he heard what had happened.' Roughie's voice came close to her ear, hushed. 'I've never seen him laugh so much.'

Philly raised her eye brows. 'Excuse me?,' she asked slowly, not believing what she had just heard. 'Bashit laughed?'

'He absolutely loathes the Thorneybushes, you see,' Roughie explained. 'And, frankly, so do I. Ghastly bunch. But, as they gave us astronomical amounts of money, we had to put up with them.'

'You're joking,' Philly whispered, feeling a bit of life returning to her body. 'Are you telling me they bought Lav's membership?'

Roughie looked over his shoulder, as if he was expecting the Thorneybushes to pounce on them. 'Yes. And have always threatened to make that public. That even our values and traditions, here at Peckers Wood, can't resist the temptation of money.' Roughie paused for a second and looked round again. 'Can you imagine how absolutely horrific if would be if that came out?,' Roughie said, while his face crumpled up in disgust. 'So Bashit had no choice as to summon you, but he'll give you a mild talking to, sort of as an official reprimand. So that, if the Thorneybushes ever found out what the Bangers did and what the club's reaction was, he wouldn't have to lie about him not having slapped you girls on the wrist.' Roughie's voice turned even more conspiratorially. 'I think he would have left it if the situation with the Thorneybushes wasn't so potentially tricky.'

Philly nodded, suddenly feeling a lot better, grasping what this all meant. 'I see. I think.'

'Knew you would. But, Philly, I do hope you, and the Bangers understand it would be far better if Lav stays kept in the dark forever. Just like everyone else. Keep this our little secret.' Roughie reached out and patted her upper arm. 'Bashit expects you to steer this in the right direction discreetly and fix this,' he said pulling away from her.

'Gosh. Thanks Roughie.' Philly felt as if tons of concrete were lifted from her shoulders.

'It's fine. That's what friends are for. I'll take you through my entrance.'

Roughie took her arm firmly, as if he was offering support. He was enveloped by the comforting smell of talcum powder and soap, reminding Philly of her father, making her feel a bit more secure as they walked towards the clubhouse together in silence until the large carved door opened with the turn of Roughie's key. Philly stepped in, noticing Lizzie hoovering the main hallway and gave her a wave.

'I just finished the President's office.' Lizzie called out. 'He's in a good mood. We've solved the *Times* crossword together.'

Philly nodded, feeling her stomach flutter as she walked towards the familiar study. The door was ajar, and she pushed it carefully, finding the President sitting behind his desk, reading a tattered *Golf Illustrated* copy and waving at her simultaneously.

'Come in, Miss Hackkett.' The shrewd eyes followed her movement without a single blink as she approached the desk, the butterflies in her stomach racing up and down. 'Do sit down.' Bashit sat back and kept on examining Philly, making her feel even more uncomfortable.

'So, Miss Hackkett. *10*. And. *8*.' The numbers were pronounced deliberately, with emphasis on the T's. Bashit paused for a moment, took his glasses off and rested his amused look on Philly. 'What an *extraordinary* achievement.'

'Yes. Indeed it is,' Philly said slowly, narrowing her eyes.

'I've taken considerable time to check our records, but it seems you have broken one of them,' the President beamed. 'No-one in our history has ever won an official match play game with that margin.' A pause followed, the interval clearly not meant for interruption. 'So. Congratulations Miss Hackkett. Please, enlighten me, us, what is your secret? Did you experience, what shall I say, some kind of divine intervention?' The President's last two words came out in a snort of laughter. 'Something to do with our celestial twins, perhaps?' Bashit was now shaking, clearly having hysterics. 'Peckers Wood Angels bringing comfort in your hour of need?,' he howled, slapping his hand on his knee.

Philly stared at the heaving old man behind the large desk, not knowing what to say or do.

'Miss Thorneybush must have been very put out. And poor Mrs Van Dycke, having to endure her eternal wrath.' The President shook his head in mock misery. 'The little devils. But I'm sure they meant well.'

A silence followed, clearly not meant for Philly to speak.

'You never suspected anything?'

Philly shook her head. 'No,' she said carefully. 'Nor did the others.'

'O my word. They move in mysterious ways.' Another roar followed.

'Please, President Bashit, it isn't funny,' Philly said, raising her voice, trying to drown out the stream of chuckles.

'No.' Bashit choked. 'It's not.' He tried to regain his posture but lost it again. 'It's bloody hilarious!,' he cried out.

'And yes, poor Varilla indeed.' Philly tried again. 'She played one hell of a game, and all she got was constant flak from that bitch Lav. We all felt really sorry for her.'

President Bashit sat up straight, cleared his throat and composed himself. 'I can imagine,' he said gravely. 'Being

Goodlie's star player and getting no acknowledgment for it whatsoever. She must have felt some malicious delight watching Thorneybush's agony.'

'I hope so.' Philly's voice had turned into a whisper.

'Righto, Miss Hackkett.' His face turned serious. 'How are you going to see to it that Miss Thorneybush will regain her true game? Get things straight again, slice hooks so to speak.'

'I'll come up with something, sir.'

'Let me help you. Let's have a think.' Bashit closed his eyes and rubbed his temples, adding drama to the gesture by humming loudly. 'You need to talk to the naughty Bangers. They were the ones who sabotaged Thorneybush's golf clubs, assisted by their beaus: Bobby the clever club fitter and Henri the handyman. If they can sabotage, they should certainly be able to de-sabotage.'

'Absolutely.' Philly nodded. 'Of course. We just need to figure out how they can they get her hands on Lav's clubs. They can hardly steal them out of her locker and bring them over to Bobby's workshop.'

Bashit grabbed his walking stick hand hoisted himself up. 'I'll leave you to sort that out, discretely. I want this to remain between us two, Miss Hackkett. Just keep me in the loop so we're on the same page.' He checked his watch. 'Well. I need to prepare for my next meeting. Men's competition and medal, clock's ticking. Only a few more weeks left. Tick tock, I told young Chipperfield, Miss Hackkett, tick tock.' His hand waved towards the door. 'You might need to reconsider your strategy, my dear. Taking all things into consideration it wasn't the walkover you assumed it was.' A finger wagged at Philly. 'So good luck with keeping your fair angels on the straight and narrow. Would be nice to see you come home with a genuine win.'

Philly stood up, squared her shoulders and cleared her throat. 'Thank you, Mr President.' She said clearly, holding her chin up, trying to look in control. 'We will bring that medal home, fair and square, you can count on us.'

Philly turned on her heel and closed the heavy door behind her, leaning towards it for a moment, contemplating what her next step should be.

They clearly meant well. Bashit's words swam in her brain, making her feel unscrewed for a moment. She closed her eyes, and the image of the Bangers popped up, sitting at Goodlie's bar, looking absolutely nonplussed and angelically innocent every time Lav's humiliation was finely pointed out. This of course happened more than once, loudly by Pru and herself, and by several embarrassed hushed whispers from the Goodlie team. Philly felt herself start to shake, as uncontrollable laughter streamed from her insides, trying to keep it silent by pushing her hands against her mouth. She breathed in deeply and exhaled, thinking about her dear childhood friends and coming up with an idea on how to punish them.

Bloody Bangers. Who would have thought they had it in them. But she had never loved them more, she thought as she started walking towards the back door and the Ladies' room outside.

CHAPTER 52

'Are you alright, Philly?,' Birdie asked, watching Philly step inside the Ladies' room and sit down at her desk. 'You look rather glum.'

'Glum? You think I look glum? Well, I suppose I have every reason to look fucking glum,' Philly said while she looked her friends in the eye, 'considering our dear President rang me and bit my ass off this evening. Lav has filed an official complaint about our behaviour during the recap of the match at drinks.'

'O.M.G. No. Were we really that bad?,' Bogey asked, her eyes large, making her look near virtuous. 'But in all honesty, it wasn't very civil of you, Philly. Mentioning her terrible score over and over again.'

'No, not civil at all,' Birdie added. 'And we felt quite sorry for poor old Gorilla. One wouldn't wish that on one's worst enemy.'

'Ah.' Philly turned towards the two sisters lying on the sofa, playing with Maggie, clearly using the little dog as a decoy. 'You felt sorry for her. How bloody compassionate of you.'

'No need to swear, Philly.' Birdie rolled her eyes. 'Language, language.'

'Listen you two. Assume crash position.' Philly raised her voice. 'I do not wish to go down in the history books as the

Lady Captain who received an official warning due to insulting an unusual hooker in the Goodlie team. So get your backsides towards Bobby Long and prepare him for another adjustment.'

The Bangers exchanged a nervous glance. 'What in earth are you on about, Philly?,' Bogey asked in a trembling voice.

'You bloody well know what I am on about.' Philly kept glaring at the two women huddled on the old sofa, now moving towards each other for comfort. 'What do you have me for, some daft twit?'

The sound of soft sobbing carried through the Ladies' room. Birdie was crouched forward, large drops fell, and Maggie was trying to squeeze herself on her lap. '*We meant well.*' The words came out in a wail.

Philly turned away, trying not to laugh. She pulled a straight face, getting into character again, making sure she sounded convincing.

'I'm sure you did.' Her own voice reminded her of her headmistress. 'Now get out, talk to that boyfriend of yours, and get it done.' She got up, held the door open and stepped outside. 'Out!,' she hissed, pointing towards the car park.

The Bangers squeezed past her and started running, Maggie at their heel, her tail between her legs, not daring to look back.

Philly's shoulders slumped, and she leaned towards a garbage bin. 'Poor things', she murmured, closing her eyes for a moment, letting laughter ripple out of her and cool down. She concentrated for a second, hearing a soft groaning coming from behind the row of bins, near the kitchen door. She pulled her mobile from her pocket and shone its flash light towards the spot she thought it was coming from, lighting up a hump that was moving up and down slightly, the motion aligned to the rhythm of the panting. A petite, hunched figure appeared in the light, sitting down, head down on pulled up knees, showing a pair of old-fashioned spiked brogues at the feet sticking out, covered in yellow withered grass.

'Mrs Pushet?' Philly moved towards the hunched woman, slowly.

The panting sound turned into loud sobs. 'I'm so sorry,' the hunched figure blubbered, 'to have to fail you.'

'Why are you outside?' Philly sat down next to the sobbing woman and pulled her towards her. 'It's bitter out here. You'll freeze to death.'

'And?' Mrs Pushet's tear -stricken face turned towards Philly. 'Who cares? I'm just a useless old biddy better off being put out of my misery.' The tears kept on coming, falling from Mrs Pushet's chin onto her already wet knees. 'What was I thinking, assuming I could contribute something to the Peckers Wood ladies, although in my heart I knew I could never play 36 holes.' She moved a little, her face distorted, clearly feeling very uncomfortable. 'Good grief, my back hurts. And my poor old knees. All my joints are sore.'

Mrs Pushet stared at Philly, her small eyes bright red. 'And all I ever wanted was to help you with your team, Philly. Just hoping to accomplish something, to contribute something meaningful. But I just can't do 36 holes.' The old lady's wrinkled little hands rushed through her silver curls. 'I saw my GP. He wasn't pleased. This is a young woman's job. You need to find a replacement, dear. Before I drop dead in the middle of the real match.'

Philly slumped down, realizing the impact of what she was hearing. 'Oh, Mrs Pushet. I'm so sorry. I never realized it took so much out of you.'

'Out of what?' A female voice suddenly appeared behind them. 'What are you two doing outside? It's so cold the pet store is selling penguins.' Pru came towards them, pulling her coat against her shivering body. 'What's going on?'

'Mrs Pushet says she can't play the Goodlie match. It's too much for her.' Philly breathed, tugging the sobbing old lady closer towards her and feeling a panic creeping up on her. 'That we need to find someone younger.'

'O bugger,' Pru whispered while she slumped down beside the other two women. 'Bloody hell.' She turned and stared at Philly. 'Now what do we do?'

The silence that followed seemed endless, none of them knowing what to say or how to act before Philly finally spoke. 'I suppose this is it. We're dead. No team. No competition. No nothing,' she groaned and rushed her fingers through her hair. 'We might as well throw the towel in.' Philly's hands pulled her head back, and she raised her eyes towards the black sky. 'What kind of section are we? Not even enough women to hold a team together, let alone become anything meaningful.'

Mrs Pushet started crying again, her sobs getting louder with each sniff. 'I am so sorry, my darlings. So terribly sorry.'

Pru pulled herself up and shook her head. 'No, Mrs Pushet. You gave us all you had in you. You made it possible we could even get started.'

'Absolutely.' Philly suddenly jumped up, realizing how she might have offended her old friend. 'You've been our life saver, and we still have a little life in us yet. We just need to be creative.' She reached towards Mrs Pushet and grabbed her hand. 'Come on. Let's get you warmed up with a stiff drink.' She pulled the little old lady up and brushed the dirt from her moist trousers. 'But we'll need to figure something out very quickly. The match is only a couple of weeks away.'

Mrs Pushet sniffed and nodded. 'Maybe young Lizzie could take over?,' she suggested innocently, her eyes unusually large and droopy, suddenly resembling a begging basset hound.

CHAPTER 53

They left Mrs Pushet in the clubhouse kitchen with Bunny, the old lady looking quite chirpy again after downing two glasses of cognac. 'I'll look after her.' Bunny had put a comfortable chair near the old range and settled Mrs Pushet down with a stash of sandwiches. 'Roughie will join us here after team practice. He can take over when we go out for our lesson.' She shooed them out. 'Go and see Lash and talk about Lizzie.'

The familiar path to the caddy shack seemed longer than normal. Philly followed Pru along the narrow bit leading behind the fourteenth, shielding her face from the icy wind blowing towards them over the long fairway and slowing them down.

'Lash told the greenkeepers to put the winter greens into play again. Hope the Idles of March won't ruin our competition.' Pru bent over and unlocked the little gate in front of the shack. 'Imagine the gales blowing over Goodlie with hardly a tree to slow them down.' She fumbled with her keys and pushed the front door open, letting the smell of violets mixed with burning oak drift towards them.

A far cry from the dry rot she inhaled the last time she was here, Philly thought to herself, stepping into the kitchen and looking round in amazement. The little cottage had undergone a magic transformation. Clearly Pru had put her own stamp on their love nest. Everything looked spotless but cozy at the same time, with soft colours on the walls and matching cushions in the comfortable looking chairs facing the little fire place. Pru's books were aligned at both sides, making the room look organized and symmetrical. The kitchen table, perched in the middle, invited her to sit down and feel homely, watching her friend rummage and get supper ready, its aroma enhancing the warm atmosphere even more.

'It looks lovely, Pru. You've made it into a home.'

'Thanks. You hadn't seen it yet, had you? I've been here quite a while now.'

Philly suddenly felt guilty. Her best friend, starting a new life, obviously very happy with a man at last, and she hadn't even bothered to come and see them. 'You're right. I'm sorry. I've been far too busy with work, Ben, the Christmas party, the competition.' A pause followed. 'With myself, I realize now.' Philly groaned and put her head in her hands. 'I haven't even seen my parents since Christmas.'

'They're fine. I spoke to your dad the other day.' Pru put a mug of black coffee in front of her friend. 'Having a whale of a time with Lizzie who can now play golf, understands poetry, beats everyone at chess and helps Bashit with his daily crossword.'

'Jesus.' Philly smiled ruefully. 'What excitement for a 16-year-old. Isn't she supposed to have raunchy adolescent fun with some boyfriend instead of hanging around Bashit and my dad? A bit odd, don't you think?'

'She's gay, Philly. So no boyfriend.' Pru stood up to get another coffee. 'Didn't you know?'

'No.' Philly stared at Pru. 'You do?'

'Of course. We all do.' Pru smiled. 'Not that it matters. But it's hard for her to meet girls, living in this village, going to a small school, not much going on.' She pulled a tin of biscuits from a cupboard and offered one to Philly who refused. 'So another reason to get more women in, especially young ones. It might help our Lizzie to get a life. Although,' Pru mused, 'she seems to like old people. She adores Mrs Pushet. And Bashit. And your dad, come to think of it.'

'Right.' Philly shook her head. 'Anything else I haven't picked up? Bushrod hasn't turned into an enlightened feminist, has he?'

'Not a chance.'

The door opened, and Lash carefully ducked to avoid knocking his head on the small door. He grabbed Pru by her belt, pulling her towards him and kissing her hard on the lips. 'Missed you, Love.'

'Missed you too.' Philly saw Pru respond, very physically, very naturally, unlike she had ever see her do before. This arrangement was clearly working out for her.

'Does Bashit know, you two living together here, that you've done up the place?,' Philly asked.

'No,' Pru replied.

'Of course he does. He just pretends not to.' Lash smiled, let go of Pru and sat down at the table. 'I watched him last week, peeking in. He passes here every day on his walk. Or his buggy ride.'

'I see.' Philly smiled. 'Well, well. Good old Bashit.'

Pru opened the fridge, put a large plate of cold cuts in front of Lash as well as half a loaf from the bread bin. 'We need to talk to you about our team. Before we start this afternoon's lesson.' She poured a beer and put it in front of Lash. 'Mrs Pushet bailed out. Thirty-six holes is proving too much for her.'

'Is it now?' Lash reached out for Pru, pulled her on his lap and fed her a chunk of meat which she swallowed down eagerly.

It made Philly concentrate on her friend, suddenly noticing she looked a little more rounded, making her more feminine. Her gaze followed Lash's hand, trailing along Pru's waist, pulling her closer against him, making them look very together, united somehow. She pulled her eyes away. 'And she suggested Lizzie should step in,' She finally said. 'What do you think?'

Lash put both his arms around Pru while chewing slowly, clearly pondering on his reply. He swallowed and moved forward again. 'I think, what choice do you have? And to be honest, this was to be expected. Seventy-five-year-old ladies shouldn't have to play 36 holes. It's inhumane.'

Pru glanced at Philly, who looked uncomfortable. 'But Mrs Pushet insisted. We didn't pressure her.'

'Mrs Pushet knew you had no alternative for the short term, but this obviously was always her plan,' Lash said. 'Why do you think she spent so much time with Lizzie? Who was actually the one who made Lizzie feel at home here? Made sure she did her school chores and get her grades up? So her mother would allow her to stay? And play?'

Philly swallowed audibly, grasping what was going on all of a sudden. 'Oh dear. You're right. And I had no idea.'

Lash grinned. 'And your parents were part of the scheme, of course.'

'I beg your pardon?' Philly stared at the large man opposite her. 'They knew?'

'Your father told me he knew Lizzie was a golfer the first time she hit a shot in your folk's back yard. He desperately wants her on the team, but he didn't want to interfere. You're the Lady Captain, not him, at least that's what he said.'

'Good Lord.' Philly slumped down, trying to take in what she just heard.

'Right.' Pru finished a piece of bread, turned towards the kitchen sink and started the stove. 'So no choice, and Lizzie's a keen golfer. That makes the decision rather easy. Lizzie it is. She'll be thrilled.'

'Just a second.' Philly joined Pru, ready to help. 'She's super young. Can she deal with the pressure of match play?'

Lash cackled. 'Are you serious? The eldest daughter to a divorced working mum, an estranged father, a witch of a stepmother who hates her, being the only girl in a rugger team, finding out she's gay and dealing with it, practically running this joint by herself when Bunny's off with you guys, getting top grades and managing to play single figure in four months' time? I think she can handle a couple of spoiled overprivileged Goodlie bitches.'

CHAPTER 54

To: secretary@peckerswood.co.uk
From: bangers@home.co.uk
cc: President@peckerswood.co.uk; phackkett@home.co.uk;
Bcc: vvdycke@home.co.uk

17th of March 2023

Subject: consider hooks sliced

Dear Secretary, darling Roughie

Just a little note from one of your besties explaining why we found it necessary to drag poor Bobby and Lash Johnsson to GHASTLY Goodlie this morning, but dear Bobby and I had QUITE a tiff, because he was absolutely certain I was exaggerating about the ABYSMAL state of the fairways. He just wanted to check for himself to be certain I wasn't in some kind of hysterical fit. (Next time we will have to invite the Goodlie girls to play at PW, so they understand what playing a real course is all about.)

But anyhoo, quelle surprise, we bumped into dear old Lav Thorneybush practicing her irons at the driving range. The POOR WOMAN obviously was struggling, do you know she bought her new clubs at Blue Hippo Golf Inc.? You are aware we are not their biggest fan and just wanted to check if she hadn't been fobbed off with totally INADEQUATE gear and guess what? Bobby took one look at those clubs and told darling Lav they were total misfit for a strong girl her. He even took lengthy time to feel Lav's biceps and core muscles to be absolutely certain. So CLEVER, how he immediately realized what was wrong. Wonderful, isn't he?

And he did a fantastic job adjusting those clubs, right there and then, fixed the problem in a flash. And Lash Johnsson, while holding Lav tight from behind against his own body, going through motion with her, he had Lav back to her whopping fine swing in a jiffy. Isn't it a MIRACLE?

Love you,
Boogs

PS: Lash Johnsson did suggest it might have been a mental problem. That Lav might be a tad obsessed with getting it down, which is understandable, when one finds out one is basically a hooker.

PPS: We also ran into Mrs Van Dycke which was really thrilling. Had a long chat about how her game was so superior to Lav's. Has Philly told you she played so well during the Thorneybush hooking fiasco? Jolly clever to hold it together under such dire circumstances, don't you agree?

PPS: Must be everything V picked up during her time at PW. We thought she might want to have a game with us here, after the competition, to cheer her up. That's okay with you, surely?

PPPS: We will invite her to lunch too, the poor thing looks ever so thin these days, like one of those bulimic Swedish supermodels. Must be the atrocious food she has to endure at her club. It really is horrendous. Even poor old Mags turned her nose up for the bite of fish cake we kept for her.

CHAPTER 55

Lizzie had looked so incredibly happy, absolutely lost for words, holding her mother's hand at the Hackkett's kitchen table while Mrs Turner had dried her eyes after a little cry, mumbling on how she couldn't believe a daughter of hers was chosen to represent Peckers Wood Golf Club. Mr Hackkett had given Lizzie a lucky pitchfork, to keep in her pocket as a good luck charm.

Not that she needed it. Philly and Pru had taken her out on a game, just after their meeting with Lash. The young girl played a super round, not bothered at all by the pressure of being grilled on how to behave on the course or in a team. When she made her last putt for 81 at the 18th, Philly had popped the question which left her openmouthed and thrilled until her face turned desperate. She stumbled that she couldn't leave the bar unattended during a Saturday, which was taken care of through a quick text message to Bunny, who said she would deal with it with Mrs Rough who had just come home from her latest trip to the Bahamas. Even the last hurdle of membership was quickly fixed by the Bangers who paid Roughie a visit and convinced Philly that all was rickety-boo, and that there was nothing to worry about. Nobody was keeping Lizzie from coming with them to Goodlie.

Philly took a deep breath, letting the unexpected warm spring air rush through her body and started walking towards the driving range for her final appointment with Simon Hot and Lash before the big match tomorrow.

The two men didn't notice her coming up the path. Philly stopped, watching Simon taking Lash Johnsson's broad shoulders into his slim hands and helping him turn slowly towards a perfect back swing. Lash's short sleeves curled up in the backward motion, showing the tattoo on his muscled upper arms while Hot moved his left hand to the head of the young man in front of him and held it still, gently pushing it a little downwards.

Philly swallowed, noticing Lash's tight shirt pop out from his trouser belt, exposing a tanned piece of skin, when his arms pulled sideways in his back swing again. She turned away and concentrated on Hot, embarrassed by the tingle in her stomach.

He looked the same as ever. Not a hair out of place, immaculate white polo-necked top and navy trousers. A pale pink cotton sweater draped loosely around his shoulders. The leather belt around his slim waist matching the clean golf shoes. His manicured hands guiding Lash back to a setup.

She started walking again and cleared her throat. 'Simon? Lash? Could you spare me a moment?'

The two men stopped their exercise, and Simon Hot came towards her. 'Miss Hackkett! How lovely to see you. Of course we can. Please.' His hand guided her towards the wooden bench. 'Sit down. Can I get you anything? I have some tea in the thermos.'

Philly shook her head. 'No, thank you.' She sat down carefully and inspected her hands. 'I just need your advice on pairing. For tomorrow.'

'I see.' Simon Hot smiled. 'You're not thinking of slicing the record breaking 10 & 8 pair up, are you?'

Lash chuckled. 'That might turn out to be the wrong angle and hook.'

'Ha bloody ha. Hilarious, you two.' Philly closed her eyes and put her head in her hands. 'Please don't make fun of me. It's a nightmare,' she groaned. 'Pru and I might have not made it to the 18th, and I am sure the whole men's section is having a field day making fun of us, the living proof that women on golf courses are disaster waiting to happen.' A pleading look went towards the two men. 'I need help,' Philly said pleadingly.

Simon pulled himself together and sat back. 'Let's take some time to evaluate this game. Let's start with the singles, how did that go?'

'Survived them. By the skin of our teeth.'

'Right.' Lash nodded. 'They had the advantage of playing their home course,' he remarked. 'Next time you will know the ways of Goodlie much better. So no worries there.'

'Yes.' Philly nodded. 'That's certainly true. We just need to be a bit sharper.'

'Absolutely. Room for improvement staring you in the face,' Simon said. 'Listen, great pairing is all about matching the right characters together. Who motivates the other to the max? Which pair makes one plus one be three? You know your teammates like nobody else, Miss Hackkett. You've played golf with them.'

Philly batted her eyelids, trying to think.

'Put Pru and Bunny together, Philly,' Lash said. 'Pru's structure and Bunny's natural feel for the ball should work like a charm.'

'Yes,' Simon continued. 'And you play with Lizzie. Your experience mixed with her length and youthful confidence, you will knock Lav and Varilla for six. And Lizzie looks up to you, she will give it everything she has in her.'

'Okay. Didn't look at it that way. But I think I can follow your line of thought.' Philly nodded slowly. 'Although that leaves the Bangers to play together. How in earth is that going to work?'

Lash stood up and stared over the range for a second. 'They might annoy the living daylights out of you sometimes, but what they share together is a very deep, very profound kind of commitment. Imagine what that could do for them, paired together in a competition.'

Philly stared at the two men for a few seconds before thanking them and nearly running alongside the clubhouse towards the putting green between the first and the 18th. She found who she was looking for, striking balls towards the little poles.

'Ah, there you are, you two. Birdie, I need a word with you. About your training schedule. Will see you in the Ladies' room in 5 minutes.'

CHAPTER 56

'What was that all about?' Bogey looked at her sister watching Philly walk towards the far end of the clubhouse. 'What have you done?,' she asked in a threatening voice.

'Nothing.' Birdie answered, annoyed. 'Not that I'm aware of.'

Bogey faced her sister. 'Did you skip lessons?'

'No.' Birdie shook her head.

'You've done all your exercises? Like Lash told you?'

Birdie pouted. 'No.' Her voice sounded naughty sweet, like liquid caramel.

Bogey sighed wearily. 'She'll give you a bollocking for that. I saw her talking to Lash the other day, and she was taking notes.'

'Shit.'

'You bet your sorry ass shit. You'd better get going.'

'I'm not a sorry ass.'

'Oh, just fuck off and face the music.'

'I hate you.'

'No, you don't.'

The tears wouldn't stop. No matter how hard she tried, they just kept on coming. Philly passed over a paper towel and poured a glass of water from the cold tap in the Ladies' room little kitchen unit.

'You don't realize what you are putting me through.'

'I do know what I am doing to you. It's for your own good. You need to confront your fears, and get out of your comfort zone. The only way to that is doing whatever you fear the most. You know you have been putting this off with every sorry lame excuse that you could come up with.' Philly handed the glass of water over. 'To tell you the truth, I am fed up. And so are the other girls.

'My life is over,' Birdie moaned.

'No, it's not, and you know it,' Philly said sternly. 'You will give it everything you've got. Let me perfectly clear on what I expect. We will win this competition.' The paper towel passed hands. 'Fair and square. *Not* by pulling stunts.'

Birdie groaned. 'We said sorry.'

'Bashit is still deeply disappointed in you,' Philly said sternly, looking away, trying to keep it together, ignoring her discomfort, knowing she was doing the right thing. 'So, you two are going to prove him wrong. Get your act together, and snap out of that sodding inferiority complex.'

Birdie stood up and wiped the last tears from her face. 'Well. If that's all, I'll be off now.' Philly nodded and tried to hide her smile by walking to the door and opening it.

'No. It's not all,' Philly said sternly. 'See you and your sister in half an hour. On the first tee. Fully loaded.'

Birdie sniffed, closed the door behind her and ran back to the putting green, finding her sister on the bench, who was eating a jam doughnut.

'My God.' Bogey said. 'You look ghastly. Whatever is the matter?'

'Fucking Philly is what is the matter.' Birdie started sobbing again. 'I'm desperate. And so will you after you know what she has demanded now.' The tears were flowing down again. 'She paired us together for the big match. And she wants to play us in half an hour. Together. As a pair. As practice.'

A long silence followed, while Birdie checked her sister's expression through her tears.

'Bloody hell,' Bogey whispered.

'Damn right, bloody hell,' Birdie hissed. 'What are we supposed to do now?'

'Did you tell her why we've never done this?'

'Of course I did,' Birdie snorted. 'I'm not dim. But she showed absolutely no mercy. She really is a cruel bitch, you know.'

'Good grief.'

'O Lord, I feel sick just thinking about it. I can't do it, Boogs, just can't.' Birdie made gagging noises. 'I think I need to throw up.'

'We could try it.' Bogey put her hand on her sister's arm and squeezed it gently. 'Just once. And see how we go.'

'But I will fail you miserably.' Birdie sobbed. 'And you will feel annoyed and frustrated at being unable to show it. You won't love me anymore.'

'Yes, I might get frustrated and annoyed. But I will always love you, you know that.' Bogey squeezed her sister's arm a little harder.

'But you are so much better at it then I am,' Birdie said in a small voice. 'It looks so easy when you do it. Like it just comes naturally.'

Bogey nodded. 'I suppose so. But you are good at other things.'

'Like what?,' Birdie asked.

Bogey shrugged. 'I dunno, loads of stuff.'

'LIKE WHAT?'

'You make Sweety happy, for one thing. That's an accomplishment. And you're good at finding those sorry companies we invest in. To make them less sorry and make us money.'

'Suppose so.' Birdie nodded.

Bogey took her sister's hand. 'Now. There is a first time for everything. We can do this. You can do this. We have been through worse, remember? Just keep your head down and your swing short. And remember to release. We will be fine. You will be fine.'

'You see!,' Birdie hissed at her sister. 'You are nagging me already. Please do not nag me. I want to vom.'

'I promise I will not nag you. If you won't whine, I won't nag. Here, finish my doughnut and get your bag.' Bogey stood up.

'Nag, nag, nag.' Birdie's eyes rolled upwards. 'I want my own jam doughnut. This one has your spit on it.'

'Whine, whine, whine. I'll spit on you directly if you're not careful. And you're driving the first.'

Mrs Pushet pulled her glasses off and turned to her young friend sitting at the table in the Ladies' room. 'I think you've solved this one,' she said, shutting the math book. 'Another A in the bag.'

'Thanks, Mrs Pushet.' Lizzie smiled at her, confidently. 'Sorry I was a bit distracted. I'm really excited for tomorrow.' She pulled her fingers through her hair and pulled a face. 'And a little nervous, to be honest. What if I fuck up?'

'Armageddon, the Apocalypse, the end of now.' Mrs Pushet made dramatic gestures, waving her arms around her. 'We all vaporize and become demons, haunting the Peckers Wood men forever.' She moved towards Lizzie and gave her a cuddle. 'Firstly, you won't fuck up, you'll be fine. And secondly, as lame as it may seem, it is just a game, Lizzie.'

'Yeah right,' Lizzie mumbled. 'But I have to prove myself to Philly, the love of my life, remember.'

'Aha!' Mrs Pushet let go and pointed a finger at her. 'That's right. And it will help you play the best game ever. As been proven today, during a daring experiment involving undying, death-defying love between women!'

'Excuse me?' Lizzie looked at Mrs Pushet with big eyes, stood up from the table and sat down on the sofa in the Ladies' room.

'You heard me,' Mrs Pushet replied while she lighted an ancient-looking fag. 'Two girls got what was coming during this afternoon's game.'

'Who?,' Lizzie asked.

'Philly wanted some testing for the foursomes. She forced the Bangers into pairing against herself and Pru.'

'O my God.' Lizzie put her hand over her mouth before speaking again. 'Were they slaughtered?,' She asked.

Mrs Pushet giggled and nearly choked on a drag. 'Slaughtered, butchered and cut up alive.'

'O dear. Are they alright?,' Lizzie asked as she poured the last of her Coke in a glass.

'The sisters are fine. They've been in the pub or an hour. Plastered by now, I should think. They came straight in from the 5th. 5&4.'

'Oh no,' Lizzie groaned. 'That's awful. How humiliating. Poor, poor girls.'

'Yes. Indeed. Poor, poor Philly and Pru.' Mrs Pushet took a puff and inhaled deeply.

Lizzie eyed her old friend and looked confused. 'Excuse me?,' she said.

'You heard me.' Mrs Pushet nodded. 'Turns out the sisters shredded them. Buried them alive. Pru told me it was quite an eerie experience. They turned up on the first tee, knocked the ball on in two and birdied. Word has it they never exchanged a single word between them, never left the straight and narrow and sank every putt within five yards, five holes in a row.'

'Wow. Really?' Lizzie pulled a packet of crisps from the box on the table.

'Lash was bloody brilliant if you ask me. He went over all our progress reports and came to conclusions and recommendations, resulting in a devious and obvious scheme, as it turns out. You know how devoted the sisters are to each other. How they cannot stand anything or anyone hurting the one or the other? That if you throw one at them you can expect it hurling back at you?'

'I do,' Lizzie answered. 'Everyone does. Realizing what they have done to the long-suffering Lav.'

'Exactly.' Mrs Pushet nodded. 'And that is precisely why they've never wanted to do this. If outsiders cause hurt, they can team up together and get back at whoever is responsible at full force. But what if you make a mess when you are already teamed up?'

'Not sure,' Lizzie said.

'Bogey doesn't want to hurt her sister's feelings, and Birdie doesn't want to disappoint Bogey. We all know what it's like, although not even being sisters. Imagine how strong that feeling is for them?'

Lizzie nodded slowly. 'I felt more concentrated and focused when I practiced with Lash.' She paused for a second. 'Wow.' She sat down, the unopened packet still in her hand. 'Philly is really clever. Birdie would rather have died than to disappoint her sister.'

'And they pulled their usual trick, of course.' Mrs Pushet giggled.

'What do you mean?' Lizzie asked.

'Hurled Philly's ploy right back at her by chopping her up,' Mrs Pushet said, with a big grin on her face. 'Poor Captain. They could have given her one hole, to be fair.'

'Hell hath no fury like a woman scorned.'

Mrs Pushet nodded. 'Two women scorned, as it turns out.'

CHAPTER 57

To: secretary@peckerswood.co.uk
From: bangers@home.co.uk
Subject: reminder, admin

17th of April 2023

Dear Secretary, darling Roughie,

Just a little note to kindly remind you we still haven't received the copy of Bunny's invoice for her admission fee we asked you about last week.

Do you remember, us explaining to you Philly put us in charge of handling the admin side, for the correct registration of membership at PW, of all our team mates, for our competition? That, it seemed only fair to let Lizzie pay the same as Bunny? As they are both staff and it would be best to save them from embarrassment, if they ever discussed their fees with each other?

So, if you do find the invoice and the confirmation of payment, please send it to us by return mail asap. We only have a couple of hours to find the appropriate funds for Lizzie, as we can hardly expect she pays for her fee herself, on the miserable wages Bushrod pays her.

Love you,
Bird & Bog

PS: If you are too busy, just let us know, we could give Bushrod a ring tonight and explain what we need. He is the Treasurer, after all.

PPS: Maybe it's a good idea if you rang us tonight first, before we approach Bushrod. So we can have a chat again on Bunny's secondary terms of employment.

CHAPTER 58

Ben gave Philly a quick kiss on his way out. 'Will speak to you tonight,' he whispered in her ear, 'after we come home with the win.' He turned and left, walking quickly towards Roughie's Land Rover waiting for him in front of the flat. The early morning pale moon hid behind dark clouds, shrouding the street in darkness.

She stared at the disappearing car. She had wished him good luck, to which he had responded they didn't need it. He hadn't returned the well-wishing, and Philly suddenly realized her match hadn't been a topic of conversation at all.

She let out a deep sigh, wishing she felt as confident as Ben did. She had a rough night, feeling anxious and annoyed at the same time, not being able to ignore Ben's steady snoring. He fell into bed and was out like a light in a few seconds, with the comforting thought he and his team were basically playing for bacon and beans today as they had won every match with a large margin so far. Bashit was, like the whole club, extremely happy with Ben's accomplishments and Simon's level of teaching. At least that was what the monthly newsletter said, before ending the long article wishing the men's premier team good luck in bringing the medal home.

She turned and hugged herself, taking in the mess Ben had

left. A half-eaten sandwich in the sink, a pair of socks hanging on her favourite blue lampshade, a wet towel strewn over her bed. His overnight bag sat next to it, half-empty, with crumpled clothes in it.

The church clock chimed. 6 a.m. Too early for Goodlie, but she had plenty of time to stop off at Peckers Wood to collect her papers, maybe even for a coffee in the Ladies' room. She jumped up and down a couple of times, trying to get her blood pumping.

Yes. Game on. Her fighting spirit was starting to pulse through her veins.

It was only three steps from the bedroom to the little bathroom, and she switched on the shower, letting the warm water run over her body before turning the tap to stone cold, the icy flow making her feel alive and tingly. Her golfing kit was already laid out. Sports bra, socks, underpants, headband. Her winning polo necked shirt. Her most comfortable slacks. All set. A quick scrub and she would be good to go. Just half an hour before she would reach Peckers Wood and set off towards victory with her friends.

She found her way without being conscious of it, her car nearly driving by itself. A fox crossed the road just as she turned towards the Peckers wood gate, and she braked hard, making sure it could jump into the dark hedge unscathed. It stopped before disappearing, the golden sly eyes staring at her in the headlights unblinkingly for a second, reminding her of Lav before slithering away through the dense foliage.

That bitch would certainly crawl today. The thought of Lavender dragging herself down the fairway face down on all fours made Philly chuckle and eager to get going. She pushed her clutch and put the car in gear, rolled through the gates and picked up speed in the lane leading towards the car park.

The day was breaking, and the first morning song of birds

suddenly appeared as she stepped out of her car and faltered for a moment, enjoying the peace and solitude. Spring was definitely at their doorstep with the promise of fresh new greenery and much-needed sunshine for the greens and fairways to gobble up. The Bangers' Jag was in its usual place, pointing towards the exit, ready for a quick departure. She passed it and parked her car in her space, right next to the Ladies' room and got out, noticing the door was slightly open.

She stepped inside, and the desk came into view, neat and tidy, pencils arranged, the notebook in its place and the drawers closed. Her fingertips stroked the tattered wood and moved towards the framed picture Bashit gave her, making her feel more confident. She had done it. Formed a team ready to play the all-important match. The old plastic desk light made a buzzing sound as the lightbulb lit up, a few flickers like lightning bolts, before giving a steady flow of yellow light.

She reached in her pocket and grabbed the piece of paper she had been doodling on during the long sleepless night. She stared at it. Her name. There it was. Loud and clear. At the top of the list. It was nearly official now.

Philly Hackkett, Peckers Wood.
Winning Captain in the hood.
And the loser, who is she?
Fucking, filthy cow Lavatory.

Her hands held her face and moved towards the back of her head. She breathed in deeply, noticing the soft sound of little feet, tapping towards her. Two little paws appeared on her shin, and she reached down, pulled Maggie towards her face, breathed in her smell and let the soft tongue lick her ear. Philly pushed her nose towards the little dog's prickly coat, holding her tightly against her. 'I love you, my sausage. We will do you proud.' Maggie gave one final lick and jumped off her lap, winking at Philly before curling up in her basket, a deep sigh escaping her with one ear folded over her eye.

The welcome to Goodlie had been awkward, to say the least. No-one was there to greet them, not in the car park or the lobby. Philly waited in line at the large desk and announced them, feeling strung, expecting Lav to pop out from out of somewhere. The receptionist had given them tokens for the driving range and keys for the lockers in the Ladies' room. Lav and her team were having a coffee in the restaurant, the girl said if they needed anything, they should come to reception, and she would sort them out.

'Right,' Philly said, looking through the glass pane wall in front of the restaurant, noticing Varilla leave a table and come towards them, looking sheepish.

'Hi Varilla.' The Bangers stepped forward and hugged her tightly, causing Varilla to gasp for breath. 'So good to see you again. So thrilling, this match.'

'Yes. It is,' Varilla finally managed to croak after she released herself. Her hands straightened her green jersey, and she cleared her throat. 'Lav's off to the putting green with the girls. I'll sort out the admin and show you the Ladies' room. Follow me.'

The room was the same as before. Spotless, tidy and lacking any kind of warmth. A few pillows were carefully placed on the modern white leather sofa, looking as if they had been inflated with a pressure pump.

Philly broke the awkward silence. 'Let's put our gear away and get cracking then.' She passed her papers to Varilla who started to tap on an iPad from behind the large empty desk.

P. Hackkett 6.8

P. Love 7.5

B. Banger (1) 7.5

B. Banger (2) 7.6

B. Snuggs 8.9
L. Turner 9.5

Philly watched Varilla's expression while she typed, secretly enjoying the other woman's eyebrows going up and down, revealing worry, registering the names and handicaps. Their hard work had paid off. All players under 10. Just as she strove for.

'All sorted,' Varilla said finally. 'Pairs noted, ready to go. Just one more thing.' She reached into her pocket and took six slips of paper out and handed them out to everyone. 'Some add-ons to the local rules. Please memorize them.'

Dear girls,

Kind reminder; no practice swings on tees and no weeing in the bushes. There are perfectly adequate loos on the 8th and the 14th.

Start with foursomes, Captains first, tee off 8:30.

Lunch 12:30 sharp.

Singles start 13:15, Captains last.

3 foursomes, 6 singles; 2 points for a win, 1 point for evens.

After the match drinks and formal dinner. Dresses, tights. Cost at actual consumption.

The field between the third and the fourth is out of bounds. Sand leading to the 10th green is part of the course.

BR Miss Thorneybush, Captain

'Right.' Philly looked round her group, who were staring at the slip of paper. 'Any questions before we go?'

'Are we allowed to poo in the bushes?,' Birdie asked innocently, while Bogey snickered.

'Don't be so bloody disgusting, goodness gracious me,' Pru said, clearly repulsed. She glanced at Varilla, expecting an angry face, but was surprised by a hunched figure, failing to hide a giggle.

‘We’ve got half an hour. I want to hit some balls.’ Philly gathered herself and stepped towards the door. ‘Lead the way, Varilla.’

They took the back stairway, leading towards the large storage area where the buggies were being cleaned by some young lads. Varilla pushed a button, and a large sliding door clicked into action, rolling itself backwards, revealing a patch of concrete and a small pathway to the shed where they left their bags earlier. They followed the sign to the driving range, noticing Lav passing buckets filled with balls to the group of women behind her, all dressed the same way in green jumpers under smart checkered green and gold sleeveless jackets and white slacks with matching gold visors stuck firmly on their foreheads. They looked identical again, each with the same streaked blond bobs and matching lipsticks.

‘What’s next?,’ Birdie whispered to Bogey. ‘Green jackets? Fucking hell.’

Lav looked up, her bright coral lips drawn into a downwards line, contempt shining from her beady eyes while she let them slide over Philly. ‘So you didn’t get the memo then?,’ she asked rhetorically. ‘On competition attire? Matching?’ The wave of her finger made the others gaze at each other, feeling awkwardly aware of their erratically put together outfits.

‘Hello, Lav.’ Philly managed to ignore the condescending remark and stuck her hand out. ‘So good to be here again and really looking forward to the match.’

Lav shook her hand, looking away the moment their palms met. ‘You’ll want to hit some shots then, I suppose.’ She pointed towards the dispensing machine. ‘Go ahead. You get 10 each.’

‘We won’t need more to beat you lot.’ Pru snatched a bucket and stomped off to fill it, the clatter of the balls causing a welcome distraction to the silence that had enveloped the driving range. ‘See you at the first,’ she shouted at Lav’s disappearing back.

CHAPTER 59

Both approaches towards the 13th green had made it to the elevated green behind the water hazard. Philly's was just a bit longer, making Lizzie's line more difficult. But she managed to get it in front of the hole, leaving a tap-in for Philly, which she made, clearly not getting it from Lav, who left hers too short, causing a challenge for her teammate. Varilla's putter came back, and she tapped. The ball seemed to hover. Philly stared at it, not daring to move. It stopped, just balancing on the hole's edge. Short.

Lav stamped her feet. 'I said, hit it, you pussy!,' she cried at Varilla, who had turned grey and waited for Philly to concede the putt before picking it up.

Philly exhaled and looked at Lizzie, who was desperately not trying to cheer. 'If we can pull off a half on the next one, it's in the bag,' she whispered.

'Tell me about it,' Lizzie replied, feeling jittery, torn between nerves and elation. 'I am to drive, right?,' she asked while she pulled her bag on her shoulder. 'Over the hump between the two bunkers?'

They walked from the green to the next tee together, feeling excited, trying to remain calm.

'Perfect. There's water on the right, but it's too near to bother you.' Philly nodded. 'Then all I have is a five wood for your slow nine iron to the green.'

Lizzie's driver came out, its hood pulled off with a firm tug. It's young owner walked to the tee, looking confident. She cocked her head, eyes on the landing point, imagining the shot, focusing on the ball's impact, feeling it in her bones. Her grip relaxed as she tightened her core, just like Lash had taught her. Her arms went back, dead straight, and she dipped her left knee before drilling down, pulling her hands towards her crotch. She turned before reaching her target, causing the ball to dent and shoot off the peg, right on spot, landing over 200 yards from her and rolling forwards.

'Wow!' Philly jumped up and down and hugged her when she stepped off the tee. 'Super shot, girl.'

Lav snorted and folded her arms. 'Just get it in the middle, will you, Varilla? If you can manage.' She looked at Philly and continued. 'Philly here might not be able to reach the 100-yard mark after a mediocre tee shot, but that's no problem for me.'

Varilla's small dark eyes tightened for a moment, and Lizzie noticed her faltering for a second before pulling her driver out and taking a large stride, reaching the tee markers and pushing her peg in slowly. She stared out over the fairway, gripped her club and swung it around her body a couple of times, like a soft ball player warming up. Her ball came out of her pocket, and she held it in front of her face, inspecting it closely for a few seconds before putting it on the peg and stepping behind it, not bothering to check her line like she usually did. Lav frowned at her teammate's unusual ritual, shrugged and sighed audibly.

One foot came down firmly, taking position an inch left of the ball while her right foot was planted a yard to the right, but more to the front, leaving the stance wide open. Varilla shook her head a couple of times and swung backwards, much higher than usual, not moving her body in the downswing. The club came down, outside in, pushing the ball from its position, causing it to curl sharply and jump into the water, skidding like a flat rock.

'You fucking moron! That's not even in play.' Lav balled her fists and shouted. 'I could have gotten it over with a bloody seven iron!'

'Bad luck, Varilla.' Philly heard a familiar voice and looked over her shoulder, seeing the Bangers' heads popping over the ridge of the last hole's green.

'We've already won,' Birdie called out. 'Seven and six. So have Bunns and Pru. See you in the clubhouse for lunch.'

Lizzie gasped, trying to keep calm and stared at Philly, now addressing Lav. 'What would you like to do, Lav? Play another from the tee or take a drop 20 yards further?,' Philly asked sweetly.

'I'll take the drop.' Lav pulled her bag towards her and marched off to the spot where she could play her ball. It fell from her hands, jumped a little and settled itself in a slight hollow. Lav mumbled something and took a lofted club out, addressed the ball and took her swing. The ball landed on the fairway, 50 yards short of Lizzie's, leaving 150 yards for Varilla to get to a spot where they still stood a chance. Her three wood came out, and Varilla addressed the ball, not even bothering with a practice swing, pulled her club up, turned and extended her body early, topping the ball, making it shoot towards a bunker, ploughing it under the lip.

'Jesus Christ!' Lav cried out in desperation. 'What in earth was that?'

Varilla narrowed her eyes, pushed her club in her bag and stared towards the green, ignoring her partner's comments.

Philly's five wood was brilliant, landing behind first and second bunker close to the green. A little chip was all that was needed to get the ball near the flag.

The women started walking, in silence, until they reached the front of the fore-green.

'Lizzie for three to the green, you for five out of the bunker?' Philly smiled at Lav who shot her a dark look and took her and wedge out.

'Just go and tell that child to get ready,' she grunted while she grounded herself in the sand. She took a large swing. The wedge drilled into the bunker's edge and left the ball motionless.

Varilla glanced at the furious woman now covered in sand and staring at the ball. She walked up to Philly and Lizzie. 'Congratulations. Wonderful game, both of you,' she said warmly while she stuck her hand out. 'Six and five. Well done.'

'Varilla!' Lav's nasal voice rang out to them. 'Get your backside over here, and take this shot!'

'I've conceded the match, dear.' Varilla didn't even bother to look at Lav. 'That's how the game is played.' She put her hand on Lizzie's shoulder. 'Come on, I'll walk you both to the clubhouse. We've got time for a long lunch.'

'So.' Pru nibbled on a piece of withered lettuce. 'We need to win two singles, then?'

'Or tie four rounds.' Philly nodded, keeping her eye on Lizzie who was in a staring contest with three boys sitting at the bar, making them uncomfortable after the lads had been eyeing them all through lunch. The Bangers were at the buffet again, stacking their plates with chips, covering them with a large dollop of tomato ketchup.

'The hummus was definitely off. And there's no pudding.' Birdie sighed, sitting down again, her plate already half empty. She nudged Bunny, who had been looking round the restaurant in wonder, not engaging in the conversation. 'Dire, isn't it.'

Bunny nodded, slowly. How could they serve lunch without sweets? Roughie would never put up with that. He had loved the treacle sponge she made him yesterday.

'Now.' Philly sat up. 'For the singles. Bogey, you are playing Varilla.' She wagged a finger at her friend who pulled a face. 'Be nice to her.'

'I'm always nice.'

'Just watch it. But make sure she begs for mercy before the 18th.' The paper napkin was tossed aside, and Philly pushed herself upwards. 'Let's go.'

They went down the steep steps on the far side of the clubhouse, dividing two patches of border with evergreen shrubs, neatly planted in even rows, the path leading out towards the little hut where their clubs were waiting for them. Bunny had taken all the water bottles and filled them at the outdoor cleaning area, adding packets of salted nuts, one each. 'For some extra energy,' she had said shyly.

The walk to the first tee was a short one, and they waited under the large standing clock. The Bangers had already finished their nuts and were doing a tossing contest, trying to throw the crumpled packages into a bin's small gap.

'Here they come.' Pru turned round, watching Lav and her team march towards them. Lav looking determined; the other women avoiding her glare.

Lizzie was up first, playing the friendly looking middle-aged woman who played the foursome against Bunny and Pru. Her short-streaked hair spread over her visor and she very kindly congratulated Lizzie on her fine first drive. Her own tee shot was only half-way, and the group saw her making a full second swing to reach the point where Lizzie needed only a pitching wedge to reach the green in two.

Bunny was done on the first very quickly, flushing two straight shots to the green, after which she spent a couple of minutes trying to find her opponent's ball in the rough who gave up with a shrug and conceded the hole.

The two following flights were also won, Philly saw Pru bending down to pick up her ball on the green while Birdie chipped in for a three.

'Lav.' Bogey grabbed her driver and flashed her teeth at Lav. 'You look like you've been struck by lightning. Maybe you should take your one iron out.' She chuckled and glanced at Philly, who shot her a warning look. 'Even God can't hit a one. Lee Trevino said that,' she whispered.

'I know,' Philly hissed back. 'Shut it, and just play, will you.'

The remaining pair watched the fifth flight tee off in silence, acknowledging both drives with a nod and getting ready themselves, letting their drives swoosh around them at great speed while they praticed their turns. The green cleared, and Philly took her drive, letting it bounce down the middle, towards the 100-yard marker. Lav followed, not much shorter, and she strutted towards it in silence.

Another putt short. Lizzie actually felt a stab of mercy for her opposite, now slumped over her putter, eyes closed, clearly not believing what had just happened. Finally she had a putt for a tie, and she left it by two inches.

'Bad luck,' Lizzie said, feeling sorry for her. 'Maybe better next hole.'

The woman gathered herself up and smiled at her young opponent. 'Luck?' She shook her head in mock misery. 'I need a bloody miracle. How can anyone hit a ball as far as you do?' She clasped her putter under her arm and gave Lizzie a friendly pat. 'But it's a delight to watch, young lady. Your Captain must be so proud of you.'

Dormie four. One point secured, two within reach. Lizzie swallowed and nodded, feeling the heat of her neck radiating towards her face. Just one more hole, and the win was in the bag. Just like the hugs and kisses she knew Philly would give her. *Keep it together,* she told herself. *Head down, keep grinding.* Lash's voice was in hear head. *Get it on the fairway. The most important shot is the next one.*

Her drive at the 15th wasn't as massive as the last ones. But it didn't matter. It was dead straight, and it bounced neatly towards the middle, leaving her with an easy eight iron. She stood aside, perfectly still, watching her competitor top her ball into the brook running alongside the fairway and dropping her club in defeat.

'You know what, Lizzie? Let's call it a day.' The older woman pushed her club in her bag and walked up to her younger adversary. 'Five and three. Congratulations.' She patted the wooden bench next to the tee box. 'And I'm absolutely knackered. Why don't we sit here and watch the others come in?'

They had a perfect view over the course and the pairs that were playing them. The 14th with Bunny landing her approach on the green, flowing along the line of ferns outside the barbed wire, Birdie on the 13th elevated green, Pru on its tee box to the far left, and a small group of women walking up the otherwise the empty first 150 yards of the 16th out towards the large water hazard.

'Lav asked a couple of lady members to come and watch,' Lizzie's opponent said. 'Not sure if that was wise though.' She winked and shook her head. 'Looks as if we're being slaughtered again,' she admitted, indicating towards Bunny who accepted an outstretched hand. 'You've got your 10 points already.'

The small crowd was now gathered at the 17th tee. Pru and Birdie had won on the sixteenth, and they had waited for Bogey and Varilla who tied, with Bogey one up for the match. She asked Varilla if she wanted to play on, knowing the overall match was already won. But Varilla held her head up high and didn't give up, saying there was always the opportunity to get at least a couple of points.

Bogey's tee shot was spot on, a perfect curve to the long par three's green and a full stop behind the flag, just a foot from the hole. Lizzie's cheer was followed by polite clapping and worried glances. Varilla took a deep breath, peeked at the expectant faces in the crowd and stepped on the tee, her heart pounding in her chest. Just one perfect shot. Just one. Her club face struck the ball right in the middle, causing a perfect flight, right to the pin.

'It's going in.' A hushed voice from the crowd broke the silence. Breaths were caught collectively as the small crowd watched the ball go, hitting the flag pole and shooting to the right, straight over the steep bunker and into the tight heather behind some low shrubs, causing a simultaneous outburst of horror to fly over the tee box. Varilla turned and held her hand out to Bogey, who accepted it with a bow before grabbing the disappointed woman in a bear hug. 'Well played, girlfriend,' she said with a big grin. 'You were quite the handful.'

'Lav wasn't.' The crowd turned to the other side, hearing Philly's voice carry towards them and seeing her walk up the ridge. 'Beat her on the 15th.'

CHAPTER 60

Where the hell was Van Dycke? Philly looked round Goodlie's bar again, eager to shake Varilla's hand and thank her for the matches. She just wanted to get this awkward evening over with and go home. The wine glasses were half-empty with lukewarm Chardonnay as bright yellow pools in their hollows. Dirty plates, streaked with half-eaten melted ice cream in pastel blotches were scattered around the table, waiting for the waitress to collect them. Crumpled paper napkins with streaks of pink lipstick were piled up on top of each other.

The noise of Lav's nasal voice piercing her brain was starting to get to her. Telling her for the umpteenth time about the new Ladies' room design, how she secured a place on the committee and the steady flow of new female members at Goodlie's door. And how pleased she was for good old Philly, now that the Peckers Wood Ladies' Section finally had accomplished something worthwhile. Fucking bitch, with that sly, evil look on her face, now really pissed and staring into a large brandy.

'Have you seen Varilla?,' Philly whispered to Pru. 'I would like to say goodbye and get this show on the road. If I have to listen to that sour loser Lav for a minute more, I swear I will be sick right here and right now.'

'She left. Sends her regards,' Pru whispered back. 'And I have had enough of this nonsense too. Let's call it a night and get ourselves out of here.' She pointed towards the Bangers and the back door.

The sisters stood up and walked towards them. 'Come on, Captain, say thank you to our dear host so we can get the fuck out of this dump.'

Philly saw Lav staring at her, cross-eyed, but still with the familiar mean look in her eyes. 'Well, Philly. I guess this was it.' Lav's pasty face moved towards her, the kiss leaving a burning sensation on her cheek. 'And again, how absolutely amazing that your bar girls did so well.' Lavender pointed at Bunny and Lizzie. 'Wonderful that they're allowed to play. She smiled, the evil look in her eyes becoming more prominent. 'Being staff.' Her face turned to Pru. 'Don't you agree, Lady Chatterley?'

'Shut your foul mouth, Thorneybush.' Bogey hissed, as she put her arms around a shivering Bunny and Birdie guided Pru away from the scene. 'One day this bar girl will buy and sell this place, so watch your step.' She reached out to Lizzie and guided the two embarrassed looking girls towards the door. 'Let's get out of this hell hole,' she said while she pulled a furious Philly towards them.

The walk to the car park cooled everyone off, and when they reached their cars they were all back to their usual selves. They gathered round and hugged each other. Philly looked round the group in front of her, huddled together. 'Well, that's that then. Medal in the bag! Mission accomplished! Anyone up for one last drink in the Ladies' room?,' she asked, while dangling the little medal in front of them.

Pru reached out, coming towards her for a last embrace. 'I think we should call it a day. We need to get home to our boys, work is waiting, and Lizzie is expected to be in school bright and early tomorrow morning. Maybe Ben will be home too, by now. Waiting for you, ready to share victories.' She kissed Philly on the cheek, released her hug and turned towards the other women. 'Come on, girls. Lizzie, I will drive you home. Let's go.'

Philly waited and waved, watching her friends get in their cars and drive off. She stared towards the gate, its image slowly disappearing as the cars turned onto the road, leaving the car park pitch black. She pulled her car door open, turned the ignition and felt in her pocket after she put the car into gear. The small round piece of metal instantly heated her hand, and she smiled broadly. This was so super good. Everyone would be so pleased. And proud. Her foot came down, and she drove home, feeling the elation somersaulting through her body, leaving it tingly and warm.

Her headlights lit up the flat's front window as she turned into a parking spot. She stretched, forced herself to look towards it. She could just make him out, slumped on the sofa, a drink in his hands, looking extremely attractive. And terribly smug. Philly turned off the ignition and stared, longing to tell him the good news to prove they had been wrong all along. Those men who would now stop snickering. Every time she walked past them. Feeling their eyes in her back. *No more silly Philly. No more silly women.* She pushed herself back, into the seat. There was no escape for them now. Time to face the truth.

He was up like a shot. He grabbed her, pushing her head against his shoulder. 'I won, darling,' Ben said softly, as if talking to a child.

Philly pulled away from him. 'Congratulations. That is so super good, Ben. You are a star.' She shook his shoulders. 'I am so proud of you.'

'So you should be.' Ben pulled away from her.

Philly held on to him, not letting him turn away from her. 'And you know what? So did I.' She heard his chuckle and felt her cheek being pinched.

'Ah yes. Your little competition. Of course. Well done you. How sweet.' The last two words were emphasized and not in an encouraging way.

'I beg your pardon?' Philly's heart skipped a beat. *How sweet? Had he really said how sweet? And little competition? What the fuck?*

Something in her snapped. The positive energy rush caused by their win made way for sudden anger. 'Excuse me?' Philly pushed Ben away from her. 'What's that supposed to mean?' She noticed a distinct glimmer of contempt in his dark eyes.

'Oh come on, Philly.' Ben reached over and tried to ruffle her hair, but she pulled back, the gesture clearly annoying him. 'You can hardly compare your competition to ours. Playing from the red, with only Thorneybush and her friends to beat. Not quite the same league as ours.' He laughed at her mockingly. 'Good Lord.'

She stepped away from him, as if she had been slapped in the face, feeling stung, and suddenly, as if struck by lightning, seeing him for what he really was. Standing there, with that familiar look of amused contempt on his face.

Her so-called boyfriend. Nothing more than a self-obsessed, narcissistic piece of shit. And she, silly Philly Fanta, had fallen for his shallow charm and the thin layer of good looks.

As the sharp realization of her own misjudgement ran through her brain, it also dumbfounded her. She stared at Ben, narrowing her eyes, repulsed, and backed off towards the small hall where the shower room was, leaving Ben to hear the water being turned on, followed by the thump of things being thrown on the floor.

Philly crouched down on the shower room tiles, her feet under her bum, her forehead against the cold blackness. A deep sob made its way from her insides, and she turned her head, letting a burning cheek rest on the porcelain's comforting cool for a moment before picking her head up and letting her other cheek cool off.

She imagined herself facing the men, feeling their embarrassed, downward stares and hearing them whispering behind her back. She could hear the snide comments that they would make. Thinking it was all frightfully hilarious, their adorable little competition. Being led on by Ben, who enjoyed belittling her, obviously not caring for who she really was at all. Or what was important to her. Fragments of the last year shot through her, forcing her to try and think of something nice Ben had done for her, without gain for himself.

She couldn't come up with anything, causing her to feel empty and angry at the same time. How could she have been so stupid? What was wrong with her? Had she actually fallen for his good looks and status at the club? Was she really that foolish?

The buzz of her mobile made her open her eyes. She reached for it and winced. *Bashit.* Oh God.

'Tell me, have you recovered from your competition?' The sharp voice bore straight into Philly's brain. 'A little birdie told me about your victory. Congratulations, well done, Hackkett.'

'Thank you, President Bashit, ' she whispered. 'We did great. Lav never stood a chance. I have the Ladies' medal in my pocket right now.'

'What's that?' The old voice was short. 'Speak up, child. I can't hear you.'

A loud sob escaped Philly. 'We won, sir, we won. Every game. We were great.'

'So I gathered.' Bashit was silent for a moment. 'Why are you sounding so miserable then?'

'I just came home to share our good news with Ben,' Philly moaned. 'But he said it was just a silly Ladies competition, that we are nowhere near his league.'

'Oh, for goodness' sake, Hackkett.' President Bashit's voice was loud now, sounding annoyed. 'Man up.'

The call ended abruptly.

Man up.

Hackkett.

Hell yes. Bashit was right. And she was done. Enough of this crap.

She slowly pulled herself off the cold tiles and drew her shoulders back, knowing instinctively what the next step should be. Her teddy bathrobe was within reach, and she pulled it around her, feeling its familiar warm comfort. She pricked her ears, thinking, with a guilty niggle of hope, she might hear Ben coming after her after the obvious blunder he made. But no, the flat was silent, except for the monotone humming of words coming from the telly.

Her feet carried her towards the small living room as if they had a life of their own, where she found Ben, now lying on her sofa, his shoes still on.

'Ben,' she said quietly.

'Shhh.' He didn't even look at her. 'I'm watching the news.'

Another snap popped. Had he actually demanded she shut up? In her own home? What in fucking hell was happening to her?

'Don't you dare shush me.' Philly stepped towards him, snatched the remote and turned the telly off, making Ben turn towards her with an irritated look on his face. 'What the hell?,' he said, slowing his words, noticing something was wrong.

'I would like you to get your feet off my furniture, get your stuff from my bed, and get the fuck out of my flat.' She tossed the remote towards the telly and rushed her fingers through her hair. 'I don't want you or your crap here.'

'What?' Ben sat up, obviously not grasping what was going on. 'Are you throwing me out? What for?'

'Yes.' She nodded. 'I am. Please leave.'

'Excuse me?,' Ben said, sounding genuinely surprised. 'What's going on, Philly?'

'You tell me.' Philly pointed her finger at him. 'Do you have any idea, Ben? What goes on with me?' Her finger shot towards her breastbone. 'You're absolutely clueless, you have absolutely no fucking idea what matters to me,' she shouted. 'Tell me, Ben, tell me what's been important to me, the last couple of months?'

'I don't know.' He shook his head, looking absolutely nonplussed. 'Something at work?'

Philly's head fell down and she dropped her hands in defeat. 'No, Ben,' she whispered. 'Please. Just get your things and go.'

'Good grief. Bloody women.' Ben grabbed his jacket and stared at her, clearly not grasping what was bothering her. 'I'll be in my flat if you need me.'

'Don't get your hopes up.' She pushed him towards the door and banged it behind him.

CHAPTER 61

Work hadn't been the welcome distraction she had hoped for. Philly stared at her computer screen, seeing the WhatsApp she just sent to Ben, after ignoring his first two.

See you at the pub at five and we will talk.

Her face fell into her hands, and she sighed. How on earth would she tell him they were over? After months of dating casually and then last year, finally moving on to something more serious? Her fingers pulled her hair back, and she sat up, trying to define what it had actually meant, something more serious. Three shags a week and a couple of meals together? As she flipped her thumb over her mobile, pictures of her parents popped up. So together, so undeniably a couple, held together by a million invisible threads. Philly swallowed, trying not to get emotional. The image rolled over to a shot of Pru and Lash, practicing on the range. Pru laughing, with her head back, Lash kissing her ear, holding her, a broad smile on his face. Both oozing happiness. Like the smitten Roughie, standing behind them, his eyes soft with love, looking at Bunny. He worshipped the ground she walked on.

Her gaze went to the right-hand corner of her screen, telling her it was nearing lunch time. She might as well chuck it in for the rest of the day. A few emails later her schedule was cleared, and she found herself driving the familiar wounding lanes up to Peckers Wood.

The car park was full. She made out Mrs Pushet's Mini Cooper, Bashit's old Mercedes in his reserved spot, and the Bangers' Jag at the far end. Her wheels turned, and she steered towards her parking space at the back of the kitchen behind the row of garbage bins, noticing the Bangers slide into the back entrance.

A cuppa with her friends. Exactly what she needed. She pulled her handbrake, grabbed her bag as she dragged herself out of her car and pushed the kitchen door. 'Girls?' The door went further ajar under her touch. 'I noticed you going in. Can I join you for a cup of tea?'

'What are you doing here? Feeling seedy? Come in.' Birdie said.

The two sisters looked up, and Bunny went towards the coffee machine to switch it on, grabbed four mugs and started to fill them with milk and sugar. Philly sat down, thankful for the bustle the Bangers were creating, throwing their coats off and searching the fridge for food.

'We bumped into Bashit and Mrs Pushet this morning.' Bogey said. 'We were hitting a few balls, and they suddenly popped up.'

Birdie nodded. 'Bashit was here bright and early and stumbled upon Mrs Pushet behind the car park.' She whistled softly. 'Good thing he found her when he did. What would have happened if she had wandered off into the woods at that hour?'

The mugs were shoved under the machine, and hot water poured into them, the sound of the old machine resembling a steam train on its last track. 'We're a bit worried about her, being all alone,' Bunny said to Philly, who nodded, not wanting to chat but just sit at the table quietly.

'She's fine. I just dropped her off at home.' The back door opened again, this time revealing the familiar figure of President Bashit huddled deeply in his loden coat, followed by Percy, looking as cold and miserable as his master. 'She told me she needed a brisk walk, couldn't sleep after yesterday's excitement.' The President looked round, taking in the scene and pointed towards the coffee mugs. 'Any more where those came from? And why are you all here and not at work?,' he said, grinning. 'Adrenaline still pumping after chopping up Thorneybush and her following?'

Birdie and Bogey exchanged a quick glance. 'We wish,' Birdie said, sounding miserable. 'Had a row.'

'A row?' President Bashit looking genuinely surprised. 'You two? That's a first. And you played so well together.'

'No.' Bogey shook her head. 'Not with each other. Of course not. We had a beastly tiff with the boys. Miserable sods.' She pulled a chair towards Bashit, invited him to sit down and passed him a large mug. 'I listened to Bobby for ages and ages about their game and when I tried to tell him about our game, he pinched my cheek and said it was jolly nice we had so much fun.' The last words were dragged out dramatically while Bogey's eyes were raised upwards.

'I see,' Bashit said, turning his attention to Birdie who pouted at him and started to speak.

'And Henri just went on and on, he drank half a bottle of cognac yakking on about their success and then said to me that us winning by such a large margin only proved that the Goodlie women should take up Nordic walking. If they wanted to grip something when allowed outside or something like that. I found myself in rather a fury by then, I'm afraid.'

A low rumble escaped the President, which he hid behind his hand. 'Right.' He raised his eyebrows for a second. 'Miss Hackkett. What about young Chipperfield?'

Oh Lord. Here we go. Philly contemplated on what to say and felt a wave of defiance coming over her.

'Oh yes. Very proud. Of himself. It never even crossed his mind to ask how I did.'

'O dear.' Bashit leaned backward in his chair, crossed his arms and looked from one face to the other. 'The poor boys did a boo-boo,' he said slowly while shaking his head. 'Sharing their good news with you, right after their game. And so enthusiastically. And what do you do, girls?'

A silence followed.

'You prove them right, by sulking, with your long faces.' Bashit ignored the surprised looks that exchanged between his audience. 'They must have been very sorry they didn't go to the pub and celebrate there, have a good time, instead of coming straight home to you whining girls.'

The women exchanged embarrassed looks over the kitchen table, none of them daring to speak.

'I agree, they could have been more supportive,' Bashit continued, again concentrating on each face for a few seconds at a time. 'But getting this medal back was a real big deal, ladies. There was humongous pressure, from the board, the whole club actually.'

'But we got a medal back too.' Birdie and Bogey whined simultaneously.

'No. You won a new medal. With one match day, against an inexperienced, new club. Which, don't get me wrong, is commendable.' Bashit stood up, looking stern. 'But ladies, that is not the same as giving it all you have five weekends in a row, against the finest clubs in the region,' he said clearly, while pulling Percy from Bunny's legs. 'If you had really wanted the boys' attention, you could have challenged them. Pro-actively. After you showed them some appreciation on their accomplishment. And asked them questions about their game, strategy, team play. That would have shown them that you really understand what the game is all about.' The loden coat was pulled tighter around the President's chest. 'Kiss and make up girls. That would be my advice. If you want it.' A stern look went towards the Bangers before the President focused on Philly. 'Finish your tea, Miss Hackkett. I want a word. In private.'

'Sir?' Philly stared back at him, feeling bewildered.

The back door opened with a sharp tug, letting in a stream of cold air carrying a gush of brown, dried up oak leaves, which twirled around the table for a while before dropping dead on the kitchen floor.

'Now, Miss Hackkett.'

They took the first few steps in silence before President Bashit halted at the wooden bench alongside the gravel path, stared at the driving range for a moment and pointed towards the roofed practice area. 'I encountered a very disturbed Club Captain over there this morning. Something to do with our Lady Captain.' His hand gestured towards the bench, inviting Philly to sit down. 'It might seem as none of my business, but when my Club Captain hurtles abuse at me, and it concerns my Lady Captain, I have no other option than to make it my business.'

Philly sat down and bit her lip, trying to control her eyes welling up.

'And the next thing I know, I find the subject abused, in the clubhouse kitchen, while she should be at work, and now close to tears.' Bashit sat down. 'What's going on?,' he asked quietly.

A big lump was stuck in her throat, but Philly managed to speak. About last night, Ben's reaction, how it made her feel. And how she consequently threw him out of her flat.

'I see,' Bashit said, slowly moving nearer to her and lifting her chin up towards him, leaving her no choice than to look in the older man's bright blue eyes. 'Listen, Miss Hackkett. I meant what I said to the Bangers just now.' He smiled for a second. 'But what they had was just an innocent squabble after a long day with too much excitement. And the four of them should stop pouting, apologize, and get on with it.'

Philly smiled back, in spite of herself, imagining the Bangers and their boyfriends.

'But this seems more than an angry argument. What's really going on?' The President's voice sounded soft and kind, his unexpected warmth making Philly spill her heart out suddenly. She started talking, letting words flow from her mouth. Explaining how she had realized the attraction was mainly physical, shallow, that she hadn't caught up on her own failure, seeing their relationship for what it really was. That she had suddenly understood they both got off on showing each other off, only wanting others to gaze at them in admiration, whenever they were together. Nothing more. Finding out so harshly that it wasn't meant to last. And how she dreaded the conversation they were going to have later today. That the mere thought made her shiver.

'I see,' Bashit said slowly before shifting his position, now facing Philly directly. 'Explain to me what exactly you are afraid of.'

The question threw her, she blinked a couple of times and swallowed, noticing a flow of relief was starting to build up inside her.

'Of his reaction,' she whispered, feeling the release of anxiety, grasping what the President was doing. 'His belittlement. How it makes me feel.' She shook her head. 'Being in a spot I don't deserve. Don't want. Ever again.'

'Right.' Bashit nodded. 'Then make sure you don't find yourself there again. See this as a practice round and go about your real match with valuable experience under your belt.'

'My real match,' Philly said quietly. 'Not quite sure what that is.'

'It will be someone that isn't interested in putting you in a place where he wants you to be. Love is about elevating your better half to where they themselves want to be. Where they can be the best they can possibly become, for themselves. And ultimately, with that, for the people around them. It's like playing a winning foursome. You want your teammate to hit the next shot from the best spot towards your shared target. Which you deliver. So you shine together.'

Philly turned her head and stared at the older man's bright blue eyes, now gazing into the space between the clubhouse and the driving range. All the tension she had been feeling flowed out of her, making way for relief. Her chin came up and determination started to build up inside her. 'He wanted me in the rough. So I would never be able to outplay him. So he could shine. Not me.'

'Let's be honest.' Bashit's voice sounded stern. 'This was never a real foursome pair. More like two singles trying to outplay each other.'

'You're right.' Philly blushed suddenly. 'I'm as much to blame for this cockup as Ben is, I know that.'

'Always two in a pair,' Bashit said. 'Do your parents know?'

An inkling of dread shot back through Philly's veins as she shook her head.

'Go and see them now. Talk to them first and tell them it's over. *For good.*' The two last words were emphasized by the President's grave voice. 'It will make you stronger talking to Chipperfield. There won't be any escape.'

'Yes,' Philly agreed. 'I know.'

'You can't boil an egg twice my dear. Over means over,' Bashit said strongly. 'He'll survive.' The President stood up and walked away, leaving Philly feeling a ton lighter than earlier that day.

Bashit turned left, following the path behind the driving range, leading up to the caddy shack. The sun was high up, its spring rays filtered between the beech trees, like gentle speckles of gold lighting up the earth getting ready for a new season. He stopped and concentrated, hearing the distant drum of a woodpecker, announcing new life with new opportunities, new challenges.

He smiled to himself and stroked Percy's head. 'Glad I'm not young anymore, old boy,' he whispered. 'So much to learn. So many mistakes still to make. Poor kids.' He started walking again, shaking his head. 'And to face the tests of love. Such hard work.'

The path led him to the tiny cottage he knew so well, and he stared towards the little window next to the front door, clearly making out Prudence Love, stirring something in a pan, looking smart in a navy business suit. He liked Love. Sharp, tidy, structured. Reliable. Predictable. He admired that in people.

He backed away behind a large oak tree, noticing Lash popping up behind Love, one hand slipping under the high-necked white blouse she was wearing and the other tugging at her hair, making her head jerk back and change the expression on her face, from concentrated to something that resembled an animal, something primal.

Bashit leaned against the tree, making sure he wasn't seen himself but was able to get a good view of what was going on in the little shack. Love's skirt was now clearly around her ankles, and Lash had pushed his pelvis towards her bottom, pumping in and out of her and slapping the right white cheek in the same motion, before Love collapsed forward and Lash arched backwards, obviously finishing what they had started. He saw his young caddy master drop down and pull up the skirt, gently kissing Love's bottom before hoisting the garment towards her waist.

Bashit reached for his scarf and dabbed his forehead. *Good Lord*, he thought to himself. Maybe not predictable after all, the Love girl. But one hell of a way to get the blood pumping as a start to an honest afternoon's work. These two youngsters were clearly getting on well together.

He reached down, leaning heavily on his walking stick to stay balanced, finding Percy's head and stroking it. 'Might be a good idea to wait for them to finish their lunch before we tap on that door,' he said quietly to the dog before backing away from the tree and starting on a detour towards the fifteenth.

Lash gave Pru a quick last kiss and pushed her out of the door, eager to get the dishes cleaned up and start his schedule. The caddy's meeting needed preparation, the head greenkeeper wanted to be informed on the members' wish list, the driving range yardage signs were long overdue a paint job, and all the tee box markers were on the list for replacement. He wiped the last spoon dry and cleared everything away, while going over his to-do list in his head. His jacket came from its peg, and he pulled the door open, nearly being knocked on the head by the President's knuckle.

'Mr Bashit. Sorry. I didn't notice you coming up the path,' he said, clearly confused. 'But come in, please.' Lash stepped aside to let the older man inside.

'No problem.' Bashit beamed at him. 'I thought I would just shoot in and out, for a cuppa. Have a quickie,' he said while he looked round. 'My goodness. You've really knocked the shack into shape.'

'Thank you, sir.'

'You've slapped quite a bit of paint on, obviously.' The President stared at Lash, making him look away. 'Quite the feminine touch, somehow. Love it.'

Lash reached for the kettle and switched it on. 'You've made your point, President,' he said with a smile on his face. 'Are you okay with her staying here?'

'Certainly.' Bashit nodded. 'Hasn't done the place any harm. But she won't be satisfied with this forever, you do realize that, don't you?,' he said, accepting the mug of tea and nodding for more milk and sugar. 'If this feels like a lasting thing you need to think ahead, my dear fellow. And I'm not only referring to the accommodation.'

Lash nodded, suddenly feeling uneasy. 'I know.'

'Righto.' The President sat up straight, clearly wanting address something further. 'Talking about the feminine touch, I would like to hear what you've been up to with the young ladies in Miss Hackkett's team. I'm actually quite chuffed they managed to put that hag Thorneybush in her place. Obviously with your help.'

'So was I,' Lash chuckled. 'Although there wasn't a doubt in my mind they would pull this off. They've really learned know how play, sir.'

'I see.' Bashit nodded, encouraging Lash to speak further. 'How? Enlighten me.'

Lash reached backwards, tilted his chair and pulled a stack of seven notebooks out of a kitchen drawer, each with a different name pasted on them. He opened the books, one by one, starting with Lizzie and moving to the others, taking Bashit through all the technical exercises, training routines, different tactics based on personality and strength, pasted pictures of the girls in a range of stances with different clubs, graphics of their performance and obstacles that needed fixing. There even were drawings of every green on the Goodlie course, complete with angles and undulations, with a near mathematical graph that stated line and speed.

'Mrs Pushet helped me with that one,' Lash said while he explained the graph to an astonished looking Bashit. 'I was thinking of showing it to Simon Hot, it might come useful to him.'

'No,' Bashit said quickly. 'That won't be necessary. Just yet.' His voice was insistent. 'I would like to speak to Hot myself first.'

'Very well, sir.' Lash closed the notebooks and stood up. 'I really need to get going. Loads to do and little time.'

'Quite,' Bashit replied, also hoisting himself to his feet. 'Just one more question. How does Miss Hackkett fit in all this? Did she make any worthwhile contribution?'

‘She did, sir. She really listened and made sure her team did the exercises I suggested.’

‘Good girl.’ Bashit nodded and reached for the door. ‘Speak to you later.’

CHAPTER 62

To: #teamPW
From: ladiesteampw@gmail.com
cc: President@peckerswood.co.uk; treasurer@peckerswood.co.uk; secretary@peckerswood.co.uk
Bcc:

1st of May, 2023

Subject: in awe

Dear and fabulous Men's Team Players,

First of all, let us apologize for our belated response to your majestic achievement, bringing the Regional Competition Medal back to our magnificent club, its only and rightful home.

Many congrats on your brilliant win!

We are so sorry we didn't address this sooner, but we were in such awe of you, just completely unable to come to any sort of suitable verbal reaction, not managing anything other than silent adoration for days on end, being overcome by your excellence.

Love you and PW forever and ever,
On behalf of the ladies team.
BBBanger

PS: How insanely clever you all are, chopping up those fine opponents, bringing them to their knees begging for mercy.

PPS: We have much to learn. Must remember asking you to show us how opponents knelt and begged.

CHAPTER 63

Philly wiped a smile off her face, checking her mobile for messages, the one from the Bangers making her feel better. She sat in her car in front of her parents' cottage, enjoying a couple of toffees, contemplating her next move. It had been quite a hurdle, telling them their blue-eyed boy wasn't as shiny as they had imagined. Her mother cried, sobbing that she had already envisioned a big wedding and a bunch of lovely grandchildren while Philly comforted her, pointing out she wasn't over the hill yet, and that she was sure she would find someone suitable soon. Someone that really loved her, instead of himself.

Her mother apologized through her tears, saying she was sorry to sound so selfish, but she just wanted Philly to have the happiness she had, with a loving husband and a daughter that was the light of her life.

Yes. Exactly. *A loving husband.* That would be nice.

Her father remained quiet all through the difficult conversation, clearly wrestling with the concept of her being single again. 'Was there no possibility of them getting back together?,' he finally asked, carefully.

'No. You can't boil an egg twice, Dad.'

He walked her to the door, clearly wanting to talk to her alone and telling her he wished they had figured this out earlier, that looking back, he had also seen the signs. And that he was sorry he hadn't talked to her about it. But that he and her Mum had been so pleased with her obviously great catch and the prospect of grandchildren, they hadn't wanted to acknowledge something was off. And that he was so sorry that she had to now confront Ben.

'You take care of Mum,' she said, getting into her car. 'She's more upset than I am.'

Her dad had nodded and rushed back inside, asking her to ring him after she had talked to Ben.

The short drive to the pub had given her time to ring Pru and tell her what she was about to do. Her long-life friend had listened in silence, not judging, not commenting, just asking her if she was absolutely sure. Philly's confirmation had triggered an unusual emotional reaction. 'God, I am glad you are dumping him. I can't stand him,' Pru admitted, adding finely that Lash thought Ben was a prick too.

'Why didn't you say anything?,' Philly asked.

Pru's answer was clear. She respected Philly's choice, just like Philly had done when she found out about Lash. Her response made Philly emotional, feeling her friend's love and respect for her. 'Just warn me if I do it again.'

Philly had laughed through her tears, seeing Ben's car pull up and turn into the pub's car park. She said goodbye to Pru, wiped her face and got out of the car, feeling relieved knowing she was about to do the right thing.

He sat at a quiet table, holding a pint, wanting to stand when he saw her coming towards him.

'Don't get up,' Philly said, pulling the chair opposite out.

'What's going on, Philly?' Ben looked annoyed, looking at her and taking a swig of beer. 'Pissed off because I didn't ask you about your precious competition?' He shook his head. 'Rather pathetic, if you ask me.'

'Yes. You're right,' she said, 'It really is.'

'Excuse me?' Ben gazed at her, looking genuinely surprised. 'So you've come to your senses?'

'Yes,' she nodded again. 'Absolutely.'

'Thank God for that.'

'I've finally grasped we are on a road to nowhere.' She looked up, finding his face. 'I don't love you, Ben. And you don't love me.'

'I do,' Ben said, sounding offended. 'And you do love me.'

'No. I really don't.' Philly shook her head. 'And you, you love the fact we're fucking, but that's about it. Your real interest in me is about zilch.' She shrugged. 'I bet you don't even know what my job is. Or my handicap, for that matter.'

'I..,' Ben faltered for a moment. 'You're a…um…and you play off…' He paused looking at her in desperation, waiting for her to say something.

But she didn't. She just stared at him, silently, wondering why she had been so attracted to him in the first place and feeling relieved by her lack of emotion seeing him struggle.

'Oh, fuck this,' he exclaimed, banging his flat hand on the table, making people stare at them. He stood up suddenly, causing the table to wobble and his beer to spill. 'I think it's better we both see other people, Philly. This obviously is not working for me.'

The key to her flat bounced on the table, and Ben stalked off, not looking back.

Philly stared at his disappearing back. 'Of course it isn't,' she whispered, wiping the spilled beer away with a napkin, letting the moisture suck into the paper. She tossed it in the nearest bin, making sure it was gone forever.

CHAPTER 64

Press release, draft
Triumph for Peckers Wood Golf Club.

The Secretary to the Board of Peckers Wood Golf Club is pleased to announce that Club Captain Ben Chipperfield and his team have brought the prestigious Regional Competition medal back to Peckers Wood Golf Club, after a year of absence from its rightful home. Chipperfield, who is highly regarded by all members at Peckers Wood, commented on his achievement as follows: 'I am delighted to have had the opportunity to lead our club towards this important victory, together with our head pro Simon Hot. At the start of my year as Club Captain, I made the promise to aim towards bringing the men's regional competition teams' exceptional standard to an even higher level. I feel deeply responsible for the development of our club and am confident that this victory proves Peckers Wood's excellence.'

Ben reached over and pulled the laptop away from Bashit and Bushrod, who had both studied it carefully. 'What do you think, gentlemen? There's room to add one sentence. If I make it any longer the newspaper won't except it.'

'I think it's excellent.' Bushrod beamed at Ben. 'Just perfect. How about you, Bashit? Anything you want to add, edit?'

The President stared out of the study's window for a moment, narrowing his eyes, concentrating on a twosome walking towards the first green, a little dog following them. 'Yes,' he said, sounding short. 'Take out the reference to Hot. And I don't think it would harm us too much if we added a line on the ladies' victory, putting ghastly Goodlie in their place.'

'Really? Is it relevant?' Ben's voice was sharp.

'Yes. It is,' Bushrod's snapped, clearly not leaving room for discussion.

'Alright. Steady on. No big deal.' Ben pulled the computer towards him and started to type. 'Like this, for instance?'

Lady Captain Filly Hackett secured her first win beating the Goodlie ladies team.

'Add the score,' Bashit said.

'Ah.' Ben looked at him, thoughtfully. 'What was it again? Can't seem to remember.'

'18-0,' Bashit replied, sounding flat, not returning Ben's look. 'They won all games, foursomes and the singles.'

'What does it matter?,' Bushrod grumbled, clearly not amused by the editing in the piece. 'And why take out Hot in favour of the Lady Captain? Credit where credit is due, Bashit.'

The President stood up, balanced on his stick for a while and walked to the window, his silence causing discomfort with the other men, who now sensed something was wrong.

'Hot is leaving us. He hasn't told me personally yet, but I know he accepted an offer from Goodlie. A very generous offer, I might add. He's confirmed he's taking them up on it.'

The silence that followed seemed to last forever. Ben fell back in his chair with his hands on his head, looking astonished. Bushrod's mouth moved, but no sound came out. His face had turned from the usual bright pink to dark purple.

'Bloody hell.' Ben jumped up and started pacing. 'And now what? Just when we have everything on track, the bastard sells us out. We're fucked without a good pro, you do realize that

Bashit, don't you?' He turned to Bushrod. 'Can't you make him a better offer? Buy him back? How are we doing anyway, financially?'

Bushrod batted his eyelids and looked uncomfortable. 'Well, I…,' he hesitated and glanced at the President, '…haven't heard back from the consultant yet, and….'

'Silence!,' Bashit thundered, causing the others to flinch and sit down. 'I want Hot out of here asap. He's clearly not dedicated to our club. Succumbing to money so easily. The miserable rat.' He stared at Bushrod. 'Take away his privileges immediately, pay what he is due and kick him off the premises.'

Bushrod nodded, knowing better than to oppose the President's order.

'But what about our team?,' Ben squeaked. 'We need to start training for next year. We can't be left to fend for ourselves.'

'Lash Johnsson will be your main man,' Bashit said.

'I beg your pardon?' Ben stared at the President, looking exasperated. 'The Caddy Master? You must be joking. Why, for goodness sake?'

'Because he too got a generous offer from Goodlie. To become the Lady Section's head pro. That hag Thorneybush offered to triple his wages. But he refused.'

Ben and Bushrod stared at Bashit, both clearly bewildered by what they were hearing. 'But why?,' Ben piped.

'Why what? Why the hag asked him? Let me think.' Bashit leaned forward and pretended to concentrate hard, frowning, finger under his chin. 'Because she was smashed to bits by the team he coached, you fools,' he shouted, waving his stick in the air. 'He obviously did an incredibly fantastic job.' Bashit's face had turned the same dark colour as Bushrod's. 'And why he will get promoted here, to work with the men's team, is because he does understand what we are about. Decency, honesty, being loyal. Understanding that life isn't always about the bloody money.'

‘Hear, hear.’ Bushrod concurred.

Bashit shot him an annoyed look and turned to Ben. ‘I have full faith in Johnsson, Ben. You will be pleasantly surprised by his approach and dedication. He managed to bring an inexperienced, scraped-together bunch from nothing to quite a decent standard in under a year. Imagine what he could do for you.’

Ben nodded. ‘I sincerely hope so, President.’ He stood up. ‘But, agreed, it is what it is. The club needs to prioritize.’

‘Yes, Ben,’ Bashit said. ‘I would appreciate it if you kept this to yourself until I’ve had the opportunity to discuss things formally with Johnsson. I would like his handshake before we make things official with an announcement.’

‘Understood.’ Ben nodded and got up. ‘I’m off. That consultant wants to interview me. Shouldn’t be late.’

‘One more thing,’ President Bashit added, pulling himself up. ‘I would like to organize an official moment, opening the prize cabinet and placing the medals in it.’

‘Medals, sir?,’ Ben asked, with an emphasis on the plural.

‘Yes,’ Bashit replied, ignoring Bushrod who pulled his eyebrows up dramatically. ‘*Medals.*’ The President hobbled out of the room, leaving the other men in stunned silence.

CHAPTER 65

Pru poked the glowing cinders and carefully placed a log on top, shivering at the same time, nearly feeling the drenches that were lashing against the trees outside. She glanced at the large figure sitting at the kitchen table, his head in his hands, the plate with the piled-up sandwiches untouched, the coffee mug still full.

She turned and reached out, touching his hair carefully, trying to get some sort of reaction. 'But it's good news, isn't it?,' she said quietly, sitting down next to him, reading the letter and agreement in front of her. 'More pay. A secured teaching place. Isn't this what you always wanted?'

A pair of troubled grey eyes found hers. 'I promised her I would be there for you.' His hands ran through his thick black hair, pushing it down and holding it together at the back. 'I don't back down on my word. It ain't right.'

Pru carefully took his hand from his head and held it. 'I know,' she whispered. 'But sometimes life asks different things from us.'

'It ain't respectful. I've never let anyone down, breaking a vow is a sin.' The familiar stubbornness was back in his voice and in his eyes. 'I'm gonna tell Bashit no deal.'

Pru moved her hand to his chin and turned his face towards her own. 'No. You are not,' she said determinedly, trying not to react to the startled look in Lash's eyes. 'You are going to stretch yourself, prove you earn the respect you crave so much.'

He tried to move his face away, but she pulled it even closer so their noses nearly touched, 'You will have this conversation with Philly and explain your situation to her. Be honest and tell her how you really feel. She'll be disappointed, certainly. But she will respect you, and become more invested in you. In us.'

Lash swallowed and stared at Pru now standing up, chucking the cold coffee down the sink and pouring a new cup for herself.

'I'll text her you're coming. She'll be in the Ladies' room in 30 minutes. And I'll be there in an hour, wanting to know how things went, before I talk to her about next year.' Pru took a sip from the hot dark liquid. 'Get your backside over there,' she ordered, clearly not wanting a reply.

The two women stared at the door, watching Lash leave with his head up high and his shoulders square, obviously relieved and a far cry from the hunched figure that stumbled into the Ladies' room an hour ago.

Pru stared at Philly. 'Thanks Freckles,' she whispered. 'Your supportive reaction was just what he needed. He felt so guilty.'

'I know. Shows he's a real gentleman.' Philly reached over and pulled her friend towards her. 'Good for him. This is a great opportunity for Lash. And you. And lucky swine Ben has gotten himself the best deal ever.' She stood up and poured herself a glass of water. 'But…what are we supposed to do now?'

The Ladies' room went silent for a couple of moments, both women deep in thought, contemplating on the decision that had been made for them.

'It will come to us.' Philly turned and looked her friend's face. 'How does it feel for you, becoming Lady Captain next year?'

'Great.' Pru's serious face lighted up with a warm smile. 'And thanks for asking, Freckles.'

'Of course. And I don't think we need to worry about the votes this time. You will be the first unanimously voted Lady Captain.'

'Let's hope so.' Pru sighed. 'You never know what could hit us in the face.'

Their stillness was broken abruptly by a gush of cold spatters blowing in, followed by two soaked figures and a trembling Maggie, who looked up at them expectantly. Two dark green hoods were pushed back, revealing the identical smiling faces, while Birdie started frantically waving a damp newspaper up in the air, Maggie following it, yapping and waving her tail.

'Philly! Look! The press has picked it up!!'

'Picked what up?' Philly pulled the plastic chair away from the small pine desk and sat down.

'Our win. Your win. As Lady Captain. Roughie sent it in, after Ben drafted it.' Birdie passed the paper over. 'Look, isn't that super? Think of all the women who will read this.'

The paper was snatched from her friend's hand, and Philly flipped it open. What press release? What on earth did they mean? 'I don't know anything about a press release. No-one ever told me.' She looked down, finding the article, with Ben's name staring at her. She read the words and sentences, elaborating on his achievements, quickly reaching the bottom of the page. She put the paper down, slowly, trying hard not to swear, trying not to believe what she saw. But it was there, right in front of her, on her desk. With the Bangers behind it, staring at her, eyes wide open with joy.

Her tongue felt dry. She tried to swallow, but couldn't. She closed her eyes. 'For the love of God,' she whispered. 'Can't even get my fucking name right.' Her head came forward and landed in both her hands. 'Bloody hell.'

Maggie whimpered, a worried glance exchanged between the other women while Bogey put her hand on Philly's back and cleared her throat. 'Never mind. The important thing is they didn't forget you, right? Last year's press release didn't even mention a Lady Captain at all.'

'No. Of course not, you dummy.' Birdie's hand shot out and slapped the back of her sister's head. 'We didn't have a Lady Captain last year, now did we? Or any year. But in all honesty, your name is rather difficult to spell, Philly,' she shrugged. 'Pateto, potato; who gives a fart?'

Her hand gave Philly's long pony tail a sharp tug. 'Come on, Lady Captain. Stop moaning. It bores me. Let's go and have lunch somewhere. Just the four of us, like the good old days.'

Yes. Stop feeling sorry for yourself. Philly thought. *This only confirms you made the right decision.* 'That actually sounds like a great idea.' She said, forcing herself to smile. 'I, we, have some news and we can discuss this.' She held out her phone, showing an email. 'Bashit's request. At least some bright spots to lighten up our day.'

Three faces stared at her.

'He invited us to join him in the clubhouse.' Philly's face split into a large grin. 'For an official prize giving. With the men.'

Birdie turned to Bogey, who was staring at Philly, open-mouthed. 'Bloody hell,' she said, sticking her hand up for a high five. 'Excellent!'

CHAPTER 66

A few strands of curls had escaped Philly's pony tail. She wound them around her finger, staring at her frenzied friends and trying to analyse her own feelings. What was it? Elation, mixed with pride? Perhaps a sprinkle of apprehension on top, knowing Ben would be there, oozing confidence and cocksureness? Would she be able to ignore him, enjoy the moment, while Bashit would address them?

'My bloody stockings are too short.' Birdie hoisted her skirt up and started to pull the crotch, hanging between her thighs. 'I hate it when this happens. Makes me want to walk like a pissed duck,' she said while strutting through the Ladies' room, her skirt on her hips, and her legs flying out.

It made Philly smile, despite the building tension surrounding them. Lizzie started to giggle, trying to get her nylons out of the packet and unfolded without tearing them. Pru looked just the part, as always businesslike, no-nonsense but beautiful. Philly watched her waving at the two sisters, who characteristically were fooling around, trying to lighten the atmosphere.

'Let your sister help you hoist those up before they get ladders all over them,' Pru said tersely.

Bogey sighed while she got on her knees to help Birdie. 'I still don't understand what all the big dressing up fuss is about.'

‘The big fuss, you idiot, is that we managed to do what we set out to do. First, we humiliated that smug bitch Thorneybush ánd brought home our medal to shine in the special cabinet, displayed personally by President Bashit, for everyone to see and admire.’

‘So?,’ Birdie asked.

Pru threw her head back in desperation. ‘So the members will realize, every time they pass through the great hall, that we *do* matter.’

Philly turned round and sat down next to Bunny, who was looking a bit sick. ‘Are you alright?,’ she asked in a low voice. ‘You look really smart in your new suit.’

Bunny nodded. ‘I’m just a bit nervous, I guess. I’ve never done this before.’

Philly’s arm went around the hunched shoulders, and she pulled the girl towards her. ‘That goes for all of us. We’re in this together. Because we accomplished this together.’

‘Yes!’ Mrs Pushet popped up from behind the shower wall, looking dapper in an army green ensemble. ‘And I am so proud of you all. Team forever!’ The words filled the room with excitement, followed by a cheer from the others.

Philly’s mobile flashed. A message from President Bashit.

“Great hall, prize cabinet, 11 a.m. You have my personal consent to use the main entrance. Bring the medal.”

Philly’s eyes moved to her watch. *10:50*. She turned round, looked at the expectant faces in front of her and stood up. ‘Let’s go chaps. We don’t want to be late.’

The gravel leading up to the paved terrace in front of the rose beds crunched under their feet as they trod carefully, not wanting to damage their shoes. A few fat drops of rain splattered down, enough for them to pick up their pace. One of the greenkeepers was tending to the borders, carefully inspecting the lavender that was starting to turn purple. Soon their hefty scent would appear, always tempting Philly to stop and bend down to touch the little flowers.

But now she went straight for her target. The heavy door squeaked as it opened slowly under the force of her right hand. Philly pushed further, and the women stepped in carefully, holding their breath but managing to keep their cool.

President Bashit was at the far end of the hall, waiting in front of the large mahogany and glass prize cabinet covering the full length of the hall's back wall, his hand up and waving them towards him.

'Ah, there you are. Right on the dot,' he beamed at all of them, nodding his head. 'And how smart you all look. Splendid.' His hand stretched out towards Philly. 'Now, Miss Hackkett. Let me have a look at that medal again.'

The little case came out of Philly's handbag, and she opened it, feeling waves of pride wash through her body as she snapped it open and pushed it towards Bashit. The hall was dead silent with anticipation, six pairs of eyes were locked on the President.

He stared at the little piece presented him and smiled. 'Well. I think I have just the spot for it.' A collective sigh rippled from the group of women to the cabinet. Bashit's blue-veined hand moved into the cabinet and opened a space between two silver cups. 'We will just wait for the men and get started. I will do Chipperfield's team first and then move over to you.' Bashit took his watch out of his pocket and sighed. 'If they show us the courtesy of being on time, for once.'

His attention turned towards the main entrance, seeing the door flying open with a forceful push, letting a group of dishevelled men in, Ben still tugging at his tie and Henri Sweet trying to squeeze himself into his sports jacket. Bobby Long looked flushed, frantically trying to force his unruly hair back with his fingers.

Ben walked straight up to Bashit, not acknowledging the women, and handed the large silver medal over, dramatically, with a large flowing motion followed by a slight bow. 'Back where it belongs, President. Thanks to yours truly and his magnificent team,' he said, while walking backwards to stand in line with the other men.

'Thank you, Chipperfield.' President Bashit's chin came up, and he stared at the men, one by one, unblinkingly. 'Whether or not you might have noticed, I asked the ladies to join us. Some recognition of their presence from your side might be civil,' he said evenly, his eyes remaining cold.

Philly noticed Ben and Bobby exchange a quick glance that looked like mutual annoyance. *Condescending fucks*, she thought, carefully taking Ben in. Still technically breathtakingly handsome, but somehow he physically repulsed her.

'Ah, yes of course,' Ben said, sounding slightly uncomfortable, still avoiding to look at Philly. 'Good morning, ladies.'

The group of men next to him followed with a low murmur that resembled a rumbled "good morning".

'Who's managing the bar?,' Charles Charmers whispered to Roughie.

'My mother,' Roughie hissed back.

'Righto. That's better.' President Bashit released his stare, turned round slowly and nodded towards Philly with the group of overwhelmed looking women behind her. 'Please, ladies. Don't be shy. Move over towards the cabinet.'

He cleared his throat, squared his shoulders and addressed the men in front of him. 'As gentlemen, we should be both gracious in defeat and humble in victory,' he said, staring at Ben. 'But, nevertheless, when it comes to this medal, we were forced to be gracious for too long.' He pulled his right arm up and pushed the medal above his head. 'Bloody well done, all of you! You have made Peckers Wood so proud!'

His shout was met with a large cheer. The men's team slapped each other on the back as President Bashit reached into his pocket for his notes and started on his speech, now surrounded by the team, leaning towards him, holding on to each other until Bashit's voice remained silent and put the prize in the cabinet, his moves accompanied by loud stomping from the men and applause from the women.

'Thank you, President. Excellent speech. Brilliant, isn't it?' Ben pushed his nose towards the glass pane and sighed. 'Bloody brilliant,' he whispered, pulling himself from the cabinet and straightening his jacket. 'Well, that's it then. We need to get going. First flight has a tee time in five minutes.'

And with that, the Club Captain turned on his heel, following the other men already waiting at the large entrance door. 'Bye, ladies. Have fun!' His hand came up in a wave just before the door opened, leaving the great hall's other occupants in stunned silence.

The door closed with a bang, making Philly jump. *That fucking patronizing piece of shit,* she thought, staring after him.

'Well.' President Bashit composed himself and glanced at the group of women, who were gazing at the door with mouths half open. 'That, frankly, was actually quite rude. My apologies, ladies. But never mind. We can manage without them.'

Philly blinked, trying to repress the surge of emotion that was threatening to water her eyes. Her mouth closed. *Man up, Hackkett,* she told herself while Bashit started to speak. Her feet stretched, forcing her legs to keep standing, letting words from the past pop up in her brain.

Not good enough, young lady. Not. Good. Enough.

Hell no. She shook her head, as if trying to shake away what kept popping up.

I will not come second.

She arched her back and looked back at the door, left open, revealing the last view of the men walking to the first tee. *Who do you think you lot are? You bloody condescending bastards.*

The clapping around her made her return to the scene around her. The President was smiling, inviting them to take a look at the medal in the cabinet and telling her he was proud of them. She watched Pru wink at her, when the President waved his finger at her and told her to keep the medal where it belonged, also for next year. She saw him nod at the Bangers and Lizzie and patting Bunny on her hair.

'Snap out of it. Party is over. Shake Bashit's hand, and get us out of here.' Pru's breath touched her ear, and her hand tugged at her arm. 'Let's take everyone to the Ladies' room for a celebratory drink. Will calm you down.'

Rain was pouring down now, turning the path leading up to the Ladies' room into a river carrying a stream of mud and gravel down to the car park. The group huddled together and started to run, shielding themselves as best they could with their jackets until they reached their familiar door. Philly reached for the lightswitch and shivered, feeling the damp that was building up in the room cling to her bones. She reached over to the electric heater, pulled its cord and tried to warm her hands while gathering her thoughts.

'My stockings are buggered,' Birdie said, while she pulled down the torn tights and threw them in the bin with a flick of her wrist. 'But jolly decent of our President, to encourage us to invite Goodlie here next year.'

'I say. Rather.' Bogey rubbed herself in an attempt to chase out the cold. 'But how are we going to manage without a pro?' She glanced at Pru who shrugged, pulled some withered daffodils from a vase and threw them in the bin with a disgusted look on her face.

Birdie turned to Philly. 'We've come so far. What if we get beaten by Thorney next year?,' she asked apprehensively. 'We'll be back to square one.'

'We're at square zilch as it is. I wanted to pop the county league question to Bashit, see if the board would support us entering, but I'm glad I didn't.' Philly sighed and shook her head. 'I don't know about you, but my earlier pride is being chopped to bits thinking about this morning. I'm just pissed off, those bloody men not even having the decency to stay and listen to what Bashit had to say to us.'

'So was I, too be frank.' Mrs Pushet handed Lizzie a Coke and patted her arm. 'One would think men are, what shall I say, empathically challenged? I'll tell you, they are totally unaware of what they just did. Silly boys. You must be so relieved you're a lesbian.' She looked up and winked at Lizzie, who choked and nearly spilled her drink over the older woman. 'There were many times I wished I was a lesbian. Much less complicated. But I just can't handle the sex.' Mrs Pushet shivered and sat down next to Bunny, who stared at her, clearly lost for words.

Philly's voice became angry. 'The rotten fucks. Probably snickering about us and our silly medal right now on their precious medal tee. And mocking it. I hope the foul weather lasts for another four hours,' she said while her shoulders drooped. 'And that half-baked press release.' She paused for a moment and looked round. 'Do you know how many inquiries I got?'

The group remained silent, obviously knowing the answer. 'Zero. And the worst thing is, Roughie told me Ben's phone just didn't stop. Even some important Royal and Ancient representative rang him, to congratulate him.'

'Perhaps we should have sent in our own press release,' Lizzie said carefully. 'Explaining what we did. To really inspire other women.'

'Yah. Maybe we should have.' Philly shrugged. 'Too bloody late now. And it still would have been our adorable little one game, playing from the red, against their obviously massive performance, playing from the real tees. Making it a real game.' She emphasized the last words, sounding bitter.

Pru nodded. 'And all communication to the press goes through the board. They would have edited to something minor probably anyway.'

The first glass of lukewarm wine was handed to Bunny, who slowly placed it on the table. 'I play from the medal,' she said quietly.

'Pardon?,' Pru asked, looking at Philly with raised eyebrows.

'Go on,' Philly said.

'All the time. When Roughie and I play together. It saves us a lot of time.'

The room fell silent, the Bangers exchanging glances with Philly and Pru, and Lizzie not knowing if she could say something.

'Right,' Mrs Pushet finally said slowly. 'And how does that pan out? Is it really challenging?'

Bunny shook her head. 'Not at all. A straight drive and one club more to the green, that's about it. I win most of the time.' Bunny grinned and gulped her drink down in one go.

CHAPTER 67

'If you want to play, you have to play with boys. If you want to stick around, you have to beat them. Annika Sorenstam said that,' Lizzy said, nodding profusely. 'You love Annika, don't you?'

Mrs Hackkett smiled. 'I do. She's wonderful.'

'I love Nelly Korda.' Lizzie sighed. 'I want to be as good as she is.'

'I know you do, and as much as I support you, you're not her. Yet.'

Sniggles let out a long yawn and rested his paws against the range, wallowing in the comfort of the Hackketts' cottage's kitchen. Mrs Hackkett put the pot of tea down and inspected the faces sitting opposite her at the table, all three with a self-satisfied look on them. 'What did your father have to say about this?,' she asked, addressing her daughter.

'That we are clearly quite mad,' Philly said. 'And way ahead of ourselves.' She glanced at Lizzie and giggled. 'And that was after Lizzie and I beat him in a nearest to pin.'

'Yea!,' Lizzie cried. 'Of course we did.'

'I see.' Mrs Hackkett leaned back. 'But this is not our back garden we're talking about. Or a retired school head. Those fit young boys really can hit that ball a long way.' She turned to

Pru. 'What about your Lash? He must have an opinion on this?'

'Mrs Hackkett.' Lizzie's chin came up. 'You know what Arnold Palmer said. Success in golf depends less on strength of body than upon strength of mind and character.'

'Quite right.' Philly nodded. 'Well, Pru, what did Lash have to say?'

Pru's chuckle sounded after a moment of hesitation, while she contemplated what was appropriate to share. He had taken her out on the driving range, pushing her to hit her driver as hard as she could, over and over, until she was exhausted and fell on the mat, begging him to let her stop, while he knelt in front of her and whispered she should be prepared to do a lot more if she thought they had any chance at all. What happened after that was certainly not for the others to hear. 'He said we might actually have a chance if we are willing to train our backsides off.'

'What about the Club Captain?,' Mrs Hackkett asked Philly carefully. 'I suppose he must consent?'

The Club Captain. Philly smirked and avoided her mother's eyes, thinking about the awkward conversation. He had knocked on the Ladies' room door right before joining a board meeting, finding her alone. He had stared at her a moment before he sat down at her desk and spoke. Commenting on his surprise, not understanding why she hadn't just asked him. That if she had, she wouldn't have to face this obvious disappointment, he could have talked her out of it. That he really didn't understand where this need to prove herself to him was coming from. Was it some sort of childish way of trying to get his attention? Was it because she was obviously frustrated he left her?

Left her? Jesus Christ. The man actually convinced himself he left her?

He had stood up and added that, coming to think of it, it was actually quite an infantile action that she dared him, assuming the girls could offer resistance to the obviously best team of the region.

The condescending twat.

Philly shuddered, jolting the scene out of her mind. 'Ben finds the whole thing frightfully amusing. But, we have set a date. The Saturday afternoon before they celebrate the handover of the Captaincy, the 17th of June, we will play against the men, from the medal tee.'

'That means you have just weeks,' Mrs Hackkett exclaimed.

'Damn right. Piece of cake,' Lizzie said triumphantly, making Philly smile.

Piece of cake it wasn't, but she was certainly motivated to see if her mother's heroine could be proved right.

The conference room's door closed behind Bunny and her coffee tray, leaving the group of men to themselves, ready to start their unscheduled meeting. Roughie opened his file, started tapping and nodded towards the Chair. A folded piece of stationary appeared, and the President opened it, slowly, as if wanting to buy time. He pushed his glasses up his nose and spoke in a deliberate voice informing the men of the content of the letter and pausing for a moment before putting the formal request forward. The paper remained between the President's fingers, and Bashit looked round the large conference table, inspecting the men's facial expressions one by one, and invited the group to come with questions. He waited for someone, anyone, to break the blackout that seemed to have enveloped the room.

'You've got to be joking. Does she have a serious screw loose?,' Bobby gawped at Sweet sitting next at his side. 'They will be shredded to pieces and she knows it.'

A circle of astounded faces turned towards him.

'Mr Long,' President Bashit injected, 'please address your thoughts and comments through me.'

'I know,' Sweet replied to his neighbour, ignoring the President's request. 'Utter humiliation awaits them. I mean, look at them.'

Bashit took the hammer and crashed it down, clearly annoyed by what was going on. 'Through me, gentlemen!,' he bellowed, stabbing his hammer towards his chest.

Bobby bit in a scone and turned his face towards the Chair. 'Sorry, President. But honestly? Why would I want to be involved in their game, anyway? I mean, come on. It's just a bit of innocent fun for them, isn't it? Something for them to do, to get out of the house now and then.'

Sweet nodded and faced the group. 'Absolutely. I once watched Lavender Thorneybush and her team on the driving range when I was on a business meeting at Goodlie. What a hoot. I could beat them with only a putter and a wedge in my bag, standing on one leg, for goodness sake.

Bobby grinned. 'The putter would be enough.'

'Thank you, Mr Long, Mr Sweet.' Bashit waved his hammer towards the other men. 'Any other observations?'

'I warned him. Allowing dogs and women?' Charles Charmers nudged Roughie sitting next to him. 'We agreed, but only on a leash. The women that is of course, not the dogs, obviously,' he whispered, making Roughie frown. 'See what happens, allowed to roam free? Leave their shit all over the place. Mr President, what are they thinking? Competitive golf? Medal tee? We might need to protect them from themselves, poor things.'

A silence followed, broken suddenly by Bobby slapping his hands on his knees, pushing himself out of the chair and started pacing. 'What a predicament. Do you understand what this means?' He walked over to Ben and stared at him, totally unaware of Bashit's dark look. 'Whichever way you look at it, we're always screwed. Or rather, we might not be for a considerable time.' He spat out while pointing at Henri Sweet and Roughie, one after another.

Roughie gasped and put his hand over his mouth, suddenly looking horrified.

'If there ever was a Catch 22, this is it, man,' Bobby hissed. 'What the fuck are we going to do?'

Henri Sweet let out a howl and slumped backwards, cupped his hands over his face and started to groan softly. Another hand went up. 'Lieutenant Retired Bushrod wants the floor.'

The large man stood, shoulders squared and raised his chin before addressing the President. 'Through the Chair, to settle the young men down, this might be beneficial. A blessing in disguise,' Bushrod said, raising his voice, building it to sound firm and determined. 'This will let them know who's boss. Once and for all. I mean, really. We're dealing with women. They relish domination. They *want* to obey.'

'Thank you, Lieutenant Retired,' Bashit said in a strong voice. 'Anything else before we vote?'

Bobby Long stared at his mobile, seeing a text from Henri Sweet pop up. *Bushrod is right. Show domination. It gets them off no end.* He eyed Sweet and nodded in agreement. Yes. Not a Catch 22 at all. This could definitely turn into a good thing.

CHAPTER 68

To: President@peckerswood.co.uk;
From: bangers@home.co.uk
cc: secretary@peckerswood.co.uk
Bcc: vvdycke@home.co.uk

Subject: brill prize ceremony

17th of May, 2023

Dear President,

Just a little scribble from two of your beloved lady members to express our gratitude for the excellent prize ceremony you organized especially for us. Winning the fab medal was thrilling enough as it was, but your warm address to us IN the magnificent CLUBHOUSE really made the whole enterprise utterly sensational.

We had a jolly good time playing the competition, even though it was at that silly ghastly Goodlie and it was indeed a walk over. The only resistance we encountered came from our dear friend Mrs Van Dycke who actually understands how to play golf. Quelle surprise, realizing her history here at our exquisite PW. Do you know she was also the only NICELY MANNERED individual at GG? Must also come from her DISTINGUISHED PW background.

So anyhoo, seeing her again made us realize how much we MISS dear Mrs Van Dycke and Roughie saw no harm in us asking her to play with us again here. And have one of Miss Snuggs's excellent shepherd's pies. And a bottle of red. And strawberries. And clotted cream. And vanilla ice cream with chocolate chips. After which it would be SUPER if we could show her where the medal is. To make certain she feels it really is in the finest of hands. That she didn't lose in vain.

Love you and PW forever and ever,
BBBanger

PS: It would be super FAB if you could accompany us and show Mrs Van Dycke the medal personally. Maybe repeat your kind words?

PPS: Thank you also for supporting us. Agreeing to the match of the century. Jolly good show. Wink, wink.

CHAPTER 69

Ben tried to keep a straight face, listening to the large, olive-skinned man in front of him stumbling over his words, clearly uncomfortable. He stuck his right hand out. 'Listen. We have a deal for coming year. So feel free to help the ladies until then. It's only a couple of weeks.'

Lash nodded and reached out, feeling Ben's strong grip around his own hand. 'Right,' he replied. 'So for now it's only the start of the observations, and after your handover to Mr Long, we will start the training schedule. If this is all, I won't keep you any longer.'

Ben acknowledged Lash's departure with a slight salute and remained seated in the large leather chair, concentrating on the last of the cappuccino in the large cup, now coloured light caramel. He picked it up and cupped both his hands around it, trying to warm the liquid, twirling it slowly. The bar was empty, except for that young help, Lizzie, who was rubbing the surface with a cloth vigorously, trying to make the old wood shine.

The smile he had been trying so hard to repress suddenly appeared, thinking of the Caddy Master Come Teaching Pro, seemingly in a bend over, what he assumed to be a conflict of interest. He shook his head and raised his eyebrows. Hilarious.

Integrity was a good thing, but one could overdo it, he thought to himself and gulped the last of the milky liquid down. It wasn't as if he was coaching the first team of a serious opponent. He glanced at his watch and stood up. One last meeting with Bashit and Roughie and then out on the course to beat a couple of mates.

'Good day, sir.'

He gave Lizzie a slight nod and closed the heavy door behind him, turned left and took the short cut to the President's study, through the back door and past the kitchen, noticing Roughie sitting at the table finishing off a plate of eggs and bacon, wiping his lips, obviously ready to go too. He tapped on the window of the study's back door and peaked in, seeing Bashit close the door towards the main hall, behind a small figure, who clearly resembled Mrs Pushet.

'What was she doing here?,' Ben asked as he stepped through the French doors.

'Just on her way out.' Bashit said, averting his eyes. 'Miss Snuggs is guiding her towards the Ladies' room.'

'Hope the recent P&L is safe and sound,' Ben chuckled, 'otherwise we may have to call in the pigs and have the old prowler locked up.'

'Safe it is,' Bashit assured him, not responding to Ben's smile. 'But sound?'

The President sat down and planted his stick beside him, carefully avoiding Percy lying under the desk. He took his glasses off and rubbed his eyes, suddenly looking tired.

Ben frowned. 'Are you alright, sir?'

Bashit nodded in silence and turned his head towards the window, clearly deep in thought and not wanting to elaborate. The study's door opened after a slight knock, and Roughie appeared, his notebook tucked under his arm.

'Sit down, gentlemen.' Bashit returned to the scene in front of him. 'I would like to get started.'

Roughie and Ben exchanged a quick glance. 'Shouldn't we

wait for Lieutenant Bushrod?,' Ben asked. 'You called for a management meeting.'

'Bushrod is unavoidably detained.' Bashit's voice clearly indicated he wasn't going to explain anything further. 'We will continue without him.' The President turned his attention to Roughie. 'And notes won't be necessary. I would like to discuss things off the record. See it as a, what do you call it nowadays, brainstorm, or something like that.'

Another glance exchanged between Ben and Roughie, both knowing better than to comment.

'I've taken the liberty to look at our quarterly finance report. By myself.' Bashit put his glasses back on and ruffled some papers on his desk. 'And gentlemen, I must confess that things, unfortunately, aren't too bright.' He paused and stared at the two silent men in front of him. 'Quite grim, actually.'

Ben swallowed and coughed in his hand before speaking. 'What do you mean by grim exactly, President?'

'Rising labour costs, astronomic electricity bills, a new fairway mower, buggies that need replacing.' Bashit leaned back in his chair. 'We had to pay Hot a, what shall I call it, an incentive to leave quietly, and Miss Snuggs is holding the coffee machine together with a piece of string and *bloody duct tape*.' The President's voice rose with each word, shouting out the last two, making Ben and Roughie sit up straight.

The shouting turned into a hiss. 'So. Rising costs. Investments to come. And income is declining. Membership count is declining. Again.'

The sound of embarrassed silence thundered through the study, bouncing from the panelled walls into Roughie and Ben's brains, now both turned into immovable pillars of concrete, not daring to move or say anything.

'I think we all three are bright enough to realize that we are actually losing money,' Bashit confessed while he shook his head in misery. 'We need to come up with a solution, gentlemen.

Otherwise our dear old friend the accountant, and subsequently the bank, will eat us alive.'

Ben cleared his throat. 'But what about the consultant we agreed upon? He must have come to some sort of conclusion by now, some kind of strategy?'

Bashit nodded and stared out of the window again. 'Yes. He did. Apparently, he reported his first findings and suggestions to Bushrod. Which, I am sorry to tell you, didn't reach me. For some dark reason.'

'I see,' Ben said carefully, slowly realizing doom was imminent.

'No, Ben.' Bashit shook his head. 'I don't think you do. Our dear fellow board member the Lieutenant dismissed the poor chap, paid him and ordered him to abort the mission. Which I found out about when, how shall I put it, a little old bird told me.'

An embarrassed long silence followed, neither Ben or Roughie had the balls to speak.

'O dear,' Roughie finally piped, turning grey, slowly understanding what this could mean. 'Now what do we do?'

A loud thump made Bashit turn away from the window. Ben had jumped out of his chair and was now fuming and pacing the length of the room. 'That fucking bastard. How dare he pass us by? It's a bloody disgrace.'

'Sit down.' Bashit grabbed his stick and pointed towards the leather club that was pushed aside. 'So we can discuss this calmly, like gentlemen.'

'Right.' Ben returned to the chair, slid it back into position and sat down. 'What's the plan?'

'We will reinstate the consultant, let him finish his job and expect his presentation the last Saturday morning of the Captaincy year. So you can be with us to reflect on it, Ben. And bring the new Captain along.' Bashit stared at the two men. 'Will you second my proposal?,' he asked in a strong voice, not leaving room for discussion.

Roughie and Ben nodded simultaneously, not daring to speak.

'Good.' Bashit hoisted himself up and pulled Percy towards him. 'That will be all, gentlemen.'

He waited for the study to become silent after the two men's departure, turned round and reached out to the bookcase on the left side of the fire place. A sharp tug made the hidden door open, and he stepped in the small room behind it. The three-quarter bed was still unmade and messy after his sleepless night, but he would deal with that later, he thought, grabbing an old rope from the wobbly bedstand and tying it to Percy's collar. He just needed a brisk walk to chase the demons out of his troubled mind.

The bookcase slid back into its lock, revealing nothing to the oblivious eye. Bashit opened and closed the French door, shivered a little and set off towards the course, trying to concentrate on the fresh greenness around him by taking a deep breath of early summer. A yellow butterfly circled around his head and flew towards the first tee, making him turn and notice the threesome waiting to tee off.

Two identical figures, familiar, beckoned him, as well as another woman, less tall but slim, putting her hand up, in a friendly wave. He set off towards them, picking up pace after a surprisingly eager Percy, who could not wait for the treat that was obviously waiting for him in more than one golf bag.

He stopped in his tracks, suddenly realizing who had waved at him. 'Mrs Van Dycke,' he exclaimed, genuinely surprised. 'I hardly recognized you. You look so…different.'

'We know. No more than skin and bones.' Birdie Banger leaned towards him and started whispering. 'It's all the stress. Poor thing is totally burned out. Can't hold her food down. At all.'

'Desperately unhappy at Ghastly,' Bogey added conspiratorially. 'Although she's too decent to admit to it.'

'I see.' Bashit moved forward and offered his hand to Varilla, looking flushed. 'Welcome back, Mrs Van Dycke. Lovely to see you again. And I gather these two want to gloat and show you the medal they managed to wrest from you.'

'After lunch,' the Bangers cried in unison. 'We're having Bunny's pie.'

'After lunch it is.' Bashit nodded. 'Just come and knock at my door.' He stepped back and gestured towards the tee. 'Please. Don't let me keep you.'

Varilla nodded and bent down, stuck her tee between the red markers and stepped back, concentrating on her line before taking her stance, firmly squared. Her head moved behind the ball and her arms went back in a straight line, before coming back in motion with her hips turning towards the pin. The ball shot off her club, dead straight and landed 200 yards further, right in the middle of the fairway.

Good Lord, Bashit thought. *Not bad, for a woman. Pretty decent, actually.* He raised his eyebrows for a second, taking in what he just witnessed. 'Good shot.' He nodded and turned towards the Bangers. 'You have your work cut out for you.' He bowed slightly and walked into the opposite direction towards the ninth green, leaving the three women to their game. The tee was clear, and he crossed the fairway, moving through the trees to the par three tenth, also deserted. Percy sniffed at the empty dog bowl and stared at his master, the President picked it up and filled it with water from the tap under the information board.

He stretched and gazed over the tenth towards the eleventh, the two identical tall yew trees half-way between tee and green stared at him, reminding him of the years passed. They were three feet high when Bushrod and himself planted them, in memory of two beloved deceased members, the digging supervised by his father, making sure they were in perfect alignment.

Bushrod. Bashit shook his head. Half-wit fool, he thought while he sauntered to the wooden bench and sat down, musing on last week's visit after receiving the information. Driving up to the little bungalow, walking up the neat garden path with the gnomes staring at him while he peeked through the net curtains, seeing his fellow board member lying in a beige-coloured lazyboy, a remote control in his right hand and a dirty plate on the little plywood side table next to him.

Mrs Bushrod was surprised and anxious at the same time to see the President, inviting him in and quickly removing her apron. They had just finished their tea, she had said nervously, and would he like a cuppa? He declined, saying he needed to speak to her husband on a confidential matter, and would she mind leaving them to it?

Bushrod nearly fell out of his chair seeing him enter the small room, grasping what his long-life friend had come to tell him. At least his, now former, board member had shown the decency to rise and stand to attention, eyes forward, listening in silence to the monologue Bashit had prepared carefully.

The President sniffed and stroked Percy's head, trying not to get emotional. He closed his eyes, pushing the welling tears back, suddenly feeling warm, comforting arms wrapping around him, followed by soft lips kissing his forehead. The image of his late wife circled around the trees, enveloping him, offering solace, telling him he did the right thing and disappearing through the tight foliage as fast as she had come to him. Some friends don't deserve you, she had whispered in his ear before she vanished. But others do.

It hadn't been a walk in the park, watching Bushrod tremble all through his speech. His so-called friend never admitted to what had happened, even lied blatantly when he stated the consultant threw in the towel himself. The whole charade made Bashit realise this man wasn't his friend and wasn't decent at all.

He had known deep down, felt it in his gut, ever since that game 20 years ago, when he, beyond any reasonable doubt, witnessed his Treasurer dropping a Titleist in the woods during a monthly medal, announcing he had found his ball. He distinctly remembered Bushrod played a Dunlop when leaving the tee. A couple of years later, Bushrod wrote a five at the 17th, while he obviously made an air shot in the rough, and subsequently claimed it to be a practice swing.

This recollection had also made it easier to stand firm this time, telling the astonished man in the lazyboy that he could remain a member, but would do himself a favour by resigning from the board. Before he would be asked to do so. Turning on his heel and leaving the bungalow had felt like a flight, to say the least. But knowing he had done what was expected of him had given him the strength to start his car and drive back to the club, his head held high. But his spirit had been rock bottom, knowing what this would do to Bushrod.

A sharp tapping sound coming from the ninth tee brought him back to the present. He looked towards the noise of laughter now reaching him, seeing Ben, Bobby and Henri walk up to the fairway bunker, ready for their approach. 'This is our cue, Percy,' he said while he pulled himself up and started to walk towards the eleventh, away from the group of young men. 'We need some extended female comfort.'

He checked his watch. If they took the short cut through the practice fairway towards the clubhouse, he would be in time for his half hour coaching young Lizzie.

CHAPTER 70

The leather creaked as Bashit leaned back and stared at the young girl, sitting in the club chair, busying herself with the items on the tray she had brought into the study. He had come to look forward to her visits encouraged by Mrs Pushet, and enjoyed the young eagerness and her obvious willingness to learn.

'Exciting news about this match Miss Hackkett is planning,' he said surreptitiously, watching Lizzie closely, trying to read her. 'Ladies versus gents. Interesting.'

A theatrical sigh reached him. 'You don't believe we can win, do you? But I am positive we can. We chopped up Lavatory and her loo brushes.'

'Miss Thorneybush and her Ladies' Team to you, young lady,' Bashit said sternly. 'Remember your place.'

'My place is on the golf course. Beating a bunch of old men.'

'Of course it is,' Bashit chuckled, despite Lizzie's defying tone. 'Use your time wisely and start hitting the dimples then. The more you practice the luckier you get.' He picked up the Times and searched for clues through his turtle-rimmed magnifying glass. 'Shakespearean lieutenant one with a lean and hungry look has nothing for us. Six letters.'

Lizzie paused for a second, holding the teapot in her right hand and the plate with flapjacks in the other. 'It should end with an O,' she said. 'Nothing. Like naught.'

'Yes.' Bashit nodded. 'And who, according to our dear William, had the look of hunger?'

'May I look it up in one of your books?'

'Absolutely. I will be mother.' Bashit took the pot from Lizzie and poured the tea, enjoying the concentrated look on the young girl's face. He munched on his Java cake, watching her dive deeply in the book she pulled from the old bookcase.

'It's Cassius,' she said triumphantly, pointing at Bashit.

'So it is,' Bashit replied. 'What shall I put down, taking your earlier point in consideration?'

Lizzie hesitated for a second before a broad grin split her face. 'Cassio.'

'Cassio it is.' Bashit scribbled the word in the crossword. 'Excellent.'

'President Bashit?' Lizzie sat down and took a flapjack from the plate sitting on the desk between them. 'I heard that our lieutenant is in the dog house.' She glanced at the old man sitting opposite her. 'What did he do?'

'Let's say he came to the conclusion it wasn't in the club's best interest to remain treasurer,' the President replied, deliberately keeping his eye on the crossword.

'I get that,' Lizzie smirked. 'But what did he do?'

'That, my dear, is between me and the good lieutenant.' Bashit turned and gave Lizzie a stern look. 'In other words, none of your business.'

Lizzie giggled. 'Bummer. I bet it's juicy then.'

Bashit eyed his young companion over his reading glasses, clearly trying to indicate the subject was closed, but her attention was suddenly focused towards the window. Her cheeks became flushed, as she followed a slim female figure with a long flowing orange pony tail.

‘How’s school?,’ he asked, a bit louder than usual. ‘Any new chums?’

Lizzie shrugged and tore herself away from the window. ‘Not really. The boys are still ignorant, and the girls…’ she paused for a second, ‘not really my types. But who needs them? I have friends here. You are my friend.’

‘Right. School. Seems a million years ago, but what fond memories.’ Bashit leaned back in his chair and gazed at the ceiling. ‘I’ll tell you a little secret. When I was your age, I was desperately smitten with our cleaning lady, Miss Miller. I can still picture her now. Glorious creature.’

Lizzie guffawed. ‘What happened? Between you and Miss Miller?’

‘Nothing, of course.’ Bashit sat up straight again. ‘It was just innocent adoration, a schoolboy crush. I was like a droopy puppy, following her around everywhere,’ he said with a chuckle. ‘Which was easy, she lived on the premises. With her sister. Who, funnily enough, looked nothing like her. But what did we boys know.’

‘How come?,’ Lizzie asked. ‘What didn’t you know?’

‘That they were lovers, of course,’ President Bashit snorted. ‘But in those days? All teaching staff knew, but just pretended not to. But this arrangement made it possible they could live together, happily ever after.’

‘Ah. I see,’ Lizzie said, feeling slightly embarrassed, but trying not to show it. ‘Poor cleaning lady, having to live a lie. Is that why you fell out of love with her?’

‘Good Lord, no. Once sixteen, my friends and I were allowed to go out, in the village. Where we met girls our own age. When Gwendoline Finley let me kiss her on the lips, Miss Miller was fast forgotten.’

Lizzie turned pink, trying to process what the President was telling her, why he was so frank all of a sudden. ‘What happened to Gwendoline?,’ she asked, eager to find out more.

'I married her,' Bashit said, the change in his voice telling her the subject was closed. 'You just mentioned friendship to me, young lady.'

'Yes. You are my friend, President, aren't you? Otherwise you wouldn't be telling me what you just did.' Lizzie felt a sense of pride, realizing this had been a rare, but special moment of confidence between them.

'I am.' Bashit nodded and pulled a drawer open. Two pieces of paper came out. 'And as your friend, I need a favour.' He passed the papers towards her, tapping on the headshot of a young woman.

Lizzie gazed at the picture, seeing an attractive face staring at her, feeling the bold look in the eyes pierce through her, making her feel strangely unnerved for a couple of moments.

'We're recruiting a new greenkeeper. And this young lady seems to fit the bill.' He looked at Lizzie, who was still fixated on the picture in front of her. 'You know how much I value good morals and character, don't you my dear?'

Lizzie nodded, not wanting to tear herself away from the photo.

'So I thought, before we go any further, you might want to assist me in the selection procedure.' Bashit reached over and carefully pulled the papers from Lizzie's fingers. 'Do some research on this girl. See if she's a good fit. A little birdie told me you can do this through that phone you seem so attached to. You could look her up on, what's it called, Instant Scam, or TrickTrap?'

'President Bashit. It's Instagram and TikTok. You know that.' Lizzie giggled, despite the funny feeling in her stomach.

'Whatever.' Bashit tried to look stern but couldn't hide the twinkle in his eye. 'I would like you to do a background check, but also meet this candidate in person. Have a coffee with her. Get to know her. So you can report back to me, informed correctly.' He folded the papers and handed them back. 'Deal?'

Lizzie nodded profusely and pulled her collar up, trying to hide the red patches that were creeping up her neck. 'Deal.'

'Good. Now leave this old man to have his tea in peace. Go and have some fun for a change. Practice your short game for that match against those ancient men.'

Lizzie stood up and stared at her old friend, understanding what he had done. She walked round the desk, put her arms around him for a second and squeezed. 'Thank you, President Bashit,' she whispered.

'Get out. And tell Miss Hackkett I am ready for our meeting.'

'I will sir.' The door opened, Lizzie slipped out, carefully making way for Philly who slid past her.

'Can I interest you in a spot of tea?' The dark, steaming liquid was poured into the porcelain cup in a steady flow before Philly could answer. 'Milk, no sugar, I presume? And please take a Java cake, will do you good.'

Philly nodded and leaned over to accept the offering, feeling confident and relaxed, knowing she had prepared well.

'Well, Miss Hackkett.' The President sat back and offered his biscuit to Percy, lying under the desk. 'You wanted to discuss next year's Lady Captain, and I want to discuss this match you are so eager to have. Please, you go first.'

'Yes, sir. I think I have found the perfect candidate,' she said assuredly. 'I would like to suggest that Prudence Love takes over.'

'Interesting. Tell me, why Miss Love, Hackkett?' The President's glasses came off, revealing the amused glint in his eyes.

'Right,' Philly said slowly, trying to ignore the sudden inkling she was being made fun of. 'Pru is extremely structured and organized, loves the game and in general, has good rapport with the group.'

'Which group? You mean our staff?' Bashit's voice trembled, trying to hold his laughter in. 'I agree she used her attributes quite effectively. Some would even say she's quite the motivator.' He paused, put his tea cup down in front of him and moved forward. 'Try again, Miss Hackkett,' he said earnestly.

Philly stared at the old face. 'Oh, alright then,' she said while returning his look, 'the Bangers are too lazy, Mrs Pushet's too old, Lizzie's too young and Miss Snuggs? Too gullible.' She blinked a couple of times, realizing what she had said. 'Sorry, President. Miss Snuggs is adorable.'

'I know what you mean. And valid points.' President Bashit's amused look turned to the window. 'So. Quite a pickle you find yourself in. What *can* you do? You might consider appointing Maggie, the dog?' Bashit moved his eyes back to Philly and started laughing.

'Ha bloody ha.' Philly shook her head, tried to remain serious but couldn't help a giggle coming out. 'How hilarious.'

'Sorry, Miss Hackkett. That was a cheap shot.' Bashit composed himself, and his expression turned serious. 'Does Miss Love have a specific goal, for her year?'

'Yes.' Philly nodded, feeling a little apprehensive. 'She would like to enter us for the handicap county league.' She glanced at Bashit, trying to gauge his reaction. 'With the board's support, that is.'

'Fair enough. Let me think about it and see what we might consider. But Miss Love it is.' He pulled himself up and leaned on his stick. 'One more thing though. Try and make it a unanimous decision. I don't think I can bear another tantrum.' He moved to the window, nodding towards Ben and Roughie getting ready on the first. 'Which brings me to this match against the men.' He waited for a moment, watching Ben tee off, hitting a massive drive.

'Confidence is the most important single factor in this game, and no matter how great your natural talent, there is only one way to obtain and sustain it, Miss Hackkett.' A pause followed. 'Work. And if this turns out to be massive deception, don't come running to me. You will need to hit a million balls, young lady. According to Jack Nicklaus.

Philly smiled confidently, knowing exactly how to respond before she turned and left the study. 'There's no sense in going to a tournament if you don't believe that you can win it.' She left a dramatic silence before continuing. 'According to Tiger Woods.'

CHAPTER 71

The familiar sound of Lash's footsteps faded away. Pru watched him until he disappeared out of her sight, after taking the turn behind the large oak trees. She looked round the caddy shack and began clearing. First the dishes, then a good scrub in the shower room, and the bed needed clean sheets. She peeked at her mobile. Another hour and a half before she would meet Philly for a round and discuss the topics for the team meeting afterwards.

This whole match against the men thing was getting more absurd by the day. She had seen the men teeing off this morning, hitting shots like cannon fire. But it seemed she was the only one having reservations. Lizzie obviously thought it was a hoot, the Bangers acted as if the whole thing wasn't remotely challenging, and Philly actually thought they stood a chance. Mrs Pushet had been a bit more realistic, commenting on the psychological part of the game. 'The mind messes up more shots than the body.' She had said, quoting Tommy Bolt, obviously an intelligent man. And Lash hadn't given up hope. 'As long as you girls keep it on the straight and narrow, you have a chance. The one who gets it nearest to the flag and putts the best will win.'

Her cloth flew over the little desk Lash used to work on his notes, and she bent over to clean between the wood and the whitewashed wall, knocking her knee against the knob holding the small doors shut. She watched the doors open, now staring at a couple of folders lying on top of a stack of books. B. Chipperfield. The sticker taped to the top folder said. She looked over her shoulder, making sure she was alone, although she knew no-one was there and knelt down, pulling the plastic folders towards her. They were all there, neatly pasted and sorted by name, one folder for each team member.

Pru took a deep breath, considering what to do. Her finger moved to Ben's name, stroking it slowly and flipping the folder open in a split second. It didn't take her long to process the information. Ben was obviously a long hitter, but seemed to have trouble striking the fairway. And missed quite a couple of short puts frequently, so it seemed. Some anger issues too, according to Lash's note in the side line.

'Well, well.' Pru thought as she put the folder aside and stared at the next one. H. Sweet. Not a lot of comments, except for a lengthy analysis on the short game. Obviously room for improvement. She reached out for her mobile in her back pocket, ready to make some pictures to share with Philly, who obviously would be thrilled to have this and put it to very good use.

She put the phone in place and stared at the photo that appeared as she switched it on. The eyes, with that look she loved so much, appeared on the screen. Oozing honesty, decency, loyalty. Suddenly reminding her of what Philly's Dad had taught them, when they were still in school, learning the rules and etiquette by reading P.G Woodhouse. "Golf is the infallible test. The man who can go into a patch of rough alone, with the knowledge that only God is watching him, and play his ball where it lies, is the man who will serve you faithfully and well."

She heard Mr Hackkett's voice in her head, instantly dropped the phone and closed her eyes for a second, feeling the shame rise to her face. The folders went back, exactly how she found them. She firmly closed the little desk, finished her chores and ran to the Ladies' room, eager to see her friends.

A little rock moved in front of her right foot against the Ladies' room door, making certain it would stay open to let the fresh air in. Philly took the broom and quickly swept, pushing out the dust and sand. Lizzy switched her mobile off, reluctantly tearing herself away from Anne van Dam's swing and started to clear leftover crumbs from the kitchen surface. A few thumps fluffed up the cushions, and Pru unfolded the plastic chairs so all of them could sit together to discuss the strategy for the coming big match.

A mobile buzzed, and Philly tapped it, listening to Bogey's voice asking her if it would be alright if Varilla stayed for a drink. 'Of course! Why not forever? She's hardly the enemy anymore, now is she?'

The next thing they knew was Birdie bursting in, pushing a clearly embarrassed Varilla forward, holding a bottle towards Philly. 'Thanks for having me, Philly, Pru,' she said, sounding genuinely pleased. 'I had a wonderful morning, lunch and afternoon.' A grateful look went towards the Banger sisters, already with their heads in the fridge, pulling chilled bottles out and putting in Varilla's gift.

Maggie had followed them, but now ran out again seeing Bunny walk up with Mrs Pushet on one arm and a large basket on the other. Birdie went towards her and relieved them of the basket, pulled away the cloth and sniffed. 'Yummie,' she said, closing her eyes. 'Sausage rolls and quiche. Heaven.'

'What did you shoot?,' Pru asked Varilla, smiling at her.

'76. The course played like a dream. Just how I remembered it. You?'

'Goodness,' Pru replied, raising her eyebrows. 'That's rather good. We certainly didn't come close to that. Both 78.' She turned to the Bangers. 'What about you two?'

'75 and 76.' The sisters started to giggle. 'Both lost a ball on the 17th.'

'And Mrs Pushet? I saw you come up the ninth?' Philly smiled and reached over to hand the old lady her glass of wine.

'Can't remember,' Mrs Pushet said. 'But I heard cheeky Charmers say he shot 76.'

'That sounds like good news,' Varilla said while she looked round. 'You might actually outplay those miserable men. You know I would give my left arm to see them get beaten by you.'

'You would?' Philly stared at her, watching her slump down and put her head in her hands before starting to speak again. 'Why?'

'I actually thought Goodlie would be more open towards us ladies,' Varilla admitted, making the others turn towards her.

'Go on,' Pru said, urging her to speak further.

'We might be condoned at the same bar, to spend our money, but our dear Secretary decided that our monthly Ladies Day should coincide with major work on the course.' Varilla reached out to the glass Birdie handed her and took a large gulp. 'Can you imagine what the men would say, if the greens were sanded during their most important match? There would be hell to pay. But we just have to put up with it.'

'Oh dear.' Philly smiled ruefully. 'That's very naughty.'

'That's one way of putting it,' Varilla said, her eyes now shooting fire. 'I would call it blatant discrimination.' She looked round the group. 'All the more reason to take this seriously. If you guys pull this off, things could really change.'

'Not only for us, as it seems.' Philly stood up, taking the lead, feeling excited. 'Imagine, we win and applications start streaming in. We might even recruit from Goodlie.'

'As long as you don't admit Lav,' Varilla smirked. 'She will be the death of you.'

'Don't worry,' the whole group replied in unison.

'Listen. Pru and I have something to share with you.' Philly sat down and pulled a plastic bag from under her seat, revealing a pile of children's clothes, pink checked trousers, a white polo necked shirt and a soft pink V-necked sweater, all faded. She put them on top of each other and nodded to Pru, who handed her a pair of heavy looking scissors.

She started cutting, pushing the scissors, making even squares. 'I wore these when Bashit and I pulled down the *'no dogs or women allowed'* sign,' she said, handing the first squares to Bunny and the second squares to Bogey. 'I was nine years old and felt so proud wearing these. And my mother, bless her, held on to them and gave them to me when I got the Captaincy.'

Six pairs of eyes stared at her.

'And now, they will be our good luck charm.' She looked at Mrs Pushet, who gave her a wink. 'Hand your pieces over to Mrs Pushet, and she will turn them into driver covers.'

The third cut passed towards Birdie, who started to weep, her crying immediately followed by sobs from Bogey. 'So every time you will get your driver out, which will be on nearly every hole playing from the medal, you will be reminded of what we can accomplish.' The last squares remained on her lap, for Pru, Lizzie and herself.

'That is a really nice touch.' Varilla said, breaking the emotional silence. 'Just the thing to remind you of your joint mission.'

Pru appeared next to Philly, holding two large glasses. 'To you, Captain,' she said warmly. 'And Varilla's right. We are on a mission together, have the best team ever, coached by the best pro ever. We will stay together, play together, and remain invincible. We are the best. Fuck the rest.'

'Hear, hear,' Mrs Pushet called out, raising her glass into the air. 'You will show those men, and the rest of the world. Let's drink to that.' She nudged Bunny. 'Come on. Raise your glass and gulp.'

‘I can’t,’ Bunny whispered.

‘Whyever not?,’ Philly asked.

Bunny started crying uncontrollably before uttering, ‘I think I’m pregnant.’

CHAPTER 72

The Ladies' room had never felt more soundless and still. Even Maggie was motionless, just like all the flabbergasted figures around her.

Mrs Pushet was the first to break the deadly quiet. 'Are you certain?,' she asked carefully.

Bunny nodded and tearfully exclaimed, 'I went to my GP because I was feeling so tired, and he told me I'm five months in.'

'In what?,' Birdie asked, looking bewildered.

'The pudding club, silly,' Bogey replied. 'It appears Bunns has a bun in her oven.'

'Holy crap.' Birdie's mouth fell open. 'So you will have a baby popping out in what, four months?'

'Yes.' Bunny's sobbing turned into a wail. 'And I haven't even told anyone. Not even Roughie.'

Philly and Pru exchanged a quick look, remaining motionless, not knowing what to say or do. 'Fucking hell,' Philly whispered.

Mrs Pushet stood up, wiggled herself next to the crying young girl and pulled her towards her. 'Sssshh,' she cooed, slowly rocking Bunny. 'It's going to be fine. Don't worry. You have your friends here.'

Another wail filled the room. 'The doctor said I need to slow down. No more than four hours of work a day, no more than nine holes a week,' Bunny sobbed. 'This messes everything up. Now what are we going to do?'

'Holy crap,' the Bangers cried out together. 'What are we going to do?'

'First of all, congratulate this new young mother.' Varilla put her glass down and moved over to Bunny. 'What fantastic news,' she said and pulled a wet cheek towards her to kiss it. 'This is one lucky little baby. To have you as a mum. And Roughie as a dad. Well done you two.'

The silence re-appeared, now filled with embarrassment, quickly followed by frenzied bustle. Philly and Pru got on their feet simultaneously, bumping into each other trying to reach over to Bunny. Birdie hurried to get a glass of water, and Bogey started to plump up a cushion to put behind Bunny's back. Maggie stretched and licked the tears from her friend's face, making her smile again.

'Tell us how you feel,' Mrs Pushet asked. 'Honestly.'

Bunny shrugged. 'Confused. Happy. Afraid.' Her look of discomfort suddenly turned into anxiety. 'I'm so scared,' she admitted, hardly audible.

A quick look exchanged between Philly and Mrs Pushet, the older woman pulled the trembling young woman towards her. 'Don't be. You'll be fine,' she whispered, stroking the long blond hair. 'More than fine.'

Bunny nodded, leaning towards the little figure next to her, nearly squashing it. 'I suppose so. But it's all so overwhelming. And I feel ever so guilty.' Her large, tear-filled eyes went towards Philly and Pru. 'You all were so excited. About our team. And our match. I've screwed everything up.'

Maggie's ears pricked up, and she started trembling, looking towards the door, clearly hearing something. The room fell silent again, and all the women followed the little dog's movement, concentrating on the sound of footsteps crunching the gravel, getting more pronounced with every step.

The door opened, letting in a stream of warm air filled with the heavy scent of Black Opium. 'Yoohoo, I'm back,' the familiar high-pitched voice rang. Mrs Rough stared at the scene in front of her, waiting for a welcome cheer but not getting it, realizing something was going on. 'From the Bahamas…'

Mrs Pushet stood up and pointed at her seat. 'Dear Cherie,' she said warmly. 'Why don't you sit down here and us girls go and walk Maggie?' Her face turned to Bunny, whose cheeks were now burning hot. 'So Bunny and you can have a word in private? I think she needs you.'

Maggie ran towards the lake between the 16th and the 18th, ready to torment the ducks that were escaping towards the middle of the water. Philly walked towards the bench and sat down, gazing at the ripples the ducks were causing and drew a deep breath. Mrs Pushet moved over next to her, the other women remained standing, silent.

'Bloody hell,' Birdie said. 'A baby. Who would have thought.'

Mrs Pushet turned to her. 'It's not rocket science, dear. You do risk getting knocked up if you have sex.'

'Mrs Pushet?' Bogey sat down next to the little figure. 'What's it like, having a baby?'

'Well,' Mrs Pushet shrugged and smirked, 'let me think. It's like playing the worst 36 holes you have ever encountered, in one day, in blistering heat, and having to carry your bag yourself. And then as a reward, you are forced to push a giant water melon out of an opening as tight as your asshole.'

'Bloody hell. Now wonder Bunns is frightened,' Birdie said, turning to her sister. 'Doesn't sound like our cup of tea at all, now does it?'

Bogey shook her head vigorously, looking petrified.

'And that's not everything.' Mrs Pushet shook her head and gave Philly a quick look. 'Oh, no. After that they suck you dry for twenty years and then bugger off to godforsaken Australia where they are too busy to pick up the phone to see how you are. Thank God I have you lot.'

Varilla cleared her throat, trying to lighten the mood. 'I'm sure Bunny's baby will be absolutely lovely.' She looked at the others, slightly embarrassed. 'It might inspire us. I want to have a baby someday.'

'Then you need to get your spurs on and ride.' Mrs Pushet waved her finger. 'You might be able to do the 36 holes easily now, but you won't have the flush of youth forever. You're not exactly a spring chicken, darling.'

'Thank you, Mrs Pushet,' Pru said sternly, putting her arm around a stricken Varilla and turning her face to Philly. 'Listen. Let's leave our perceived offspring for now, as delightful as they might seem. We need to think about the match now Bunny is obviously not able to play.'

Damn right they did. It was the first thing that shot through her brain after Bunny's reveal, Philly thought, feeling a tiny pang of guilt pierce her conscience. Baby okay, but couldn't they have timed it a little more carefully? 'Now what?,' she asked rhetorically. 'I think we've run out of household angels to save us.' She eyed the Bangers, who were staring at Varilla, looking as if they were in some kind of parallel universe. 'Any bright ideas anyone?'

Pru shrugged. 'We're doomed,' she said. 'Without some kind of miracle.'

'I feel lost.' Mrs Pushet shook her head. 'Maybe this is the divine telling us to lay down our capes. Our elegant escape, to back down gracefully and return to our humble beginnings.'

'No.' Birdie's voice came up suddenly, sounding resolute. 'We've come this far.' She walked over to Varilla and stared at her. 'We've had lunch together. Spent the day together. And had a super time.’

‘Have you come home, Varilla?,’ Bogey asked in a grave voice, touching a trembling Varilla, who nodded profusely.

‘Welcome back.’ Birdie pulled Varilla towards them and hugged her tightly.

CHAPTER 73

To: secretary@peckerswood.co.uk
From: bangers@home.co.uk
cc: President@peckerswood.co.uk;
Bcc: vvdycke@home.co.uk

4th of June 2023

Subject: pitter patter

Dear Secretary, darling Roughie,

What excellent news! A ROUGH BABY!

We cannot wait for the sound of pitter patter little feet, running around your mansion. How clever you are making Bunns and your fab mother so deliriously happy. We DO ADMIT we were in shock for a quite a while, realizing Bunny will not be able to spend MUCH TIME WITH US anymore.

WHAT are WE going to do now? WE will be so MASSIVELY bored. Maybe we can hang out with YOU much more? Like ALL DAY, EVERY DAY? Help you run our exquisite PW? Because you will be MASSIVELY bored too not having Bunny at your disposal ALL the time? Doesn't the prospect of US AT YOUR FEET ALL DAY sound ABSOLUTELY DIVINE?

Let's hope we don't acquire a potential new friend and get distracted by some lost soul, keeping us occupied and TEARING US AWAY FROM YOU. Because we feel the desperate need to save someone who has seen the error of her ways, wandering a fair way on a lost course, confused, waiting for guidance towards the path of righteousness, how to return home to her flock?

Love you,
Boogs & Birds

PS: Did we tell you we bumped into Mrs Van Dycke the other day, when you were on the course with that delightful Charles Charmers, when you both shot 80 and us girls came home with 75?

PPS: We actually had quite a jolly day together, even though V had a meltdown on the tenth when we asked her how she was fairing at Ghastly. Turns out to be far more dire than anyone could imagine. Poor V. We gave her all the love we had in us and she's alright now.

PPPS: Question. How would that bitch Thorneybush feel if our continuous TLC would lure our potential new friend back to her real flock?

PPPPS: Imagine the look on TBush's ugly filthy face reading the draft resignation letter you find attached? We thought it might help V to stop wandering and keep her following us on our path towards the fairest way. What do you think?

PPPPPS: By the way, we noticed you were putting short on quite a few holes yesterday? (When we followed you on your path? Being so bored without our potential friend?)

PPPPPPS: The greens are fast this time of year, but not THAT fast. Pitter patter, darling Roughie, pitter patter.

Attachment
Resignation letter. First and final draft.

Dear Miss Thorneybush, darling Lav,

The great artist and golfer A. Cooper once said: 'Mistakes are part of the game. It's how well you recover from them, that's the mark of a great player.'

How inspiring. And comforting. And what a guiding principle, nearly divine.

I have made a humongous mistake. But I have found my road to recovery. And unsurprisingly enough, this road leads me towards the gate of heaven through which I have gone before, and will pass through again, leading me to my fellow great players, to whom I truly belong. My real sisters, who achieve greatness on their course and off, but understand this is worthless without the things that really matter, like decency and honesty.

If you are wondering what I am on about, which, knowing your brain is as painfully slow as your game, could be the case, I am leaving Ghastly Goodlie and returning to Divine Peckers Wood.

In other words, my dear Lavender, good bye, au revoir, auf wedersehen, fare well. I wish you go far and hope you will stay there.

Yours sincerely,
Mrs V. Van Dycke

Ps. Please don't bother to reply to me. The mere thought of having to read your poison makes me feel rather sick.

PPs. You might have heard about the future Mr and Mrs Rough expecting. Which makes me the latest team member. So thrilled. Have forked out for the most adorable Tiger baby outfit ever.

CHAPTER 74

Philly turned towards her side and stretched, realizing how much she enjoyed being alone in her bed. She pushed the duvet away and slipped out to the small kitchen, wanting a cup of tea to calm the nerves that were now really building up. Just a couple of hours before the big day.

The water started to boil, and she poured it over the used teabag in her mug, watching the liquid go dark. She sat down at the small kitchen table, cupping the mug with both hands and closed her eyes, letting her thoughts drift back to last week's events.

Mrs Rough's elation about her becoming a grandmother had turned to frenzied over-excitement wanting to arrange the wedding of the century before the baby was due. This burst of crazed fever was quickly but firmly turned cold by an unexpectedly resolute Bunny who clearly put that she was having nothing of the sort, pointing out she had no desire to spend her wedding day absolutely exhausted and looking like a hippo that had swallowed a yoga ball. After she had safely delivered the baby, there was more than time enough for her future mother-in-law to come up with whatever she fancied for a fun packed wedding. But for now, Roughie and herself were setting a date for a quick registry office arrangement, and nothing further.

Philly smiled, remembering Mrs Rough's astonished face and consequently long pout which was taken care of by a lengthy walk around the course with Mrs Pushet and President Bashit. Apparently the promise of full ownership of organizing the wedding and the commitment of the whole Ladies team to be bridesmaids had calmed the waves. Move over Windsors, here come the Roughies. Mrs Rough was probably arranging the horses and carriages already. The mere thought of the whole team clad in probably light pink princess gowns with massive bows above their bums, clutching Bunny's train while climbing some cathedral's steps made Philly giggle.

After the sensation of Bunny's pregnancy had died down, she and Pru had called the team together to concentrate on the next steps towards their match. Bunny had taken the opportunity to have a good cry, realizing she really wouldn't be able to be part of the team playing the men, but hugged Varilla and made her promise she would do everything she possibly could to win. Since then Pru and Varilla had played together as much as they could, finding out how to motivate each other. The Bangers were dividing their time between helping out in the kitchen and bar together with Mrs Rough, and practicing their putting. Lizzie was on a tight schedule, doing her homework with Mrs Pushet after which she would be found on the driving range, more often than not accompanied by Philly's father, who seemed to massively enjoy the progress of his new eager pupil.

President Bashit had reinstated Varilla without a fuss, making her promise to lure her husband back as well, which she did with success. Roughie told her he swore he saw skid marks in the car park where Virgil's car was, as if had jumped in his car and bolted from Goodlie to Peckers Wood as fast as racing in a Formula 1 match.

Philly turned her head and rested her chin on her knees. She needed to be realistic. Chances were slim, to say the least. But at least some good had come out of last year. Varilla was back where she belonged, and Bunny and Pru had landed their loves.

The remainder of the tea went down her throat, and she got up, stretched, took a deep breath and went back to bed.

CHAPTER 75

President Bashit wiggled his right foot, nudging the furry lump at the end of the bed, telling the dog to wake up. Percy's large droopy eyes looked at him, and the dog rolled over, knowing it was time to crawl off the warm patch and wait for the rope to be tied to his collar. The duvet was folded backwards, and the President's feet hit the floor boards. He sat still for a moment, contemplating the long day ahead of him. The meeting, the match, the hand-over party with the men. His right arm stretched, reached for his toilet bag, and pulling it under his arm while tying Percy to his rope with his left hand.

'Come on, old boy. Let's go before the light comes.' He stood up and opened the door to his study, listening to the quiet around him. It was so early in the day not even the birds had started to sing yet. He took his familiar route to the men's room and took a long shower, relaxing under the hard stream of hot water gushing over his body. He soaped his face and shaved, using the old razor, his hand knowing what to do by instinct. Next in the routine was a firm brushing of teeth and turning the water from hot to stone cold, leaving him feeling invigorated while drying off with one of the rough towels from the warm airing cabinet.

A brush appeared from his bag, and Percy flopped over, ready for his buff. Bashit knelt down and stroked his friend in long movements, from head to tail, announcing the final brush with a kiss on the dog's long snout. 'Time for walkies,' he said while he pushed his bag in his locker. 'And then breakfast, before we go and see what news our friend the consultant has for us.'

'What's the matter?' President Bashit peered over his glasses, towards the bent figure in front of him. 'You haven't said two words while you've been in here in my study.'

A dark look came towards him. 'I said "good morning." That's two words. Or can't you count?'

'I think I will ignore your rude sarcasm for now, Lizzie. Knowing the circumstances.'

'What do you mean?' Lizzie put the plate in front of the President and held the tray in front of her, like a shield.

'I can understand the fact you're nervous. For this afternoon.'

The tray came up higher, now blocking Lizzie's entire frame. 'Why should I be nervous?,' she said defensively. 'I'm never nervous for a game. That's for lame sissies. I'm not a sissy.'

'I see.' Bashit started slicing his bacon. 'Am I right in assuming you have your phone on you?,' he asked while he looked at the confused face in front of him. 'Do me a favour and google 'Woods Tiger nervous quote.'

Lizzie's phone was jerked out of her trouser pocket, and she started tapping.

'What have you found? Anything interesting?,' Bashit asked casually.

'"*If you're not nervous, it means you don't care.*"' Lizzie's voice was hardly audible. '"*Quote by Tiger Woods.*"'

'What's that?,' Bashit leaned forward and held his hand behind his ear. 'Speak up child.'

"*There's nothing wrong with having your goals really high and trying to achieve them. That's the fun part.*" The words came out in a fast flow, and the tray fell on the floor. Lizzie's shoulders slumped, and her hands flew to her face. 'President Bashit, I am so shaky I don't know what to do. What if I fuck up and make a fool of myself? Philly will be so disappointed. You will be so disappointed. And Mr Hackkett….'

'Shut up and stop whining. That sounds lame and doesn't suit you.' The President folded his napkin and sat back. 'Listen, my young friend. If I am not mistaken, our dear friend Tiger also said that disappointment is part of the game, and how one handles it defines one as a competitor.' He stood up and walked up to Lizzie, still frozen in front of the desk. 'I know you will give it everything you have. Just play fair and square. That's all that counts.'

He scooped up the tray with the handle of his stick and pushed it towards Lizzie. 'Now. Let me finish my breakfast. Go and check the conference room. My guest will be here any minute.' He turned the girl round, gave her a slight push and walked her to the door. 'Do as Tiger does. Smile at obstacles. It makes them go away.' The door opened, and he waved at the young girl, telling her to leave him.

Bashit opened the door and walked towards Roughie, who was bent over, plugging a large cable in the screen above the conference table and setting his laptop up. Ben was rearranging some chairs and greeted him with a slight nod. 'Refreshment are on their way, sir,' he said. 'And so is our guest. Bobby is picking him up now.'

'Good show.' He sat down in his usual spot and looked round. The place could do with a proper dusting, he noticed. And the curtains looked tired too, suddenly. Just like the wallpaper. He smiled to himself, in spite of the fact the decor made him feel a little depressed. Might be a good job for the ladies, he thought. Getting their teeth into redecorating, if the consultant had some good ideas for bringing in the much-needed cash.

Bunny came in, looking big but beautiful and started on setting out the tea and coffee. He caught her eye and winked at her, which was rewarded by a shy smile. A knock on the door made her quicken her pace and she left, squeezing herself past Bobby and a crisp young man coming up towards him with an outstretched arm, followed by the usual 'How do you do?'

He started the meeting with the customary pleasantries and invited the consultant to start his presentation, taking in each slide as the delivery continued, making notes, waiting for the young man to wrap up with his final recommendation.

'Thank you very much,' Bashit said slowly. 'For these remarkable insights.' A black-out silence followed with embarrassed glances moving between the other men. 'However, something tells me we've heard this all before. Or am I having a really powerful case of the déjà vu's?'

The consultant looked bewildered. 'Would you like me to go over my recommendation again? Explain some more?'

'No.' Bashit shook his head and stood up. 'It's crystal clear to me. Thank you very much for your time and send your invoice as soon as you can. To me personally, please.' The President's hand came forward, and the consultant shot towards him to shake it. 'Good day. Mr Long will show you out.'

Bobby stumbled to his feet, reached over to assist the confused consultant gather his briefcase, and they made their way out, leaving Ben and Roughie looking embarrassed. Bashit hobbled towards the laptop and pulled the cable out with a sharp tug, fading the blue light out. 'Well, well.' He leaned on his stick and started to hum. '"Low-hanging fruit," the young man said. Where, in earth, have I heard that before?' He turned round, hearing the door close behind Bobby coming in, who was looking agitated, sensing there was trouble to come.

'Tell me, boys.' Bashit gripped his walking stick. 'Did I actually hear that recruiting 75 women during the next three years would cause considerable financial spinoff and should balance the books towards a sound profit?' The stick came up and hit the table with enormous speed, sounding like a whip coming down.

'Yes, sir,' Ben whispered, knowing better than to try and contradict Bashit. 'That is, in effect, what the consultant said.'

'And for that insight, our club now is thousands of pounds the poorer?' His voice bellowed across the room, causing the others to duck. 'What a fucking joke!'

The room remained silent, as if trying to recover from the outburst.

Ben finally managed to clear his throat and put his hand up. 'If I may, sir?,' he piped, while he tried to sit up straight, not feeling the confidence he needed right now. 'We might not feel inclined to follow the recommendation. How we run our fine club is up to us. What we communicate to our members is up to us.'

'Absolutely, yes,' Bobby said, wringing his hands, looking at Roughie for support but failing to catch his eye. 'I mean, come on. What does this chap think, anyway. He obviously hasn't a clue.'

Ben nodded. 'Right.' He stood up and started pacing. 'You're right, Bashit. This is a joke. What was the man on about? For goodness sake, what a moron to come up with this nonsense.'

'Sit down.' The stick came down again, this time even faster than the first time, making Ben cringe and run back to his seat. 'And bloody well shut up.' The President's face was bright red, specks of froth that had started to form in the corners of his mouth now flew across the room as he jerked himself towards Roughie. 'Look up the minutes of the meeting when our ladies joined the board meeting. I would like to hear again what they came up with.' He spun round and stared at Ben. 'And I am certain our soon to be former Club Captain is eager to hear it too. See if he still thinks the consultant's idea is, what is the word again, moronic.'

The chilly silence after Bashit's words was broken by soft tapping of the keyboard, and Roughie started to speak, his voice trembling as he read what was in front of him, aware of the embarrassed looks Ben and Bobby were exchanging.

Bashit crossed his arms over his chest. 'Well, gentlemen, let me explain, as you lot obviously don't grasp what the joke is. Or first, what it is not.' He moved forward, not moving his arms. 'It's not that we should consider a larger ladies section. No. The joke is we are going to fork out money, our members' money, money we really do not have much of these days, to pay for a consultant who comes up with a recommendation we already have possession of.' The bald head shook, Bashit's face looked distorted. 'How in earth are we going to explain that to our dear members? And what in hell's name will our new treasurer think?'

'Why should we explain?,' Ben asked. 'I mean, nobody reads the bloody minutes anyway. And who says we need to share this presentation?' His shoulders came up in a dismissive shrug. 'And we haven't appointed a new treasurer yet. So what's the damn fuss?'

Bobby's hand came up, accompanied by a conspiring look at Ben. 'Yes, President. Now you mention it. What is the status on the new treasurer? Any candidates?'

'Well, gentlemen.' The sarcasm in Bashit's tone was sharp enough to cut through steel. 'One might assume that, from somewhere deep down in our membership base, some fine nominee would have popped up, at least one hopeful contender approaching me with actual sound suggestions on how to run our, in your words, great institution's bloody finances and make this club, or what is left of it, ready for the future. But up to now, zilch, nada, nothing.' Bashit slumped backwards. 'So, like everything else here, I have to deal with the blasted shambles myself.'

Ben and Bobby eyed each other and rose their eyebrows simultaneously, understanding not to react and turning to an uncomfortable Roughie obviously chewing on something he wanted to share. Ben pushed his arm out and checked his watch. 'Could we come to an end? We need to grab some lunch before we tee off for that match against the Ladies. And we want to wrap up some things for the celebration later.'

Roughie opened his mouth, put his finger up and started to speak. 'We could consider following up on the consultant's report,' he said carefully. He blushed and added, 'I mean, to be quite fair, I've rather enjoyed playing with Bunny. If I'm honest, I miss our rounds, now she can't play.' He turned to Bashit. 'And Bunny and I are really fond of Lizzie. Like our President is too, aren't you?'

A load groan erupted from Ben and Bobby's side of the table. Both the men slouched back and put their hands over their eyes. 'Good Lord.' Bobby started to chuckle. 'Jellyfish.' He hoisted himself up and moved towards the door, followed by Ben, also snickering.

'Let's park the subject for the moment and put it on the agenda for our next meeting,' Ben added in a cocky manner, making Bashit frown. 'Something will come to us. It always does. See you for drinks later.'

The door closed behind them with a loud bang, leaving the President staring at his Secretary in silence.

CHAPTER 76

200 yards to the entrance. Please drive slowly.

Philly suppressed the nervous tingles creeping up her spine by shaking her hair backwards and clenching her teeth at the same time, nearly driving on auto-pilot as she made the familiar turns. Her car's engine rumbled, the low roar sounding like a long-satisfied grunt after being pushed to its climax, making her feel the thrill of the wheels skidding, and the wind blowing in her face, enhancing the strange mix of fear and elation, as she concentraded on what was ahead of her.

150 yards to the entrance. Please drive slowly.

Her foot hit the brake at the familiar gap along the 15th. Philly stopped, closed her eyes for a couple of seconds, remembering the times with her father again. A distant woodpecker's drum ran towards her, its melodious sound soothing the tension in her muscles. Her mind drifted to Ben, her afternoon's opponent, waiting for her body to respond with some sort of physical reaction. It didn't. The only thing she felt was that she was ready. For the best game in her life.

Her eyes opened and became fixed on the mirror, checking her face and reassuring herself she looked exactly the way she wanted, before turning back towards the road. The final familiar bend came into view, towards the lane leading up to the gate. The thick maythorn hedge was still nearly hiding the coloured sign post on the left.

100 yards to the entrance, please drive slowly.

The cast iron gate appeared and opened. The two ancient oak trees' branches were swaying, as if they were waving her through. Philly shifted gear and drove to the far end and parked her car in her Lady Captain spot, realizing it would be the last time. From tomorrow onward, Pru's car would be here.

They already had a little ceremony together, sharing some bottles of rather decent white wine and a tray of snacks Bunny had smuggled from the kitchen. The Bangers had tied a bow round the chair behind the little desk with Pru's name on it, and Mrs Pushet had stood up and said some really kind words, making them all a bit emotional.

But before her year was really done and dusted, the grand finale was yet to come. She looked over the car park, making out Mrs Pushet's old Mini in her familiar spot, next to the Bangers'. Varilla's shiny BMW was there, next to Pru's dependable Volvo. She got out to pull her bag from the trunk and noticed her father had also arrived, most likely to give Lizzie some last pointers.

Before his young protegee was fed to the wolves. Shredded to pieces. Left for dead. Like the rest of them. Back to being the laughing stock. Forever into eternity. Because Silly Philly Fanta, along with her stupid women, needed to prove a point.

Ha bloody ha.

Philly looked down at her shoes, suddenly feeling sick, grasping what she had forced her friends into. Her earlier confidence flew away from her, like a jet plane shooting off a runway.

They were fucked. She was fucked.

There wasn't a chance in hell they would be able to come anywhere near those men. What had they, she, been thinking? She inhaled deeply through her nose and exhaled, letting the air out through her mouth, slowly, suddenly feeling her mobile buzzing in her front trouser pocket. She pulled it out and concentrated on what popped up in front of her. Mum, it said, revealing her mother's smiling face. She tapped, waiting for the message to pop up.

Hi darling. Thinking about you and remembered
something your dad's favourite said.
"I look into their eyes, I shake their hand, pat their back,
and wish them luck, but I am thinking, 'I am going to bury you.'"
Remember? Seve? Good luck. Go bury them. X Mum.

Her thumb moved over the screen, caressing the words that now floated in front of her, thinking about what her mother had sent. Philly pulled herself up, blinked away her tears and jerked her shoulders back, feeling her fighting spirit return. Her mother was right. Seve was right. The only thing they needed to do is keep it on the fairway and don't get intimidated by the length of the men's drives.

Who needs to be a long hitter? The woods are full of them.

She pulled her chin up again and started walking towards the driving range, suddenly feeling a whole lot better.

CHAPTER 77

The last basket was stacked, and Lash shoved them next to the ball dispenser, checking his watch at the same time. He turned round and watched Pru do her routine, pushing her groin towards the target with a club stuck between her arms. Philly was rearranging her tee pegs, Varilla was selecting a marker, the Bangers were munching on a Mars bar, and Lizzie was keeping a ball high with a seven iron. They never looked more ready than they did now. And however this turned out, kudos for them to at least give it a try.

'I'll see you in 15 minutes, ladies,' he said. 'Need to push the crowds off the tee before I start you off.'

'Yeah, right,' Lizzie smirked. 'We wish.'

Pru turned and walked up to him. 'Thanks for the lesson, darling.' She hoisted herself up and kissed him quickly. 'I suppose it's up to us now.' Her voice trembled slightly, and she bit her lip. 'I just hope we manage to scratch some holes towards us.'

'You will.' He brushed her cheek with his thumb and left them, taking the shortcut by crossing the ninth towards the first tee, seeing a group gathering under the starting hut. He made Bashit out, Percy lying at his feet and the stack of score cards in front of him. Mr Hackkett was there, next to Mrs Pushet with Maggie on her arm and Mrs Rough and Bunny, chatting to Mr Graham the head greenkeeper, who was standing beside Lizzie's new friend Cath.

He greeted them with a smile and a nod, before stepping onto the tee box, checking if the yellow markers were aligned perfectly. His right-hand dived into his back pocket, finding the coin he had saved for the toss. The first fairway was clear, he saw the last twosome teeing off at the second, just like he arranged it.

His eyes went towards the clock, eleven to one. The first pair, Lizzie and Charmers, were due at one. And once they had reached the green, he would invite Birdie and Sam Spoon, followed by Bogey and Sweet, Varilla was facing Bobby Long, Pru would play Roughie and then the most interesting pair, Philly and Ben. Captains playing Captains.

He looked over his shoulder, noticing the women coming over, Philly walking up to him and announcing herself on behalf of her team. Ten minutes before the starting time, on the dot. He glanced at Mr Hackkett, on his way with the score cards, reaching out towards his daughter, pulling her towards him in a big, warm hug. He turned towards the car park, hearing the sound of a car boot being slammed shut, the noise followed by Charmers pulling his bag straps over his shoulders and hurrying towards them.

'Hi there,' Charmers said to Lash, hardly acknowledging Lizzie, who walked up to him. 'Am I up first?' He pulled his driver from his bag and grabbed a ball and a tee. 'Rest are on their way. Finishing their lunch. Will be here any minute.' He bent down and teed his ball up.

'Mr Charmers.' President Bashit's voice suddenly bellowed, making them all jump. 'Wait for the toss. And seeing the Captain isn't here yet, I will stand in for him.' He looked at Philly and gestured her towards him. 'Heads or tails, Miss Hackkett?'

'Heads.'

Lash balanced the old coin on his thumb and flipped it, causing it to fly high up into the air before it dropped at their feet.

‘Heads it is.’ Bashit stared at Philly. ‘It’s up to you. First or second?’

‘First.’ Philly nodded and turned her face towards Charmers. ‘Would you please be so kind as to remove your ball?’ The sarcasm was undeniable, making Lash smile and look away.

‘Bloody hell,’ Charmers grumbled. ‘What is this? Frigging Ryder Cup gone goddamn woke or something?’ He bent down and jerked the ball towards him, nearly falling against Lizzie, who was beaming at him.

‘Hello, Mr Charmers.’ Her smile widened, she pointed her right hand at him and pulled him towards her. ‘Good luck,’ she said, while she patted his back and stared into his eyes unblinkingly. ‘I’m playing a ProV one, with the letter L on it.’

‘Alright. Good for you. Callaway for me.’ He stepped backwards and waved at a group of men hurrying towards them. ‘There they are. Let’s get this over with. Back before tea.’

‘Yes,’ Lizzie replied, pulling the pink hood from her driver. ‘Absolutely. Let’s.’ She stepped onto the tee, gripped her club and pulled it back. The speed of the practice swing following through sounded like jet plane taking off.

Lash nodded at her, winked and put his hand up. ‘Silence please.’ He called out.

Lizzie’s drive was perfect, the strike and impact so hard nobody managed to follow the flight of the ball landing in the middle of the fairway. She stepped back and gestured at Charmers, whose jaw had dropped. ‘Not my best by far, Mr Charmers, but it will have to do.’ The beaming smile was back again on the young face. ‘I’m sure yours will be way further than mine. So be it.’ She shrugged. ‘I’m just a wee girl.’

The collective intake of breath was audible as far as up to the clubhouse when Charmers’ ball sliced over the trees onto the ninth fairway. He averted his look chucking his driver in his bag, and he took off, marching towards his ball, leaving Lizzie to pull her cover back over her driver with Mrs Pushet coming towards her.

'Great drive, my dear.' The old lady reached up and pinched Lizzie's cheek. 'I do realize it's not really your thing, but,' Mrs Pushet smiled, making her eyes disappear between the wrinkles, 'promise me you will fuck that bastard so hard he won't be able to walk upright ever again.'

Lizzie choked and nearly stumbled over her bag. 'Jesus Christ, Mrs Pushet,' she whispered.

'Promise me.'

'I promise.'

'Good show. Better be off now. May the fours be with you my darling.' Mrs Pushet returned to her group.

CHAPTER 78

Ben stared at Philly stepping off the tee after hitting a dead straight drive. To say the atmosphere was awkward was an understatement. They had hardly exchanged half a word since they teed off at the first, walking along the fairway as far apart as they could possibly manage. And her level of golf, for crying out loud. He couldn't believe how she played, again her tee shot was hardly twenty yards shorter than his.

He squinted towards the movement on the tenth tee on the other side of the thick row of pine trees and saw Varilla bend down, pick her ball from the cup and step backwards, making room for Bobby to make his putt. Ben closed his eyes for a second and returned to the scene, watching his teammate shrug and scoop his ball up with his putter from the edge of the hole. *Bloody hell*, he thought. This match was turning out tougher than he imagined.

Philly nodded towards the ninth green. 'Seems we're in for a wait at the tenth.' She stopped walking, slid her bag off her back and selected her club quickly. Her back swing and the sound of impact told him she hit another cracking approach. The ball jumped once and stopped dead behind the flag. Polite clapping followed from the small group gathered between the ninth and the tenth.

'Damn,' he whispered, staring at his lie. Not bad. Not brilliant. With the branches of the old oak tree just in his line. He took his stance, opened his left foot and closed his grip. The ball flew exactly like he intended it to do, in a perfect draw straight at the flag. Another round of polite clapping followed his steps towards the green.

Philly took her putter and parked her bag against a tree behind the ball washer, nodding at President Bashit, who was waving at her while he strolled up to Ben. She followed Bashit, keeping a safe distance.

'Well.' President Bashit looked up to his Club Captain. 'How are you doing? Enjoying yourself?' He peeked over Ben's shoulder for a second and nodded, acknowledging Philly standing a couple of yards behind him. 'Nothing beats playing some really good golf on a warm summer's afternoon. Everything okay?'

Ben stared at the older man, suddenly feeling apprehensive. 'What do you mean, Bashit? There's something in your amused tone that tells me some things aren't what we expected. And you are wallowing in it.'

'Aha. I must admit I am experiencing a touch of schadenfreude.' The President put his hands behind his back and nodded slowly. 'Shall I enlighten you?'

'Yes, man.' Ben sounded desperate. 'What in hell's name is going on? I'm one down, for crying out loud. If this goes on, my *life*, as I know it, is over. Fucking hell, she's tearing my balls off.' His hand brushed over his hair and he shook his head. 'Please tell me the others are okay?'

'Ben, you know, *life* is, like our dear friend Bobby Jones said, like golf. You get good breaks from bad shots and bad breaks from good shots. But in the end, we have to play it as it lies.' He pushed his Panama hat back and stared at the man in front of him, who was clearly lost for words. 'Up to now you've had fantastic breaks, the wind in your favour. And bugger, you reach the turn and find your wind has changed. Well, tough luck. But that's *life* for you.' Bashit shook his head slowly and tutted. 'Sometimes you just have to adjust your sails to find your course again.'

'Fucking hell, Bashit. Spare me the bloody quotes,' Ben cried out. 'What's the score?'

'Mmm. Let me see.' The President pretended to think, putting his finger on his lips. 'Charmers is being thrashed by young Lizzie, he probably won't make it to the sixteenth. Spoon is playing, in his own words, the game of his life and is one up. And the rest came through all square. So up to now, knowing your score, it's one for the ladies up to now.' Bashit pointed towards the ninth green. 'Your opponent is waiting for you to putt, dear man. Don't slag. So annoying, slow play. Chop, chop.'

'Fuck me.' Ben stared at the amused face and pulled his putter towards him.

'See you at the 18th, Ben,' the President said while he wandered off towards the clubhouse. 'Play it as it lies.'

Philly halted, looked towards the green, making out the group gathered at the far end. The flag in front of them was limp, there wasn't a breath of wind and the afternoon's heat had hardened the fairway curving around the lake. She pushed a strand of hair behind her ear and stepped towards her ball, ignoring Ben who was leaning on his bag. The obvious silent treatment and the annoyed glares during the last three hours hadn't bothered her. On the contrary, it had helped her concentrate and keep to herself, not becoming distracted by idle chit chat.

Lizzie won, I lost 1 down, rest square. Pru's text message had said when Philly checked her mobile walking from the 17th green. *We're waiting for you at the 18th.*

Philly had looked at the text what seemed like a hundred times, not believing what she saw, but slowly comprehending what had passed during the last hours. The only couple she had seen conceding and walking back towards the clubhouse were Lizzie and Charmers, who finished at the 15th. A nervous chuckle escaped Philly, making Ben glare at her. Lizzie had beaten Charmers. 4 and 3. What a hoot. And all the others had played on, which meant, inconceivably so, that they were still alive. But now it seemed they were more than alive.

All square. With one to go.

They were kicking ass.

This was fucking unbelievable. She shook her head and squeezed her fingernails into her palm, as if wanting to prove she was not stuck in some weird dream. Realizing the scene was real. Slowly understanding what was happening. To her. To her friends. That they weren't thrashed. At all. That they stood firm, showing what they could do. That all their hard work was paying off. She inhaled deeply, held her breath for a moment and squared her shoulders before letting the air flow from her mouth, and recollected her thoughts. Her chin went up, her ponytail tickled the spot between her shoulders and electric energy shot through her body, tensing it, making it tingle.

'Come on, one last approach. You might hole the damn thing and bloody well win,' she whispered to herself while straightening her back and loosening her neck by moving her head from right to left a couple of times. She saw Ben staring at his ball, a couple of yards from her, in silence, obviously annoyed, as he had been the last couple of holes.

Her hand went towards her six iron, she pulled the club towards her and held it towards her body for a couple of seconds, feeling her stomach doing somersaults. Calm down, she tried to tell herself. Even if she would hit her worst shot ever, they would go down with their heads held high. Her head shook, as if she was trying to force the nervousness out.

No. Don't get uptight. Relax.

This was a shot she had done a million times before.

Concentrate. Imagine it.

Her feet were planted firmly in the grass, and she wiggled her bum a couple of times, looking at the green, seeing her friends and the men's team. Her knees slackened, and she inhaled taking her club back, pushing it towards the grass again in motion with her hips turning towards the ball, forcing herself to keep looking down, hardly feeling the club's contact with the ball, and she knew instantly she had hit the sweet spot, feeling the thrilling sensation of perfect rhythm down to her groin. The ball flew forward, cleared the front of the green and stopped dead, two feet behind the flag.

Philly closed her eyes and exhaled dropping her chin down, feeling the thrill of the shot and the applause coming towards her. Her head came back up after a second, and she turned towards Ben, who was selecting his club and starting his usual practice swing routine, pretending to ignore her. But the grimace on his face said enough. He took two steps back, one last look at the flag and took his stance.

His arms came back, but his back swing was not as short as usual. Philly noticed his head came up a split second too fast, and his club head made impact too high, topping the ball towards the flag in a low flight, causing it to bounce once towards the elevation, shoot up into the air and come to a full stop in the fringe in the fore green.

Oh my God. He missed it. Bloody hell. Philly held her emotion inside herself, tried not to cheer, grasping what could be next. A tap in for her, a very difficult chip shot for him. Could this actually be true? That she would beat Ben? And with that, they, the women, would actually win? Apprehension shot through her, mixed with elation, causing her to feel lightheaded.

The stunned silence from the group was an acknowledgment of what Philly suspected. Ben had botched up his crucial shot, just when she needed it the most. She glanced towards him but he was already on the move, obviously not wanting to walk to the green alongside her.

Her bag was on her back again, and she strode towards the green purposefully, still trying to make sense of it all. How should she be feeling? Like a good sport? Sorry for Ben? Or just good for herself? She thought about her mother's message again, quoting her father's favourite player, his face popping up in her brain. What was the other thing he said?

"If you ever feel sorry for somebody on a golf course, you better go home. If you don't kill them, they'll kill you."

End this game, Philly Hackkett. By holing that put and shaking his hand for the win. Of their match. Of *the* match, she told herself.

The thought of the possible outcome made her insides go funny again, and she concentrated on Pru, looking at her and giving her the thumbs up. Her hand went back and she pulled her putter out over her head, walking to the back of the green, waving towards her friends while a voice popped up in her head.

There is no shortcut to success.

Philly clenched her teeth and pictured the woman who said this. Boy, had Annika been right. They had fought so hard. But some annoying niggle at the back of her brain told her this wasn't over yet.

Ben stopped and stared at his ball dumbfounded, not believing what had just happened. He hadn't topped an iron in years, not even under severe pressure. He shook his head, trying to shake off the emotion, turning his focus on how to play this next shot, just how he had been taught to do during all the mental training sessions he had taken with the team. It ain't over till it's over, he knew that. The fat lady hadn't sung just yet.

Not a terrible lie, he thought while he crouched down behind the ball and peered at the flag. What club would be best? A slow pitching wedge? Bump and run with a 7 iron? Just hope for the best, get it within half a yard and pray Philly would suddenly get the yips and leave hers short?

His gaze was went towards Bashit who looked expressionless. His eyes were drawn to Roughie who, standing between the President and Varilla, seemed to be trying to catch his attention by moving his arms and staring at him intently. He narrowed his eyes and watched the movement, the slow folding of hands over his friend's chest. Right hand went towards left arm. Four fingers rested on his sleeve. Left hand towards right arm. Very slowly. Three fingers.

Their eyes locked, and he selected his club. It felt good, lying steady in a light grip. A little tap, not too much. Just right. Ben kept his head slightly tilted while his club head touched the ball, making it jump over the fringe and roll towards the flag in perfect pace, in perfect arch towards the flag.

It was going in. For birdie. He could feel it. He held his breath and closed his eyes, hearing the blissful soft plopping sound of the ball dropping over the edge of the cup.

He gasped. The group at the back of the green gasped. His team leapt up simultaneously, starting to cheer and he arched back, lifting his putter over his head, realizing what had happened, feeling a surge of relief flowing through his body and he managed to control himself, gesturing the crowd to be still and let Philly try and make her putt.

He watched her crouch down quickly, as she placed her ball behind the marker, concentrated and pulled herself up, then walking towards him, bending down for the line again and returning to her ball, taking her stance. The ball left the putter from the middle of the club face and it hit the back of the cup, the result of an absolute perfect strike.

The ball dropped.

The crowd roared.

All square.

Ben shook his head and walked up to her, his hand outstretched. 'Well done. Amazing game,' he said earnestly before turning and walking towards his teammates.

CHAPTER 79

Philly drew back from Birdie's tight embrace and watched President Bashit gather the men together and walk towards the clubhouse. 'I can't believe it,' she said, covering her burning face. 'I'm starting to realize they tied the match with a fluke chip in.' Her hands fell down, and she stared at Pru, who started to laugh nervously, releasing the tension she had been feeling since she walked off the 18th green.

'We did great.' Varilla stepped forward and gave Philly a hug. We could have won.'

'We could have won,' Philly repeated slowly, taking in what had happened. 'We could have won,' she said again with a whisper, shaking her head and feeling herself being pulled from Varilla towards Mrs Pushet for an embrace. 'Imagine if we had. Imagine.'

'What a wonderful achievement. Those men finally grasped what you are capable of.' Mrs Pushet reached up, pulled Philly's face towards her and gave her a big kiss. 'Extraordinary accomplishment, all of you.' She let go and turned to Lizzie, standing next to a puce faced Bunny. 'And you, beating the crap out Charmers, how did he react?,' she asked while a wicked smile crept on her face. 'He's still walking upright, I see.'

Lizzie grinned. 'Actually, he was,' she paused for a second, catching the attention of the group of women standing together, 'very good about it.' Her hand dived in her pocket and she pulled a shiny blue-and-white-coloured marker out, 'I made my winning putt, he scooped his marker up, put it in his right hand and squeezed it into mine.' Lizzie looked round and held her hand out. 'Then he congratulated me, said I played a cracking game and said I could keep the marker as a memento. It's supposed to be collector's item.'

The circle around her drew tighter as everyone inspected the little token on her palm, the St Andrews logo clearly visible. 'What a lovely thing to do,' Pru said. 'Well done, Charles.'

Lizzie nodded. 'And that's not all. He asked me if I would be interested in another game. Invited me for next Sunday, as his partner, for a four ball better ball.' She said, glancing at Bunny. 'But I have to work, of course.'

'Bollocks.' Bunny's response was unusually loud. 'You are with playing him. I'm not on my last legs just yet, I will manage. Just make sure you are the better ball.' She leaned towards Mrs Rough. 'And you can help out, can't you? Take a break from shopping for baby clothes. The poor mite will have to change 20 times a day to wear it all,' she said firmly while pointing towards the clubhouse. 'And talking of work, we ought to get going. The changeover party will start soon, and we need to get ready.'

'Right.' Philly nodded. 'We will leave you to it. Let's see if we can find a moment for a little celebration.' She took Pru's arm and turned towards the Varilla, the Bangers and Mrs Pushet standing together. 'We'll go to the Ladies' room, change and see if we can order a pizza or something, good idea?'

'Excellent idea,' the Bangers cried before running off the green.

The Ladies' room was empty, but somehow something felt different. Pru looked round, trying to figure out why. The chairs were still as they left them, their bags were stacked on the sofa, the mugs she had rinsed earlier were still on the kitchen towel. Her eyes moved towards the small pine desk, and she noticed its chair seemed to be in a different angle from how she usually made certain it was. She reached over to push everything in right order to find a folded yellow sticky note taped to the silver-framed picture of Seve Bashit had given Philly. She fumbled the note open, read it and peeked inside the small fridge. Six bottles of chilled Champagne appeared in front of her with a card attached to one of them.

'Chaps,' she said, peering over the fridge's door. 'Come and have a look.'

Bogey was the first one to reach her. 'Don't tell me we're low in wine. I've never wanted a drink more in my entire life.'

'No.' Pru's shook her head, slowly, trying to figure out what was in front of her. 'They asked us to bring these with us and to join the gentlemen in the club lounge.'

Bogey grabbed the note from Pru's hands and stared at it. *"Let's finish this day off with a bang. President Bashit."* She passed it over to Philly, who stared at it for a few seconds before passing it to Varilla.

'Bloody hell,' Philly said. 'This day really is full of surprises.'

'What are we waiting for?,' Birdie shrieked. 'This is fucking brilliant. I've been dying to find out what it's like in there.' She pulled her sister towards the changing room. 'Come on. Put your frock on, and let's go. Last one there is a loser.'

CHAPTER 80

Peckers Wood Club Lounge.

The bold, curved letters above the heavy panelled door stared at them. Philly reached for the brass knocker and thumped it twice, looking over her shoulder for support, trying to ignore the sensation of her heart racing. The women waited for a few seconds and watched the shiny doorknob turn slowly, opening the door to find President Bashit with a huge grin on his face.

'Ah. There you are. Wonderful.' He stepped aside and swung his right arm towards the large room in front of them. 'Please, ladies. Do come in.'

Philly stepped over the threshold, attentively, followed by the her friends, also remaining silent. They paused, huddled together and looked round, taking the scene in, looking and feeling overwhelmed by what they witnessed. The large open fire was blazing, champagne glasses were arranged on a mahogany table beside it. All the leather club seats were empty, and the men's team was standing in front of the large bar, dressed in their blazers and slacks, wearing their Peckers Wood ties. The long dining table was laid out with the club's special china and silver.

Bobby Long stepped forward, held out his hand and reached over to Philly. 'Lady Captain Hackkett,' he said, with a genuine smile while turning to Pru, 'and soon to be Lady Captain Love. I believe congratulations are in order.' He bowed his head slightly and shook Philly's hand before reaching out to Pru's. 'Well done, Ladies. You were absolutely terrific.'

Loud clapping and a cheer erupted from the bar. President Bashit held his hand up, silencing the men and gesturing the women towards him. 'Come over here, ladies, join me for a moment. Let's open those bottles so I can say a few words. And fill the ladies up first.' He passed the glasses over to the astonished group of women in front of him while Bobby and Henri began pouring the champagne.

President Bashit stepped forward, held his glass up and cleared his throat, immediately silencing the room. 'I will keep this short. And with what I am about to say, I hope I will have said it all.' He slowly looked over his shoulder, staring at the group of men, before turning towards the women in front of him. 'Sam Snead once said, "of all the hazards, fear is the worst."'

A collective groan rippled through the men's team. 'Here we go,' Charles Charmers said sounding desperate, but with a smile on his face.

'It is the oldest and strongest emotion mankind has,' the President continued, 'especially fear of the unknown.'

A dramatic pause followed, and the President raised his glass. 'To the Ladies Section. For teaching us a lesson, in more ways than one.'

'To the Ladies Section!' The men followed the President in his cheer and stepped forward to shake the women's hands, one by one.

Bashit put his arm around Philly and led her towards the bar. 'I must admit I didn't see this one coming, Hackkett. Well done.'

Philly managed a smile. 'That makes two of us. I still can't believe it.'

'And I never thought I was ever going to say this, but I am rather enjoying having you here in the lounge.' A boyish glint appeared in the President's eyes. 'It's been a while since I had a night out with a couple of nice young ladies,' he whispered while looking over her shoulder and winking.

Philly turned her head, seeing Mrs Pushet who came towards them and beckoned Bashit, who nodded and leaned towards the bar for support. 'Just nipping out with Mrs Pushet. She needs a breather after all this excitement. Back in a moment. And I would like to invite you to sit next to me for dinner, Hackkett. I need to pick that sharp brain of yours.'

'Yes, President Bashit.' Philly nodded. 'Of course. I am honoured.'

'Righto. You join your friends, and we will talk shop during dinner then.' The President put his glass to his grey lips and finished off the last of the champagne before grabbing Mrs Pushet by the arm and guiding her outside onto the terrace.

Philly stared at the group at the other side of the bar, wishing she could hold on to this blissful feeling forever. It was the most amazing rush. They were actually here, invited deep into the inner sanctum of the prestigious Peckers Wood old boys network. Henri held on to Birdie, with a look of drunken bliss on his handsome face. Bobby whispered something in Bogey's ear, making her throw her head back with laughter, Pru chatting with Charles Charmers, looking relaxed and smiling at Lizzie who was busy behind the bar. Her attention was drawn to a hunched figure, standing alone next to the fire place, as if trying to avoid everyone. 'Varilla?,' Philly said carefully, approaching her. 'Are you alright? You look a bit worse for wear, to be honest. What's wrong?'

Varilla cringed, nearly folding over. 'Not sure, sorry. Feel a bit nauseous, that's all.' Her eyes closed, and she exhaled.

'What's up with her?' Bogey's voice popped up. 'Too much booze already?'

‘No.’ Varilla sighed. ‘I just feel sick.’

‘Oh dear.’ Birdie had also appeared. ‘And we’re having dinner in half an hour. We need to get you sorted out.’ She put her arm around Varilla and tugged at her sister’s arm. ‘Come on, let’s go to the men’s room and stick you on the loo. Something just needs to come out, one way or the other, that’s all.’ She pushed Philly aside. ‘You go and get the others, we need to get her back on her feet.’

CHAPTER 81

Varilla heard the soft click of the loo's door, shutting out Birdie's voice, telling her to try to relax and give a shout when she was done. A wave of nauseausness rushed through her, and she put her head in the loo. She tried to be sick but nothing came, except cold shivers combined with hot flushes. She took a deep breath, smelling the faint chlorine of the loo's water and knowing this wasn't going to give her any relief from her agony. Her hands were on the floor, cold and sweaty. She tried to pull her heavy, throbbing head back from the cold porcelain rim, and she slumped backwards towards the door, folding her arms around her aching stomach as tight as she possibly could.

'Varilla?' Bogey's voice sounded, clearly worried, followed by a thump. 'Are you okay?'

She managed a groan, opened her eyes slowly and looked round, trying to locate her handbag, with her dear possession. It was just beside her driver's license, right where she left it half an hour ago. Her trusted bible, her guide and lifeline during the most complicated situations she had ever encountered.

'We are opening the door now, Varilla,' Birdie called out. She tugged at the door, causing her friend to fall backwards, right into Bogey, who was pitched forward by the impact.

'Thank God,' Birdie whispered, crouching down beside

her and pushing her sister to the side. 'We thought you flushed yourself down the loo.' She pointed towards Varilla's right hand. 'What's that?,' she asked while she raised an eyebrow. 'R&A rules? Do they help you poop?'

She shook her head, slowly. 'No.' The book opened slowly, shaking under her trembling hands. 'I just wanted to check something, about today's match.'

The Bangers looked at Philly and Pru standing behind them, eyebrows raised. 'What in heaven's name are you on about, old girl?,' Bogey said. 'Why on earth would you want to do that?'

Varilla's tremble turned into a violent shiver. There it was, the paragraph, again. She read it, again. Yes, it was quite clear. As it was the last four times before she looked it up in between the bouts of nausea.

'Look.' She passed the book to Philly with trembling fingers who squinted to read the handwriting in the margin out loud:

'For giving advice, remember you are allowed to discuss things that are commonly known – You may not tell someone how to play his/her shot, the best approach to take or what club to hit unless they are your partner in a team or match play event. Rule 8-1 prohibits a player from asking for advice from a spectator but does not prohibit a player from receiving unsolicited advice because the player can't control such an act. There is no penalty when an authorized party gives advice, but the player should take action to stop this irregular procedure.'

Philly finished reading, and she looked at Pru whose eyes were wide with alarm. 'We all know this. Why should this bother us now?'

'Ben played a bump and run,' Varilla whispered. 'I saw it.'

A flash of terror shot up Philly's spine. *Was the bloody woman honestly pulling the rule book out? Now? When they had finally achieved what they longed for?*

A look of despair exchanged between the others, now joined by Lizzie and Bunny.

'We noticed you leaving. What's going on?,' Lizzie asked.

'Discussion about a bump and run,' Birdie replied. 'Yes. Sure he did, somewhere. We all do once or twice during a round.'

Bogey nodded. 'Not the prettiest shot in the book, but useful sometimes. What's the problem with that?'

'The problem is that Roughie might have suggested it.' Bashit's voice came towards them, and the group flinched, perfectly in sync with the dark vocal rhythm. The President carefully closed the men's room's door behind him, hobbled towards the six women sprawled over the floor, pulled one of the chairs towards them and helped Varilla sit up, making certain she was alright before carefully taking the small book from her hands. 'Not with so many words, but I saw it too.' He pulled another chair over and sat down. 'The question is, now what do we do?' he asked, leaning backwards and looking at each woman, one by one.

'What the bloody hell happened?,' Philly asked, her tone threatening. 'I don't like the sound of you two.'

'No.' Pru stood up and brushed herself off. 'Nor do I.'

'Please.' Bashit looked at Varilla. 'Mrs Van Dycke. Tell us what's been bothering you.'

Varilla swallowed, closed her eyes for a second and started to speak. 'We were on the side of the 18th green,' she said slowly. 'Recovering from the shots Philly and Ben made.' Her voice quivered, but she pulled herself together. 'Ben walked up to his ball, checked it.'

'Yes,' Bogey said, sounding impatient. 'We know. We were there.'

'But then, he looked up, into the crowd,' Varilla continued.

'There's no harm in that,' Birdie said.

'I know.' Varilla nodded again. 'But something happened,' she said, while her head dropped in her hands, and she started to sob.

'What?,' The Bangers cried out together, sounding desperate and looking at Bashit, who remained motionless.

'Roughie caught Ben's attention, signalled him with seven fingers,' Varilla blurted out. 'After which he chipped in with the bump and run and secured the half.' A big tear welled up and dripped from her nose.

'So?!' Another desperate cry erupted from the two sisters, who were now standing next to each other, looking despondent.

'The rule is clear.' Varilla's voice was hardly audible. 'There's no question about it, none *what so ever*, as always, clear as a whistle.' A deep sob escaped her. 'No room for interpretation whatsoever.'

'Fucking hell.' Bogey dropped down on her knees, trying to take the information in.

'Are you suggesting Ben lost the hole?,' Bunny asked, sounding earnest and moving towards the now astonished looking Lizzie. 'Meaning *we* won the match?'

'You tell me.' Bashit finally spoke, leaning forward, making the women jump again. 'I'm actually very interested in how you perceive this situation.'

This wasn't happening to her, Philly thought, clenching her jaws. Or to her friends. Not now. They were not returning to being the butt of every pathetic joke the men would make. Or would be so very entitled to make, if she didn't nip this idiocy into its miserable bud.

'Give me that bloody rule book,' she snapped while she yanked it from Bashit. She closed the book firmly and tossed it onto the nearest bench, clearly dismissing it and reached over to Pru, pulling her friend's head towards her mouth, whispering softly enough for Varilla and Bashit not to hear what she was saying, but feeling her friend nod in agreement before she pulled back and addressed the group. 'We don't know Ben hit a seven iron,' she said, her head held high.

'No,' Birdie replied, relief visibly flooding from her. 'We did not.'

'But he played a bump and run! With the seven-iron

technique Lash taught us,' Varilla hissed, starting to cry again and running her fingers through her hair. 'O my God. What are we going to do?'

'It's obvious,' Pru said calmly. 'We do what we always do. We do the right thing.'

'Damn right,' Bogey nodded. 'Which in this case is…?'

'Nothing.' Birdie said. 'I can hit that bump and run with any club in my bag, for goodness sake.'

Philly nodded. 'Damn right again. Give me my three wood, and I can do it. Or my five iron. Or my wedge.' She shook her head. 'No. And Roughie was just a bit chilly, Bunny wasn't there to hold him so he hugged himself, that's all.'

'But.' Varilla stuck her finger up. 'Imagine what would happen if it turned out we won? If we would walk back to the lounge and announce the win?'

'Yes.' Pru nodded, looking stern. 'Imagine that, Varilla. Just imagine that.' She paused and leaned forward towards the stricken woman. 'Just what would happen, exactly?' She pulled herself up and brushed herself off, in slow movements, leaving a long silence.

This nonsense had to stop!, Philly thought, forcing herself to stay collected and in control. She obviously had to spell it out. 'Listen carefully Varilla.' Her voice rose, causing the others to straighten and focus on her. 'Remember what Sandra Jane Haynie said. "In golf, just as in life, no one can tell you what to do. We are presented with options; it's up to us to decide which one suits us best."'

'Or will serve us best,' Bogey added.

'Oh my god.' A desperate cry finally erupted. 'No.' Varilla's eyes became large, and she inhaled sharply, staring at Bashit with a terrified look on her face. 'Our true victory down the drain. The one we worked so hard for," she blurted out, her cheeks now puce with shame.

Thank God. She finally grasped it. Philly sighed with relief inwardly, closing her eyes for a moment, pushing away the image of astonished, horrified men, turning to each other silently, acknowledging they had been right all along. That clearly women didn't understand what it was all about. And should be banned forever. Which would have materialized if Varilla hadn't gotten into her thick skull what she was causing. 'Damn right,' she said firmly. 'We do not know which club Ben played. End of story.'

'Yes. Absolutely.' Varilla wiped her nose. 'Of course. I get it now. And you are so right.'

All the women nodded determinedly. 'Absolutely right. Yes. Definitely. End of story.'

'End of story it is.' President Bashit hoisted himself up and pulled Varilla to her feet. 'The club remains a mystery.' He held out his arms and beckoned the women towards him. 'I second your excellent ruling, my dear Peckers Wood members. Made in the spirit of the game, well done.' He hugged the women, one by one. 'I'm so proud of you. Now let's get back to the fun.'

CHAPTER 82

'Well. We're back. Ready to get this party properly started,' President Bashit beamed at Mrs Pushet, waiting for him to guide her to the club lounge dinner table. 'Sorry I left you so long. At my age a visit to the little boys' room takes forever.'

'Doesn't matter, Harry.' Mrs Pushet smiled back at him. 'I'm having a wonderful time with all these boys and girls.'

'Good. Glad to hear it. Please, sit down. And Miss Hackkett, at my other side,' he said, greeting Philly and gracefully waiting for her before nodding towards the other men to take their seats and sitting down himself. 'Again, Hackkett, wonderful game. Well played. Again.' He smiled broadly.

'Thank you, President.' Philly nodded and leaned towards Bashit. 'And again, it was close,' she whispered.

'Yes. It was. What a year, Hackkett, what a year,' he said slowly, shaking his head. 'You've come far, I'll give you that. A steady section, competition medal, tie against the men. You must be very proud with how everything worked out for you.'

Now it was Philly's time to beam. 'Yes. To be honest, I am.'

Bashit moved towards her, suddenly with a grim look on his face. 'One thing, Miss Hackkett.' He cleared his throat. 'That handicap league I heard you were so keen on....

'Yes?' Philly stared at him, suddenly feeling apprehensive. 'What about it?'

'I'm afraid it's not going to happen. I can't support it.'

'Mr President? What do you mean? And especially after today?' Philly's heart dropped, but she detected a twinkle in Bashit's eye.

'I've taken the liberty to enter you for scratch league. Much more appropriate, don't you think?' Bashit's face lit up and a large grin split his face. 'Gotcha!'

Philly's hands shot to her cheeks and she stared at the President. 'O my God.' She blurted out. 'I nearly died.' Her hand moved towards Bashit's arm and she squeezed it for a second. 'Scratch league. Wow. Thank you so much. The girls will be over the moon.'

Bashit patted her arm. 'You get what you deserve, Captain. It can get lonely though,' he mused, 'Being a leader.' The President looked at Philly carefully. 'Like this silly game we love so much. Hale Irwin said it's the loneliest sport because one is completely alone with every conceivable opportunity to defeat oneself.' Bashit shook his head slightly. 'It brings out our assets and liabilities as a person, and the longer one plays, the more certain one is that a man's performance is the outward manifestation of who, in his heart, he really thinks he is.' He ended the quote with wag of his index finger.

'Or who she is.' Philly smiled, while her finger waved back at Bashit.

'Or who she is.' Bashit nodded gracefully. 'I'll certainly give you that. You've manifested yourself, and your ladies, rather well as the year progressed. How, Miss Hackkett, would you describe your journey? How did it make you feel?'

Philly was silent for a moment, thinking of what she read so often under a photo of Arnold Palmer on her father's small desk. 'It was,' she faltered for a moment, 'like golf. Deceptively simple and endlessly complicated; it satisfied my soul and frustrated my intellect.' She turned and stared Bashit straight in the eye. 'It was at the same time rewarding and maddening. Like the greatest game mankind has ever invented.'

'Right.' Bashit batted his eyelids a couple of times, trying to hide his emotion and move Philly's attention to his liver-spotted hand by covering hers. 'I've taken the time to review the whole year myself, had a good think.' The hand left with a squeeze. 'About my strategy, for the coming years.'

'That's always a good idea,' Philly said. 'Like my mother says, "fail to plan is plan to fail."'

'Excellent advice.' President Bashit cocked his head. 'I think, Hackkett,' he said conspiratorially, 'in order to get the club back on its feet, we need to recruit more women. About 75? During the next three years?' A fat wink followed. 'What are your thoughts on this?'

Philly stared towards him open mouthed, raising her eyebrows slowly, not knowing how to react, annoyed or with feigned ignorance. She choose the latter. 'Sounds excellent, dear President. Where ever have I heard that idea before?'

'Hmmm. Haven't the foggiest. But it will come to me, I'm sure.' Bashit smiled, while he patted her hand. 'Some smart birds must have told me.'

Philly felt a squeeze and she stared at the old hand leaving hers while a wave of triumph flowed through her body, making her feel warm and tingly. He hadn't forgotten. The whole experience in the conference room came back to her, but now with a sense of accomplishment, instead of agonizing shame.

'Righto, something else, my dear.' The President's smile turned into a frown, but the boyish look of amusement remained in his eyes. 'Now that Miss Love is relieving you from your Captaincy duties, might I assume you have some time on your hands? To help me?'

Now it was Philly's time to frown. 'What do you mean, President? Something needs fixing?'

‘Yes. It certainly does. If you are game, that is.’

‘For what?’

‘For doing me the honour of appointing you the new Peckers Wood Golf Club Treasurer.’

THE NINETEENTH HOLE

'Any good?,' Bashit asked.

'Excellent,' Mrs Pushet answered while she handed the spliff over to him. 'Here. Try it yourself. Splendid stuff.'

Bashit took the glowing stub, inhaled deeply and exhaled slowly, closing his eyes for a moment. Mrs Pushet reached out and pulled the roll up from his fingers. 'Watch it with that. We don't want to set the place on fire. We're baked enough as it is.' She pushed it into the ashtray on the wobbly nightstand, after taking a last long drag. She flipped to her side and pulled her friend towards her, feeling his chest hair tickle the space between her shoulders, and his hand cupping her breast.

'I have more where that came from,' Bashit whispered into her ear and pulled her closer towards him.

'Good.' Mrs Pushet sighed and closed her eyes. 'As long as you come with me on a regular basis too.'

'Christ Almighty,' Bashit chuckled. 'How eloquently romantic you sound, my poetic goddess.'

They lay in silence for a while, relaxed, enjoying the moment, half awake and half asleep together, feeling joined, their lie keeping them interlocked.

'We've had quite a year, haven't we?,' Bashit whispered after a while. 'But I'm pleased. About how things turned out.' He paused for a moment. 'Tell me. What was your high point? The fitting prank the Bangers pulled?'

Mrs Pushet shook her head. 'No. Frightfully entertaining though. They still think you were really pissed off. Poor things,' she said, giggling at the same time. 'And they meant well.'

'They always do,' Bashit said softly. 'I love them to bits. Always have. I just can't help myself.' He sighed. 'They're like three-month old puppies, tearing everything apart, weeing on your favourite carpet, shitting on your bed and leaving you still want to cuddle them to death.'

'I know.' Mrs Pushet sighed too. 'Amazing. It's a gift.'

Bashit's thumb went up and down, stroking the breast under his hand. 'Bobby and Henri are doomed, aren't they?,' he whispered.

'Absolutely. Those two puppies will stay together in Dimple house until they turn into grey old smelly bitches, glued together wherever they go. And they will probably die together on that worn out sofa with their greasy fingers in a packet of salt and vinegar chips, wearing matching frayed polos and watching a rerun of some Open.'

'There are worse ways to go,' Bashit said, sounding earnest. 'And bless them for bringing the Van Dycke woman back. Imagining the look on Thorneybush's face while she read that resignation letter had me smiling for weeks.' His voice had turned light again. 'What about Lizzie?,' he continued. 'The magic transformation from a sulky teenager to a young woman with brilliant prospects.' Pride was now obvious in his voice.

'Nope.' Mrs Pushet shook her head, making Bashit sneeze as her soft curls brushed his nose. 'Being coached by us, the Hackketts, learning the game with Lash and the girls, it all helped. But she already had it in her. We just jabbed it to come out a little quicker.'

'Right.' Bashit's hand moved downwards, now stroking the soft flesh beneath Mrs Pushet's belly button. 'Let's move on to the liaison between my protege Lash and the seemingly frigid Prudence Love he managed to thaw out. How high do they score?'

'High on the entertainment ladder.' Mrs Pushet shook, laughing. 'I know you've seen them at it, you filthy old bugger.'

'I beg your pardon?' Bashit pinched her, making her flinch. 'You found it very educational, too.'

'I certainly did.' She stroked the hand that lay on her belly. 'But I hope lust will turn to love. They both deserve it. And could be great together if they manage to keep it together.' She was silent for a moment. 'But it won't be easy for them. She's a complicated little number, and he's a stubborn piece of work. We need to observe them carefully and help them whenever we can.'

'I agree. Which leads us to our Miss Hackkett. Complicated too?,' Bashit asked.

'Good grief, no,' Mrs Pushet replied. 'As simple to read as first grader's math assignment. Predictable too. She will end up married to someone slightly more decent than Chipperfield. They will spawn three annoying, ill-behaved kids they claim they adore but secretly don't, live in a Victorian too expensive for them, exploit some long-suffering foreign nanny because their careers exhaust them and can't keep dumping the kids on poor granny Dorothy, all for the desperate need to keep up with the Jones's, and maybe, if he's extremely lucky, hubby will be allowed a round Sunday mornings. If he doesn't get caught bonking the foreign nanny, that is.'

'Good lord. Do you really think so? Sounds like pure hell,' Bashit said, sounding concerned. 'Is there something we should do?'

Mrs Pushet shrugged. 'Yes. I suppose we should. Don't quite yet know what though. Pretty pigheaded, Philly. But it will come to us. It always does.'

Her fingers grabbed Bashit's, and they intertwined. 'I know what your high point was. I've never seen so much joy in your eyes, as when you held that baby girl for the first time.'

Bashit sighed and closed his eyes, remembering that afternoon, nearly smelling the little bundle that was passed to him, the moment she opened her eyes and looked right through him, exactly like his father used to do. Bernice had never looked more beautiful, Roughie never more proud and Cherie Rough? As happy as a thousand clams at high tide. 'You're right. I can't get enough of the little thing. Thank God they take her with them to the club every day and let me take her on my daily tours.'

'She'll hit a five iron before she can walk.' Mrs Pushet smiled. 'And beat every one of us before she goes to kindergarten.'

'I'm not that bad.' Bashit squeezed the flesh between his fingers. 'I just hope there's room for lots of fun in her life. Like we had. And still have.'

'Hell, yes.' Mrs Pushet snuggled closer, enjoying the comforting warmth radiating from the body beside her. 'We lucky ones did have fun, didn't we? All the partying, trying out exciting new things, unafraid and unabashed.' She remained quiet for a while. 'I hope they all have the wonderful times we had. Enjoying life, grabbing it by the balls and doing some good.' She sighed. 'I feel sorry for the young. They seem so uptight nowadays, so stressed all the time, and the poor mites take themselves far too seriously. Such a waste of precious time.' She rolled over to the nightstand and checked her mobile. 'Talking of which, I think it's time for my fun,' she said, giving her old friend a wink.

'Yes. It is.' Bashit pulled himself up. 'A deal is a deal. You won the bet, fair and square. I did appoint a female member to the board within a year, and I did sign the membership agreements for more women.'

'Yep. Good thing I found that balance sheet before it was too late.'

'Indeed.' Bashit gave his friend a long stare. 'I'm still trying to work out how you got your fingers on it.'

'It's a gift.' Mrs Pushet stared back. 'My darling.'

Bashit turned away, pulled the duvet up and looked down. 'Righto. Here we stand. How shall I deliver?'

'I'll be starfish.' She pushed herself down on her back, kicked the duvet back and spread out her arms and legs. 'So you can have your wicked way with me to which I will obey to willingly.'

'As you wish, your highness.' Bashit sighed and mockingly rolled his eyes, the familiar twinkle shining through as he moved downwards. 'Some things just never change.'

GOLF TERMS EXPLAINED

Ace: A hole in one.

Albatross: Three under par score.

Approach: Short or medium shot to the green.

Better Ball: Best score on a hole by partners.

Birdie: One under par score.

Bogey: One over par score.

Break: The curve the ball due to slope of the green.

Carry: Distance a ball travels in the air.

Chip: Short shot played to the green.

Divot: Turf / sand removed when hitting a shot.

Dogleg: When a fairway bends right or left.

Dormie – Having a lead equal to the number of holes remaining to be played in a match play game.

Draw: Right to left shot with a slight curve.

Drop: When the ball is lost or unplayable, a ball is dropped from arm's length at knee height onto the course.

Eagle: Two under par score.

Fairway: Short grass area between the tee and the green.

Follow-through: The final part of the swing from impacting the ball to completion of the swing.

Fore!: Shout of warning when a shot may hit another player within reach of the ball's fight.

Four-Ball: Group four golfers each playing their own ball.

Foursome: Group of two pairs of golfers playing shots alternately with the same ball.

Free drop: When a player may take a drop without a penalty stroke.

Gimmie: Very short putt near to a hole, awarded/ given by other players in match play, or in friendly golf.

Grain: Direction in which blades of grass grow and might influence the speed and roll of the ball on the green.

Green: Final part of the hole with very short grass, meant for putting.

Gross score: The number of actual strokes played within a round, before handicap is deducted.

Ground under Repair (GUR): An area of the course under maintenance identified by stakes or a line.

Half Shot: Reduced, short swing for shorter shots.

Hole out: To finish a hole by getting the ball in the hole.

Honour: Granting the right to tee off first on the next tee box to another player.

Hook: Shot that curves strongly from right to left.

Hosel: Hollow part of club head where the shaft meets the club face.

Lie: Where the ball sits on the course, hence a 'good lie', or 'poor lie'. Or worse.

Links: Golf course situated on the coast with sand dunes and very few trees and shrubs, exposed to the wind.

Lip: The edge of the hole.

Lip-out: A putt that catches the lip of the hole and causes the ball not to fall into the hole.

Marker: Thin, flat item used to mark the position of a golf ball on the green to prevent your ball obstructing other player's putts. This also refers to a person who keeps the score in a match.

Match Play: Competition scored by the number of holes won or lost.

Medal play: name for 'Stroke Play', keeping the score on every hole. In this type of competition, the full 18 holes are always played.

Mixed: Man and woman playing together, as a team.

Mulligan: Opportunity to replay one's last shot, granted in a friendly game.

Net score: Score after the handicap is deducted from the gross score.

Out of Bounds: Area outside the regular playing area of the course, usually marked by a white line or white stakes, or structures like walls, fences or railings.

Par: Standard average number of strokes for each hole.

Penalty: Extra stroke(s) added to a player's score for violation of the rules, loss of a ball, ending up out of bounds, or other unfortunate events.

Pin: Flag stick in the hole on the green.

Pin-high: A ball which is level with the pin.

Pitch: Shot used to approach the green.

Play Through: When a group of slower golfers or players trying to find lost balls allow players behind them to pass them.

Driving Range: Practice area.

Relief: Permission to pick up and drop the ball without a penalty.

Rough: Longer and thicker grassed area of the course.

Sandie: Making par on a hole after being in a bunker.

Shank: When the ball catches the hosel of the club instead of the club face which causes the ball to go sharply right.

Slice: A shot that curves violently to the right, like a banana.

Thin: A shot between a top and a well-struck ball.

Top: To hit the ball above the centre of its mid-point, making the ball roll instead of fly.

Turn: The halfway point on a golf course.

Unplayable lie: When it is impossible to play a shot because of its lie. The player may drop the ball to another area, with penalty.

Up and Down: Not managing to reach the green in regulation, but getting a par with an approach shot and one putt.

Whiff: To swing and completely miss the ball, also known as air shot.

Yardage: The distance between the ball and the target.

Yips: Fear of missing short putts.

THOUGHTS AND THANKS

First of all, let me thank Bobby Jones. As many golfers agree, golf *is* the closest game to the game we call life.

Alas, sexism is one of the parallels and has been since the Middle Ages. For instance, the prosecutors that lead Mary Queen of Scots to her death in 1587, pointed out that she'd played golf just days after her husband died and that hitting the links so soon after his demise proved her poor and suspicious character. *Really?* Would her widower's time on course have been viewed the same way? Or would it have been accepted as solace for a man in mourning? That question was totally irrelevant. Mary, being a woman, shouldn't have been on the course. *(source: Newsweek.com)*

Moving on, in the mid-20th century, Royal Liverpool's club secretary was heard saying *"No woman has ever entered the clubhouse and, praise God, no woman ever will." (source: Dailysports.com).* Not a great comment in today's brave new world, but certainly not uncommon in the nineteen forties.

It got a lot better as time went on. Or didn't it? *Maybe not.* Apparently, as recently as 20 years ago there were still signs hanging outside clubhouses that read *"No dogs or women allowed."* They since have been removed, but a large group of women believe they were taken away out of respect for dogs. (source: HuffPost)

It all seems so strange, considering the fact that technically golf could be the most inclusive sport in the world. The handicap system and the way the playing field is adjusted to a players ability ensure that virtually anyone can play against any opponent and experience fair competition.

Is it really about the game in itself, or is it about something else? According to the New York Times, when the head of the Royal & Ancient Golf Club of St Andrews in Scotland was asked in 2013 why racism is unacceptable but sexism is not, he replied that *"excluding women was a way of life that some people rather like."* (source: HuffPost)

His comment might seem outrageous, but let's flip this one as well, like in Mary's case. What if some important female rights woman would have said this about excluding men at an all-women's event? Would we have been just as outraged? Let's be honest. Probably not. And that, in my opinion, is not okay. I believe that striving for inclusiveness goes both ways, not only when it's convenient for the underdog.

I honestly get that men don't always want women around, and vice versa. We are equals, but we are not the same. And that, in my opinion, is fine. Personally, am not against all male golf clubs. Or any club or organization that selects on gender. But I do believe that if you do decide your activity is inclusive, you should act upon it.

When I first started toying with the idea for the book, I wasn't quite certain how big a topic sexism in sports, especially golf, was anymore. Somewhere deep down, I was hoping we had moved on, forgot about all the nonsense and that wonderful female golfers like Annika Sorenstam and many others, had proved that golf was the most inclusive game in the world. But next to my hope, there was also a niggle that we might not be where we want to be just yet.

It isn't as bad as 25 years ago, but on my golf travels during the last 10 years I certainly experienced women still having lower status, sometimes very obvious, sometimes more under the surface. This was confirmed on many occasions, like in the autumn of 2022 when I finally got the opportunity to play one of the beautiful UK links courses that had been on my bucket list since forever. After forking out on a massive green fee, I set off towards the lovely old clubhouse to change into my golf kit. Feeling all excited, I went through the grand main door and was kindly but firmly stopped by a gentleman who requested me to remove myself and use the entrance at the back. A bit rattled I turned round, scuttled outside again towards the back entrance and found a door between the garbage bins where I was allowed to enter. It wasn't because I was a green fee player, it turned out to be the entrance for the ladies. What a bummer. But what great inspiration for my book. Thank you for that!

During my research I have interviewed lots of women golfers, who I want to thank for their openness and their often-humorous reflection on the subject. Most of these ladies experience blatant sexism in one way or another, like not being allowed to play on weekends, not being allowed in certain committees, only getting part time memberships; all based on gender. I distinctly remember one lady, who walked away from her club in 2021 because she could only get a membership for playing on weekdays while her husband could get a full membership and was allowed to play all days. She was the one working from Monday to Friday while her husband was retired. The board didn't seem to grasp that it isn't the nineteen fifties anymore and most women, like most men, work full time and use golf to unwind during their time off. Which turns out to be during the weekends, for the most of us.

If you are interested in some formidable lady golfers who challenged male domination in golfing arena's in Scotland, try and watch the documentary '*Iron Women*'. Great stuff about daring and bold women. We need to continue their work. Things have improved so much, but we are not there yet.

Writing this book was a long bumpy journey that involved the support and encouragement of many individuals, men and women. I would like to express my deepest gratitude to those who have contributed to the creation of this work and have shown such genuine interest in its progress.

First and foremost, I want to thank my husband for his unwavering support throughout this process. His love and understanding have been my anchor, and I am grateful for his understanding silence during the countless hours he was left to fend for himself while I was immersed in this project. Thanks darling, you have been so supportive.

I extend my sincere appreciation to my golf buddies, male and female, who provided many valuable insights. Your perspectives and enthusiasm have enriched this book in ways I could not have achieved alone. My gratitude also goes to the management of the lovely club and its beautiful course where I am fortunate enough to play, I have always felt so welcome and hope to stay a member for a very long time.

A heartfelt thank you to my editors, Matt Price and Greta Timmers, whose expertise and guidance have been instrumental in shaping and refining the manuscript. Their attention to detail and commitment to excel have truly elevated the quality of this book. Next to Matt and Greta, a big thank you to Victoria Heath Silk who has done an amazing job on the cover design. Her artistic flair has truly brought my vision to life.

I am indebted to all the professionals who generously helped with their expertise in the world of golf and publishing, online and offline. Your willingness to share your knowledge has been invaluable, and I am fortunate to have had the opportunity to learn from you.

I inherited the golf bug from my father, a keen player, a true gentleman and certainly funniest man I have ever met. With every page I have written, my darling Dad was standing behind me in spirit, watching me over my shoulder, coaching me through difficult moments. I owe some of the characters to him, he was the one who created Bashit, Bushrod, Prudence Love, Rough and Hackkett in the nineteen seventies when he wrote hilarious columns for his golf club's magazine. All I did was fluff them up a bit and bring them to the 21st century.

Finally, a special thank you to my sister, the better version of me, on the golf course and off. Her sense of humour and her love and friendship over the last 50 years are the backbone of this book.

With heartfelt gratitude,

Emma Briggs

ABOUT THE AUTHOR

Emma Briggs is a writer and civil servant from the south of the Netherlands, happily married to her husband who fell in love with golf at a later age but is making up for earlier years lost. Emma is half Dutch, half British. Her father emigrated from London England to Eindhoven the Netherlands in the early sixties, after being a reporter for *Golf Illustrated* for a couple of years. He caught the golf bug from Emma's grandfather, a keen low handicap golfer. Her grandmother, who started playing after she turned sixty, was a small Lady section's Captain in the mid nineteen eighties.

Emma started playing golf in her late teens. She was quickly followed by her younger sister who became, and still is, the far better player and owns a high-end club fitting business and golf shop with her life partner. Emma and her sister are both members at the same golf club.

Printed in Great Britain
by Amazon

60200053R00262